A Disposable Spy

Paul Bushell

First Published in Great Britain in 2023

A CIP catalogue record for this book is available from the British Library

ISBN 978-1-7392266-0-2 (paperback)

ISBN 978-1-7392266-1-9 (ebook)

Cover Design by Creative Covers

Typesetting by Book Polishers

Published by Centage Media Ltd

30 Orange Street

London WC2H 7HF

For Lorna

May be we are not such fools as we look. But though we be, we are well content, so long as we may be two fools together.

Lorna Doone, by R.D. Blackmore

South West London, 1917

It was warm for April. The rays of the early morning sun played on her thin cotton dress as she bent down to place the note between the empty milk bottles. Normally, a simple folded note was adequate. Not today. This note required an envelope. After a moment's deliberation, she decided not to lick the flap, tucking it in instead so the milkman would read it straight away.

She straightened up, hesitated, then bent down and pulled the envelope out to check the wording once more. Satisfied, she replaced it between the milk bottles, each one washed till it shone like new, checked that it was held firmly in place then went back inside. She left the door unlocked.

Wanting to cause as little inconvenience as possible, she went about her remaining tasks in her usual manner - methodical, efficient, above all, conscientious. From the drawer in the hall table, she picked out two envelopes, sealed this time, and propped the smaller one against the flower vase in the centre of the table. The other, a foolscap envelope, she took into the kitchen, placing it in the centre of the kitchen table.

Returning to the table in the hall, she gazed longingly at the two framed photographs that stood beside the flower vase, one on each side. She picked up the first one, a photograph of a Naval Officer in full uniform and gave it a long kiss. The second one, of a young blonde-haired boy, she hugged to her bosom before kissing it. When she had replaced them, making sure they were in exactly the right position, she noticed that one of the tulips in the vase was slightly crooked and eased it back into its correct place. As she did so, she heard the front gate creak on its hinges. Through the window, she saw the familiar face of the local Police Sergeant, a man who had gone out of his way to be kind to her. She rushed to the front door, opened it and stepped outside to greet him, shutting the door firmly behind her.

'Hello, Sergeant,' she said in an accent that still bore traces of her native country. 'How are you this lovely morning?'

The Sergeant saluted to show his respect for this woman who had suffered so much.

'I just wanted to check that you're alright. The way those people treated you was a disgrace'.

'That's very kind of you but I assure you I'm fine.'

'When I complained, they warned me I'd be sacked if I mentioned it again. Terrible people. No decency at all.'

'Well, it's kind of you and I do appreciate it. But you mustn't put your job at risk. You've got a family to feed.'

'Don't you worry about that, Mrs Fawkes, I won't let them stop me making sure you're alright.'

The Sergeant saluted once more and, with a cheery, 'see you tomorrow, no doubt,' retreated behind the squeaky gate.

She waited till he was several houses down then turned to go back in, only to find the door shut behind her. Remembering she'd left the back door unlocked for a particular reason, she went down the side return, through the kitchen and into the hall.

The inconvenience she would cause still bothered her, almost enough to make her waver. Almost, but not quite. She climbed the small step ladder, placed the rope around her neck, shut her eyes firmly and kicked the ladder away.

Chapter 1

The South of France, July 1939

THREE MINUTES TO seven.

The sun, though slipping behind the hills, still made its presence felt. The waiters, their polished shoes scrunching across the gravelled terrace, brought out the canapés and opened the first bottles of champagne. A minuscule breeze gently wafted the scent of jasmine across the terrace. The cicadas maintained their ceaseless accompaniment.

Jean-Paul Durand checked the watch his uncle had given him for his bar mitzvah, signalled to the band to start playing and took up his position to one side of the French doors. As he slipped the watch under his cuff, his first guest, a young American, stepped out onto the terrace. Catching sight of the watch, he pointed to Durand's cuff.

'That's a beautiful watch you have there, Monsieur Durand.'

'Monsieur Wade, I'm so glad you could join us. It was a present from my late father on my twenty-first.'

'He had excellent taste.'

Durand smiled appreciatively.

'I hope you're enjoying your European tour.'

'Having a wonderful time,' said Brandon. 'I'll be sorry to go home.'

Arming himself with a glass of champagne, the American wandered off to admire the view.

Hotel L'Hirondelle des Iles had opened four years ago and was doing well. Summer holidays along the Riviera were becoming popular and the larger towns were rapidly expanding. Tourist hotels, casinos, luxury villas. But L'Hirondelle had been built away from the crowds, on the edge of Fort Sarrasin, a small resort east of Marseilles. Cobbled streets led down to a tiny port, once home for fishing vessels, now full of private yachts. The hotel overlooked sandy beaches, flanked by the long road that wound its way eastwards through a succession of sharp curves overhung with cedars, pines and mimosa. Behind the hotel, the land rose, gently at first, then steeply into tree-covered hills. In the far distance, the rocky brown and grey slopes of the tallest hills protected the area from the worst of winter. Its position gave it all the advantages of the Riviera without being swallowed up by the commercialization despoiling the coastline further east. As a result, it was favoured both by those who preferred to avoid the vulgarity of the main resorts and by those who could not afford that vulgarity.

Durand was pleased with the hotel's success and pleased with life. Some believe if a man's name is Durand, there's a strong possibility he has changed it from something else. In Jean-Paul's case, they would have been right but he had developed a self-effacing manner so people saw him as a reserved but gentlemanly fellow, not someone with a secret. Tonight, however, an observant onlooker would have noticed a change in his manner. In between greeting his guests, he repeatedly stole a swift glance across the terrace towards the hotel entrance, always checking the watch he was so keen to lie about.

The hotel's speciality, the Tuesday evening cocktail party, was underway. Soon, other guests followed the young American who, from his position on the far side of the terrace, cast an eye over each set of newcomers. Several groups had formed, all talking amongst themselves, but not to the others, and in a variety of languages.

Durand had noticed this on the first of these Tuesday evenings and seen it as a serious flaw. It never dawned on him that the guests rather liked the arrangement. They had found the perfect cocktail party, one where you didn't have to speak to the other guests. You could discuss them without fear of offence, and they could discuss you. The hotel quickly acquired a group of regulars for whom the cocktail parties alone were a sufficient attraction to lure them back each year.

This year, they had someone new to discuss. While everyone else was wearing evening dress, the American wore a pale linen suit and a white, soft collared shirt, open at the neck. His outfit quickly drew mutterings about *les Américains* from the other men. Not so their wives. Towering over the other men, his unusual dress sense, shock of brown hair, gentle brown eyes and the early stages of a beard gave him an air of glamour altogether lacking in their husbands. A glamour assisted by the rumour that his family had recently sold their business and Brandon was now a gentleman of leisure with the means to go with it.

In a village deep in the hills, another young man, not so stylishly dressed, sat in a well-worn armchair. The room he sat in was panelled in lime-washed oak and had walls so thick that, even at this time of the year, he found himself shivering. There was nothing he could do about it, it had never occurred to him he would need firelighters in August. Besides, he would be gone in a few days and he needed the neat stack of logs by the fireplace for another purpose. He didn't want to light the newspaper either. Franciszek Koslowski was lonely and scared and the Polish newspaper was the one thing that reminded him of home. That and the box by his side. He never let that out of his sight.

Brandon was starting to get bored. The procession of guests had all but dried up and he was thinking about dinner when a group of latecomers, three unaccompanied women, caught his attention as they stepped through the French doors. Two of them, obviously mother and daughter, strode confidently towards Durand. The third walked with tentative steps, seeming to hang back as if reluctant to join the party. She didn't look like the other two. A friend of the daughter's, he guessed.

The young woman looked at the strange sight of all the little groups and noticed an underdressed young man looking straight at her, holding her gaze for more than the permitted second or two. With their eyes firmly fixed on each other, neither noticed Durand stealing yet another glance at the front door, as he stepped forward to greet the new arrivals.

Delighted when the young woman addressed him in French, Durand responded warmly. The mother, not to be left out, quickly joined in the conversation, constantly touching Durand's sleeve, which her young companion assumed was the French way. The introductions completed, the family followed established procedure and made a little group by one wall of the terrace. From here, they could look out across the masts of the yachts, towards a tiny island which, from time immemorial, had guarded the bay from invaders.

'It's gorgeous. Do people live there?'

Audrey and her mother were delighted by their guest's reaction.

'Yes, not many though. Most of the people are holidaymakers, there for the day. We can take a boat across, if you like.'

Audrey and her mother accepted a glass of champagne then turned round to look at the other guests, checking to see how many had returned from last year. The young woman took a glass of orange juice and continued to admire the view. With the sun setting, the heat of the day was slowly dissipating. The air was clear. The small island looked inviting.

Audrey whispered to her mother.

'Who's that man in the linen suit? He can't be a guest, surely.'

Juliette Poitrenaud looked across at him.

'From the look of his clothes, I'd say he works here. He must be the gardener. He does a wonderful job. Perhaps Jean-P,' she corrected herself, 'Durand let him join us as a treat.'

Realising they were talking about the man who had held her gaze, their young guest turned round.

'His clothes look too expensive for a gardener. Don't you think?'

'Not necessarily, we French know how to dress well. No, he's the gardener, I'm sure. I remember him from last year. Which is more than I can say for this dance band.'

The man Juliette had decided was the gardener had come to a decision of his own. Smiling at the other guests as he weaved between them, he slowly moved towards the three women. He was within a few feet of them and about to introduce himself when someone beat him to it.

This year, with a view to helping, indeed forcing his guests to mix with each other, Durand had introduced the novelty of a dance band. To set things in motion, he announced a snowball waltz, a dance which required those on the floor to change partners at the end of each tune by picking someone from the onlookers. He needed a partner for the first dance. Who better to choose than the charming young woman he'd just spoken to? There could be no question of starting the dance with her older companion, Madame Poitrenaud.

Unaware of what lay in store for her, the young woman watched Durand advance towards their little group.

'Mademoiselle, will you do me the honour?'

Engrossed by the view, she'd paid no attention to his announcement. A small band was playing but nobody was dancing so what on earth could the rather sweet Frenchman mean with his beseeching look? Determined to spend the holiday acting like a woman of nearly nineteen, she suddenly felt like an embarrassed girl of eighteen and was about to decline his offer when the look of pleading in his eyes stopped her. Instead of a childish refusal, she gave him her hand and followed him onto the floor where he quickly set out to put her at ease.

'You speak French very well. Have you been to France before?'

'No, this is my first visit but my mother spent some time here during the war and is fluent. To be honest, I'm terrified of making mistakes.'

'Well, in the north, they frown on foreigners making mistakes but it's different in the south. We're much more relaxed so you can relax too.'

And relax she did. By the end of their short dance, she'd told him about her family life, her love of riding and sport and even confided her big ambition to him. Then the music stopped and they were required to leave the floor to find new partners.

Until the arrival of the three women, the young American had been surveying the other guests without any great interest. Not anymore. The older woman's behaviour in front of Durand, the repeated sleeve touching, the lingering eye contact, hadn't passed unnoticed, nor had the young woman now dancing with Durand. She had a physicality that took his breath away. When the music stopped, he knew he should wait to be asked by someone already on the floor but he wasn't taking any chances and wandered casually into the path of the young lady just released from Durand's arms. She'd hoped to disappear into the crowd but he was too quick, too determined. He'd hoped she might not be French but he'd heard her speak French to Durand and decided he'd just have to do his best.

'May I have the pleasure?' he said in passable French.

'Ô' she replied. Oh my, she thought, the gardener is asking me to dance. Will he understand my French as well as Durand?

She noticed his firm grip as they started to dance. Strong hands and arms from all that gardening. Hoping her French would be up to it, she decided to compliment him on his work.

'The gardens are beautiful, you must be very proud.'

'It's the gardener you should compliment. I only arrived today from Milan.'

'Oh, I'm so sorry, I've been misinformed.' She blushed. 'I'm afraid I don't speak Italian.'

'Nor do I.'

'But I thought you said....'

The music stopped. It was time to change partners. He knew what he ought to do, release her and let someone else experience what he was now experiencing but his arms were in control and they wouldn't let go.

'I think we're supposed to change partners now.'

She said it with amusement in her voice, not irritation, as if it was an observation rather than an instruction. The decision was taken for them when the music resumed.

'Look, my French is rather limited, you don't speak English by any chance.'

'Just a little,' she laughed.

'Hey, you speak my language.'

'No, you're speaking mine.'

'I guess that's so, I stand corrected. I'm Brandon by the way, Brandon Wade'.

'I'm Mary Ballantyne.'

'That sounds Scottish. Where are you from?'

'I'm half Scottish. My mother's English. I live with my parents in England, a little village called Woodstock. And you?'

'Boston, Massachusetts. I'm touring Europe, next stop London.'

All too soon, the music stopped. This time, he had to let her go.

'I'd better get back to my gardening.'

She blushed again.

'You must think me an awful fool.'

He held her gaze and smiled.

'That's not what I was thinking at all.'

As he walked off the floor, he passed Durand and smiled at him. The Frenchman didn't notice. His glances towards the entrance hall had finally been rewarded when a taxi drew up and two men stepped out. Now he could stop looking over everyone's shoulders and concentrate on being a good host. He tried to return Brandon's smile but the American had already walked away.

In the village house up in the hills, there were no drinks, no canapés and no dancing. Franciszek Koslowski, his Polish newspaper half on and half off his knee, lay slumped in his armchair by the unlit fire, sleeping the sleep of the just.

Chapter 2

EARLY NEXT MORNING, two men slipped out of the hotel as inconspicuously as they had slipped in the night before and now stood in front of the window of a hat shop in the narrow, cobbled lane that ran behind the promenade. Giving its display a cursory inspection, they pushed on the door. Crooked with age, it needed a firm push but the bell managed a lively tinkle, causing the elderly owner to look up from dealing with a lady needing a sun hat for her grandson. The younger of the two men signalled that there was no hurry, allowing the older of the two men a moment to reflect on how he had come to be standing there.

When he'd arrived at Marseille railway station the previous evening, George Heywood had stepped off the Blue Train clutching the ticket he'd been handed by his head of department, a present to celebrate his retirement.

'Everything will be paid for. It won't cost you a penny.'

When he tried to protest that this really wasn't necessary, his boss held up his hand.

'No, my dear fellow, think nothing of it. After your years of loyal service, it's the least we can do. In fact, we'll even lend you a linen suit from our wardrobe. You'll have to return it when you get back, I'm afraid, but feel free to wear it as much as you like,'

Heywood looked at the ticket.

'This gets me to Marseille railway station. What happens then?'

'Someone will meet you off the train and take you to a hotel.'

Assuming that the 'someone' would be from the Consulate,

he stood on the platform as, one by one, the other passengers disappeared through the barrier. The guard whistled, the train steamed off down the track. Had he got off at the wrong station? He glanced anxiously at his ticket. It said Marseille, so did the painted wooden board on the platform wall.

Deciding the person meeting him must be in the ticket hall, he was about to pick up his bag when he heard a familiar voice behind him.

'Welcome to Marseille.'

'Where the hell did you spring from?'

'I was on the same train as you. Got off just as it was leaving. Call it a precautionary measure.'

'If this is just a holiday, why do we need precautionary measures?'

Both men knew it was a rhetorical question and the younger one didn't answer it directly.

'Let's have dinner in the station restaurant. We can catch up.'

It had been a while and Heywood was delighted to see young Freddie Fawkes again. And a little alarmed. On his last day in the office, he'd been given an envelope to give to the "someone" picking him up. Now he knew who that "someone" was and given the nature of the business they were in, he knew this trip would involve more than just acting as a postman.

The restaurant was having a quiet night, only three tables occupied. Freddie chose a table allowing him to face the door and well away from the other diners. Once they'd ordered, he knew his old friend would have a lot of questions.

'Fire away.'

'When you disappeared from Broadway Buildings and stopped coming over for Sunday lunch, I assumed you'd resigned in a huff. To be honest, I was disappointed you'd left without saying goodbye. It wasn't like you.'

He eyed his old friend up and down.

'What happened?'

'Z Section.'

'Sounds like the title of a bad film. What's it for?'

Seeing the waiter approaching with a basket of bread, Fawkes sat back, nodded his thanks, let the waiter depart then got down to business.

'Real spying. As things deteriorated in Europe, it became obvious that our agents were useless. We used the Passport Officer at each embassy as our main man and everyone knew it. They were all retired military men, too busy drinking away their pensions to keep their fingers on the pulse. We had a secret service that didn't provide any service and wasn't even secret. C told Dansey to set up a parallel section using people with real connections in their area. Thanks to him, we are now well informed about European matters. More to the point, my career is on the up.'

'Claude Dansey? I thought he was fired for embezzlement. Surely you're not mixed up with him.'

'The embezzlement story was just a cover for him to set up Z section in Bush House, well away from Broadway.'

The fact that his young friend, under-appreciated in Broadway Buildings, was now enjoying a richly deserved recognition was welcome news to Heywood but how did he, a retiring desk man, fit in to whatever was going on? Before he could find out, the waiter appeared with the first course. Being a patient man, he waited till it was safe to resume.

'What's this got to do with me being given a retirement holiday? Apart from it obviously not being a retirement holiday.'

'No, it is a holiday. Of a sort. It's just that I'm here to do something and you are the perfect person to help me do it. We're going to be the archetypal Englishmen abroad.'

Fawkes was forced to sit back while the waiter approached yet again, this time with more bread.

'You've got something for me?'

Heywood handed over the envelope and waited for more details. In vain. Pocketing the envelope, Fawkes set about his meal.

'I'll explain the rest tomorrow. Right now, let's enjoy the food. I couldn't leave my compartment and go to the restaurant car in case we met. And you never know who else is on these trains. I'm starving.'

Heywood's thoughts were interrupted by the hat shop owner. Having successfully concluded the sale of a sunhat, he made a display of accompanying his customer to the door before returning behind his counter, straightening the few loose items on the counter top then looking up at the two men. The younger one placed a business card on the table in the name of Frederick Fawkes, London Films Production Limited.

'Bonjour, Monsieur. Deux châteaux de panama s'il vous plaît.'

The shopkeeper assessed the man standing before him. He was expecting an Englishman but the tall, blonde-haired blue-eyed man looked decidedly German. And a little on edge. Debating whether to end the conversation, he turned to his companion. Short with thinning hair kept in place with Julysia hair cream, George Heywood looked like a man in his mid-sixties, in the process of handing over his responsibilities to the younger man. He also looked calm and by hanging back a little, aware of the need not to seem intimidating. Reassured, the old man decided to address his comments to him.

'Ah, les panamas. Oui Monsieur, bonjour, un moment s'il vous plaît'.

He went into the back of the shop, reappearing with two hats. In English, he said, 'you're lucky. They've just come in.'

The Englishmen tried them on and pronounced them perfect. No price was mentioned but an onlooker would have been surprised by the large wad of francs that the younger man handed over and by the speed with which the old hat-seller slipped the wad into his back pocket. Both parties to the transaction wished each other the customary bonne journée as the bell over the door signalled the end of the transaction. Once out in the lane, Fawkes turned to Heywood.

'Glad that's over.'

'I noticed you looked a little tense.'

'He deals with both sides all the time. People like him have their uses but you never know how far you can trust them. That's why I wasn't given his contact details until you handed them over in that envelope. That reminds me, I must burn the letter as soon as we return to the hotel.'

Fawkes smiled and placed an arm on his old friend's shoulder.

'Time to start looking for film locations.'

Heywood had other ideas. Spotting a narrow gap between two shops and a glimpse of sea at the other end, he led his companion through to the seafront where they surveyed the almost empty beach. When he spoke, an expert would have detected an East End accent, softened by years of exposure to men from the upper ranks of society but defiantly holding its own.

'Perhaps a paddle first, away from prying ears. Just a few more questions.'

'Fair enough.'

Fort Sarrasin had a history stretching back for centuries but when it came to tourism, it was a newcomer. The row of buildings on their side of the road contained just one restaurant, one clothes shop for women and one for men. The rest of the buildings remained, as they had done for several hundred years, as fishermen's cottages with nets drying in the sun and cork buoys piled up by each front door. But things were changing. At the far end of the row, one of the cottages had a sign announcing that it was being converted into a café. A shame, thought Heywood. Right now, there was a perfect balance between the old and the new but for how much longer?

Crossing the road, they walked down a short flight of wooden, barnacled steps onto the beach. With socks and shoes removed, they rolled up the legs of their linen trousers and set out across sand that was already heating up beneath the morning sun. At this hour, the beach contained only the most ardent sun worshippers and a few children. Even so, they went as far out as the shallow water would allow. Once he was sure they were out of earshot, Heywood got down to business.

'London Films. Aren't they a real film company?'

'Indeed they are, run by a man called Korda. In return for finance from Z section, he lets us send people out in their name.'

'What's my role in all this?'

'To add credibility. You're obviously not a spy.'

A lesser man would have bridled at this obvious reference to his desk-bound career. Heywood laughed

'Thank you very much.'

'No, that's the whole point of the London Films set up, it's real and so are you. You saw how that man preferred to deal with you rather than me. You look decent, honest and straightforward, everything you really are. You said you were hurt not hearing from me, well I didn't like it either but I had no choice. You're the only man in Broadway I really trust. I shall be sorry when you're gone.'

While Fawkes kicked away a minuscule crab menacing his big toe, Heywood continued his questioning.

'Panama hats. I may not have had a top-class education, we didn't quite stretch to that sort of thing in the East End, but even I know the difference between a chapeau and a château. What was all that about and do you usually place your business card on the counter when buying a hat?'

'All part of the process. Anyone could have come in and asked for two panama hats. No one else was going to ask for a couple of châteaux.'

'What are the hats for?'

'They contain the map coordinates for our rendezvous. Half in one hat, half in the other.'

Fawkes saw the look on his friend's face.

'I know what you're thinking. Your sole function is to provide a second head for the all-important second hat. Not so. You have an essential role to play. On my own, I'd stand out like a sore thumb. Together, we're just two Englishmen abroad. Out of our depth and there to be laughed at.'

Both men looked down at the six inches of water that threatened them and laughed.

Heywood moved on to the next item on his agenda.

'It's good to see you so happy.'

'I was fed up with the snobbery in Broadway and their refusal to even consider that the department might be penetrated by communists. They think their sort would never betray their friends. Moving to Bush House is a new beginning for me. I feel much more optimistic about the future.'

Heywood knew he was on thin ice with his volatile friend but he needed to say something.

'A word of advice?'

'You know how much I value your advice even when I don't have the good sense to follow it.'

'You had plenty of reason to feel aggrieved in Broadway but, let's be honest, you're not exactly noted for your tact and diplomacy.'

Fawkes laughed.

'I don't need tact and diplomacy in Z Section. There's none of that 'you're not one of us' nonsense, it's strictly business. That's why I fit in so well. I've played a vital role in setting up a network of agents all over Europe. Broadway may not appreciate me but they do.'

This wasn't going to be easy. Heywood watched over Fawkes's shoulder as a group of children arrived. The oldest boy, indicating he was the boss by holding on to the beach ball they were going to play with, started to divide the little group into two small teams. Like Heywood, he was struggling to get his point across as the children argued with his selections. When, finally, everyone was happy, they marked out a crude football field in the sand, using jumpers as goal posts. Oh to be that age again, thought Heywood. Then it was back to the task in hand.

He tried another tack.

'When war comes, Z section may be merged with Broadway. There's a big difference between you in the field, calm, collected and capable and you back in the office putting everyone's backs up. They resented your attitude then you resented their resentment.'

'That's because they saw me as someone whose past made him vulnerable, someone they could use. I tell you, if they ever order me back to Broadway Buildings, I'm off to join the army. They can bloody well manage without me.'

A sergeant in the Great War, Heywood had served four years on the Western Front. When his CO joined the SIS, he'd invited Heywood to join him as a desk man, someone who'd make the SIS run as smoothly as he'd made the regiment run in the trenches. He and Fawkes had hit it off from the moment the younger man had joined the service. He understood his young friend and knew how to handle him. He'd tried tact and diplomacy but the tactless, undiplomatic Fawkes had failed to take the hint. It was time to step up the warning. His East End accent, smoothed at the edges but still distinctive, found favour with his friend. Not for the first time, he put it to good effect.

'Don't be so damn silly. You were born for this type of work but you need to play the long game. Cooperate and move up the ladder. Make your point about communist penetration when you have the authority to do so.'

Expecting an explosion to match the large chip on his friend's shoulder, Heywood was glad their location ensured it would be muted. Aware of his surroundings, Fawkes took his anger out on the water, splashing about and frightening the tiny fish away. It seemed to work, and not just on the fish. When he spoke, his voice was calm.

'What am I going to do when you retire? You're the only one who keeps me sane.'

Heywood threw caution to the wind.

'Well, for a start, you could get yourself a wife. Your perspective is too narrow. A wife will do you a world of good, broaden your outlook. It worked for me. Knowing I had a wife and children at home kept me going when I was in the trenches.'

'There's no chance of that. No woman would have me, not with the kind of life I lead. Besides, where would I find one? I'm either in the office or in the field. I'll never find a wife in the office and I certainly won't find one in a place like this.'

'You'll meet someone. The question is, when you do, will you open up to her or keep your feelings bottled up inside? The right woman will only come your way once. When she does, if you don't tell her how you really feel, you'll lose her.'

Having said his piece, Heywood changed the subject.

'So what are we doing here?'

Fawkes circled his feet under the water, stirring up the sand. When he looked up, he gave Heywood a triumphant smile.

'Back in January, I joined our codebreakers for a meeting in Paris with some Poles. They only brought me along because of my German then sent me back to the hotel when they realised everyone spoke English.'

'They're a secretive lot.'

'They're a bloody rude lot.'

'How do you mean?'

'The man we're going to meet, Koslowski, drove me back to the hotel and we had a long chat. The purpose of that meeting was to exchange information on breaking German codes but neither side trusted the other. On top of that, our people called the Poles ignorant and foolish. Not surprisingly, both sides went home empty-handed.'

'Is he here in the south of France?'

The triumphant smile spread a little wider.

'Koslowski thinks his people should have revealed more. He's come here to hand something over but only if he deals with me. Don't ask me what it is, I don't know a thing about codebreaking but if I can pull this off, it will be the biggest thing the Service has ever done.'

Confident that they were secure while standing out in the open, the blow to the back of his head caught Fawkes by surprise. After falling forward with a loud curse, he steadied himself and turned to face this unknown enemy. Instinctively, he sought to protect his friend by standing between Heywood and the threat. As he did so, the smallest boy, acting on orders from the biggest, ran across from the makeshift football field and held out his hands. Behind the shaken Fawkes, Heywood picked up the beach ball and, lacking much in the way of French, handed it silently to the boy.

Wisely, Heywood didn't seek to make fun of Fawkes's reaction to being hit by a beach ball. Fortunately, Fawkes himself saw the funny side.

'Seems the Germans are recruiting younger and younger spies. I'll deal with him later.'

'Good idea. We could infiltrate their network by joining in the soccer game.'

Heywood patted Fawkes on the shoulder.

'Anyway, back to business. It sounds as though your career really is on the up.'

'As long as the mission succeeds. In this game, you're only as good as your last success. This one's really important to me.'

Even with the light sea breeze, the early morning sun was already burning through Fawkes's jacket. He took it off and slung it over his shoulder. His colleague ignored the heat. Enough of the fatherly advice, he wanted to know what the plan was.

'So, our cover is that we're looking for film locations. Where are they and how are we getting there? By bus?'

Fawkes didn't reply immediately. He was looking down into the clear water and watching the crabs crawling across the sand. They were tiny but they had claws. When he looked up, he could see his friend was waiting for his reply.

'No, we have to collect something. We can hardly sit in a bus with it on our laps. We need a car and I'm hoping for a few civilians to join us as extra cover. Before we do that, we need to identify this village by checking the coordinates on our map.'

Fawkes looked at his old friend, ankle deep in water, trousers rolled up, panama perched on his head. The old sergeant from the

Great War had been a beacon of sanity amongst the self-serving careerists that surrounded him. He might be an admin man but he always had a wise comment to make when they discussed things over Sunday lunch at Heywood's house in Kennington.

A tiny crab, braver than the others, made it as far as Fawkes's big toe, giving it the tiniest of nips.

'Let's get out of here before these monsters eat us alive.'

In the double room forced upon them by their skinflint employer, the maid had started the daily clean as soon as she was sure they had gone down to breakfast. It didn't take her long to find the letter Fawkes intended to burn. As instructed, she noted down the only words it contained, the address of the hat shop, folded the note into her uniform pocket and set about her chores.

Later that morning, she went out to the laundry area at the back of the hotel, emptied the trolley full of dirty linen then wandered over to the gate that opened onto the road. A man emerged from the shade of a doorway on the other side of the road, strolled nonchalantly over, exchanged a pair of bank notes for the note she had made and disappeared back into the shade.

Chapter 3

THE YOUNG WOMAN who had made such an impression on the jaded palate of Brandon Wade threw on a pair of slacks and the first blouse she came across in her drawer. Her roommate Audrey, who'd taken more trouble to less effect, looked at her enviously. The hairstyles of the time suited Mary's naturally wavy hair which clung to her head, looking both fashionable and natural. Her oval face and straight nose drew the onlooker towards her grey blue eyes while the light dusting of freckles on her fair skin gave her the look of a country girl come to town.

'It's not fair, you look fabulous and you're not even trying.'

The compliment passed over her head. She had other things on her mind.

'Do you think we'll be able to play some tennis while we're here? I'm dying for a game.'

Laughing, Audrey linked her arm in Mary's and led her down to join Audrey's mother for a late breakfast on the terrace. While Juliette poured the coffee, Audrey surveyed the almost empty beach and pointed at two men paddling in the water. One looked to be in his sixties, short with thin brown hair, the other, probably early thirties, was taller with thick blonde hair and blue eyes. With the right woman to tell him how to dress, she thought, he'd be quite presentable. As it was, both men wore white office shirts with the obligatory stiff collar, combined with linen trousers rolled up below their knees, the ensemble topped off with panama hats.

'Will you look at those two. Surely they can't be guests.'

'I rather think they are,' said Juliette. 'I saw them arrive last night during the cocktail party.'

'I wonder what nationality they are,' said Mary. 'The younger one looks German.'

Juliette laughed. 'I think it's fairly obvious, don't you? They're typical Englishmen, out of their depth in a foreign country. No offence, my dear.'

But she was offended. Not by Juliette's remark but by the presence of her fellow countrymen. An only child from a small village, she was enjoying the sophistication of her surroundings. By making a laughing stock of themselves, they were, to her young mind, making a laughing stock of her. She determined to keep well away from them.

Pulling up in front of L'Hirondelle des Iles, Harry Ransome applied the handbrake of his Wolseley, switched off the engine and turned to his wife.

'It took longer than I expected but we got here in the end.'

'Now we are, you've got work to do, my man.' She stroked the mop of mousy brown hair that had tumbled over his forehead. 'You've had your epic car journey and you've enjoyed moaning all the way down about your boring job. Now it's my turn. I want my baby. Starting tonight.'

Harry looked at his wife and smirked. 'Madam, your demands are onerous but I shall obey. Just as soon as I've checked the oil.'

'No you bloody well won't. I've had enough of sitting by the roadside while you fix the latest problem. The next few days will be dedicated to my needs, not yours. And certainly not this bloody car's.'

'We wouldn't have had so many problems if they hadn't hoisted her on and off the ferry. It upset the old thing. I really ought to check the oil.'

'Give me the keys.'

'What?'

'You can have them back when you've done your duty.'

Harry smiled at his wife.

'Seems a fair exchange.'

They looked up to find two men standing in front of their car, noting the British registration.

'Good morning,' said the younger one, raising his panama. 'Staying long?'

'Only four days, I'm afraid. We hope it'll be long enough to find something interesting to do.'

'I'm sure it will,' said Fawkes. Then, as if the thought had just occurred to him, 'I say, why not join us for a drink this evening? We can fill you in on the possibilities.'

Heywood noticed that, in addressing the couple, he'd altered his tone, speaking with more of a drawl.

'That would be delightful,' said Harry.

As the two men went into the hotel, Lydia made a face at her husband. Once they were out of earshot, she said, 'fill us in on the possibilities indeed. I haven't come all this way to have a drink with a couple who look as if they've stepped straight out of your insurance company. The only possibility they'll know about is where to buy a copy of yesterday's Times.'

'Don't worry, it'll be just a drink and then we'll be shot of them. Besides, we need to know where to buy a copy of yesterday's Times.'

'Oh, God.'

As soon as they entered their room, the two men they'd just spoken to removed their hats and peeled back the sweatbands to reveal a piece of paper in each with a series of numbers. Fawkes unfolded his Michelin map, read off one set of numbers along the side, another set across the top. Where they crossed, he noted the name of the village. He made no mark on the map, wrote nothing down and ate the rice paper on which the numbers had been written. When he spoke, the drawl he'd adopted for the Ransomes was absent.

'La Dame Brave. It's some way inland. We'll certainly need

transport. I'll have a word with our man before we meet the young marrieds for that drink.'

'One thing, before you go.'

Fawkes gave him a puzzled look.

'Roll down your trousers or they'll think you're a stupid Englishman abroad.'

'The perfect cover, old boy. Works every time.' As he made for the door, he added, 'and you must do the same.'

Keeping his trousers rolled up, Fawkes went down to reception, slapped the map down on the counter and demanded to see the manager.

'The room's a disgrace, make sure you give him my name and room number.'

He was shown into an office that was dark, cool and decorated in the art deco style. Durand sat at an inlaid wooden desk, a bakelite wireless at one end, a Peruvian statue at the other. Behind his head was an original Tamara de Lempicka. To anyone else it was modern and glamorous. Fawkes felt he'd wandered onto a Hollywood film set and said so. Durand laughed.

'Well, you should know.'

He sat back and surveyed the latest man to be sent out from London.

'And how is the film business?'

'Coming into focus but we need your help. We have to go up into the hills to sort things out and need some cover.'

Durand wandered over to the window where the Venetian blinds still let in a chink of light. He closed them completely, returned to his desk and turned on the lamp. Unfolding the map, Fawkes pointed to the village. Durand smiled.

'La Dame Brave. I know it well. What exactly do you need to do?'

'We have to collect something. It'll be safer both for us and the person we're meeting if we go as a crowd. What can you suggest?'

'Collect *something*, you say.'

Durand returned to his desk, absent-mindedly stroking the

Peruvian statue. They didn't want him to know what they were collecting which meant they didn't trust him. He'd been in this game a long time and tackled the problem head on.

'How much do you know about me?'

Fawkes had been briefed by Dansey who'd told him he was trustworthy but sensitive about his origins. 'Let him tell you his story. He'll like that.'

'Just that you're our man down here and I'm to place myself in your hands.'

The Frenchman said nothing for a few moments, giving Fawkes's eyes time to adjust to the gloom.

'I wasn't born French. I'm an Egyptian Jew. Three generations of my family have worked for British intelligence since long before it took on its current form as the SIS. We helped the British buy shares in the Suez Canal Company and were with Kitchener at Fashoda during his stand-off with Captain Marchand. Some other time, I'll tell you what Kitchener said to the British Press when he came out of his tent.

'As a reward for our services and because things were getting rather hot for us in Cairo, the British relocated us here when I was a child, changed our name and turned me into the Frenchman you see today. When your Mr Dansey formed Z section, he contacted me and renewed our relationship.'

He leaned forward, his eyes brightening the gloom.

'Dansey wouldn't have done that if he didn't trust me. If we're going to work together, you've got to trust me too.'

'It's not a question of trust, believe me. I don't know what I'm collecting and the fact that they haven't told me means it's really important. For your own sake, it's better you don't know either.'

Durand had made his point and, as Dansey had predicted, felt better for it. With a shrug of his shoulders, he got down to business.

'The village has a small perfumery. I can organise a little trip for a few guests, enough people to make it look innocent, not enough to get in your way. How big is this object?'

'I'm told it should fit under a car's back seat.'

'At the perfume factory, the guests will buy souvenirs so it won't look suspicious if their cars are loaded up with various packages at the end of the visit. Better if you travel back to the hotel in a different car from the one with the package.'

'As long as the person with the package doesn't disappear with it.'

'We'll have to use one of your jolly decent British chaps then, won't we?'

Fawkes refused to rise to the bait.

'How will you arrange this?'

'The guests are used to little trips like this so it will come as no surprise. Can you get hold of a car?'

'I'm working on that. We're having a drink later with one of those jolly decent British chaps you were talking about. He's just checked in with his wife.'

Durand smiled. The Englishman could give as good as he got. He liked that.

'I suggest we plan to leave at 10 o'clock tomorrow morning. Let me know when you've got a car.'

He returned to the Venetian blinds and reopened them a fraction, signalling that the discussion was over. The Englishman made for the door then stopped.

'What was it he said?'

'Who?'

'Kitchener, at Fashoda. What did he say to the British Press?'

'Out of my way, you drunken scum.'

'Well I'll be damned. Those were the days.'

Fawkes left Durand's office looking like a guest who hadn't had his complaint dealt with.

'Is everything satisfactory now, Monsieur?' asked the anxious receptionist.

'He thinks he can fob me off with a trip to a perfume factory.'

Chapter 4

'THING IS, OLD boy,' Fawkes drawled, 'we're a trifle pressed. We're in the film business and need to inspect a location up in the hills but don't have a car. Then I heard there's a visit to a perfume factory in the very place we want to go. Amazing coincidence.'

The rooftop bar of L'Hirondelle des Iles was in a round turret at one corner of the roof terrace. Though not as grand as the terrace below, the view made it popular with guests and passing trade. Harry and Lydia wanted to enjoy that view. Fawkes wanted to sound like a high-powered film executive, the sort of man whose needs must always come first.

It was seven o'clock. In an hour's time, the temperature would be perfect. Right now, all four of them were glad, not only of the shade that the turret afforded but of the draught that wafted through the open windows on either side.

'We could take you if you like. Lydia would like to look at a perfume factory wouldn't you darling'.

'I thought we'd had enough driving for a few days'.

'Yes, but this sounds fun and Mr. Heywood and Mr. Fawkes need our help.'

'Oh, George and Freddie, please.'

Lydia knew where this was heading but she didn't want to give in too easily.

'You just want an excuse to do some more driving.'

She was right but Harry also wanted to curry favour with an important man in the film industry. His job in the insurance company was secure but boring. Fawkes, or rather Freddie, might be the answer to his prayers.

'I'll be frank with you Mr, er, Freddie. My father wouldn't let me take up my place at Cambridge because we were too poor. I've been stuck ever since in a boring job in insurance. Are there any openings in London Films?'

Fawkes noted the stifled surprise on Lydia's face.

'I'm sure there are, especially for someone like you. The film industry is full of people who started out in something quite different.'

He pulled out a business card. 'Take this and give me a call in September. Has your lady wife considered auditioning for a film part?' He might as well have her eating out of his hand while he was about it.

'I'm afraid that is of no interest to me whatsoever, Mr Hawkes.'

That's more like it, he thought. He particularly liked the way she deliberately got his name wrong. No "Freddie" nonsense for her. If she wanted a job in his real line of business, on the other hand…

'I'll tell old Durand we're all fixed up.'

'Old who?' said Harry.

'Sorry, I should've said, he's the manager and a first-class fellow.'

'Then you mean young and rather good-looking Durand,' said Lydia. 'Will he be coming too?' she asked mischievously.

'I shall insist on it.'

'I suppose I could force myself,' she said playfully.

'Shall we say 10 o'clock tomorrow morning?'

Durand needed volunteers for the trip. He was confident Mme Poitrenaud would agree, together with her daughter and the young English woman. The American had a car so he proposed to rope him in as well. They would have his car, the American's and whatever the British agents could come up with. Heywood and Fawkes would look a little less like two standout Englishmen on a spying mission.

'Agnes, ask Mme Poitrenaud if she would kindly come to my office.'

Giving Durand her usual warm smile, his receptionist picked up the phone. Juliette kept him waiting for half an hour before striding into his office without bothering to knock.

'Finally you condescend to summon me. I suppose I should be grateful you can find the time.'

'That's not very nice of you is it, Juliette?'

Mme Poitrenaud wondered how many other women were entertained in his office. She was feeling anything but 'nice'. The Venetian blinds were wide open.

'I've been here since yesterday and, apart from a brief chat at the cocktail party, you've completely ignored me. You know my husband arrives next week. How could you be so cruel? You think you can do as you please and I've got no choice but to put up with it.'

'My dear Juliette, it is you who does as she pleases and I who have to put up with it. I don't know from one year to the next if you're coming and any time you decide to go elsewhere, I shall have to accept the situation with good grace.'

He walked over to the blinds and closed them completely. The bakelite radio and the Peruvian statue were no longer on the desk. He started to unzip Madame's dress.

'Well, you'd better make up for lost time.'

'There's something I need to discuss with you'.

'Afterwards'.

'As Madame wishes.'

Chapter 5

DURAND WAS RUNNING late. Due to dine with the hotel's owners at eight o'clock, he needed to speak to the American first but Juliette had been determined to make him pay for his lack of attention. Once released, he went to Reception to ask if the American was in his room.

The receptionist answered with an intimate smile. 'I think he's in the roof bar.'

'Thank you, Agnes,' Durand replied, without smiling back. He arrived on the roof to find Brandon waiting to catch the lift down.

'Monsieur, I'm so glad I caught you.'

He steered him back towards the bar.

'I'm arranging a little group to go to a village in the hills where they have a small perfumery. I was wondering if you'd care to join us. I think you'd find it interesting. Of course, there would be plenty of free samples to take away.'

'Thanks for the offer, old sport, but I doubt it's my kind of thing. When is it?

'Tomorrow at 10 o'clock. I know it's short notice but these trips aren't easy to arrange. So many people want to go on them. When a vacancy occurs, we have to act quickly.'

'Ah well, I'm playing at the tennis club tomorrow morning. What a shame,' he said, trying to sound convincing.

'Yes indeed, it is a shame. If, by any chance, you change your mind, let me know at breakfast. In the meantime, have an enjoyable evening.'

Durand thought he knew what would change the American's

mind. While he allowed time for him to return to his room, he asked the bartender how things were going.

'Fine. Every year, we seem to get more people in off the street. There isn't a bar in the area with a view like this one.'

'What are they drinking this year?'

'Cocktails, mainly. The americano is very popular. It's funny how cocktails have caught on. The Americans invented them to mask cheap, bootleg liquor, now everyone in Europe is drinking them. Europeans think it's a stylish American drink, Americans think it's a stylish European drink. We win either way.'

The barman spread his shoulders, expecting praise for his commercial nous but Durand had already picked up the phone. Brandon was surprised to hear from him so soon and wondered if he'd forgotten to sign his bar tab.

'Monsieur Brandon,' Durand hoped the American would like the mixture of respectful formality and slight intimacy, 'this is very impolite of me,' a slight pause for effect, 'I find myself in an embarrassing position. It was presumptuous of me, but I was counting on the use of your car as I promised Mme Poitrenaud I would take her, her daughter and her companion. I'm not sure if you remember the young British lady. I believe you had a dance with her yesterday. Or was it two dances, I can't remember.'

Brandon could certainly remember but even though he was alone, he affected a blank expression, as if recollecting last night was a struggle. Durand made no attempt to help. What he'd just told him would either spur him into action or not.

'It would help if I knew something about these people.'

Durand prepared to reel him in.

'Of course, my apologies. They are a French family from Paris. Madame Juliette Poitrenaud and her daughter Audrey will be joined next week by Monsieur Poitrenaud when his work permits. In the meantime, they have come down with a British girl who is the daughter of an old family friend. That is a story in itself.'

'She speaks excellent French, I notice.'

'Indeed she does. As I say, there is a charming story to that.'

'I don't want to let the other guests down.' Brandon sighed to make it look like a reluctant decision. 'So yeah, sure, I'll come along. There's just one thing though. My car is a two-seater. I can only take one passenger.' That bit was true. The next bit wasn't. 'And I don't speak French.'

'In that case, you'll just have to take the young British lady.'

Chapter 6

With his mind firmly on breakfast, Fawkes was slow to recognise the old man from the hat shop, standing in the hall, anxiously rotating one of his hats by the brim. Skipping the bonjours, Fawkes ushered him outside.

'Don't tell me you gave us the wrong hats.'

'Of course not.' The old man puffed himself up indignantly. 'I've had a message.'

Fawkes watched him reach into his jacket.

'Not here.'

Grabbing hold of his arm, he placed a hand under the man's armpit and steered him through the door and across the road towards the harbour wall. The sandy beach lay on one side of the wall. On the other, a collection of large rocks had been piled up to act as a breakwater. At the far end stood a freshly painted lighthouse. Struggling with the pace, the old man asked plaintively, 'is this necessary?' Fawkes was worried the old man was coming to tell him the mission was off. Recognising that he shouldn't take it out on the old fellow, he released his grip.

'I'm sorry but I didn't want anyone in the hotel seeing or hearing our conversation. Let's just stroll slowly towards the lighthouse. Then you can tell me what this is all about.'

The few fishermen who still used the port had already returned from their night's work and were unloading their catches as a ferry from the island slid past them. The first sunbathers had already arrived on the beach. An old man was wading ashore from his early morning swim. It all looked very peaceful, very safe.

They strolled round to the front of the lighthouse. Surrounded by water, Fawkes smiled at his companion. The old man took this as a sign to pull an envelope out of his well-worn linen jacket and hand it to Fawkes.

'Your client contacted me to check you had collected the coordinates. When I told him there were two of you, he sounded pleased and said he would send me a letter with details of your meeting. This is it.'

Fawkes pulled out two sheets of paper. The first was a detailed map of the route from the main square in the village to the house where the Pole was staying. It was complicated. The second was a letter instructing Fawkes to send his companion to the house which would be identified by a green cloth on the doorstep. He must carry a briefcase. Fawkes was to go to the perfume factory where the real handover was to take place.

He turned and looked out to sea, his eyes squinting in the glare. A sailing skiff passed by in front of the lighthouse. Some boys were climbing on the rocks with a makeshift fishing rod. Standing there amidst all this innocence, Fawkes pondered this change of plan as the sun burnt through his shirt. Though used to risking his own life, he felt uncomfortable putting Heywood in the same position and was reluctant to agree to any arrangement that separated the two of them. On the other hand, doing so would greatly increase the chances of the handover going undetected. Better still, if there were any Germans, they would go back with a story about the handover of some papers. Everyone, even Dansey, would be happy and if Dansey was happy, he'd have a good chance of surviving the reorganisation that Heywood had warned him about.

'Why do you think he's changed the plan?'

It was perfectly obvious why but Fawkes wanted a second opinion. The old man didn't like expressing opinions. That wasn't his role. But the young fellow was tense and that made him tense. He looked away, as if to distance himself from his own words.

'As he says in the letter, he thinks he's being followed. If he is, the plan seems a sensible precaution.'

Fawkes sighed.

'It's hardly a surprise but at least we know where we stand.'

Another gaze out to sea then he turned and faced the old man.

'Alright, we'll do it his way. Thank you. I'll make sure London is told of your assistance. Best if you wait here while I go back to the hotel.'

They shook hands and the old man watched him depart, glad to have no further part in the matter.

A cry of triumph came up from the rocks as the boys caught a fish at their first attempt.

Chapter 7

THE OLD MAN opened the door of his shop and sighed. He was glad to be back in his little world of hats and wanted nothing more to do with this particular plot. When he was young, he'd fancied himself as a spy but that was long ago. He knew he wasn't and never had been any such thing. He was simply a conduit, used by all sorts of people to pass information on to all sorts of other people, no questions asked. The extra income didn't make him rich but it kept the hat shop going.

The young Polish gentleman had contacted him a month ago to say he was coming to the south of France to meet the British but didn't want to reveal his exact location till the last moment. The old man had known Durand's family for years and had been happy to use the hat routine. He'd also told the Pole about the unique characteristics of a village in the hills called La Dame Brave.

Handing over the hats had been no problem, nor was telling the Englishman that the Pole wanted to meet him. Having a conversation in public was another matter. Everyone in this kind of business, for that's what it was to him, a business, knew what he did and knew he never possessed any useful information. He operated in no man's land and that was where he wanted to stay.

The sight of his shop window helped him relax. The display hadn't changed since the Great War and the straw hats were yellow with age. But he'd recently found the solution. The entire window was now covered in a sheet of yellowy brown film to shield its ancient contents from the sun. Proud of his ingenuity, he stopped to admire the sight before entering his domain. The bell over the door welcomed him back as he turned the sign over.

He went through to the storeroom to make himself a cup of coffee. A set of imaginary accounts, kept for the taxman, rested on a shelf next to the hat ribbons, an old ledger even more faded than his hats. He really ought to make a few entries but he'd just taken a first sip of coffee when the bell over the door announced a customer. A woman, attractive but not beautiful, was browsing. Grateful to her for sparing him from bookkeeping, he slipped behind the counter.

'Good morning, Madame. May I be of assistance?'

'I hope so,' she replied in accented French. 'I'm from Sweden and I need a sun hat. What would you recommend?'

The old man produced three straw hats. As she took the first one, two men came in. He turned to them and told them he would be with them in a moment. They gestured that there was no hurry. He turned his attention back to the charming lady. Three other men were outside looking at the window display and pointing to one of the hats. It was going to be a busy day.

'This one is perfect but I don't like the red ribbon. Do you have some blue ribbon instead?'

'Of course, Madame. I'll just go into the back and get some.'

If only he'd stayed in the shop in full view of passers-by. As soon as he'd disappeared into the storeroom, the two men locked the front door and put up the 'Closed' sign while the woman followed him into the back. She remained charming.

'Perhaps you could help me with one other thing.'

Hearing the front door lock, he turned, startled to see she'd followed him. She could smell the fear.

'Relax, you know why we're here. We saw you at the lighthouse. Just tell us what we want to know and we'll be on our way.'

The men joined her in the back room, one grabbed him from behind, pinning back his arms.

'Gently, gently,' she admonished him. The man let him go. The hat seller staggered back, knocking his coffee over the ancient ledger.

'That was entirely our fault. Heinrich, mop it up at once.' Heinrich, a bear of a man, more used to breaking people's backs than performing household tasks, found a sheet of blotting paper and grumpily did as he was told.

'Now, where was I? Ah, yes, the gentleman you were talking to by the lighthouse. We know who he's meeting but not where. Perhaps you can help us.'

'You people in the Abwehr know I'm never told that sort of thing.'

She whispered in his ear, 'but we're not Abwehr.'

Oh God, he thought, they're SD, real Nazis.

'Perhaps not so gently now.' Once more, the old man felt himself gripped, this time more tightly. Unable to control his bladder, he looked pitifully at the woman. This was the Englishman's fault. If he hadn't insisted on going to the lighthouse, they wouldn't have been spotted together. His survival was at stake. He owed the Englishman nothing. Wanting to get rid of them, he told them the name of the village.

'Well, that's a start but whereabouts in this village?'

'They're meeting in a house, I don't know why. You know I'm never given that sort of information.'

'When?'

He thought of saying tomorrow but they'd come back when they found he'd lied. Tell them the truth and they'll leave him alone.

'Today.'

'And the address. As you've been so helpful, you might as well tell us.'

'There was no address. Just a map. I gave it to the Englishman. You'll have to follow him.'

They'd find out one way or another. If he cooperated, it might be good for future business. When he'd finished, the woman smiled warmly and patted him on the back.

'I think that's all for now, except for one thing, of course.'

'There's nothing else I can tell you, I swear.'

'No, no, you misunderstand. Where's the blue ribbon?'

The old man, though still held in a firm grip, felt a surge of relief.

'Up there on the left.'

'Why, thank you. That's exactly what I need.'

She reached up for the ribbon, folded it into a double thickness and wrapped it swiftly round the old man's neck. She paused before tightening it. 'I don't want to do this but you broke the rules. You shouldn't have gone to the lighthouse. I can't risk you telling the Englishman we've been here. I'm sorry.' Using the old man's pen, she tightened the ribbon like a garrotte. He could have struggled but he knew it would only delay the inevitable by a minute at the most. He had better things to do in the remaining moments of his life than waste them on a pointless struggle. He knew who and what to think about as the silken garrotte tightened round his neck.

When it was done, she told one of her accomplices to fetch the three men waiting outside. The five of them stood over the lifeless body waiting for her orders.

'Make it look like a robbery gone wrong then go up to this village, find the street he was talking about and keep an eye out for the Englishmen. We don't want a diplomatic incident so no rough stuff. Follow them when they leave and don't let them out of your sight. I won't be far away but I don't want them to see us together in case I need to work my charms on them later.'

'It would help if we knew what we were looking for.'

'Don't you think I know that? We know this Pole has brought something for the British. Everyone in the department thinks it's documentation about our Enigma machines but I'm not so sure. I think the Poles are on to something but no one in the department believes me. If I can prove them wrong, we'll all benefit so just do as I say, OK?'

'Where will you be?' asked Heinrich.

'I'm going to check on that hotel with the funny name. Sort things out here and make sure you lock up before you leave.'

She folded the ribbon, picked up the hat and walked out.

'She's tetchy,' said one of the men.

'Berlin have got it in for her,' said Heinrich. 'If she messes this one up, Fraulein Mirbeth is for the high jump.'

'If this mission is so important, why put a woman in charge?'

Heinrich gave the questioner a pitiful look.

'They think the mission is bound to fail because there's nothing to find but if it turns out there was something, she can be blamed for not finding it.'

'What if there is something to find and she does finds it?'

'Her boss will claim the credit. He wins either way. Ambitious men need others to pin the blame on when things go wrong. Who better than a woman? They shouldn't try to do men's work.'

When the others sniggered, Heinrich held up a hand to silence them.

'If she fails, she'll take us down with her. It's in our interest to make sure she doesn't.'

They spread the old man across the desk, broke open the petty cash box, shut the door to the back room and let themselves out.

The sign continued to say *Fermé.*

Chapter 8

HEYWOOD WAS HALFWAY through breakfast on the terrace when a grim-faced Fawkes finally strode across the gravel. As he reached the tables, his face switched to become wreathed in smiles as he gave every guest a cheery wave. Until he reached Heywood's table.

'Trouble?'

'Yes and no.' He told him about his encounter with the hat shop man.

'If the Germans are on to us, Koslowski's plan makes sense but I think it would be better if you stayed behind. The Germans will know what he does and can guess why he's here. If things get nasty, I'd rather you weren't involved.'

Heywood buttered a croissant and added a dollop of apricot jam. He appreciated his friend's concern for his safety but he wasn't fooled. Fawkes knew he'd insist on coming along and was probably counting on it.

'If all I have to do is sit in a house in a Provençal village, I doubt I'll be in much danger.'

He popped a piece of croissant into his mouth and swallowed it. Wiping the flakes from his mouth with his napkin, he continued.

'The Pole's plan makes good sense. If we split up in the village, it will confuse him. I say 'him', do we know how many there are?'

'Koslowski's note only mentioned one.' Fawkes selected a croissant from the basket. 'But you never know. Are you sure you want to do this?'

'Definitely. Besides, if there is only one of them and two of us, we'll both be safer.'

Fawkes hid the relief he felt by busily reaching into his jacket for the directions to the house.

'These instructions are complicated. Once we've dropped you off, try and get along pretty quickly. If he follows you, he'll be some way behind to avoid being noticed and there's a good chance you'll lose him down this maze of streets. I'll tell Durand.'

He was about to add 'but I won't tell him about the lighthouse meeting,' when he was distracted by a new arrival on the terrace.

'Christ, will you look at that.'

Heywood turned to see Brandon make an entrance in a safari suit and an extra day's growth of beard. 'Who does he think he is, Ernest Hemingway?'

'Perhaps he thinks there are tigers up in the hills,' said Fawkes. 'Mind you, if he's armed, we might need him later on.'

'I doubt that. He's dressed to impress that young British girl.'

'Really? Which one?'

'That one over there, they can't take their eyes off each other. Haven't you noticed?'

'Strangely, no. I've had other things on my mind.'

'Well, they told me to look upon this as a holiday and that's what I'm doing. You should be grateful I'm so observant. See for yourself.'

Fawkes turned to look at the object of the American's interest. He could only get a three-quarter view of her but it was enough. If he'd been a real film executive, he'd have signed her up on the spot. Then she giggled at something her companion said and the spell was broken. Beneath the beauty, she was just a child and, though he didn't know it, a child who was laughing at him.

Determined to distance herself from the two embarrassing Englishmen, she'd watched the younger one as he crunched across the gravel.

'He's wearing a starched collar. Probably planning to catch the 8.32 to London Bridge.'

'Now, now, Mary. You shouldn't be so catty. It's not their fault they lack French sophistication.'

Mary's laugh had a false edge to it. Juliette was enjoying her discomfort too much and her comment only emphasised how much of an embarrassment the two men were to a young lady aching to match Juliette's savoir-faire. When the two men stood up to leave, she didn't bother to lower her voice.

'At least we'll be able to get away from them for a day. I can't wait for this outing to start.'

Fawkes knew who they were referring to. As he passed their table, he gave them a courteous smile. When Mary ignored him completely, he gave himself a pat on the back for his convincing disguise.

By ten o'clock, the guests were assembling in the foyer. Juliette had made the trip to the perfume factory twice before and would have been happy to give it a miss but felt obliged to show Mary, currently giggling with Audrey, the beauty of inland Provence. Then the Englishmen appeared. Mary, assuming they were on their way out, was tempted to make a display of displeasure when, to her horror, Durand introduced them to the rest of the group.

'Ladies and gentlemen, joining us today are two representatives of one of Britain's finest film companies, London Films. They're looking for suitable locations for their next film and La Dame Brave has caught their attention.'

At a stroke, the two men went from being the height of embarrassment to the height of chic. People to know rather than avoid. Noticing the look of irritation on Juliette's face, Mary ostentatiously joined the others as they gathered admiringly round the two men. Juliette, equally ostentatiously, kept her distance.

'Do you need any extras for this film, gentlemen?' asked Harry Ransome. Everyone laughed but he was only half joking. Their conversation in the rooftop bar had set him thinking about making a career switch. Now, two men who could make that happen would be travelling in the back of his car. What a stroke of luck.

Relieved the two Englishmen were no longer an embarrassment, Mary was wondering if Brandon would be joining them when a flash of green metal swooped up the drive, coming to a halt with a handbrake turn in front of the hotel. Seeing it was a two-seater and anxious to reach the car before anyone else, she strode swiftly through the door, nearly colliding with a woman, attractive but not beautiful, coming the other way. In a contest of politeness, each woman stepped aside for the other then stepped out again at the same time. Finally, the incomer insisted on letting Mary through with a 'please, I prefer that you should go first.' Mary thanked her as they passed but by the time the encounter was over, everyone else had caught her up. For a moment, all seemed lost then Durand led her to Brandon's car.

'As my car has a small back seat, there is only room on it for Mme Audrey, would it be possible for you to take this young lady?'

'Of course, M. Durand, but I hope you won't mind being stuck with Mme Poitrenaud.' He gave him a wink and patted him on the arm before turning to help Mary into his car. She'd looked good dancing in a check gingham dress. In slacks and a somewhat tight blouse, she was stunning.

Watched by the woman Mary had encountered, the two men from the film company climbed into the Ransomes' Wolseley.

'Welcome aboard, gentlemen.'

Fawkes, still pondering the wisdom of what he was about to do failed to respond to Harry's greeting. Heywood gave his young friend a reassuring pat on the shoulder.

'Let's try and enjoy this, shall we?'

Lydia Ransome heard the comment. 'Don't you like looking for locations Mr Hawkes?'

Fawkes switched on the drawl.

'Usually, but today could be rather tricky. I have to view this perfume factory you're all visiting and do some hard bargaining with the owners while Hey, er George, goes off to discuss accommodation with the owner of some empty houses. On these trips, the scenery can be lovely but the negotiating side can be rather stressful.'

Heywood nodded his admiration.

As the convoy drove up the hill behind the hotel, Mary started to appreciate how old Fort Sarrasin must be. The road was cobbled and narrow, so narrow cars had to mount the pavement to pass each other. Most of the houses had been converted into shops on the ground floor but the accommodation above looked unchanged since the Revolution, even the paint looked original. At the top of the hill, they passed the fort itself. Much of it was dilapidated but the tower in the centre had stood the test of time, still dominating the bay below. Beyond it, lay the village graveyard over whose entrance, a Latin inscription read *Hodie Nobis Cras Vobis*. As they swept past, Mary wondered what it meant but decided there was no point in asking an American playboy.

Remembering what Durand had told him, Brandon decided it was time to learn more about his passenger.

'Durand says your family have known the Poitrenauds a long time.'

'Our mothers met when they were serving in a field hospital during the Great War. I suppose being surrounded by the dead and dying created a bond between them.'

'That's a great story', said Brandon. 'Is there a Monsieur Poitrenaud?'

'He'll be down next week.'

'It can't be much fun being stuck up in a hot city when everyone else has gone away.'

'Audrey says he's used to it. I'm guessing he rather likes a week on his own and Juliette certainly likes her week before he comes down. Yesterday evening, she was really happy.'

'I'm sure she deserves it.'

'What about this car then? It's rather smashing. Did you hire it for the holiday?'

No, it's mine. I bought it when I arrived in Southampton. It's a British car, a Jaguar SS. The man who sold it to me said they'd only made three hundred or so of these with an extra powerful engine. It's taken me all over Europe.'

'What a shame we're stuck behind Durand, you won't be able to show me how fast it goes.' The challenge was accompanied by the look she'd given him when their eyes first met at the cocktail party. He laughed.

'I'm not falling for that. Durand is the only one who knows the way. You'll just have to take my word for it that this car is fast.'

For several moments, she studied her hands, clasped together in her lap, while she debated whether to say what was on her mind. Finally, she spoke.

'You're not how I expected an American to be.'

'And how did you expect an American to be?'

'You know.'

'No, I don't.'

'Well, brash, showy.'

'Well, if I'm not brash and showy, what am I?'

'Understated, almost cultured.'

'You flatter me. Well, at least I'm not showy.'

'Apart from the car.'

'That's British.'

'You know what I mean.'

'Well, I suppose I'll have to settle for almost cultured. At least it's better than being how you expect an American to be.'

'Don't be horrid. I'm trying to pay you a compliment.'

He turned to look at her and smiled.

'The attempted compliment is accepted.'

'I shouldn't have spoken.'

'Yes, you should. In fact, that's just about the nicest thing anyone ever said to me.'

He judged, correctly, that it was time to change the subject.

'Anyway, poodling along behind Durand gives us time to talk about you. What are your plans? You must be very popular with the young men in, where was it you said, Woodstock?'

'I'm not interested in that sort of thing.' She didn't want to tell him she'd just left school so she told him about her ambition. 'My first love is show jumping. I want to concentrate on that full time and compete in the 1940 Olympics.'

'Good for you,' said Brandon. 'I admire a young girl who doesn't want to go down the well-trodden path to domesticity. Don't give up on your dreams.'

'You're not travelling with anyone?' Mary tried to sound as casual as possible.

'No, we sold the family business this year and I'm taking the opportunity to tour Europe before war starts.'

'You think there'll be a war? I know it's in the papers all the time but surely no one would be so stupid after the last one.'

'As soon as the harvest is in, I'm afraid. Still, let's not talk about that now. We're here to enjoy ourselves. While we can.'

Chapter 9

THEY DROVE THROUGH the coastal vineyards then up into dense woodland. Here and there, Man had tried to carve out small areas for his own use but the overwhelming impression was of nature untamed and untameable. As they climbed higher, the trees themselves gave up the struggle, yielding to a landscape of giant rocks, black with age but with areas where the original pink sandstone glowed defiantly.

A road that had been gently winding now turned into a series of hairpin bends with sharp drops on one side, jagged rock face on the other. Then they rounded one more bend, the ground levelled out and the bare landscape gave way to dazzling fields of lavender, row upon row, as far as the eye could see. Beyond it lay La Dame Brave, its ancient walls, a tower and a church, perched on cliffs of solid rock. The convoy drove through the gates and climbed into medieval streets lined with houses that varied in age from the seventeenth back to the fourteenth century.

At the top of the hill, the little convoy arrived in the tree-lined village square. In the centre, a dusty boules court was occupied by a group of old men. To one side, a group of tables and chairs were occupied by chess players, both young and old. Most of the shops lining the road that ran around the square catered for the needs of the villagers but Fawkes noticed that some now offered tourist merchandise. It was a shame, he thought, but if this hadn't become a tourist destination, they wouldn't have been able to come here in this convenient little convoy.

As soon as the cars had parked up, one behind the other,

Heywood stepped out, smoothed the creases in his suit and walked off, clutching Koslowski's directions in one hand, nothing in the other. As he disappeared around the corner, Mary noticed him steal a quick glance back, as if he didn't want them to see where he was going. Happy to acknowledge the existence of her fellow countrymen she remarked on this to Brandon.

'Why has the old one gone off on his own? I thought they'd look at film locations together.'

'The old guy's obviously the boss,' said Brandon. Perhaps he's trying to do a deal to rent some houses for the film crew. There's more to making a film than just setting up a camera.'

Once everyone had assembled, Mary conferred with Audrey. 'Perhaps they're not really looking for film locations,' whispered Audrey. 'Maybe they're a couple of spies on a cloak and dagger mission. That would make Mummy even more furious.'

Mary walked over to the Ransomes.

'Why do you think the old one went off alone?'

Harry seized the opportunity to sound knowledgeable about what he hoped would be his future line of business.

'They told us in the car. The old guy is looking for accommodation for the film crew while the young fellow looks at the perfume factory as a location. They seem rather decent chaps to me.'

Durand had overheard the conversation and laughed. 'That's right. They have to rent a house and don't want the owner to know it's for a famous star or he'll put the rent up. As for them being spies,' continued Durand, 'if that's the best the British can do, then heaven help us.'

Fawkes looked down the hill. No one seemed to have followed them. He hadn't expected Heywood to disappear from view so quickly and wished he'd been able to see where he'd gone but, as the real changeover was to take place elsewhere, it shouldn't be a problem. Time to get into character as a location finder. He examined his surroundings.

From a film maker's point of view, they couldn't be better.

The bluest sky he'd ever seen contrasted with the walls of the houses, some yellow, some pink, all with rustic tiled roofs. The light was so strong, every shutter of every house seemed to have been closed to keep it out, every head covered with a wide brimmed hat. But he was a spy, not a film maker. For him, the wide hats made it difficult to pick out any possible enemies and the narrow streets were places to hide but also places to be ambushed. He felt the usual tightness in the stomach, the need to look around all the time without seeming to do so. He was where he belonged.

The conversation about the 'spies' had taken place beside the Ransomes' Wolseley. Glancing into the car, Mary spotted the briefcase she'd seen Heywood carrying out of the hotel.

'Oh, he's left his case.'

She reached in, pulled out the surprisingly light case and made off down the lane in pursuit of Heywood. Brandon, never one to miss an opportunity, rushed after her.

'I hope you don't mind me accompanying you to find Mr Heywood, Miss Ballantyne.'

'Not at all Mr Wade. As long as you don't hold me up.'

'I'll do my best. You shouldn't go off on your own like this. These streets are a maze. You could disappear forever. I wouldn't like that.'

Mary's face flushed at the barely hidden compliment.

'Oh, I'm sure you'd soon get over it.'

'You're probably right. The fact remains, a beautiful young woman like you can easily attract attention from the wrong sort.'

'You mean someone like you?'

At that moment, a man brushed past them, pushing Mary into Brandon. He steadied her with a firm grip. It reminded both of them of their dance.

'More someone like him, I think.'

'He seems in a dreadful hurry.'

'Perhaps he's chasing our man too.'

'Didn't I tell you they were spies?'

'You did, indeed.'

'You can release me now.'

She said it reluctantly. He obeyed with even greater reluctance. She looked up the lane.

"Now where's Mr Heywood. I can't see him anywhere.'

'If they're both spies, we'd better follow that gorilla.'

She laughed. He looked at her seriously.

'You have a lovely laugh.'

'Thank you.'

'No, I was being serious.'

'So was I.'

The silence that followed came as a welcome relief to the young country girl. Like the characters the two film men had adopted, she was out of her depth in a foreign country. Fortunately, following the gorilla paid dividends as she spotted Heywood at the far end of a long, narrow lane. She turned to Brandon.

'There he is.'

When she looked back, Heywood had disappeared.

Holding the map in front of him, squinting at it in the glare and wishing he'd brought sunglasses, Heywood turned two more corners. There, at the end of the lane, as described in the map, he found a set of wrought iron gates opening onto a small courtyard containing eight identical houses, each with a flight of stone steps leading up to an oak front door. Generations of feet had hollowed out the steps, the centuries had blackened the oak. Walls that had originally been plastered in Provençal pink were now mottled in a black and green stain with only the edges still showing the original colour. He guessed they must be the oldest houses in the village and had once belonged to artisans, each specialising in his own craft. Feeling he'd stepped back in time, he picked his way over the ruts from the wheels of the wagons that had carried their wares and made his way towards the line of doors, each identical, each firmly shut against the sun.

No sign of a green cloth. Not until he heard a panting sound and turned to see a dog standing behind him, the cloth hanging from its mouth. With a triumphant look, it scampered off, leaving him wondering what to do next. Standing in the blazing sun, he was on the point of confessing defeat when one of the doors opened and a silhouette beckoned to him. Relieved not to have failed right at the start, he climbed the steps and followed his host across a small hall and into an oak-panelled room. As his eyes accustomed to the gloom, he saw that the room was dominated by a stone fireplace, beside it a pile of logs, neatly arranged.

The cool room provided a welcome relief from the heat. It was plainly furnished with a table and four chairs in the middle and a dresser against one wall, all in lime-washed Provençal style. A single armchair stood by the fireplace. The oak floor was so uneven, he had to be careful not to stumble as he picked his way across. His young host had no such problem and strode swiftly towards the logs, removing the top layer to produce a pile of sheets of paper. Only then did Heywood remember the briefcase, still lying in the back of the car. He'd have to carry them back in his hand.

'These are for you to take back. They're a Polish translation of War and Peace and can safely be allowed to fall into the wrong hands.'

He smiled at the elementary deception then got down to business.

'Has your colleague told you what to do?'

'Wait here for an hour or so then leave.'

'Precisely.'

Koslowski felt more relaxed now things were underway. He smiled at Heywood.

'I expect you think what you're doing is a waste of time but it's just as important as the rest of the operation. They'll probably give you a medal one day.'

'I'd sooner have a larger pension.'

'Are you about to retire?'

'When this is over. This is a sort of paid holiday given to me as a leaving present.'

'Well, enjoy it then. I expect you deserve it.'

They shook hands and Koslowski left the room. Heywood heard him go into the kitchen but never heard him leave and assumed he'd found a way out without being seen. Left to his own devices, he sank into the armchair and turned his thoughts to the game of cricket and the current Test series.

Still wondering where Heywood had gone, Mary and Brandon came to a meeting point for four narrow lanes but no sign of him. Looking for a clue, they saw the brute who'd barged into them scurrying down the lane that led off to the right. Brandon looked at Mary.

'Follow that spy?'

'What choice have we got?'

Laughing, they set off. The narrowness of the lane and the height of the ancient buildings shut out the sun. Hoping they'd chosen correctly, they enjoyed the light breeze that seemed to follow them down the lane. The sun bided its time until they reached a dead end in the form of a courtyard. Then, unrestrained, it blazed down on them as they considered a row of identical houses. Ahead of them, the gorilla seemed to have the same idea. When he saw them, he hurried round the side of the courtyard and disappeared.

'Do you think he went in one of these? Shall we try each one?'

While Mary studied the house, Heywood, enjoying a brief lull in his imaginary conversation, wandered over to the window. Seeing him, Mary waved the briefcase and made for the door. While she waited for the door to open, she noticed a worn carving on the doorpost.

'Sorry to interrupt, we found your briefcase in the car and thought you might need it.'

'That's very kind. Silly of me to forget it. I'd invite you in but you know how it is.'

'Of course, you get back to your negotiations. We'll see you later.'

Brandon put an arm round Mary to guide her down the steps,

forgetting to remove it until they had worked their way out of the maze of lanes and reached the welcome sight of the square.

Fawkes was itching to move on to the factory but Durand had to attend to the needs of his guests and that meant a leisurely drink. In the heat, there was little demand for coffee. 'May I suggest the sirop de citron à l'eau?' Juliette suggested. 'I find it ideal on days like these.' The women accepted her suggestion, the men had beers. All except Fawkes. He needed the caffeine. God, he needed the caffeine.

After a few sips of the bitter drink, Audrey confessed, 'actually, I like to add sugar.'

'Good idea,' said Lydia. 'I'll join you.'

Fawkes had watched expressionless as Mary and Brandon chased after Heywood, leading anyone watching straight to him. He drummed his fingers on the table until he became aware of Juliette's eyes on him.

'Damn fine coffee, Madame Poitrenaud.'

The drawl was accompanied by a beaming smile.

'You really should have tried it.'

Juliette smiled nervously. If everyone in the film company was like him, how on earth did they get any films made?

Fawkes's fears were confirmed when they returned, minus the briefcase.

'Sorry to keep you all waiting,' said Mary. Juliette noticed her face. Was it flushed from exertion or from the pleasure of going for a stroll with Brandon?

'It was a complicated route and we weren't helped by a man who overtook us and kept obscuring our view of Mr Heywood. For a minute, we wondered if he was going to the same place but he kept on walking.'

'Probably just a local,' suggested Fawkes.

'I doubt it,' said Brandon. 'He certainly wasn't dressed like one and had a pale skin. Definitely a foreigner.'

'You said he looked like a gorilla,' said Mary gazing adoringly at her companion.

That settled it. Signalling to Durand, Fawkes went through to the back of the café.

'I wish they'd stayed out of it. They've been followed. We've got to keep him out of the factory. Bugger.'

Durand picked up the phone on the wall and slipped a token into the slot. 'I'll tell the factory one of the women is receiving unwelcome attentions from a man and ask them to keep him out.'

Fawkes found little reassurance in the Frenchman's words. It was his own fault. He'd left too much in the hands of Koslowski. Heywood was alone and he was heading for a rendez-vous in a place he knew nothing about. He barely gave Durand time to put the phone down.

'We should leave now. We'll need to make some decisions when we arrive so you and I better travel together. The French lady and her daughter will have to go with the Ransomes.'

Durand was all smiles as he addressed the guests. 'Ladies and gentlemen, I'm sorry to rush you but the factory wants us to go there right away. Mr Fawkes and I will be travelling together. I hope that won't inconvenience you Madame Poitrenaud.'

The French lady, restricting herself to a brusque 'not at all,' took a last sip of sirop de citron and stood up.

Chapter 10

THE FACTORY WAS perched on the eastern edge of the village, overlooking the lavender fields below. The main part was a tall Provençal house with yellowed walls and a roof of clay tiles, overlapping in a double layer to ensure it was watertight. It didn't rain very often in this part of the world but when it did, it was torrential.

The height of the main building was emphasised by two single storey wooden outbuildings, one on each side, with sturdy oak beams and distinctive tiles with rounded ends. The rear of the factory ran right up to the edge of the rock on which the village had been built, offering a magnificent view from its windows. For the tourists, it was an enchanting sight, for Fawkes, a nightmare. When the Pole had suggested a handover in the factory, he'd imagined something modern behind high walls. Confronting him was a set of rustic buildings approached through a farm gate set in a low, dry stone wall.

'Christ, it's completely open. How are we going to get this thing into the car without being seen?'

Durand had stopped in the entrance, the others behind him. 'Why the delay?' muttered Harry. 'Perhaps we're too late,' said Lydia.

There was plenty of space to park on the left but Fawkes needed to get the cars out of sight. He pointed to the right.

'Park behind that shed. That way, he'll only be able to see us if he's hiding in the lavender fields. We'd better get a move on or the guests will become suspicious.'

'It's a bit late for that.'

As Durand led the group into the factory, Juliette set to work.

'Did you enjoy your chat with your important new friend? Are you sure you have time for us? We don't want to put you out.'

Durand made sure everyone could hear. 'I apologise, Madame, we were discussing how to negotiate location rights with the factory owners. Apparently, it can cost a lot of money.'

He led them to a window at the back of the factory. It had the desired effect. Symmetrical rows of lavender stretched out as far as the eye could see. Here and there, sections had been devoted to jasmine, the white flowers enhancing the splendour of the lavender. The atmosphere lightened perceptibly as they appreciated the stunning sight. Fawkes appreciated the lack of cover the low bushes would give the enemy. Durand prepared to explain how the factory worked.

'The village is named after a woman who was burned at the stake and is one of a few in France where everyone is Protestant. To protect themselves against government raids, they developed a network of tunnels, carved out of the rock on which the village is built.

'As you can see, this is a very old factory. It uses distillation methods that are unchanged since it was first built and prepares both lavender oil and water and also jasmine wax. You will have seen some jasmine in the fields. This is just the tip of the iceberg, so to speak. There are over four thousand small jasmine growers in Provence. Every day, they harvest the flowers at dawn, before the sun damages them and, every day, the plants replace the flowers, except for one day each year when, for reasons which no one understands, the jasmine plant takes the day off. The flowers are soaked in water. Once the excess moisture is removed, they produce a wax with a perfume that is identical to the flower from which it is made. Now, if you will follow me.'

Had he been gabbling? God, the needy Englishman made him feel nervous.

He led them up a flight of wooden steps to watch the newly

harvested stalks of lavender being tumbled into a wooden still. Beneath it, a boiler, originally from a steam train, sent up a steady flow of steam to extract the oil from the plants. An elderly clerk with a white beard and pince-nez glasses, sat at a high desk, recording each bundle of lavender in a foolscap ledger. In front of him, a large window overlooked the lavender fields.

'This is exactly like the view from my office desk in the City,' said Harry. Lydia gave him a sympathetic look and stroked his arm.

The guests might be happy, Fawkes wanted to find Koslowski. For that, he needed Durand. The Frenchman ignored his signals for as long as possible then, with an audible sigh, made his excuses and led Fawkes down the steps.

'That man is never there when you need him. He really can be most inattentive to the needs of his guests.'

While Lydia raised her eyebrows at the remark from a surprisingly touchy Juliette, Brandon stepped forward to fill the gap. He knew nothing about perfume but had no inhibitions in finding people who did. A trip to the boiler room was followed by a stroll amongst the lavender then it was back to the factory to watch the packing line.

Fawkes led Durand away. He'd left Heywood on his own. Koslowski was nowhere to be seen. As soon as they were out of earshot, he expressed his frustration.

'Where's the bloody despatch bay? They must have one.'

Durand led him towards the shed next to the cars.

'Well, there's no sign of him.'

'Relax Mr Fawkes, I'm right behind you.'

A smiling Koslowski seemed to have appeared from nowhere. He was carrying a carton and looked questioningly at Durand. Fawkes took the hint.

'I'm sorry old boy. Thank you for your help but I've strict instructions not to let you witness any of this. Don't take it personally. Like I said in the hotel, it's for your own safety.'

'Of course.' Durand wanted to stay and part of him did take

it personally. He resented the fact that he, a long serving agent of the British but a foreigner and a Jew, was not considered sufficiently trustworthy to be let in on the secret. But he was a professional and Fawkes was right. The less he saw, the safer he was. With a polite bow of the head, he withdrew gracefully.

Fawkes looked at the box, expecting Koslowski to open it. The young Pole made him wait.

'When you came to the meeting in January, how much did you know about codebreaking?'

'Nothing at all. I was only there because I spoke German. As soon as my team realised I wasn't needed, they sent me back to the hotel. Thank you for driving me back, by the way.'

'I enjoyed it. You weren't like the others. That meeting was a failure because we codebreakers are like you spies, we keep what we know to ourselves. But time is running out and someone has to do something.'

He placed a hand on the shoulder of the British spy.

'When I say someone, I mean you and me.'

As Heywood had pointed out, so much of Fawkes's time was spent sitting around, waiting. It was moments like this that made it all worthwhile. Koslowski was preparing to give him information that his superiors didn't want to reveal. Was he looking for money or was he acting from principle? The golden rule in these circumstances was to let the source say his piece. He nodded and waited for the Pole to continue.

'The Germans encode messages using a machine that looks like a typewriter.'

'I'd heard rumours of this.'

'The first ones were similar to the commercial machines and were easily broken. Now, they're using a more sophisticated version with too many combinations to be broken manually. They named it after the Enigma Variations by the British composer Elgar.'

'Presumably, there aren't too many of these machines, if they're so complicated.'

Koslowski laughed briefly then his face turned dark.

'The factory has orders from the German armed forces for over 100,000. They will communicate with each other in complete secrecy. All the spies in the world won't help you.'

'But what you've brought today will?'

Like a magician reaching the climax of his act, Koslowski opened the box and pulled out a metal disc.

'My people found your people too stuffy and arrogant.'

'Welcome to the club.'

'My people are not much better. They're holding back too much information. That's why I've brought you this, it's a rotor from an Enigma machine. There are five of them in this box. They show you the wiring of the Enigma rotors and, if you know what you're doing, you can work out how the machine encodes each letter and build a machine to do the reverse.'

Fawkes had two speaking styles. One was a pastiche of what foreigners expected from an English gentleman, a drawl peppered with public school aphorisms and understatement. In the right circumstances, it served him well. On this occasion, however, he spoke in the other style, hard and direct.

'I don't understand. If the codes can't be broken, how will a machine help us to do it? Surely a machine can't do more than a human brain.'

'Don't take offence, Mr Fawkes, but you don't need to understand. Just get these rotors into the hands of people who do. The old way of making and breaking codes is over. You need a machine that can handle a large number of combinations in a short space of time before the message is out of date.'

Through dark rings of sleeplessness, his eyes blazed, his face was alight with excitement. Code breaking was his whole life.

But it wasn't Fawkes's and he was struggling to take it all in. He wanted to believe everything the Pole was saying if only because of the benefit it would bring to his career but the claimed significance of what was being handed to him made him suspicious. The old doubts returned. He looked round the room to make sure there was no one else around then moved a little closer to Koslowski.

'Why are you giving me this?'

Koslowski screwed up his face as if the answer was causing him real pain.

'I love my country, Mr Fawkes, but it's run by ultra-nationalists who've lost touch with reality. They're convinced Poland can withstand a German attack and don't want to let go of their great secret. Germany will attack soon. When they do, we'll be defeated. We Poles are a clever people but we can't do everything ourselves. We've designed a machine to break codes on an earlier version of Enigma but the Germans have made the machine more complicated. I know you British have been working on something similar but time is running out. As a patriot, I believe I have to pass on to you what we know in the hope that you can improve on it in time.'

'Will my people know how to use these rotors?'

Koslowski visibly relaxed as he returned to matters technical.

'Like all the best toys, it comes with instructions.' He fumbled inside his jacket and produced two handwritten sheets of paper. One was a wiring diagram, the other contained twenty lines of numbers and letters, nothing else.

'They won't make head or tail of this,' said Fawkes.

'They will with these instructions. The future of code breaking lies not in language but in mathematics.'

Fawkes was a language man. As soon as Koslowski started talking about maths trumping language, his doubts returned and not just in the ability of a machine to replace a man. Like an actor going off for a change of costume, he walked away from Koslowski and looked briefly out of the window while he pondered the situation. What if the Germans had set the whole thing up to send the British codebreakers on a wild goose chase? Why were they only being followed by one German? His career already hung in the balance. Get this wrong and he was finished for good. He switched speaking styles.

'The thing is, old boy, I don't quite understand why we're doing this here, such a long way from either your home or mine. It's all a bit tricky, isn't it? I'd be the first to admit that we're a trifle pressed when it comes to codebreaking but we don't want to be taken to the cleaners.'

He waited for Koslowski to react to his pomposity. The Pole rose to the occasion. Looking him straight in the eye, he spoke quietly but with great force.

'Mr Fawkes, let me make one thing clear. The Germans must never, under any circumstances and whatever the cost, find out you have these rotors. They know their enemies will spend countless hours trying to break their codes. They know that, sooner or later, some of their machines will be captured. But they are certain that the number of combinations is so great, the codes themselves will never be broken.'

He moved closer, placing his hands on Fawkes's shoulders and his face inches from the Englishman's.

'If they find out about these rotors, they will realise their confidence has been unjustified and will make the codes even more complicated. If that happens, you will lose the war. You must do whatever is necessary, make whatever sacrifices are necessary, to ensure they don't.'

Fawkes exhaled sharply. Relieved, a little ashamed but above all, reassured. He dropped the drawl but Koslowski did not release him from his grip.

'In other words', said Fawkes, 'the greatest strength of the German machine is also its greatest weakness.'

'Now, perhaps you understand why I've gone to a lot of trouble to conceal this handover. Anyone watching the house will think you're getting some notes on their coding machine. If they think they know what's going on, it will be easier to fool them.'

Fawkes smiled. 'I thought you were a code breaker, not a spy'.

'I deal in riddles. It's just a question of applying it on a larger scale.' He stepped back. The confrontation had served its purpose for both men. The Pole picked up the box.

'Which car are we using?'

'The one on the left, it's got a good rear seat. I examined it on the way here and it will lift easily. We just need to get the box out without being seen.'

With a quick 'stay here', Koslowski disappeared into a side room to emerge dressed in an overall and wheeling a trolley laden with samples. He placed the box amongst them then wheeled the trolley out to the cars, loading a set of samples into each of them. In the middle of all this, he opened the door of the Wolseley, lifted the seat and slipped the box in. In little more than a minute, he returned, smiling at a job well done. Then he stopped smiling. He had one last message for the Englishman.

'Tell your masters I will never tell anyone I gave you these rotors. No matter what they do to me. You have my word on that. You may need to know that one day.'

Fawkes had one more test, a question he needed to ask. The answer would tell him whether these rotors were genuine. He dreaded getting the wrong answer but had to ask it. He tried to sound as casual as possible.

'What will you do now?'

'Go home.'

'To Poland?'

'Of course.'

'Will you be safe?'

'Probably not but it's my homeland. I must be there when the time comes to defend it.'

This was what Fawkes wanted to hear. It made it less likely Koslowski was peddling junk in return for asylum. He hid his relief but his conscience was troubled. He made a quick decision.

'Why not come back with us? I'll get you into Britain and make sure you can stay there. You'll be useful, something you won't be in a Poland that won't last a fortnight when the Nazis invade.'

'Out of the question. I must go home, it's my duty.'

With that, he kissed Fawkes on both cheeks.

'That was a test, wasn't it?'

Fawkes nodded.

'A word of advice, what I have given you today is of the greatest value. Your people will soon see that. Whether they tell you is another matter.'

Chapter 11

A LATE LUNCH in the main square gave Durand an opportunity to relax. Everything had gone according to plan, allowing him to resume his role of jovial and considerate host.

'Permit me to suggest a typical Provençal dish, la Daube Provençale, perhaps with a side plate of Tapenade. Washed down, of course, by a bottle of vin rosé from one of the vineyards we passed on the way here. I think you will enjoy it.'

Fawkes had suggested they start without his fellow film executive, which was just as well as there was no sign of him. He tried to play the role of location manager but the longer he waited for Heywood to reappear, the more worried he became. Mary noticed this and used it to open a conversation with him.

'You look worried, Mr Fawkes. I'm sure your colleague is alright. He looked fine when we left him.'

Brandon didn't like the film executive having Mary all to himself and joined in.

'Tell Mr Fawkes about your show jumping. That'll take his mind off things.'

'He's not interested in that.'

'No, please, I'd love to hear about it.'

'There's nothing to tell, really. I love riding and I've been kindly lent a wonderful horse to practise show jumping. I hope to make the team for next year's Olympics. I think we should all do what we're best at, don't you Mr Fawkes? I expect you're best at being in the film industry. No one should rob the world of their talents.'

He tried to laugh at the wisdom of this young girl but it reminded him of what he was supposed to be best at. Dropping the worried expression, he flourished a business card and played the role he'd been allotted.

'You have a wise head on young shoulders, Miss Ballantyne, and a very pretty one. Have you considered a career in films?'

He was saved from having to offer her a job by the arrival of his colleague, strolling around the corner, briefcase in hand, not a care in the world. Heywood pulled up a chair and poured himself a glass of rosé.

'Sorry about that.' He took a sip. 'There was a lot to discuss and I didn't notice it was so late. I hope you all enjoyed the factory.'

Fawkes's relief at his safe return was short-lived. On the other side of the square, a man was leaning against a wall, nonchalantly reading a newspaper. He bore a marked resemblance to a gorilla.

Seeing Fawkes's worried expression, Juliette placed her own interpretation on it. He'd realised his older colleague had been doing a bit of business behind his back. She decided to stir the pot.

'We had a wonderful time, Monsieur Heywood,' said Juliette. 'But you need to keep an eye on your young colleague, he disappeared for a long time. I don't know what he was up to.'

Freed from a lifetime sitting at his desk, Heywood relished the opportunity to play the master spy and needed no encouragement to join in the repartee.

'I'm sure the young lad was doing his best for the company. You'd be surprised at the strange people he meets but that's the film business for you.'

'And what were you doing?' If there was a hint of accusation in Juliette's voice, Heywood ignored it.

'I was finding a suitable house for the star of our next film. It wasn't easy, she can be very demanding.'

'Who is it? Do tell us.' Lydia placed her hand on his to encourage a little indiscretion from the old fellow.

'All I can say is she's just been making a film in Hollywood, a civil war epic.'

Though irritated by the attention the two men were receiving, Juliette wasn't one to fight a losing battle.

'How did you come to be in films, Mr Fawkes? Was your father in the same line of business?'

'Good Lord, no. He was in the Navy. He was killed in the Battle of Jutland.'

'I say old man, what bad luck,' said Harry. 'You must be frightfully proud of him. Has your mother ever recovered from her loss?'

Fawkes hesitated before replying, a hesitation so brief, none of the others noticed. Except Heywood.

'She died of cancer, a short while later.'

Irritated by the sympathy this generated, Juliette changed the subject.

'Are you going to Cannes, Mr Heywood?'

Juliette's question caught Heywood off guard. There was nothing about a can in his notes from Korda. But he knew film was kept in cans and swiftly recovered.

'Yes, Madame Poitrenaud, we always keep each roll of film in a can.'

Juliette laughed.

'No, I don't mean a tin can, I mean the place Cannes. Aren't they holding some sort of film festival there, starting on the first of September?'

'Oh that. I don't think we'll bother. Even if it goes ahead, I doubt it will be a success. I can't see the point of it. No, they'll cancel it, you mark my words.'

Small talk wasn't Fawkes's strong point and he was glad Heywood was doing a good job. It gave him time to think and not just about the mission. Since their conversation on the beach, he'd been stewing over Heywood's warning that there would be a merger between Z section and Broadway. Mergers were an opportunity to cut out dead wood. For all his bravado about walking out, the job was his whole life. Though he didn't fully understand what Koslowski had been telling him, he had no doubt the rotors were of great significance. Bringing them back to London would be the making of him. The mission had to succeed. Failure was not an option.

But what to do with the gorilla? Perhaps the silly girl's intervention had done him a favour. When it was time to leave, he leaned over to Harry.

'Slight change of plan, old chap. I have to go to Marseille to meet another of our contacts so I won't be coming back just yet. Thundering nuisance, frankly, but never mind.'

'How will you get back?'

'Don't worry, I'll get the bus there and the train back.'

'Be back in time for the fireworks,' said Lydia.

'Wouldn't miss them for the world, dear lady.'

Steering Heywood into the back of the café, he brought him up to date.

'Why were you so long?'

'I stupidly left the map in the house. It's a complicated route even with the map. Without it, I took several wrong turnings.'

'Doesn't matter, we won't be needing it again. I'm more worried about the man who followed you. That silly girl led him right to you.'

'She was only trying to help.'

'She just wanted an opportunity to flirt with the American. At least he will have seen the briefcase and will assume it's what we came for.'

He gestured towards the cars.

'We can use it to draw him away from the Ransomes' car but that means splitting up. I'll take the briefcase to the Consulate in Marseille while you travel back with the package.'

'Where is it?'

'Under the rear seat, where you'll be sitting.'

For a moment, Heywood said nothing. Fawkes hoped he was accepting his assessment. When, finally, he spoke, Fawkes reeled under the impact of his words.

'I didn't mention it on the beach but one of the things they say about you is that you take unnecessary risks with your own life. We both know why that is.'

He paused.

'Don't let the past cloud your judgement. You don't have to prove anything.'

'To Broadway?'

'To yourself. If there's only one of them, there's no need to take this risk. I think we should travel back together.'

As a sop to Fawkes's pride, he added.

'I'd feel safer that way.'

But Fawkes's ambition counted for more than his pride.

'No, it's important I draw this man away while you stay with the package. You'll have to take my word for it but I've learnt enough about it to know it's more important than my safety.'

Fawkes smiled at his old friend and placed a hand on his arm.

'I'm only doing my duty. There's nothing melodramatic about it. It's what I signed up for.'

Before Heywood could reply, he changed the subject.

'Your concern for my safety means a lot to me. You've been wasted all these years in a desk job, you know.'

While they were speaking, Mary emerged from the Powder room. Realising they were talking business, she stayed back in the corridor to pick up hints about the film world.

'What did you think of Koslowski?'

'We only spoke briefly, but he struck me as a decent and sincere chap who believes in what he's doing. The odd thing was how he got out of the house. He was there one minute, gone the next. What did you think of him?'

'Much the same. I was worried he was trying to cheat us but he has real fire in his eyes and he's taken one hell of a risk coming here.'

'Do you think this package really is important?'

'I do. Whether our masters agree is another matter.'

He patted his companion again.

'Good luck and I'll see you back at the hotel.'

Mary waited till the two men had walked out into the sunshine then followed them out. Their conversation had made no sense to her but what really struck her was the change in the younger man's manner, from empty-headed to hard-headed. It was as if he was a different person.

This time, Audrey had insisted on travelling back with Mary in Brandon's flashy car. The back seat was an uncomfortable bench but she didn't care. Why should Mary have all the fun? This left Durand alone with Juliette. She wasted no time.

'What on earth possessed you to abandon us like that?'

It had been bad enough knowing a German had been following them all day, exposing the guests to danger. The last thing Durand needed was a possessive woman sounding off.

'I had to help the Englishmen,' he sighed. 'They're our guests too, you know. They never speak foreign languages. Besides, I'm hoping there'll be a little something in it for me.'

Juliette had more salt to rub into the wound.

'I doubt that. Look what happened at the factory, your slavish attention to his needs wasn't exactly rewarded, was it? I saw how quickly he got rid of you and we both know why that was.'

Durand was alarmed. How much had she seen?

'I don't know what you're talking about?'

She moved in for the kill.

'He got rid of you because he didn't want a Jew interfering in his business arrangement.'

Durand was about to dismiss the remark as nonsense when he realised it gave him an opportunity to bring the subject to a close. He adopted a pained expression.

'Well, that's just something I have to live with.'

Satisfied with the exchange, Juliette sat back and lightened the conversation.

'Funny the older Englishman going off like that.'

'Yes, you'd think the film locations were more important than renting a house.'

'They sound pretty useless at film making, if you ask me,'

said Juliette.

'I think they're just pretty useless in general.'

Durand was half afraid his words had a ring of truth to them.

Lydia had wanted to say much the same to Harry but was restrained by the presence of Heywood, sitting in the back.

'We had a lovely day didn't we, darling.'

'Yes, the Wolseley went rather well.'

'Stupid man,' she said, fondly.

Confident their pursuer would follow him, Fawkes watched the trio of cars set off for the hotel and started to relax. But Juliette wasn't the only one to assume Heywood was the boss. On the far side of the square, two cars were parked in the shade of a plane tree. The driver of one car, Fräulein Oberst Ingrid Mirbeth, was leaning into the rear window of the other to give her orders to the four men inside.

'The handover of the briefcase from the boss to the younger man was too obvious. There's probably nothing in it but we can't take any chances so one of you find Heinrich and follow the younger man wherever he goes. The rest of you should follow the boss in the car. He'll have what he came for on him. When he gets back to the hotel, we've got to get him on his own so don't let him out of your sight.'

'What about you?'

'I'm going to have a look inside that house. There may be something there.'

'What about the Pole, how will you handle him?'

'If he's got any sense, he'll be long gone. Then I'll join you back at the hotel.'

Confident his own plan was working, Fawkes concentrated on drawing the gorilla towards the bus and failed to notice another car tucking itself in behind the convoy as it set off for Fort Sarrasin.

Fawkes boarded the empty bus, paid his fare and looked around to see where best to sit. The strangely shaped bus had an open standing area at the back, protected by a brass rail running around in a curve. A useful exit should the need arise. He sat in the back, next to the opening and waited for one particular passenger to join him.

The bus was in no hurry to depart and slowly filled up with passengers who had been to market and were bringing their purchases home. The woman opposite had a bag of clothes, the man next to her some sausages which reeked of garlic. A large woman struggled along the aisle carrying two dead chickens, flopped down next to Fawkes and held the chickens up for his approval.

'Formidable, Madame. Vous avez très bien fait.'

Pleased with his ability to converse with the natives, he turned back to find a man standing over him. His hands were large and scarred, his body short but powerful. And he'd brought a friend along. When he leered at Fawkes, Fawkes had good reason to smile back. There had been two of them after all but he'd drawn both of them away from the cars. His ruse had worked. Heywood was safe.

The driver had started the engine when a voice shouted from across the square. 'Attendez.' Everyone looked around to see a group of nuns, walking fast but not running. They boarded the bus at the rear leaving those standing with no alternative but to move down the aisle towards the front. One minute, Fawkes had a thuggish German standing over him, the next he was looking up at an elderly nun. Offering her his seat, he stepped out onto the open area at the back. The German was now at the far end of the aisle, twenty passengers between him and his quarry.

With each stop, the number of passengers reduced, allowing the German to work his way towards the back. Fawkes held the briefcase in one hand, the handrail in the other as the bus started the run into Marseille.

As the bus approached the station, the German made his move. Pushing his way past the nuns, he stepped out into the open and swung a scarred fist. Fawkes ducked and the fist smashed into the window behind his head, sending glass flying over the nuns. That was the signal for everyone to start screaming and yelling.

Holding the briefcase in front of his face, Fawkes launched himself against the man, knowing he had to neutralise the danger from the man's fists. The man responded by throwing him against the low railings and trying to grab the briefcase. When Fawkes clung desperately to the railing, the man simply picked him up and threw him and the briefcase across to the other side. As he landed, the briefcase burst open. This brought the second man out from the body of the bus to try and gather the pages as they fluttered in the breeze. His efforts prevented his colleague from continuing to throw Fawkes around just as the bus pulled up at the station.

Seizing his opportunity, Fawkes jumped over the railings, ran across the road and into the station. Ignoring the ticket collector, he dashed onto the platform. One train had just arrived on the opposite platform. Another was approaching the platform he was standing on. He could hear footsteps pounding behind him.

The ticket collector had been caught by surprise when the first man ran past him but he was ready when a second man tried the same thing and grabbed him firmly. His reward for doing his duty was to be punched in the throat and stomach with two powerful blows.

Belching smoke, the approaching train grew nearer, the clank of its pistons drowning out all other sounds. Fawkes had seconds to decide. Calculating his chances, he darted across in front of it just as his pursuer reached the platform. Hidden from view, he scrambled up the steps on the wrong side of the stationary train to join the line of passengers disembarking.

'Keep walking,' he told himself. 'Don't look round.'

Lost in the throng, he left the station the way he'd come. Safely inside a taxi, he looked round to see both men dodging the traffic as they gathered up the last of the pages. The Englishman may have escaped but it didn't matter, they had the documents he'd planned to take back to London. Mirbeth would be pleased.

In the Consulate, the Passport Officer was less than welcoming.

'I wasn't told there was a mission underway on my patch.'

'Well, that's disgraceful. I'll make sure it goes into my report.'

'So why are you here?'

'Actually, I'm not sure I'm allowed to tell you.'

'Can you at least tell me if you've had any luck?'

'So far, so good. We've got the merchandise.'

'So where is it?'

'Safe and sound.'

The Passport Officer looked sorry for himself.

'Nobody ever tells me a bloody thing. I just sit here doing nothing and trying to look important.'

'Well, you've succeeded there.'

When Fawkes gave him a consoling look, the man took it and ran with it.

'Are you in a hurry?'

'No hurry at all. My number two will be back at the hotel soon. They're having a fireworks display there tonight. I've never been keen on that sort of thing.'

'Sorry to disappoint you but we're having one here too.'

'Good God, whatever for?'

'It's an experiment. They think it'll be good for trade, attract more holidaymakers.'

Fawkes was not impressed.

'It'll never catch on. Do the trains still run during the fireworks?'

'Of course, you'll be back around the time they end. Before you go, can't you even give me a clue as to what you're up to?'

'Alright, but keep this to yourself. We've obtained details of a new German bombsight. Can't say I understand how it works but I was followed here so it must be important.'

'How many followed you?'

'I thought there was only one of them but it turned out there were two.'

'You were lucky. They usually hunt in packs of four or more.'

Fawkes tried to look unconcerned but his blood froze.

Chapter 12

FRUSTRATED BY THE slow speed of his companions on the journey out, Harry Ransome made sure he was at the front, on the way back. His new-found freedom meant the others were soon left behind, along with their frustrated pursuers. What Harry saw as a bit of fun in his beloved Wolseley was interpreted quite differently by them. The sight of the leading car pulling away confirmed their suspicion that it contained the senior British spy.

'Careful, darling, you may have something precious on board.'

Lydia's remark alarmed Heywood until he saw the smirk they exchanged. But it worked. Harry slowed down, allowing Heywood to relax and review the day. Not much excitement but he'd played a worthwhile part in the operation. Fawkes was welcome to hobnob with the staff at the consulate. A bath, followed by a drink on the terrace, was infinitely preferable. He might try one of those americanos the barman was always going on about.

'Enjoying the drive Mr Heywood?'

'Immensely, thank you. You drive very well.'

'Do you drive?

'Fraid not. I have a simple bus journey to work and weekends are spent on my allotment. I don't really need a car.'

'Where do you live?'

'Kennington, do you know it?'

'Gosh yes, we live in Balham so we're practically neighbours. Have you been to France before?'

'Just the once, but it was for quite a while.'

He looked out of the window to signal an end to that conversation. Lydia took the hint and changed the subject.

'We usually go to Cornwall.'

Heywood's laugh put the other two at ease.

'We usually holiday in Birchington, at Mrs Leadbetter's boarding house. That's why I'm looking forward to a cocktail tonight. In Birchington, our treat is a trip to Forté's milk parlour for a knickerbocker glory. Not quite the same.'

Running his hand over the leather seat, he studied the instruments on the dashboard. If they gave him a retirement gratuity, perhaps he'd buy a little Austin.

They were near the coast now, the grey of the rocks beneath the village and the dense woodland had been replaced by brown and dusty earth. Amid all the browns, there was an abundance of green vines.

'I always thought vineyards were large affairs with huge châteaux but these are tiny. Some aren't much bigger than my allotment and there isn't a grand house in sight.'

'It hasn't stopped the owners giving their tiny terroirs rather grand names,' laughed Lydia. Harry turned to look. 'Eyes on the road, darling. I don't like these great big ditches that run down the sides.'

'It may not be a château,' said Harry, 'but there's a big house up there on the right. Let's take a look. Alright with you Mr Heywood?'

'Absolutely,' he lied. The americano would have to wait.

At the top of a dusty track, Harry swung the Wolseley into the forecourt of the finest vineyard in the area. The price of rosé was so low, the Ransomes bought six bottles in a wooden box. Wondering where to put it, Harry decided the space under the rear seat would be perfect.

'I don't think that would be a good idea, actually,' Heywood tried not to sound too alarmed. 'It could get rather hot down there and the wine might spoil.'

'There's little likelihood of that.' Harry smiled conspiratorially.

'Actually, 'I want to hide it from UK Customs. Underneath this seat is rather a good place don't you think?'

Lydia joined in.

'Mr Heywood might be right, darling. Put it in the boot for now.'

Once they were back on the main road, with his secret cargo still safe, Heywood could relax. His thoughts had turned once more to buying a little car when there was a loud bang. Instantly, the Wolseley careered into the drainage ditch, settling at an angle of forty-five degrees. Heywood was thrown against the rear door from where he could see blood running from Harry's forehead.

'Where've you been hit, old boy?' he asked anxiously.

'My head grazed the rear-view mirror but, otherwise, I'm fine. How are you darling?'

Though Britain didn't have these ditches, the occasional tyre failure wasn't unknown to Lydia and she took it in her stride. What puzzled her was Heywood's reaction. He seemed to think they'd been attacked.

'I'm sorry. I must have drifted off before I heard the bang. Perhaps I was dreaming about my time on the Western front but my first thought was that someone had shot at us. I'm afraid I haven't had much experience in cars.'

Harry reassured him.

'Don't worry, old boy, you must have had a terrible time in the war doing your bit. Your reaction is quite understandable.'

Heywood eased the rear door open and stepped out into the ditch. While he was mopping his brow, three cars went past without stopping. When a fourth car approached them, he assumed it would do the same. Instead, it came to a halt behind them. The three men who got out were all heavily built.

'Finally, someone's stopped to help us,' said Lydia.

Heywood wasn't so sure that helping them was what the newcomers had in mind.

The men had almost reached them when another car came around the bend and drew up beside the Wolseley. Seeing who the driver was, they stopped and hung back dutifully. An elegant woman stepped out and lowered her sunglasses.

'Are you alright? You must be terribly shaken.'

Lydia, who'd thought nothing of the arrival of the three men, was immediately mistrustful of this woman with so much poise and elegance. Harry thought she was rather smashing.

'Thanks awfully for your concern but it's not as bad as it looks. We've had a puncture, that's all. I need to change the wheel.'

'Pulling the car out of the ditch looks like a job for several men. Those men are driving a car with a German registration. I'm Swedish but I speak German. Shall I ask them, or do any of you speak German?'

'I say', said the bedazzled Harry, 'that's awfully nice of you. None of us speak a word of the old krautspeak.'

Heywood had been sitting on the edge of the rear seat, his feet in the ditch. As the men approached, he stood up and saw the seat had become detached from its usual position. The edge of the box was clearly visible, the men a few feet away.

When they came right up to him, he staggered back in a mock fainting fit, pushing the seat back into place. Fearing they'd guessed what he'd been up to, he was surprised when they lifted him up gently, dusted his suit down and made him rest against the side. One of them produced a flask of brandy.

'I must have had a dizzy spell. I'm alright now.'

When he declined the offer of the brandy, the German shrugged and took a sip himself.

The Swedish woman gave Harry a warm smile.

'I think I've seen you at the hotel.'

'Gosh, have you? Well I never. I'm surprised I haven't noticed you there. How long are you staying?'

That was quite enough for Lydia.

'We've been up in the hills visiting a perfume factory. It was organised by the manager.'

'I tried to join it but I was too late. Was it enjoyable?'

'Marvellous, it was in a beautiful spot. The only problem was the way the manager disappeared as soon as we arrived. But it didn't matter. We saw everything.'

'Wasn't he feeling well?' She asked casually.

'He was trying to help a colleague of this gentleman,' Lydia gestured to Heywood. 'They're in the film business. I saw them both in conversation with a young man in the loading bay.'

Worried the three Germans might speak English, Heywood joined in.

'We're down here looking for film locations. When we heard there was a visit up here, we thought we'd tag along.'

'I hope you had a successful day.'

With the car righted and the wheel changed, the three men drove off with a cheery 'Auf wiedersehen'. All three looked at Heywood as they spoke. 'Not if I see you first,' he muttered to himself.

'Safe journey,' said the Swedish woman as she drove off.

Once she was safely out of the way, Lydia was prepared to admit she'd been helpful.

'It was silly of me, I know, but those Germans seemed rather intimidating.'

'Oh, I never thought they intended us any harm,' lied Heywood. 'But it was lucky the Swedish lady spoke German.'

'Yes, her turning up like that was certainly a stroke of luck,' said Harry.

'Get in the car,' said Lydia. Harry obeyed.

The temperature had dropped and the light was fading as Heywood stretched out in the back. Unlike Fawkes, he had a wife and two children. His daughter had recently presented him with a first grandson and retirement held many attractions for him. He started to make plans but, as the car rolled along, his head slowly dropped and he drifted off.

He woke to the sound of Harry's voice.

'That puncture has rather messed things up, I'm afraid. Would you rather walk from here, Mr Heywood? It's going to take us some time to get through this lot.'

They'd arrived at the top of the cobbled street that led down to the quayside. It was already dark and the street was blocked by sightseers attending the firework display.He didn't fancy making his way through the crowd. They'd got back safely, there was no hurry.

'Don't think I'll bother. We can see the fireworks from here.'

He looked out of the window. Everyone was facing the harbour waiting for the start. Everyone except three men, spread across the tightly packed crowd. Three men he recognised. One of them was pointing at the car.

He had to think fast. If he stayed where he was, they would take him, probably take the Ransomes and certainly find the box. In the general hubbub, no one would even notice.

He had to draw them away.

'Actually, I think I will walk after all. Thanks for the lift.'

As he leapt out of the car, the Ransomes looked at each other.

'That was a bit sudden,' said Harry.

'Must be desperate for his americano or whatever he called it. Are they any good?'

'You're not having any alcohol my dear. Not in what I hope is your condition. I thought it was funny when he talked about his holidays. Would a film executive stay in a boarding house in Birchington?'

It was twenty years since Heywood had felt bone chilling fear. On the Western Front, it was a daily occurrence, one he'd accepted but never got used to. Afterwards, the job, his family and his allotment had been rocks to which he'd clung. Now that fear returned, spreading to every part of his body. But he also felt something else. He'd allowed himself to be lulled into a false sense of security. He was angry with himself and his anger sharpened his senses.

On the way out, he'd noticed the ruined fort, built on the highest ground to provide protection from Saracen invaders. Off to his right, a long flight of shallow tread steps led up to it. The fear he'd experienced long ago had returned but so had his determination. He had no choice. He would have to become a soldier again.

Scurrying up the unlit steps, he hoped it would be a moment or two before they spotted him. But he was old and they were young, it wouldn't be long before they caught up. Just get as far away from the car as possible. Taking the steps two at a time, he was surprised how fast both his legs and his mind worked as he leapt over the uneven cobblestones. His progress was accompanied by a loud bang signalling the start of the firework display and the end of the darkness that hid him. All he could do was run as fast as he could, drawing his pursuers away from the car and its secret.

The steps led him into the remains of a courtyard. One wall of the fort ran along the right-hand side, a low, crumbling wall to his left. At the far end, a high wall with a wrought iron gate. He ran towards a gap in the crumbling wall and stared into the pitch black, unable to see what was on the other side but desperate enough to take the risk. As he prepared to squeeze through the gap, the fireworks lit up the sky and he found himself staring down at a forty-foot drop. He drew back, trembling. That left the gate. He crept towards it. It opened without a squeak. He hid behind the wall, gasping for breath. He wouldn't last long like this.

He crouched behind a statue, trying to control his breathing. The statue cast a shadow in the fireworks but his pursuers ignored it. They knew the path was a dead end and thinking he was a field agent, they concentrated on the cobbled alleyways that would allow him to escape down to the town. Once he decided he'd lost them, he sat at the foot of the statue and began to breathe more easily. He'd drawn them away from the Ransomes and their car. If he could just find a way out. Easing himself off his stiff old knees, he leaned forward to peer through the gate just as a series of explosions lit up the sky. Night turned into day, casting his shadow across the gateway.

One man took a last look towards the courtyard, saw the shadow and shouted to the others. Cursing himself for his stupidity, Heywood ran down the path that led to the main tower of the fort. The entrance stood at the top of a short flight of steps. Exhausted, he used his hands and feet to scramble up the steps and collapsed through the door, kicking it shut with his feet then feeling the surface of the door for a lock, bolts, anything that would secure it. But there was nothing. He was in a dead end of his own making.

Before they'd set out that morning, Fawkes had produced two revolvers from his suitcase.

'Surely we're not going to need them.'

'I hope not old chap but I never take chances. I always assume the worst and try to prepare for it.'

'Well you can carry one but I won't. I'm not trained to use it.'

'You survived four years on the Western Front. You've had a lot more "training" than I have.'

He held the gun out to his friend.

'If we're separated, I'd be happier if you had this. It's a Webley British Bulldog, five bullets not six and completely reliable. Nothing complicated to jam unlike those pistols the Germans are so fond of. The .45 calibre bullets will stop anything in their tracks.'

Noting the attractive pearl handle, Heywood had reluctantly slipped the short-barrelled revolver into the inside pocket of his Airey and Wheeler tropical suit, a pocket wide and deep, as if designed for an Englishman abroad who might need to carry the odd revolver now and then.

The ground floor was bare. Stone floor and walls, no furniture he could push across the door. In one corner, he could see a spiral staircase, wide enough for one person at a time. He dragged himself over and peered up. Half a dozen steps led to a small landing. He sat on the top step, pulled out his revolver and waited. Sweating from exertion and fear, he removed his panama, wiped his forehead and stared at the hat. Noticing his shaking hand, he tried to take his mind off things by making a mental note to have his suit cleaned when he got home. Then he remembered being told the department wanted it back and would probably charge him for the cleaning.

Knowing the tower was a dead end, his pursuers ignored it at first. With the only sound coming from the fireworks, his hopes started to rise. Then the door creaked open and a flash from the fireworks cast three shadows.

He stood up, his adrenalin in full flow. Catching them by surprise, he shot two of them before they had time to react. One, shot through the heart, dropped silently where he stood. The other was hit in the stomach and started to choke on his own blood, a sight Heywood had witnessed too many times in the war. With a .45 bullet inside him, he wouldn't last long.

He turned and ran up the steps. The remaining man, realising he must be dealing with a top agent who had deliberately lured them into a trap, waited a few moments then followed.

Two bullets fired, three left.

When he reached the top floor, he found himself standing under a small trapdoor that led to the roof. If he could squeeze through it, he could look down on the German as he came out from the narrow staircase. He tried to push it open but in his sweaty hands, the catch wouldn't budge.

The German rounded the corner. Both men fired. Neither shot found its target. As the sound echoed round the enclosed space, the German retreated.

Two bullets left.

He gave another heave at the door but the effort caused him to lose his footing. The Webley slipped from his grasp as he fell to the floor. Hearing him fall, his opponent rounded the corner and took aim. For Heywood, everything seemed to slow down as he wondered if he would hear the explosion before the bullet killed him. But there was no explosion, only the click of the gun jamming, just as Fawkes had said. Grabbing his old-fashioned revolver, he fired his fourth shot. He'd killed his last opponent with a bullet to spare.

Instead of feeling elation, he was hit by a wave of extreme

tiredness. It was good work for a desk man but it had drained him completely. He wondered if he had the strength to make it back to the hotel.

Steadying himself against the wall, he brushed the medieval dust off his suit, another reason to get it cleaned, and made for the steps. His calves ached more walking down than they had going up and he had to stop several times to prevent them cramping up altogether. By the time he reached the last flight of steps, he was on the point of physical and nervous collapse. The firework display seemed to have finished, the atmosphere was one of complete silence.

He stumbled across the stone floor towards the door and pulled it open. The charming Swedish woman was standing there. As he tried to adjust to this surprise, he encountered another one. She was pointing a gun at him. He had one bullet remaining.

But she was a woman and he hesitated.

She didn't.

He felt the thump in his chest. As his legs gave way, he put his hand inside his jacket and felt the sticky blood on his fingers. Sinking to his knees, he leaned against the stone wall of the tower, a tower that had stood for centuries but had never seen any fighting until tonight.

He rested in this kneeling position to gather his strength. Trying to come to terms with what had happened, he remained calm and collected, reviewing recent events, as if preparing a report for his superiors. He wondered what his family were doing back in London and how he would spend his retirement with them. Something told him he needed to think about a great many things in a short space of time. How important was this package? Would there really be a war and would what he'd done tonight affect its outcome?

He looked up at her. She was smiling. He looked down at his suit and wondered how much it would cost to get it cleaned.

Still wondering, he felt his life ebb away.

Chapter 13

THE RESIDENT PIANIST was tinkling away as Brandon strolled through the bar and onto the terrace, where the Poitrenauds were taking coffee. The sun had set but the air was still warm and scented with jasmine, the pink of the bougainvillea still vivid in the fading light. He waved to them as he walked over to an empty table. Juliette beckoned him over.

'We have a spare seat; would you care to join us?'

'Are you sure you haven't had enough of me for one day?'

Brandon sat down before Juliette could give a truthful answer. She'd noticed the star-struck look on Mary's face as soon as he appeared through the French doors. But one has to do the right thing.

'You didn't dine in the hotel tonight?'

'No, I dined at a restaurant on the beach front. Durand recommended it to me. You should try it. The owner, a guy from Senegal called Yann, is a keen yachtsman.'

He turned to Mary.

'Did you enjoy your trip to the heart of Provence?'

'Very much. I thought it would be rather dull but I was wrong. I couldn't believe how much things changed when we drove inland. It's so wild and untamed. And that village, it was like stepping back in time.'

Audrey piped up. 'You enjoyed the trip in the car too, I think,' she smirked. Juliette gave her a sharp look but there was no stopping her. 'And taking the briefcase to the old guy, that must've been fun.' Juliette deftly changed the subject.

'You handled the trip to the perfumery wonderfully, we hardly noticed Durand had abandoned us. You must tell us more about yourself. Have your family been in the States long?'

'I'm third generation. My grandfather came to Boston and made a lot of money in the railroad business. My father diversified and we just sold the business so I'm now a man of leisure.'

His eyes wandered across to Mary. She was wearing a dress in two shades of blue which enhanced the colour of her eyes, eyes that returned his gaze. When he turned back to Juliette, his words took the three of them by surprise.

'But not for long.'

'Let me guess, you're going into politics.'

'There's going to be a war and soon. I'm going to London to join the RAF.'

'Doesn't your Neutrality Act forbid American citizens from fighting for foreign powers?'

'Well, they'll just have to arrest me then.'

'So, you can fly,' said Audrey.

'Yes, my family owned a small airline, I started flying in my teens.'

Brandon's arrival presented Juliette with a quandary. She was due to meet Durand but her duty to Mary's mother meant she shouldn't leave the silly girl alone with the young American. He was certainly a smooth operator, presenting himself as a hero like that. How many other girls had he used that line on?

She was debating what to do when one of the porters appeared at her side.

'Excuse me Mme Poitrenaud, there's a phone call for you.' Juliette followed him over to the reception desk. A familiar voice spoke.

'Where are you?'

'On the terrace trying to get away but we're stuck with the American.'

While she was away, the smooth operator took up the conversation, focusing, not on Mary but on Audrey, and her life in Paris. A thrilled Audrey went into every tiny detail of life in the arrondissement where they lived. Brandon listened attentively, glancing occasionally at Mary. Her eyes remained fixed on him until Juliette returned.

'Was that Daddy?'

'No, it wasn't for me at all. I don't know why they thought it was.' She turned to Brandon. 'It's been a long day and it's getting late. I'm afraid we'll have to bid you goodnight.'

'Of course, sleep well.'

Brandon followed them into the bar. As she stood by the lift, Mary watched him lean over the pianist to request a tune. It looked as though he planned to stay.

Having seen the girls to their room, Juliette made towards her own, veering off to the lift at the last moment and pressing number six. While Audrey waxed lyrical about the brave young American, Mary searched for something.

'Bother, I've left my gloves on the terrace. I'll have to go back.'

'I'll come with you.'

'Don't bother, I'll only be a moment.'

Mary rushed off, leaving a puzzled Audrey. Puzzled because she hadn't noticed Mary carrying any gloves. She summoned the lift but it had gone to the sixth floor so she turned and ran down the stairs. At the bottom, she paused to compose herself before strolling across to the French doors. Her thoughts were innocent. She just wanted to enjoy the moment.

Someone had beaten her to it. A tall, heavily built black man was sitting at the table they had just vacated, wearing a pair of dark blue sailor's bell bottom trousers and a white tee shirt. A bottle of whisky sat between him and Brandon. Each man had a glass in one hand and was gesticulating with the other as they spoke. Jealous of the man's good fortune, she stood in the doorway, listening to their conversation. The stranger was expressing himself forcibly.

'There will be a war, no doubt about that and if the boches come here, I will fight them with every last drop of my blood.'

'Good for you Yann. This won't be a traditional war about territory, it'll be a war against tyranny. Everyone has a duty to fight for freedom. That's why I'm joining the RAF. We've got to beat these bastards.'

Mary walked nervously towards them. As soon as he saw her, Brandon stood up and greeted her with a broad smile.

'Well this is an unexpected surprise. Won't you join us?'

'I left my gloves on my chair. I won't disturb you.'

'Oh, come on, now you're here it would be a shame to rush off.'

He pulled out her gloveless chair.

'May I present Yann Philippe, restaurateur, yachtsman extraordinaire and patriot. Yann, this is Mary Ballantyne from England.'

Yann stood up and kissed Mary's hand.

'Mademoiselle, it is an honour. Can we tempt you with a glass of scotch on this lovely evening?'

If there was one rule Mary always kept, it was never to touch alcohol. She watched Yann pouring her a glass.

'I really shouldn't.'

Yann handed her the glass.

'Just a little taste, you don't have to finish it.'

She sat down, raised the glass to her lips, tasted the amber liquid, made a face and hastily put the glass down.

'It's not very nice.'

The men laughed.

'Try it with a little water,' suggested Brandon as he diluted the fire water. 'It'll open it up.'

She tried it. 'That's not so bad but I still don't like it.'

She sat back in her chair feeling rather adult. 'You two seem to be having a lively conversation.'

'Monsieur Brandon and I think war will soon be declared and we're both determined to fight for the cause of freedom.'

'Well, you'd better be wrong. I want to take part in the Olympics next year.'

Brandon gave her a sympathetic look.

'So you were telling me. I hate to be the bearer of bad news but I doubt they'll be going ahead.'

'That can't be true,' she said, glancing across at the hotel entrance just as the man from London Films reached the top of the drive. Brandon saw her looking at him intently.

'There's your plan B, I think.'

She glared at him.

'What on earth do you mean?'

'Come on, don't pretend you haven't thought about the possibilities. When you first saw those two crazy guys, you found them acutely embarrassing. Your attitude changed completely when you heard they were in the film business.'

'My goodness, you have been studying me carefully, Mr Wade.'

Brandon laughed.

'Enough to know you've certainly got the looks to be a film actress. And, from your performance right now, I'm beginning to think you don't need acting lessons.'

As he approached the front door, Fawkes glanced across at the terrace, hoping to see Heywood. All the tables were empty except for the one occupied by an unusual threesome. That the British girl and the American were having a drink didn't surprise him, they'd been eyeing each other all day long. But who was the other man?

He was surprised to see Mary stand up abruptly, as if annoyed. Hurrying through the hall to intercept her, he found her scowling.

'Hello, young Mary, did you enjoy the day.'

Mary dropped the scowl and smiled sweetly.

'Lovely thanks but I must be off to bed now.'

'Of course, I won't detain you. I was planning to have a drink with Brandon but I see he's not alone.'

'No, he's with Yann, the owner of the restaurant he dined at this evening. He's very nice but set on fighting the boches with all his might. Just as well there aren't any Germans around.'

With a wave, she disappeared into the lift. As the lift door closed, Fawkes dropped all pretence and started a frantic search of the hotel.

Chapter 14

WHILE THE LIFT made its way to the sixth floor, Juliette asked herself the usual questions: 'How long can this go on? Why am I doing it?' She knew the answers: 'As long as possible' and 'because I need it.'

"It" had already gone on for four years. She'd never done it before, would probably never do it again but, from the moment they'd met, she'd known it would happen. She needed him and felt entitled to him. It was only fair.

It had started on the third evening of that first holiday. He'd caught her eye immediately. Probably caught every woman's eye. There was a slight look of the Levant about him, Jewish perhaps? It made the fruit seem doubly forbidden. Why wasn't Charles here to protect her?

Durand had a routine. Every evening, he went up to the roof bar to pay his respects to the guests before wandering to the far end of the roof. She assumed he wanted to enjoy the view and the warm evening air on his own. It was a while before he told her he was looking towards the land of his birth.

She knew the rules but with her husband arriving at the end of the week, she didn't have time to play by them. She edged towards the solitary figure.

'Are your guests so objectionable you like to get as far away from us as possible?'

He hadn't heard her approaching and flushed, stumbling on his words.

'Not at all Madame, I thought I'd walk over here for a few

moments. If I'd known you were there, I would have stayed.'

'That would have been a pity. We wouldn't have had this opportunity to be alone.'

Durand had sworn never to compromise his position but the truth was, the handsome hotelier was lonely. He'd devoted every waking moment to establishing the hotel as one that guests would return to year after year but there had been a price to pay. The simple fact was, he had no social life. The only people he met were guests who came, stayed for a while and left. The only people he dined with were the hotel's owners. Of course, some of the female guests hinted at the possibility of a dalliance but none were worth the risk. Until Juliette. He couldn't say why she was different, she just was. He couldn't say why he took a risk with her he wasn't prepared to take with other guests, he just did. Perhaps there was a hint of loneliness in her expression when she thought no one was looking at her, a loneliness that matched his own. Whatever it was, they both felt it and, once it had started, neither wanted it to finish.

His solemn brown eyes gazed into hers.

'Can we meet?'

'Aren't we meeting now?'

'Somewhere private.'

'Where would we go?'

'Room 643 is empty. Wait ten minutes then join me.'

'I'm in safe hands then?'

'Most assuredly, Madame.'

That was on the first holiday. Four years later, room 643 had received many such visits, particularly on firework nights. Tonight, she noticed there'd been a few particularly loud explosions but paid them no attention. Her annual relationship with Durand had become the centre of her life. Wanting it to last forever but knowing it wouldn't made her determined to enjoy it even more.

'I'll have to go, darling. I need to check the Englishmen got back safely.'

'For goodness' sake, they're mad. The older one's not too

bad but the younger one is very odd.'

'Yes, but I ought to check they're alright.'

She needed to keep Mary away from an American playboy; he was worried about some Englishmen. It was not how she'd pictured the holiday when she'd boarded the train in Paris.

Durand came out of the lift to find Fawkes darting around.

'Where's Heywood? Have you been celebrating on the roof with him?'

Durand steered him into his office.

'He's nowhere to be seen. Why have you been so long?'

'I had to stay at the consulate for a while. I wanted to keep my pursuers occupied long enough for Heywood to get safely back.'

He stopped abruptly and went silent. Durand was alarmed by the dark look on his face.

'What's the matter?'

'I'm wondering if the man in the consulate was right.'

'What do you mean?'

'I said there were only two men following me. He said they usually hunt in a group.'

Durand sat down at his desk, absentmindedly stroking the Peruvian statue while he digested Fawkes's remark.

'The Ransomes' car is in the garage so the box must still be in it but if Heywood's nowhere to be seen, we've got to be realistic. If they've caught him, they'll come after you next.'

Fawkes paced up and down. On the journey back, he'd been imagining the warm reception he'd get back home. Now, all he could say was 'Christ, what have I done?'

'It's not what you've done that matters now, it's what you do next. You've got to make yourself scarce and quickly.'

'I've got to stay and find him.'

'You can't possibly stay and you know it.'

'I can't leave without the box.'

'There's no question of you leaving with it. They know who you are and they probably know where you are. I admire your loyalty to Heywood but the mission comes first. I don't know what it is you've been collecting and I don't want to know but you'll never be forgiven if this mission fails because you put your colleague before your country.'

Seeing the anguish on Fawkes's face, he softened his approach.

'I'll get the box out as soon as the Ransomes come down in the morning then I'll sort something out with the Passport Officer. I'll make sure it gets back to London.'

He pointed to a door to one side of the lift. 'That door leads to the garage. Get your things together and meet me in there. We'll go in the laundry van. You'll be in time for the overnight train.'

In the room he'd shared with his colleague, Heywood's things were neatly laid out for his return: razor and brush by the bed, pyjamas neatly folded. Consumed with guilt, Fawkes remembered telling him in the station restaurant that the Blue Train made thirteen stops each way from Paris to Menton.

'Unlucky for some,' Heywood had remarked.

He packed up his things and took the lift down. On the way to the van, they walked past the Ransomes' car. Durand saw the look on his face.

'Don't worry, I'll get it in the morning.'

He ushered the tense Englishman into the van and drove him to the station. On his return, he checked again that the Wolseley was safely locked up and went to bed.

Next morning, Agnes greeted him with a warm smile. He greeted her with an instruction to ask the Ransomes for their car keys.

'They've already left. They went very early.'

'For God's sake, why didn't you tell me? Where did they say they were going?'

The receptionist came close to tears as she watched his face blacken. Why was he so stressed over such an everyday occurrence?

'I'm sorry Monsieur Durand. You don't usually ask to be told these things.'

Durand recovered his composure and placed a comforting hand on her shoulder.

'It is I who should apologise. It's just that they had some perfume samples for the other guests in their car. Did they say where they were going?'

'Only that they were making their way slowly home.'

An hour later, a car drew up outside. A man Durand knew well stepped out. When he'd shut the door to his office, the receptionist stood outside straining to hear the conversation between her boss and the police inspector.

'Charles, how goes it?'

'I'm fine J-P but we've got a bit of a mess on our hands. Who've you got staying in 117?'

Durand pretended to consult his room sheet.

'An Englishman in his sixties. I haven't seen him around since yesterday afternoon.'

'Hardly surprising. He was found in the tower of the old fort this morning.' Charles paused for effect. 'With a bullet in his chest and the key to 117 in his pocket.'

'That's awful. He seemed such a nice old fellow. About to retire, I believe.'

'Well, he's retired now and he "retired" three men with him. They seem to have had a gunfight.'

'Surely, someone must have heard this?'

Durand's performance was effortless.

'It must have taken place during the fireworks. No one realised they were hearing gunshots.'

As he spoke, Charles glanced around enviously at the ultra-stylish office, so different from his own back at the police station.

'What else can you tell me about him?'

'He said he was from a film company. He was here with another Englishman who went home yesterday.'

Heywood's fate didn't surprise Durand. What Charles said next did.

'It's not the only murder, you know. The old hat shop man

was strangled in his shop yesterday.'

'That's terrible.'

Durand liked the old man and had dealt with him for years but his death would draw attention away from the hotel.

'Will you be able to keep the hotel out of it?'

'Don't worry, our little town is just getting going as a tourist resort, I'm well aware of the damage a scandal like this would do. This is one for the Intelligence boys. They'll keep it quiet.'

Chapter 15

SHE KNOCKED, SOFTLY at first, then harder. A sleepy-eyed Audrey opened the door to her mother.

'I've had an idea. It's a perfect day, let's make an early start and go to the island. Look sharp, the first ferry goes in thirty minutes.'

'What about breakfast?' Audrey thought her mother had gone mad.

'We'll have it on the island. It'll be lovely.'

And it was. But it took a lot of grumbling from the two girls first. Once Juliette had left them to get up, Mary was as fractious as Audrey.

'Why can't we go after breakfast? What's the hurry?'

She stumbled over to the window. The sun was up and a slight mist hung over the island, the sign of a perfect day. She started to brighten but Audrey was still grumbling.

'It's your fault. She just wants to get you away from the American. She's fed up with you making eyes at him non-stop.'

Mary didn't see herself doing anything of the sort and it had never occurred to her that anyone else would either. Audrey's comment pierced her like an arrow and she dressed in silence. If they were aware of the way she looked at him, he must be too. She wouldn't make that mistake again.

Carrying the hamper she'd been given by the hotel, Juliette heard the ferry sounding its horn and urged them along the harbour wall. As they chugged out of the harbour, Mary gazed at the receding coastline and the hills beyond. A scene that had barely changed for a thousand years was slowly disappearing.

Along the coast, the signs of change were everywhere. Things looked more natural inland but how long would that last? She was glad she'd come here before it was too late.

She made her way to the front and a scene that was more pleasing to her country girl eyes. A narrow shelf of flat rocks surrounded the island, forcing the assortment of dinghies, small sailing craft and the occasional speedboat to anchor offshore. Within a few feet of the gravelly sand, the trees took over. Nature, not man, was in charge. Audrey came up and stood beside her.

'What do you think? Bit of a shock?'

'It's so unspoiled.'

They disembarked and walked up a flight of steps to a stony path. Juliette ushered them off to the right. 'There's a lovely little cove round the bend, it's not far.'

The sound of the cicadas accompanied them as they worked their way round the shoreline to a cove overhung with pine trees, their lowest branches dipping into the pale blue water. They scrambled down a gravel strewn slope that led to a flat shelf of rock, water lapping at its edge. Audrey laid out the rug, Juliette produced the croissants and coffee. The cicadas, the way the trees ran down to the shore, the gentle lapping of the waves.... for a country girl like Mary, this beat breakfast on the terrace, Brandon or no Brandon. She showed her gratitude through a mouthful of croissant.

'I know why you've brought us here but you don't have to worry, I know how to behave.'

Juliette was glad of the opportunity to pass on the wisdom of her own experience.

'Darling, it's the way of the world for men to show their admiration for women. We women must be more circumspect. It's one thing to receive the attention of men, it's quite another to return it. *Ça se fait pas.* You've led a sheltered life, which is as it should be but you're beautiful and you've reached a stage in life where you're going to meet a lot of men who will desire you. You must be careful only to encourage the right ones, not everyone who gives you admiring glances. It's easy to get carried away when you're down here and get involved with someone when you shouldn't. It can happen to any woman. Brandon's obviously a playboy with no intention of settling down. Any woman who thinks she's landed him is in for a shock.'

Mary hadn't expected a full-on lecture. Her gratitude started to diminish.

'I'm not taking him seriously. I'm flattered, that's all. Where's the harm in that? I came on this holiday to have fun. First, everyone's told me my show jumping dreams will be cancelled by a war, now you're telling me not to have anything to do with the only attractive person here.'

Realising she was wasting her time, Juliette changed the subject.

'Never mind that, I've got some real news.'

She gave Mary a triumphant look.

'You know those two Englishmen? Well the older one was shot dead last night. Can you believe it?'

'What happened?'

'I only know this from Agnes, the receptionist. Apparently, he was found dead with three other men who'd been shot by him in a gunfight in the fort.'

She sat back with a satisfied look on her face.

'So much for them being in films. They were obviously gangsters.'

Mary was torn between shock at the older one's death and shame at them being gangsters.

'Perhaps they were in films and he was shot in a dispute about the money for a house rental.'

Juliette wanted to sound magnanimous in victory but she needed to ram that victory home.

'That's not the French way, my dear. No, they were gangsters. I thought so all along.'

'No you didn't,' piped Audrey. 'You thought they were just a couple of out-of-their-depth Englishmen.'

'What about the other one?'

'He's cleared off. Believe me, we're well rid of them.'

Juliette tried to sound serious but her delight at this turn of events was all too evident. Mary was furious at being betrayed by her fellow countrymen but they weren't there any more to be the target of her anger and she could hardly direct it at Juliette. She stood up.

'I think I'll explore. I could do with some time on my own.'

Once she'd scrambled up the bank and disappeared into the trees, Juliette turned to Audrey.

'Let her have a wander. I don't know why she's so touchy. I thought I handled that rather well. Young women need to learn how to behave themselves. She's an only child. Her parents spoil her.'

'I'm an only child.'

'Yes, but that's different.'

'You mean I'm not beautiful like her. It's her looks that irritate you.'

'What do you mean?'

'Down here, you're used to being the centre of attention. She's stolen that from you and you don't like it.'

'Oh, shut up and eat your breakfast. We should never have brought her on this holiday.'

Still feeling the effects of the whisky he'd drunk the night before, Brandon needed some sea air and asked reception for some suggestions.

'Why don't you take a trip to the island sir? There's a ferry every hour. Actually, you've just missed one.'

'Is there no other way I can get there?'

'You could hire a speedboat. My brother has one.'

Like every other member of the staff, Agnes knew Brandon was well heeled.

'But it's expensive. Shall I call him?'

'You do that.'

After twenty minutes and the handing over of a wad of francs, Brandon was heading across the water in a Gar Wood speedboat, the wooden deck glistening in the sun, the wind and salt lashing his face. By the time he'd dropped anchor, all traces of scotch had been purged from his system. Standing on the shingle to consider his options, he opted to head off to the left. When he came to a fork in the path, he faced another choice: climb the steep hill to the top of the cliff or walk along a level path beneath and sit in the sun. A stone seat carved out of the rock looked inviting. He decided to sit and do a little thinking.

He'd be the first to admit that he was used to a certain type of woman. With his wealth, that was inevitable. Such women didn't live in small villages and dream of the Olympics, they were sophisticated and knew the rules of the game. So did he and he had no trouble handling them.

But the encounters were meaningless.

Now, in that acme of sophistication, the south of France, he'd met someone from a small village, someone who dreamed of show jumping, not men. Right from the start, he'd known she would be different, that a relationship with her would have real meaning.

The trouble was, he'd become so used to dealing with the other type of woman, he had no idea how to handle someone like her. He'd messed up last night when he'd teased her about becoming a film star, something he could do with the other type, not with her. Sure, she was a bit spoilt and naïve but that was because she was young. As she matured, she'd lose all that and become a lovely woman. He was beginning to realise he needed to be there when that happened. For the first time in his life, he'd met someone he really wanted to be with.

While these thoughts ran through his head, he sat fidgeting on the seat. He preferred action to stillness and needed to find something to do. He looked at the steep hill, wondering what lay at the top. Only one way to find out.

And it was steep. To his left lay the rocks and the vivid blue sea, to the right, a vineyard with neat rows of vines stretching all the way to the top. When he came to a gate, he opened it to wander among the grapes. Bending down to examine them, he weighed a bunch in his hand, ripe and ready for picking. He stole a look around then tried to steal a grape. The entire bunch came away. Hurriedly eating the evidence of his theft, he continued up the hill.

As she wandered inland, Mary could see this was not the wilderness it appeared to be from the ferry. There was order and method at work. Some of the trees were tall, some short. Space had been created to let in the light. Whoever was running this place knew what they were doing.

Having reached what she guessed was the middle, she had to decide which direction to take. In front of her stood a solitary dead Aleppo pine. A single, long branch pointed up the hill. Taking it as a sign, she set off.

The ground rose steadily until she emerged into the open to be confronted by a monastery, dominating the highest point of the island, overlooking land and sea. No wonder the place was well kept. Halfway between her and the monastery door was a well with a leather bucket hanging by a rope from a simple roller wheel. She wandered over and peered down the deep dark shaft.

Brandon was half way through the bunch when he reached the highest point of the vineyard and discovered he'd stolen monks' grapes. He was about to throw the rest away when he saw someone peering into a well, just yards away. He wandered over, smiled sheepishly and proffered the bunch.

'Care for a grape?'

'What are you doing here? Has anyone seen you?'

'It's only a bunch of grapes. I doubt they'll burn me at the stake for stealing it.'

'I mean has anyone from the hotel seen you. We shouldn't be meeting like this.'

He smiled and walked over to her.

'Relax, the Poitrenauds don't own you. And they certainly don't own me. Where are they?'

She pointed behind her. They looked at each other in silence. He moved closer.

'It's nice here,' she said, stepping back.

'Yes, these monk guys must have a great time living on a desert island like this, don't you think?'

'It's lovely but it's not for me.' She looked around. 'There's nowhere to ride.'

'You're keen on that, aren't you? Well, you'll soon be back home with your horses.' He took her hand in his. 'But as Yann and I were trying to explain to you, there won't be any Olympic Games next year. I'm sorry, I'd have gone to Helsinki to watch you in action.'

Leaving her hand in his, she looked at him, unblinkingly. She shouldn't have done that. He'd intended to behave himself but that look had been too much. Which was bluer, the sea, the sky, or her eyes? He pulled her to him. As he kissed her, the grapes burst, staining his shirt and her blouse. She pushed him away.

'What on earth are you doing?'

'I'm sorry. I shouldn't have done that.'

Then he stiffened his resolve.

'To hell with it, I've wanted to do that since the moment I first saw you.'

She knew what she wanted to say but Juliette's words had hit their target.

'I think you're lovely but we're on holiday and we'll soon be going our separate ways. Besides, I'm too young for this. Go home. If there really is going to be a war, you'll be glad to be back safe in America. Let's forget this ever happened.'

'I've already told you, I'm staying and joining the RAF. Why won't anyone believe me?'

'Because you're a playboy. You just say whatever will get you the girl.'

She saw the crestfallen look on his face.

'Look, even if you mean it, it doesn't change anything. I'm too young, I'm sorry.'

Giving him no chance to reply, she rushed off into the pine trees leaving him with his grapes and his dreams, both crushed.

Mary told Juliette she'd brushed up against the grapes in the vineyard. As soon as they were back in the hotel, she rushed up to change her blouse while Juliette and Audrey sat on the terrace watching Brandon swoop into the bay in his speedboat. When he walked up the hotel drive, he seemed deep in thought. As he drew near, the stain on his shirt was plain to see. He smiled, waved but hurried past. Juliette turned to Audrey.

'What has that girl been up to?'

Chapter 16

'I'M AS DISAPPOINTED as you are.'

Brandon did his best to sound convincing as he selected a croissant from the buffet. Juliette tried to hide her relief.

'When are you leaving?'

'Tomorrow morning. I'm going to London to join the RAF. Things are moving fast. I need to do the same.'

'That's very noble of you.'

She'd started to walk back to her table when, magnanimous in victory, a thought occurred to her.

'We must do something special tonight.'

'Leave it to me, I'm finalising the details this morning. In the meantime, don't book anything and be ready at eight o'clock. I've asked Durand along too.'

'Sounds intriguing.'

At eight o'clock, everyone had gathered in the foyer. Everyone except Brandon. They were wondering where he was when they heard the gentle clip-clop of hooves and saw a horse drawn tram at the end of the drive with Brandon atop, sitting next to the coachman. He beckoned to them.

'We're going up the hill to the old town. I hope the poor old chap will be able to make it.'

The horse ignored the remark. He'd been doing this all his life. He waited patiently till they were all on board then set off at a gentle pace.

Halfway up, the tram drew to a halt beside an oak door set into a wall that ran beneath the tower where Heywood's holiday and life had come to an end. Brandon swung down to the ground, opened the door and led the way onto a lawn fringed by cypress trees and a weeping willow. In the centre, a table was covered in a white cloth and laid for dinner.

'Brandon, this is exquisite,' said Juliette. 'What a clever man you are.'

'The Town Hall hires it out cheaply if you ask nicely. Monsieur Durand suggested it, arranged the staff and kept quiet about it too. He's good at keeping secrets.'

Mary gazed at the man she'd turned away, knowing that tomorrow, he'd be gone. It was sad but she accepted they would never see each other again and that Juliette had given her good advice. For her, the evening was a rite of passage, one in which Durand played his part. He hadn't forgotten her help in putting dancing on the menu at his soirées and showed his gratitude by treating her like an adult. He talked to her of her family life in Woodstock and of her ambitions.

'I suppose you think it rather childish to take riding so seriously.'

'Not at all, Mademoiselle. The world is changing fast and nowhere faster than in the role of women. This generation will be like no previous one.'

Taking it for granted that Brandon would only want to make table talk with her, Juliette was surprised when he told her he believed the law was the one thing that kept mankind civilised. She didn't agree.

'Of course, a sound legal system is essential but it's so easy to corrupt the system and make laws that remove our freedoms. Look at Germany. Everything the Nazis have done has been done in accordance with the law. That's what is so terrifying about their success. Would you uphold the law there or would you see it as your duty to break the law in the defence of freedom? If it can happen in Germany, it can happen anywhere but everyone is so content with things the way they are, they don't want to consider the possibility.'

Juliette had surprised herself. She'd listened to many dinner party conversations of this kind but had never contributed herself. In Paris, it was considered *de trop* for women to offer up such opinions. How liberating these Americans were.

'When it comes to defending freedom, we're going to have to do a lot more than break a few laws,' said Brandon. 'We're going to have to fight and pretty soon now.'

'We?' Juliette looked more than a little cynical. 'So, you really mean to join the RAF. Your fellow Americans seem determined to stay out of it.'

'My country may be, I'm not. If there's a war, I won't stand idly by. This will be a fight for freedom. Everyone must play their part.'

By the time he'd finished, he realised the others had stopped talking to listen. In the silence, Durand signalled to a waiter to bring champagne then rose to his feet. Mary, breaking for the second time her rule of only taking soft drinks, accepted a glass.

'I hope the other guests won't mind if I speak on their behalf and thank Monsieur Brandon for this most charming gesture. This has been a memorable evening, one I'm sure we will all treasure in the years to come, whatever those years may bring.'

Brandon rose to reply.

'Friends, I hope I may call you that, the pleasure is mine. I will treasure my memories of this holiday for the rest of my life. With the storm clouds gathering around us, none of us knows what the future holds and I am reminded of the poet's words, "they are not long, the days of wine and roses." We must make the most of them while we can. I've also been listening to some wise words from Madame Poitrenaud about our reluctance to face reality when it doesn't suit us. They put me in mind of something a fellow American, Upton Sinclair, said recently. "It's hard to get a man to understand something when his salary depends upon his not understanding it." We're all finding it hard to understand that a terrible war is about to be unleashed because our comfortable lives depend upon us not understanding it. Let us hope we wake up to reality in time.'

He paused to let his words sink in.

'But enough of that. Friends, I've been honoured to make your acquaintance and who knows, perhaps one day we'll all meet again. If that day comes, let us hope it will be on an evening like this and in this magical spot.'

He raised his glass. As he did so, he looked at Mary. As soon as their eyes met, she looked away. Juliette smiled at her and nodded approvingly.

Chapter 17

FREDDIE FAWKES SAT in his compartment staring blankly at the scenery as the Train Bleu worked its way inland from Marseilles. Though trained to go about his business as normally as possible, there were occasions when someone might try to kill him or he might be the one doing the killing. This caused him no discomfort. He believed in what he was doing. That Heywood was almost certainly dead, however, had left him profoundly shaken and not just because it reflected on his own judgement and handling of the mission. Fawkes knew he wasn't the most sociable of men, knew his line of work exaggerated rather than diminished that trait. He'd had the good fortune to meet Heywood soon after he'd joined the service and had been taken under his wing, often going back to Heywood's home in Kennington for a meal at the weekend. Unlike his young friend, Heywood's life was like that of any other office worker, except that the business he worked for dealt in secrets rather than insurance policies, deception rather than bank loans. He worked regular hours, went home to his wife each evening and grew vegetables on his allotment at the weekend. Over the years, he'd become an important part of Fawkes's life, acting as a bridge between his world of secrets and the real world around him.

Being British, it never occurred to either of them to call each other by their Christian names. They remained Heywood and Fawkes right to the end. Even so, long before they arrived in France, Heywood had become an essential counterweight who enabled Fawkes to arrive at a better balance in his unusual life. His impending retirement had not been welcome to Fawkes but he'd consoled himself with the knowledge that their Sunday lunches would continue. Now that too was gone and it was all his fault. First his mother, now Heywood. He felt and was quite alone.

Riven with guilt at his failure to protect his friend, he sat pondering the future as he gazed out of the window. The mission had been a disaster. Even if the rotors reached London, he'd be sacked on his return. He wondered if the Navy would take him back but didn't frankly care.

Hearing the carriage attendant announcing dinner, he wandered along to the dining car, found a seat at an empty table and picked up the menu. Before he'd had time to choose, he became aware of someone standing over him. Without looking up, he spoke in French.

'Would you mind coming back in a while? I haven't decided yet.'

'Actually, I was wondering if I might join you.'

He looked up. A woman stood over him, hands elegant, immaculately dressed in a peach coloured linen dress. He worked his way up to her face. She wore no hat on her blonde hair but a pearl necklace glinted in the light from the lamp on the table. Her blue eyes had a friendly expression.

He gestured to her to sit down, assuming that would be the full extent of their conversation. She picked up her menu and started to read it.

'Do you have any suggestions? I haven't been on the Blue Train before. Have you?'

'I came down on it,' he replied. 'I'm afraid I get a bit lost amongst all the fancy descriptions. I'm going to stick to the salad. But you can always ask the waiter for advice.'

He smiled at her and she took it as a cue to launch into the story of her trip to Menton, where she said she'd joined the train. She told him she was Swedish.

Attractive without being beautiful, she would have convinced anyone else. But Fawkes, an expert on accents, thought she spoke French, not with a Swedish accent but with the lilting tones of a German from Bavaria. Blonde hair, blue eyes, very Nordic, not necessarily Swedish. Then again, Bavaria, southern Germany, not so Nordic. He hadn't ruled out the possibility he would be spotted joining the train and had already decided not to go to sleep during the night but he was surprised by this direct approach. And so soon into the journey.

What was the plan? Lure him back to her compartment or simply occupy him while her companion searched his? He took a quick look up and down the car. The two gentlemen whose acquaintance he'd made on the bus were nowhere to be seen. Perhaps she really was just a Swedish woman on a train.

As he considered the possible scenarios, he realised she was speaking to him.

'Are you German, by any chance?'

This was one question he hadn't expected.

'No, actually. Why do you ask?'

'You speak French very well but with a slight accent. I was thinking maybe you were German. I'm so glad you're not.'

'You don't like the Germans?'

'They're such bullies. Don't you think?'

He responded by switching from French to English and going into full Englishman abroad mode.

'I couldn't agree more, Madam.'

He leaned forward. She did too. Her perfume wafted across as he looked into her eyes.

'Between you and me, I think they're the most frightful people.'

He sat upright again. That perfume was just a little too intoxicating.

'And that Hitler chappie. Well, really, what a buffoon.'

'You're so right.'

She smiled sweetly with her mouth but her eyes were hard as she forced the words out. He started to enjoy himself a little too much.

'Don't worry, there are no nasty German secret police here. Just a very beautiful Swedish lady and yours very truly. The name's Freddie, by the way.'

'Ingrid.'

She held out her hand. He kissed it. That perfume again.

'That's a lovely accent you have. What part of Sweden are you from?'

'Actually, I'm from Norrköping.'

She pronounced it correctly as Norrsherpping.

'That's a strange name for a town, madam,' said the Englishman abroad.

'Not really, it means north market. You have the same thing in England, I believe. Chipping Norton and Chipping Camden, for example. Chipping or Sherpping, it's the same Norse word for market.'

Had his talent for accents let him down? Would a German agent from Bavaria really have known all this? Perhaps the Swedes from Norrköping speak with a lilting accent. He started to doubt himself. Wanted to doubt himself.

'Did you enjoy your holiday?'

As she spoke, she looked out of the window, as if she was merely making conversation. He had to be careful. If they'd made Heywood talk, he would have told them he was in the film business. He had to come up with something else.

'It wasn't a holiday, I'm afraid. I'm in the beer business. My employers sent me down on an important job but it didn't go very well. I don't think the French are civilised enough for British beer. Still, I hope your holiday was enjoyable.'

'I was working too.'

'Good Lord, what a coincidence. I hope you had better luck than me.'

Once again, her reply took him by surprise.

'I doubt it. I work in the hotel trade. My bosses sent me to negotiate the purchase of a hotel in Menton but I messed up and I'm not looking forward to going home. They've never really liked me.'

She placed both her elegant hands on the table.

'Simply because I'm a woman. I'm not one of their little group, not one of the boys. Unless a miracle happens, I face the sack.'

'I'm sorry to hear that.'

He leaned forward again. He really should stay away from that perfume.

'Actually, I think we're in much the same position. My bosses are all upper-class toffs. They use people like me as hirelings to do their dirty work. People like us are disposable, I'm afraid. It looks like we're both on the way out, you from the hotel trade, me from the beer business.'

'Yes, it's hard to believe, isn't it?'

She played with her pearls.

'Unless something unexpected turns up.'

Innocent Swedish woman or German agent? At least he'd given her the impression his mission had been a failure. But he'd always assumed a German agent would adopt a manner of extreme self-confidence and belief. And be a man. What worried him most was that he found it strangely therapeutic to find he had so much in common with someone who might be planning to kill him. If he was starting to think like that, perhaps it really was time to get out of this line of business.

'We seem to have a lot in common. Even if I'm not sacked, I'll never be promoted beyond a certain point.'

She put the menu down and looked at him. The mission had been a disaster. They had assumed the older man was the boss and that, if they captured him, they'd either find something on him or torture him till he talked. Instead, he'd killed three of her men. When she'd come face to face with him, she'd had no choice but to shoot him before he shot her. A search of his body had proved fruitless. The younger man was her last chance to save the mission and her job. One of her men had identified Fawkes from the fight on the bus but the other wasn't sure. It didn't help that he was using his Englishman abroad act to hide his reactions to everything she was saying. And it was working, she couldn't read him at all. She tried a different approach.

'I heard there was a big gunfight in one of the smaller resorts.'

The news hit him like a punch in the solar plexus. His best poker face couldn't hide his shock.

'Really? I must have left before it happened.'

'So did I but I heard someone talking about it on the train. I hate violence. Don't you?'

'Good Lord yes. Not my cup of tea at all.'

While she read the menu, his mind worked furiously. No one on the train could have known about the gunfight. Now he knew two things, what had happened to his friend and what they had in store for him. She was trying to unsettle him and it was working. The two gentlemen whose acquaintance he'd made on the bus must be with her. He considered what would happen next and how to deal with it.

Her mind was working just as fast. She must return to her carriage. There were arrangements to be made. That was one shock even his face couldn't disguise. Pity, it was rather a nice face. Almost German, in fact.

She sighed then smiled at him. Gathering her gloves and handbag, she stood up.

'Actually, I think I'll skip dinner. Monsieur, I mean Freddie, it's been a pleasure. I wish you a safe journey back to England.'

He stood up and kissed her outstretched hand.

'I hope your journey back to Sweden is equally safe.'

He watched the folds of her linen dress ripple as she walked away but as soon as she was out of sight, he sat back to consider his situation. Know your enemy was the first rule of his trade. She'd set out to frighten him and it had worked. They were a better team than he'd given them credit for. On the plus side, he hadn't got the rotors with him. They were in Durand's hands and would get back safely to London. The only thing at stake was his life. For a professional like him, that was a considerable plus. It meant he only had one thing to concentrate on: staying alive.

He was tempted to stay in the restaurant car for the rest of the journey but quickly dismissed the idea. If they couldn't make their move on the train, they would take him on arrival. He had to confront the danger now, deal with it now. He felt for his Webley, stood up and headed back to his compartment.

As he entered the carriage containing his compartment, he noticed the attendant knocking on the door of the compartment next to his before using his key to enter and lower the bed for the night. If they were waiting for him, the attendant's presence would complicate matters, might even deter them altogether. As he drew alongside that compartment, the attendant appeared in the doorway. Fawkes turned to smile at him. The second it took to recognise him as the other man on the bus allowed him to avoid the neck chop that would have at best knocked him out, at worst killed him. As it was, the blow landed on his shoulder, sending a shooting pain down his left arm as he was hauled into the compartment. Using the back of his foot to slide the door shut, the man hurled Fawkes across the compartment. If his head had connected to the wall, he would have been knocked out and that would have been that. Instead, he landed on the soft body of the real attendant and for a brief moment found himself staring into the surprised eyes of the dead man.

As the German raised his hand to deliver a fatal chop, Fawkes kicked him, aiming for his knee but hitting him in the crotch. The German grabbed his foot and twisted it, lowering his head as he did so. With the pain shooting his knee, Fawkes grabbed the man's head and tried to break his neck. Seeing the danger, the German released his foot and stood up to swipe his hand across Fawkes's face. Fawkes felt the ring on the man's finger rip through his cheek. Seeing that he had drawn blood, the German grabbed Fawkes by both feet, pulling him onto the floor as he drew out a knife.

Needing something to protect himself from the knife thrust, Fawkes pulled the dead attendant across in time for the knife to sink into the poor man's chest. While the German pulled the knife out of the attendant, Fawkes slid from under the attendant and pulled out the Webley. Firing it wasn't an option. The sound of the shot would bring the train to an emergency halt and half the staff to the compartment. Stepping aside, Fawkes brought the revolver down hard on the German's face then swiftly forced his head back, snapping his neck. The man slumped lifeless onto the floor, next to the attendant.

All this had taken place with the compartment door shut but unlocked. Fawkes quickly locked it. He was exhausted, ached all over and had blood dripping from his cheek. And he had two dead bodies on his hands. Clearly, they had intended one of those bodies to be his, with him being blamed for the murder of an attendant who had died valiantly defending himself.

The German's clothes were on the seat, neatly folded. He thought of dressing both men and leaving them, side by side, the German taking on the role that had been intended for him. He quickly discarded that plan. As soon as they were discovered, the train would be halted and everyone on the train would be questioned. His bruised and bleeding knuckles and the bleeding cheek would lead any jury to convict him of both murders. They still used the guillotine in France.

A better plan was needed, one that involved disposing of both bodies. He remembered that, on the way down, there had been several tunnels on this part of the track. He stripped the German of the attendant's uniform then looked out of the window. He couldn't be sure but it looked like a tunnel lay ahead. He'd have to move quickly. Sliding the window right down, he waited till they entered the tunnel then heaved the attendant up. The man was heavy and he was exhausted but, once his trunk was out, the legs could be swung over. Any sound of the body dropping was drowned by the roar of the steam engine in the tunnel. He sat back, dripping in sweat. Not knowing how long the tunnel was, he couldn't afford the luxury of a rest. Grabbing the German, he repeated the process. Using his last ounce of strength, he slid the window up just as the train left the tunnel. Exhausted and trembling, he sat down.

He'd survived one attempt on his life but there were still two people on the train who wanted him dead. He was a long way from safety. Gathering up the attendant's uniform, he slid the door open and peered cautiously out. No blonde, no second man. Back in his own compartment, he packed the uniform into his suitcase. No time to waste. With his panama pulled low over his face, he cautiously slid the door open and made his way to the cheap seats in the middle carriages.

As he sank onto the hard seat, exhaustion hit him like a sledge hammer. He hadn't slept since his last night in the hotel but the woman and the gorilla he'd fought on the bus might come looking for him at any time. Sleep was out of the question while he was still on this train. He couldn't even risk closing his eyes.

The next stop was Lyon, at 6am. When he felt the train start to slow as it approached the station, he went into the lavatory and changed into the attendant's uniform. Emerging as the train clanked to a halt, he peered out of the nearest window then hurriedly stepped back. The woman and the gorilla were standing right beneath his window, scanning the platform. The whistle blew. He turned to move down the carriage to the far exit and came face to face with a man. Were there three of them?

'Here, take this.'

The man handed him a suitcase.

'Quickly, man. The whistle has blown.'

With his own suitcase in his left hand and hoisting the man's case on his right shoulder to cover his face, he clambered down the carriage steps, onto the platform and straight past his pursuers, so close, he could smell the woman's perfume. He heard her saying, 'get back in. He must still be on board.' Fawkes noticed she was giving the orders. A woman in charge. Hard to imagine that happening in the SIS.

The man who, unknowingly, had saved his life, gave him a tip and made for the exit. Taking his own case into the lavatories, he changed back into his suit. He was tempted to keep the uniform but if he was arrested, it would be damning evidence. Stuffing it out of the window over the cistern, he disappeared into the restaurant buffet to eat a decent breakfast and wait for the next train to Paris. This one had no first class and was used only by workers who referred to it defiantly as the Red Train. As he picked up his coffee cup he sighed and, though not religious, made a small sign of the cross.

'That's for you, George. Rest in peace.

Chapter 18

HARRY AND LYDIA Ransome reached Dover after an excellent journey home which, for Harry, meant that every time the Wolseley broke down, he'd been able to mend it. On one such occasion, he'd had to pull into a garage near Limoges with clutch failure. While discussing the problem, he removed the rear seat to show the mechanic the access panel to the rear differential. A carton filled the space. The garagiste lifted it up with a puzzled look and asked him what it was.

'I've no idea. I certainly didn't put it there.'

Harry opened the carton to reveal five strange discs. He was debating whether to throw them away when Lydia walked into the workshop.

'What do you think this is, darling? I found it under the rear seat.'

'Is it a repair kit supplied by Wolseley?' Then she thought for a moment. 'You don't suppose it's something to do with those two men from the film company? Perhaps they wanted to get it back to the hotel then forgot about it.'

'Madame, whoever hid this under your seat did not do so for honest purposes. I suggest you go to the local police station and hand it in.'

Harry bristled at the suggestion. 'No, no, you don't understand. They weren't criminals, they were Englishmen, jolly decent chaps, actually.'

His convictions were not shared by the garagiste.

'Only the other day, an Englishman shot three men. It's in the papers. Take my advice, give it to the police or throw it away.'

Harry held the future conduct of the war in his hands while he pondered his options. He was about to throw it away when Lydia took it from him.

'Let's put it back and hand it to the police in London.'

'Good idea. Are you happy with that?' He turned to the Frenchman who shrugged.

'It's all the same to me,' he said, but he'd made up his mind to get these people off his hands as quickly as possible. Borrowing parts from the Mayor's Citroën, he worked all night to finish the job. Harry and Lydia were able to drive off early next morning, leaving the garagiste to explain to the Mayor why he wouldn't have the use of his car for another week.

As soon as he arrived in Paris, Fawkes phoned Durand to check that he'd retrieved the rotors and arranged for their despatch to London. Durand's receptionist, ever protective of her boss, reluctantly put the call through from a man now known to have been part of a two-man team of British gangsters. When Durand told him the rotors were wandering around France, he exploded.

'Why didn't you stop them?'

'Don't start blaming me. This is all your fault for changing your plan. Heywood's dead by the way. I had a devil of a job explaining that away.'

The long silence from Fawkes made Durand take pity on him.

'Can't you intercept them at Dover? There can't be too many cars coming from the continent and they're all hoisted off the ferry by crane. The Ransomes' car will be easy to spot.'

Taking Durand's advice, Fawkes stood on the quayside in Dover and watched three ferries come and go before he spotted the Ransomes' car being off-loaded. A quiet word with a Customs officer, then all he could do was wait.

'Just routine, Sir,' the smiling Customs officer told Harry. We don't have many cars off the cross-channel ferry so we like to check them. Why don't you pop into the café over the road?'

In the Customs House, Fawkes looked at the box with a

mixture of relief and loathing. The complete mess he'd made of things had ensured the box would reach London without the Germans' knowledge. If he told his bosses this had been the plan all along, he might not be sacked after all. They might even praise him for his ingenuity.

In Balham, Harry unloaded their cases and brought them up to their cosy little flat. Knowing he was about to return to a job he loathed, the journey had given him time to think. If war was avoided, he'd definitely get in touch with those film people.

'Well, that's the lot then,' he said.

'Don't forget that strange box,' said Lydia. 'I'll help you.'

They lifted the rear seat and stared at the empty space.

'The garagiste must have taken it,' said Harry. 'There he was, telling us not to have anything to do with it, and all along he wanted it for himself.'

Taking a leaf out of the Frenchman's book, they shrugged their shoulders and soon forgot all about it.

While Brandon was on his way to London in his fast car, Mary prepared to enjoy the rest of the holiday and Juliette prepared for the arrival of her husband. She was a well-bred woman who knew the rules of the game. When she left room 643 for the last time, she didn't look back. For the remainder of the holiday, the family Poitrenaud and their young British guest enjoyed the relaxed informality of the south knowing they would soon be returning to the more formal ways of the north. Nothing lasts forever, least of all a holiday, and for Mary, there was no sadness when it was time to go home, only pleasure at the prospect of more riding. She would never forget the man who'd given her a holiday to remember. She wished him well in his future life.

The day after the Poitrenauds left, it rained for the first time in two months. Hearing the rain hammering the pavement outside his office, Durand took the lift to the deserted roof. He looked down at the yachts with their hatches battened against the rain and at the wet sand from which the last and most determined bathers were now departing. In the distance, the island was barely visible. He thought about recent events with a growing sense of foreboding. The spying game had been rather good fun and quite lucrative up till now but the old hatter's death had shocked him. He was beginning to regret getting caught up in it.

He turned around and walked back to the lift. He was soaked to the skin.

Chapter 19

THE ROUTE HAD been straightforward, A40 from Marble Arch all the way to Oxford. Someone at the Embassy had advised Brandon to join the Automobile Association and he now had a silver AA badge on the radiator. As a result, he soon discovered the AA men on their motorbikes. They were everywhere and each and every one saluted him. The Embassy man hadn't warned him about this. Unsure how to react, he saluted them back until he noticed nobody else did.

As he drove out of the London suburbs, he was surprised by how new everything was. Central London was old and grimy, just as Americans had been told it was. Further out though, new factories lined the roads, new houses filled the streets. He'd heard about the workers' protest marches in the north. Down here, the country seemed to be recovering strongly from the depression.

The mighty Jaguar swooped down the hill into High Wycombe and zoomed effortlessly up the much steeper hill on the other side. He was in open country now with farmland on either side and horse drawn ploughs at work. Every village had a blacksmith. As he came through Stokenchurch, he found himself looking down briefly on the vale of Oxford before disappearing into the winding, tree-lined road down to the plain below. He ignored the sign for Oxford. He had more important matters to deal with.

His arrival in Woodstock was announced in the usual way, a flash of green metal and the sound of rubber gripping tarmac as the Jaguar turned into the High Street. Alerted by the sound, onlookers watched the car come to a halt and a man dressed as

Ernest Hemingway step out. The first person to catch his eye was a farmer dismounting from his horse.

'Excuse me sir. Do you happen to know where the Ballantynes live?'

The farmer looked at him.

'That's a nice car you've got there, son. I didn't know you Scottish could afford cars.'

'I'm not Scottish, sir. I'm American.'

'That explains it. Well, if you can afford a car, you can afford to pay for information like that.' He smirked at Brandon.

A woman overheard the conversation and stepped in.

'Don't pay him any attention, young man. He just wants you to pay for his booze. Is it Frederick Ballantyne you're looking for?'

'It's his daughter Mary, actually.'

'Well she'll be out riding her horse at the moment. The Duke lets her use the palace stables.'

'How do I get to them?'

'You mustn't go through the front gate. You'll have to drive round the back of the palace grounds until you come to a sign.'

She pointed him back the way he'd come.

Brandon looked past the stocks, towards a sign saying "Palace Entrance". It seemed a lot easier to follow that sign.

'Thank you, ma'am. I appreciate it. What does a pint of beer cost round here?'

'Ninepence.'

Brandon gave the man a shilling. 'Here you are old fella. Enjoy yourself.'

He climbed back into his car and said to the woman, 'I'll just turn round up there.' She smiled at him and said, 'I hope you find her,' before rushing home to tell her neighbour that a handsome American had been asking after the Ballantynes' daughter. If she'd stayed a little longer, she'd have noticed that Brandon had gone round the corner towards the palace gates but hadn't come back.

He drove through the gates and sailed up the drive. Round

the back, he came to a greenhouse with a gardener inside. Shabby and stooped, his cardigan full of holes, the man looked as if the Duke worked him hard and paid him little.

'Pardon me. I'm looking for the stables. I have to meet someone there.'

The gardener looked at him. 'American?'

'Yes. I don't suppose you get many of us round here.'

'Only my mother.'

He directed Brandon to the stable, touched his cap to him and watched him drive off. As the car drove away, a footman rushed up. 'Is everything alright, Your Grace? I don't know how that man got in here.'

'American y'see,' said the Duke as he resumed his potting.

There was no one in the stables, just the leathery smell of the tack room, the sweet smell of hay and the distinctive odour of horses. He swung his legs out of the car and scanned the mist-covered fields for signs of life. The Jaguar made cracking sounds as the engine cooled. He was thinking about driving across the fields in search of her when he heard the low, thumping sound of hooves. As the sound grew louder, a horse and rider emerged through the mist. Even with a hat on, she was unmistakable.

He saw her expression change as she caught sight of him. Bringing the horse to a halt, she looked down at him.

'What are you doing here? I thought you'd be halfway across the Atlantic by now.' Her voice had a hard edge.

The stable smells faded into insignificance as he looked at her. To begin with, that's all he wanted to do, look at her. But she wanted an answer.

'It's like I said, I've decided to join the RAF. As this is my last day of freedom, I thought I'd look you up. I hope you don't mind.'

'That's very flattering but, if this really is your last day before joining up, I'd have thought you had better things to do than waste your time with me.'

He said nothing while she dismounted, giving her time to think.

'I'm sorry, I shouldn't have said that. It's good of you to bother. What are you doing for the rest of the day?'

His hopes rose a little.

'That rather depends on you. Could we go for a drive?'

Mary looked at the car and remembered the drive up into the hills to La Dame Brave. It seemed a long time ago. It would be nice to relive the memory and it wouldn't do any harm. It would just be a drive.

They drove west into the Cotswolds. Though the traffic was light, progress was slow. At regular intervals, tractors would swing out of fields without looking. When the tractors weren't holding them up, they would find their path blocked by flocks of sheep winding their way from one field to another. Then, for what seemed like miles, they followed a brewer's dray pulled by two white shire horses, the wooden barrels, piled impossibly high, looking anything but secure.

'I hope they don't roll on top of us, said Brandon.

'They won't. That's why they go so slowly. In any case, we're nearly there.'

Brandon saw a sign for a village called Bibury.

'Your Mr Henry Ford liked this place so much he tried to buy one of the streets and ship it over to Michigan.'

'You mean there's more than one? Looks pretty small to me.'

'One pub, one shop, one tearoom. What more do you need?'

Nervously, she took his hand and led him towards the tearoom. Brandon entwined his fingers with hers. She started to regret her simple gesture but rather admired the way he exploited it.

'I hope they have a spare table.'

'I doubt if there's anyone here at all. The tearoom is part of the local post office and stores. It would never survive on its own. Not many farmers come into the village for a cup of tea, they head straight for the pub.'

A pheasant ambled past them without a care in the world.

Brandon glanced up and down. There was no one around.

'It's like the wild west but in a different setting. Instead of a dry and dusty town in the middle of nowhere there's a soft green village in the middle of nowhere. But the setup's basically the same. Any minute now, the big landowner will ride up with a six gun in his holster, hitch his horse to a post and swagger into the saloon.'

As he finished speaking, a man rode up on his horse, wearing a tweed cap and jacket instead of a stetson and leather jerkin. A broken shotgun rested across the saddle. He tied the horse up and strolled into the pub.

'See what I mean? They just took the life they knew, got on a boat across the Atlantic and reproduced it on the other side.'

She laughed then gazed at him, rather more adoringly than she'd intended.

'You're very perceptive, aren't you?'

'Not really, I'm just stating the obvious,' he protested, but not too much.

As the only people in the tearooms, they were served with extra scones and cream. That was before the people in the adjoining shop heard Brandon's American accent. No one had seen an American in the flesh before. Soon, every table was taken and the owner started to regret being so generous with the scones.

Unaware of the interest they'd aroused, they talked freely. The journey had given Mary time to think. Half the time he was trying to make it look as though this was just a casual call on an old friend. The other half? It was time to find out.

'Where's this leading?'

'Well, I thought after tea, we could go to the movies in Oxford.'

'You know what I mean. And the pictures aren't open on a Sunday.'

When he leaned across the table and took her hand, the onlookers leaned across their tables to get a closer look. If he was an American, he must be an actor. That much was obvious.

They must be rehearsing a scene from a moving picture. The dialogue quickly confirmed this.

'Mary, we've both known where this was leading from the first time our eyes met on the terrace of the hotel. You know we're made for each other. Do you honestly think I would go to all this trouble just for a bit of fun?'

'I rather think you would. You cut quite a dash at the hotel and I doubt if zooming up here in that fancy car of yours was much of a chore.'

She leaned back and looked him in the eye. She wanted to talk seriously but, for him, that look only intensified his desire.

'Even if you are sincere, there are so many obstacles in the way. You'll be going home soon.' He started to protest. She held up her hand. 'Oh, I know you want to fight for freedom and all that but my guess is as soon as war breaks out, you'll be on the first boat home. And if you really did go off to war, we'd be apart anyway.'

She was trying to work up to what she needed to say but it was so hard to get the words out. She looked away for a moment then leaned forward and took his hand. 'Look, I'm very young and I still dream of a career in show jumping. I'm not ready for marriage.'

The onlookers (by now there was a full house) were surprised by the line about show jumping. That didn't seem right for a Hollywood picture. One of them whispered to the others 'That line will probably be cut from the final version'. He'd read a magazine called Motion Picture in the barbers and regarded himself as something of an expert. They waited eagerly for Brandon's reply.

'That's because, instead of seeing me as an opportunity, you see me as a threat, a threat to the fulfilment of your sporting dreams. You may not become a champion but we can have a wonderful life together. I'm really serious about you. I just need a chance to prove it. Please say you'll give me that chance. You won't have to borrow a horse from the Duke, I'll buy you one of your own. You'll have the best of both worlds.'

With every word he spoke, every look he gave her, her resolve weakened. She tried one last move.

'If there is a war, I'd rather you were safe on the other side of the Atlantic. Then, when it's over, you can come back and we'll take it from there.'

As Brandon tried to think of a reply, a voice boomed across the room from another table. The speaker wasn't a local so everyone assumed he was part of the rehearsal. A History don from Oxford, he came out to these tearooms every Sunday because he usually had the place to himself.

'Your companion is giving you good advice, young man. There will be a war and very soon. If I were you, I'd start making plans to return home. You won't want to be here when the bombing starts.'

He placed a shilling on the table to cover the cost of his tea plus a generous tip and walked out. This was obviously the climax of the scene. The audience did what any audience would have done in the circumstances. They applauded.

The two actors looked at each other in amazement then burst out laughing.

'I think it's time to go,' said Mary.

Brandon paid the bill. As they made for the door, a young woman held up a piece of paper and a pencil. He gave her a puzzled look until he realised she wanted his autograph. He thought of explaining he wasn't a film star, decided it wasn't worth the effort, shrugged his shoulders and signed.

'I thought you British were supposed to be a restrained lot.'

'Well, it's not every day we get to meet a real film star.'

Everything that could be said had been. They drove back to Woodstock in silence. When they arrived at her house, she took his hand.

'I don't care what that man said. The world couldn't possibly be so stupid as to start another war, I just don't believe it.'

'You mean you want to go to Helsinki with your horse and

you don't want any distractions in the meantime.'

She let go of his hand and in that moment, he knew he'd lost her.

'If war comes, don't fight in it. Go home then come back when it's over. I'll be waiting.'

He leaned over and kissed her. This time, unlike their encounter on the island, she made no objection. He made it last as long as possible. Saying, 'no need to see me to the door,' she jumped out and was gone.

On the drive back to London, he tried to convince himself she hadn't rejected him but he knew she had. Joining the RAF, fighting for freedom, all his plans had been centred around her but she'd sent him away. He felt directionless again.

When he arrived back at his hotel, he found a note asking him to call at the American Embassy. He knew what it was about. His father was using his influence to get his only son back home before war broke out. Twenty-four hours ago, he would have torn the note up. Now, he walked around the corner to the Embassy and was shown straight up to the top floor. Ambassador Kennedy didn't waste words.

'War is about to be declared, Brandon. Everyone who can get out is doing so. I can't tell you what to do but I strongly urge you to leave now.'

He pushed a ticket across the desk.

'The Queen Mary sails tomorrow morning, loaded up with gold bullion. That shows you how much confidence the British have in their future. With any luck, it'll be a short war.'

He pushed the ticket further across the desk.

'We're at the dawn of a new age, Brandon. Things are changing fast but you need to go home now.'

'There are things I want to do over here, sir.'

'And you'll soon be able to do them. There are going to be big opportunities for American industry in the new Europe that will emerge from this war. A man in your financial position will be able to seize the opportunities with both hands.'

Brandon looked at the ticket. If Kennedy was right, he'd be back in six months. Surely Mary would be impressed if he returned to claim her. He needed one more nudge. Kennedy came in on cue.

'I went to a lot of trouble to get that ticket for you, Brandon. Your father is a good friend. I did it for him. Don't let us down.'

He sighed and picked up the ticket.

'I guess you're right. Thank you for the trouble you've taken, Mr Ambassador. I appreciate it.'

As a last pretence that he was coming back, he booked his car into storage, paying for six months' rent. 'I look forward to seeing you on your return, sir,' said the garage owner as Brandon stepped into a taxi for the short ride to Charing Cross station. As the taxi pulled away, the garage owner phoned his solicitor. 'How long do I have to wait before I can claim ownership of a car a client has abandoned?'

The Ocean Terminal in Southampton was packed with people. Some had just arrived and were desperate to get back into the country, others just as desperate to get back out. Once he'd settled into his cabin, Brandon made his way to the side of the ship where he joined other passengers leaning on the rail, taking a last look at a country about to go to war.

'If you ask me, we're getting out just in time.'

The opinion was expressed by an elegantly dressed American woman in her mid-fifties.

'These people have no idea what they're in for. I feel sorry for them.'

'I guess you're right,' said Brandon. 'But I feel we should be doing something to help them.'

'Definitely not. We should stay out of Europe's endless squabbles. Let them fight it out amongst themselves, I say. It's not our job to prop up the British Empire. Anyway, I rather like this Hitler. I wish we had someone like him back home, instead of that pathetic Roosevelt. He's too fond of communists for my liking.'

As he stared aimlessly at the crowd on the quayside, a line of children crossed in front of him, walking away from another liner and towards the pier building.

'They're Jews,' said the woman. 'The Captain of that liner over there delayed sailing from Cherbourg to take them on board. I suppose he thinks he's doing them a favour. I can't see the point myself.'

As Brandon watched them walk by, one of the children, a little girl, no more than eight years old, looked up at the Queen Mary. Perhaps he was imagining it but she seemed to be looking at him reproachfully. As she did so the ship's loudspeaker announced that the gangplank was about to be removed.

The look on the child's face combined with the announcement jolted Brandon into action. He felt as if he'd woken from a trance and could see clearly now. Without saying a word, he ran towards the gangplank. One of the crew tried to stop him. 'We're about to sail, sir.'

He ignored him and ran down the steps. The crewman shouted after him.

'What about your luggage sir?'

'Keep it. I won't be needing those clothes where I'm going.'

He stopped to take one last look at the great ocean-going vessel then walked into the Terminal building. A man in a Cunard uniform stopped him. 'Do you need directions, sir?'

'Not any more. Now I know exactly where I'm going.'

Chapter 20

THE TOP FLOOR of Broadway Buildings wasn't a grand affair. True, unlike the floors below, there was a carpet on the landing but it was worn and in need of replacement, rather like the man sitting at his desk in the large office that looked over the back of the building, towards St. James's Park.

The head of the SIS, the man known as C, was a shadow of the man he'd been when he'd taken over the top job and he and everyone else knew it. His last gift to his country had been the purchase, with his own money, of a large house in Buckinghamshire to house a code-breaking unit. A year earlier, he'd written a detailed dossier about Hitler that revealed the dictator's true character and the threat he posed. It had been badly received by a Foreign Office anxious to see Hitler as a man with whom they could do business.

Since then, he had declined rapidly. It was time to pass the baton to a younger man. Which was why he had summoned the man sitting in the chair on the other side of his desk.

'I'm going into hospital tomorrow for an operation.'

'I'm sure it will go well.'

'Not a chance. I'm on the way out and I don't just mean out of this office.'

He shifted from one side of his chair to the other, trying to ease the pain. It didn't work. The sooner he got this over with, the better.

'Which is why we're having this meeting.'

His deputy tried to hide the lively sense of anticipation

that swept through him but his boss could see the gleam in his junior's eye. In an ideal world, there would be a better successor for him to choose but this world was far from ideal. Which was the second reason he'd called this meeting.

'The FO ignored my warnings about Hitler, thanks to that fool Henderson. Now we're at war, I don't need to tell you of the dangers we now face.'

However, the old man knew he did need to tell him and proceeded to do so.

'We've gone to war assuming we can rely on the French military and political leaders to hold Hitler on land while we control the seas. The second part may be true but not the first. Too many of the French elite share Hitler's views. They're hiding it for now but the truth will out. If I'm right, we face a war of attrition that we simply can't afford.'

'Surely Hitler can't afford it either.'

'He can in the short term. Germany will do what it did in the Franco-Prussian war, it will steal train loads of French gold and ship it back home. They'll do the same to every country they invade. We've assumed all along they'll run out of money but every penny they've spent will be recovered from their victims. We're the ones who will end up penniless. We've made a terrible mistake and we must do something about it. That's where you come in.'

The pain was now so great he had to stand up. Leaning on the desk he gestured to his deputy and spoke in a whisper.

'Bottom drawer. Pills.'

The younger man went round to the other side of the desk, opened the drawer and produced a bottle of pills. He looked up enquiringly.

'Four.'

He tipped four tablets out then went over to the sideboard underneath the window. Ignoring the carafe of water, he poured a glass of whisky. When the old man had swallowed the pills, both men returned to their chairs.

'I want you to take over.'

The younger man affected to declare himself unworthy but C silenced him.

'The final decision is not mine, of course, and I'll be dead anyway but I'm confident they'll respect my wishes.'

With the help of the pills, he summoned up the last of his strength.

'Now listen carefully. You can play a vital role in avoiding the disaster that is about to unfold by using our lines of communication with the anti-Hitler movement.'

'You mean anti-Nazi.'

'No, many of these men are anti-Nazi but some of the big players are more anxious to overthrow the man rather than the movement. We can't be fussy, we have to cultivate both.'

'What do you mean?'

'We have to do a deal to stop the war in its tracks.'

The younger man didn't agree but said nothing that might jeopardise the promotion that would take him to the top of the tree.

'I understand, sir. We'll talk more about this when you come out of hospital.'

'One more thing. The young fellow who fetched the rotors. I'd like to see him. Thank him personally. Bletchley Park were very excited when they got their hands on them. Tell him to visit me in hospital.'

'Shouldn't it wait till you're out of hospital?'

The old man laughed and waved him away.

The first thing that caught his eye was a sign for the morgue. Not a good start. Fawkes didn't like hospitals but he hated morgues. They brought back memories he'd spent half his life trying to forget.

He'd been told to use the back entrance and go straight to the third floor. When the briskly efficient ward sister ushered him into the private room, he was shocked by the sight that greeted his eyes.

He'd returned from France expecting to be debriefed in Bush House by Dansey but things had moved on while he'd been away. Z section was no more. Merged with his original department, it had moved back into Broadway Buildings and he had a new boss, a man called Lestocq. Expecting to be debriefed by this man, he was surprised and pleased to be told to report to dear old C himself.

After his transfer to Bush House he'd seen nothing of C for over a year and wasn't prepared for the sight of the man in the bed in front of him. There had been rumours the old man wasn't in the best of health but nothing had prepared him for the terrible decline in the one man he greatly admired.

'How are you sir?'

'Not at my best, I'm afraid, but they're operating on me tomorrow. I should be back to full strength soon. But never mind me, I wanted to have a word with you about your mission. I hear you did a grand job.'

'That's kind of you sir but I lost my partner and must take the blame for that.'

'These losses are always regrettable but sometimes, they are unavoidable. You mustn't blame yourself.'

C shifted slightly, wincing with pain as he did so. The sight moved Fawkes as much as the old man's kind words.

'I asked you to come here because I want you to have no doubt of the importance of those things you brought back. Damn clever of you to do it in the way you did, by the way. Much of the coming war, I've no doubt, will be like the last one, but not all of it. What you brought back will help us to have a clearer idea of the enemy's intentions. I don't need to tell you how important that is.'

Once more, the old man winced with pain. This time a nurse came in.

'You must leave now,' she said to Fawkes. 'He needs to get his strength up for the operation tomorrow.'

'Just a few more moments, nurse,' said the old man. When she'd gone, he continued.

'You've got a real talent for this line of work, I spotted that in you right away. That's why I recruited you. You've also got ambition. That's good too but you mustn't let ambition affect your judgement. Talent and ambition are fine but they're not enough. You've got to learn how to get on with the people around you. Less of the one-man-band approach to everything.'

'It's difficult for me.'

'Everything about this job is difficult. You know that. Why should this part be any different from the rest?'

The nurse returned. Fawkes stood up and made to leave. As he did so, he felt C grasp his arm. The strength and urgency of his grip took him by surprise.

'I feel guilty about what happened. We acted with the best intentions but what we did to your mother was unforgivable. It was thoughtless and cruel.'

The old man shifted himself until he was sitting upright.

'It never occurred to us that she would do that. Please remember that and that we thought what we were doing was for the best.'

The memory of what had happened to his mother filled Fawkes with anguish but he had no idea why the old man was talking about a wrong that had been committed by the Navy, not the SIS. It must be the painkillers doing the talking. Even so, it was the first time anyone in the service had expressed any sympathy for Fawkes's tragic loss and he was touched by C's concern for the wrong that had been done. The old man was clearly very ill so he played along.

'Don't worry about it, sir. It was a long time ago. Just concentrate on getting well. We need you back in the office.'

His words had no effect as the old man continued to grasp his arm firmly and continued to speak with a guilty look in his eyes.

'You have a lot to offer the department. If you take any setbacks in your stride and handle them diplomatically, you'll go far.'

Fawkes was lost for words. It was as if he was saying a final goodbye. He gently removed the old man's hand from his grasp and laid it back on the bed.

'Good luck tomorrow, sir. We need you back to strength.'

He emerged onto the street with his mind in turmoil. Not from the shock of the old man's deterioration or from the praise for a job well done. It was the cryptic apology for the death of his mother. But he'd been a child at the time. The terrible event that had shaped him was years before his recruitment to the Service. Had it just been the drugs talking or was there something he didn't know, something he'd never been told?

There was only one person he could speak to. When he left the hospital, he took the Tube to Hammersmith and walked the rest of the way.

Chapter 21

SHE WAS WAITING for him. She always was. As he walked through the entrance to Fulham Cemetery, the memories and the guilt came flooding back. Memories of how she had always protected him when he needed her, guilt that he had failed to protect her when she needed him.

The guilt had started before that terrible April day. He'd always been proud to have a British father and a German mother he adored. It gave even a boy as young as him a certain cachet with his peers. Then war was declared in 1914 and everything changed. Although their adult neighbours behaved very well towards her, his friends enjoyed teasing him. His young mind struggled to cope with conflicting thoughts. He still adored her but she was also an embarrassment.

In June 1916, his world collapsed when his father was killed at the Battle of Jutland. Riven with guilt, he witnessed the shattering grief that gripped her as they clung to each other. In the months that followed, she had taken him to visit the grave, telling him how lucky the two of them were that, although his father had died in a great naval battle, his body had been recovered, giving them the consolation of a grave to visit, a consolation denied to so many others in this terrible war. He would stand next to her and listen while she talked to his father's headstone, the tears coursing down her cheeks. For a brief time, a time he would remember for the rest of his life, mother and son were as one.

Then one day, there was a knock on the door. They had come for him.

They, whoever "they" were, had graciously allowed mother and son three months to mourn the death of his father but by September 1916, a new school year beckoned. It was time to remove the boy from his German mother's influence.

Sent to his room as soon as they had arrived, he had crept out to the bannister on the landing. Pressing his face against the spindles he'd listened to the two men giving his mother a terrible choice.

'You have to face reality, Frau Fawkes.'

'Mrs Fawkes,' she interjected in her German accent.

The man from the Ministry ignored her remark. The local police sergeant who had accompanied him looked away, embarrassed.

'You are a German national and this country is at war with your country.'

'Britain is my country.'

Again, he ignored her. His instructions were clear. It was more than his job was worth to ignore them.

'You are German, madam, and as such, you should be interned. In that case, your son must accompany you into internment.'

Either through embarrassment at what he was saying or because he needed to remember what he'd been instructed to say next, he paused and looked down at the piece of paper in his hand. He decided it would be safer to read out the words in front of him.

'However, in view of your husband's service to the nation, we are prepared to allow you to continue to live here in this house, on condition that your son is handed into the care of the Royal Navy.'

He could hear his mother speaking calmly and politely.

'For how long?'

'Permanently, Frau Fawkes.'

The police sergeant finally had enough.

'It's Mrs Fawkes. Her husband died for this country, for God's sake, you heartless bastards.'

He too was ignored.

'Look, it's up to you to decide your son's future. As the son of a Naval officer, he has every chance of an excellent career in the service. What future will he have if he's interned along with his German mother?'

The conclusion was a formality. His mother came upstairs and told him he'd been offered a wonderful opportunity to be educated at Naval College and she was sure Daddy would have wanted him to go. No mention of what she wanted.

'Will you come and visit me?'

'Of course,' she lied.

He'd heard what they said, known it wasn't what she wanted, known she needed him by her side, but had said nothing. A hug and a kiss and they parted, forever. It was over so quickly.

In the six months that followed, though he settled into life at Naval College, his performance was undistinguished. When, one fine day the following April, he was called into the College Commander's office, he assumed it was to be reprimanded.

No attempt was made to conceal the truth. The Commander almost relished his words.

'I'm afraid your mother has hanged herself. Obviously, I'm sorry for your loss. I know you've struggled to settle in but, given her instability, they were right to rescue you and bring you here. I'm afraid she won't be buried in consecrated ground. That's always the case in such situations.'

Perhaps his tone would have softened if the conversation had continued. Hearing the Commander's words but barely able to understand what he was saying, Fawkes ran out of the office, across the Parade Ground and into chapel, not to pray but to climb the circular staircase to the top of the bell tower. The coldness of the stone was welcome to a heart that seemed on the verge of boiling over. As soon as he reached the top, he climbed without hesitation onto the ledge by the bell. Beneath him the hard surface of the Parade Ground offered a solution, a way to calm his raging mind. As he gazed down at it, a wonderful calm came over him. His head cleared of all the thoughts that had confused him since he'd arrived at the college. It was quite simple, he should have refused to go to Naval College and gone into internment with her. To put that right, all he had to do was jump and he could join her and his father.

As he shuffled nearer the edge, a voice behind him called his name, a voice he recognised so well. He turned round and there she was, holding out her arms, beckoning with her hands. Without hesitation, he climbed off the ledge and ran to her.

Much later, he climbed down the staircase and re-joined his fellow cadets. While he tried to pay attention to the condolences they offered, something the Commander had said nagged at his brain but he couldn't remember what it was. Then it came to him.

Why did the Head say, "they" rescued him, not "we"?

He was told to catch a train up to London where he was met by the local Police Sergeant.

'Someone has intervened to allow your mother to be buried next to your father. Quite right too, the way they treated her was a disgrace. I never understood why.'

By the time they reached the graveside, the whole street had assembled there. Two men, one of whom he recognised, were standing apart, looking far from happy at the turnout. After the service, a long-time neighbour and friend came up and hugged him. Pointing to the two men, she didn't pull her punches.

'They killed her.'

The men signalled to the police sergeant to move her away and hurried Fawkes into a car. Remembering the Head's words, he asked, 'who are you?'

The men exchanged looks as the car moved off then the one he'd met before replied.

'Just a couple of civil servants. People who have your interests at heart. It's thanks to us they allowed your mother to be buried alongside your father. The Church and the State were against it but we made them see sense.'

When they arrived at Paddington station, Fawkes made to open the door but one of the men placed a restraining hand on his shoulder.

'We're not monsters. We realise she was, in her own way, a victim of the war but our priority was you and your future. It had to be. You'll never put this behind you but you can learn to deal with it and the best way to do that is to bury yourself in work. Your father was a brave man. You owe it to him to work hard.'

The man smiled a rare smile.

'Now hoppit.'

Back at Naval College, he threw himself into his work and was transformed from an also-ran into a star. When he moved on into the Navy, his career prospered, his future seemed bright, until he was inexplicably stitched up by absurd charges and a blatantly biased court-martial. He had no doubt someone had taken against him for having a German mother.

He was due some luck and it came in the shape of the SIS. On the day he left the navy, he received a tap on the shoulder and an invitation to visit an office building near St James's Park. To his surprise, he found himself in a job he both enjoyed and was good at. Once more, in London, he resumed his visits to his parents' graves and let them know how fulfilled he was by his new job.

Which brought him to the reason for this visit. For all the skills he had acquired, he was quite unable to decrypt C's words. The more he thought about them, the less sense they made. As he explained this to his parents, it became clear that the only rational explanation was the obvious one. The old man's drugs had been doing the talking.

He knelt over the headstones, kissed each one and whispered, 'I just want to make you proud of me.'

Barely a week later, he was summoned to another meeting. The old man hadn't survived the operation, his funeral had been held and a new C appointed. He and another man, an unfamiliar face, looked up as Fawkes was brought in. With the firm jawline of a man who would remain calm under fire, the man looked a different sort from the usual Broadway lot and not just because he wore the uniform of a Commander in the Navy. When he lit his pipe, a familiar fug greeted Fawkes's nostrils.

'Come in, Fawkes. This gentleman is from our decryption branch. He wants to have a word with you.'

With a quick 'good morning, Commander,' Fawkes shook the proffered hand.

The Commander smiled at the man who'd brought him the precious rotors then got down to business.

'Quite simple really. I want a brief report on what happened in France. You met the Pole in a village in the hills, correct?'

'Yes, sir, he arranged quite a complicated handover, involving two locations.'

'Why was that?'

'He was nervous, sir. Suspected the Germans knew he was there and wanted to give them the impression he was merely handing over some papers.'

The Commander looked surprised.

'Is this in your report. I haven't been shown it.'

'I was told not to make one, sir.'

'Tell me now, then.'

'He arranged a bogus meeting in the house where he was staying and a genuine one at a perfume factory.'

In meetings of this kind, Fawkes had learnt to watch the interaction between the other people. Short or long exchanges of looks often replaced words. Not once did the Commander look across at C. His eyes remained on Fawkes throughout.

'They tell me you were the only person he was prepared to meet.'

'That's right, sir. He mentioned the January meeting in Paris, saying it didn't go well as neither we nor the Poles were willing to give anything away. Apparently, they took a dislike to everyone except me but I was sent packing when they found my German wasn't needed. That's why Koslowski chose me to receive the rotors. I'm not trying to be impertinent sir. I'm just telling you what the Pole said.'

'No, that's fine. I want his actual words, not a sanitised version. So, he told you they were rotors. Did you understand what he meant?'

'Not until he explained it to me. He said they were from an Enigma machine and would help us build a machine to decode Enigma. Claimed we were working on something similar but were going about it the wrong way. That we badly needed the rotors because decoding will decide the outcome of the war.'

For the first time, the Commander gave C a quick glance. As he did so, the door opened and Control's secretary poked her head around it.

'Sorry to interrupt but Mr Lestocq needs Mr Fawkes. He says it's urgent.'

Fawkes noticed the Commander didn't seem at all put out by this intervention, as if it had been pre-arranged. He looked across at C who nodded. When he stood up, the Commander rewarded him with a smile.

'I used to know a Fawkes in the navy. First class fellow, died at Jutland.'

'That was my father, sir. Actually, your tobacco, St Bruno Flake, reminded me of him.'

'You must be very proud. You've got quite a name to live up to.'

The Commander stood up and held out his hand.

'Look, I'm afraid the Pole was misinformed. Once we had a chance to look at them, it became obvious that the rotors won't be of any use but you did a grand job in bringing them in. I don't think C will mind me saying that you're due a significant promotion.'

Fawkes took the stairs down to his floor to give himself time to digest what he'd been told. The old C had summoned him to his death bed to tell him how important the rotors were. Now the Commander was saying the opposite. Would he really be given a promotion if the mission had been a failure? He remembered Koslowski warning him he wouldn't be told the truth.

Did it matter? A promotion was a promotion and God knows he deserved it.

Once Fawkes had left, the Commander came straight to the point.

'Interesting things, those rotors.'

'Are they genuine?'

'Definitely. I don't know if it's because they liked Fawkes or because we've finally guaranteed Polish sovereignty but our last meeting was a real step forward. That and these rotors showing the Enigma wiring, are enormously helpful. Your young man did a grand job when he brought them in.'

The Commander drew on his pipe.

'Which makes him a bit of a problem.'

'You told him they were useless.'

'Yes, but he wasn't fooled. I may have convinced him the Pole was exaggerating but, er.'

'What?'

'Has he spoken to anyone since his return?'

'Only my predecessor. He visited him in hospital.'

'Well, there you are. A dying man anxious to give praise where praise was due while he still could. It's a shame you allowed the visit to go ahead.'

'I couldn't stop it. My appointment as his successor hadn't been confirmed. I wasn't going to do anything to prejudice that. Does it matter?'

'Definitely. You can't let a man with his knowledge go into occupied territory. What if he's captured?'

The Commander tapped his pipe on an ashtray and started to re-fill it. As he did so, he looked towards the window.

'Is he a valuable asset?'

C watched the Commander re-light his pipe, with its tiresome odour.

'He's unorthodox, not quite what we're used to but I expect we'll need plenty of that in the coming war.'

'He must be good. Did you realize he'd learnt so much from the Pole?'

'For security reasons, we told him not to file a report.'

'Well, it's lucky I spoke to him. Thankfully, he didn't know about our recent meeting in Pyry Forest but he already knows too much. You'll have to keep him out of harm's way, for now at least. Perhaps permanently. If he fell into enemy hands, we both know what they'd do to him. You'll be doing him a favour.'

'He won't like that. You've just promised him a promotion but if I keep him in the office, he'll put everyone's backs up. He's always banging on about communist penetration of the department. He infuriates Lestocq.'

'Who?'

'Joined us last year. First class fellow, knows all the right people because he's one of them. I'm grooming him as a future C.'

'I don't care if Fawkes puts whatshisname's back up.'

'Lestocq. Scion of one of Britain's oldest families.'

'If you say so. The point is, Fawkes possesses information that must never be revealed to anyone else in the department. Give him something useful to do in another location, something that makes use of his fluency in German. If it isn't really a promotion, make it seem like one.'

'I'll have a word with him.'

'I'm sure you'll handle it with your customary tact but under no circumstances link it to what he knows.'

As the Commander stood up to leave, he sighed.

'If the Poles are cooperating because we've guaranteed their sovereignty, I'm afraid they're in for a shock. We can't possibly help them. What a country we've become.'

Before summoning Fawkes back, C decided to have a word with Lestocq, partly because he was Fawkes's superior, mainly because

C knew he would enthusiastically endorse his departure.

His normal practice when someone entered the office was to carry on writing and, without looking up, gesture to the incomer to take a seat. As soon as Lestocq entered, he stood up and invited his socially well-connected protégé to join him.

'Lestocq old man, we need to decide what to do about Fawkes.'

Adopting a solemn expression, Lestocq prepared to play the role allotted to him.

'It's a difficult one, sir. He's got his good points, of course.'

'But?'

'He's not a team player, never has been. In the SIS, you're either an insider or you're an outsider. Fawkes positively enjoys seeing himself as an outsider.'

C also had a role to play in this conversation, one carefully crafted to arrive at the right conclusion.

'He gets on well with his agents and has gathered a lot of useful information when we needed it most.'

'Not always. They tell me his last mission for Z Section, supposed to be straightforward, was a failure and his partner was killed. Who knows what really went on there?'

C ignored the invitation to tell Lestocq what really went on there and continued his mock defence of Fawkes.

'I'm sure his behaviour was entirely above board even if the outcome was unfortunate.'

'I'm not suggesting his being half-German should be held against him but things are different now we are at war.'

Having cornered his quarry, Lestocq moved in for the kill.

'Then there's his obsession with communist penetration of the department. We don't need such negativity right now.'

C nodded.

'I'll admit he goes too far when it comes to communists.'

'He'll be accusing you and me before you know it. Considering your predecessor rescued him when he'd been thrown out of the Navy, you'd think he'd show a little gratitude.'

The conversation was going well. Now was not the time to correct that version of events.

'Even so, I feel a little guilty about pushing him aside.'

'That's generous of you, sir and I'm not suggesting we push him out altogether. There must be other work he can do, work that makes use of his languages but keeps him out of our hair.'

'I'm glad to hear you say that. We mustn't be too hard on him but I take your point. I'll see where we can send him.'

Lestocq concealed his pleasure. C would have expected nothing less.

'It would make my task easier if I could tell him we're looking into any possible communist penetration of the service. You're the ideal person to carry that out. No need to put everyone's backs up but see if you can find someone suitable amongst the dead wood, if you get my drift.'

Lestocq avoided giving his boss a conspiratorial smile.

'Rest assured I shall be discreet but thorough.'

Once his protégé had left, C sat staring at the wall for several minutes before coming to a decision. Both the Commander and Lestocq had made the same point - give Fawkes a job that made use of his languages. He picked up the phone, had a brief conversation with the person on the other end, then asked his secretary to summon Fawkes.

The summons to return to the top floor came as no surprise. He'd followed Heywood's advice to be diplomatic, the meeting had gone well and, though a promotion wasn't within the gift of the Commander, he couldn't see why else he would be called back. No stairs this time, he wanted to get there as quickly as possible. When he arrived back in C's office, a new, diplomatic, Fawkes smiled at him.

'You wanted to see me, sir?'

'Sit down, Fawkes.'

C felt guilty. The man sitting opposite had done good work, vital work and didn't deserve what was about to happen to him, nor could he be told the real reason. His voice was gentle. Fawkes was encouraged.

'As the Commander said, you handled your last mission well. It's not your fault the rotors proved to be useless.'

Having been told by the dying C that the rotors were anything but useless, the old Fawkes would have angrily challenged this claim.

'It was a disappointment, sir but you were right to send me to collect them.'

It was hard to tell which man was more astonished by these words. Both the deliverer of them and their recipient maintained expressionless faces as C hastily moved on.

'You deserve a promotion and you shall have one.'

This diplomacy stuff really works, thought Fawkes. Oh God, what am I turning into?

'I have an important job for you. You were the only person who could carry out your last mission and the same applies to this one.'

Recognition at last.

'We're equipping a mansion to house captured German officers. It will be the last word in luxury with the intention of putting them at their ease to loosen their tongues. What they won't know is that there will be listening devices everywhere. Their every word will be recorded.'

Fawkes felt a first frisson of unease but played along.

'Sounds like a good idea, sir.'

'I'm glad you like it because you have a central role to play. We're going to need men who are fluent in German. This means two things, their German must be tested and, as we plan to use men of German origin, displaced Jews, that sort of thing, they will need to be vetted by someone skilled in recruiting agents. We have to be able to trust their translations. As I said, it's vital work and you're the only man who can do it.'

Fawkes said nothing and, for a moment, C thought he'd got away with it.

'So, I wouldn't be working in the department anymore?'

'No, you'd have to be on site.'

Fawkes knew what he ought to do – continue with the diplomacy, accept that the new job was important, above all, pocket the promotion.

'How long will the mission last? Will I return to the department when it's over?'

'I can't say how long. It could be quite a while but we'll certainly find room for you somewhere when it's over. Not sure where exactly.'

During the long silence that followed C was encouraged. It looked like the man would go quietly.

'How could you do this to me?'

'Do what?'

'I'm the man who brought back those rotors, who successfully pulled off the most important mission ever conducted by the SIS. And don't give me that guff about them being useless. I heard how valuable they were from old C's own lips. *He's* never lied to me. Not once.'

Momentarily irritated when he realised he'd been seen through so easily, C soon relaxed. This was more to his taste. He could handle this. Used to dealing with disgruntled employees on his estates, he changed tack and addressed Fawkes as if he was a trainee gamekeeper's assistant being let go because he hadn't come up to scratch.

'Listen Fawkes, you've been doing your best but now we're at war, things have changed. We need a united team with no room for individualists. Fact is, I'm going to have difficulty finding a role for you here. Even your best friends would never call you a team player and being half German complicates things, makes it difficult for your colleagues.'

He regretted the words as soon as he'd uttered them but his pride wouldn't let him row back. Fawkes's pride helped him row forward. This was more to his taste too. He could handle this.

'The Service saw it as an advantage when they recruited me.

Your predecessor made quite a thing of it at the time. I should have thought I'd be even more useful in a war.'

'As I say, things have changed. There are issues about your background. We both know what I'm referring to. They've led you to take too many risks in an effort to prove yourself. We've put up with them till now but what was acceptable before, isn't any more.'

Wondering what to say next, C shuffled in his chair. The ever-reliable Fawkes came to his rescue.

'He was a good man.'

'Who?'

'Your predecessor. I trusted him.'

Any residual guilt C was feeling evaporated.

'Now you listen to me, Fawkes. You're a half German who bangs on about the communist threat. Across the channel, we're going to war with a whole German, alright an Austrian, who also goes on about the communist threat and has used it to tighten his grip on power and silence all his opponents, not just the communists. In these circumstances, keeping you on is too much of a risk.'

Years of stored-up bitterness rose eagerly to the surface.

'The only reason Koslowski gave us the rotors was because he trusted me and no one else. Not you, not Lestocq, me. It's men like Lestocq who pose a risk because they don't know what they're doing.'

It occurred to C that the tiresome fellow was giving him an opportunity not just to exile him but to sack him, deal with the problem once and for all. Just keep needling him and he'll go too far.

'That's quite enough of that. Your German will be useful but not in this department. You'll be living in luxury accommodation and you'll remain on our payroll.'

He paused.

'But only if you accept this posting.'

Seeing Fawkes was about to explode, he realised he'd allowed

Lestocq to manipulate him into an unnecessary confrontation. If Fawkes stormed out, the department would lose control of a man who knew too much. He moderated his tone.

'You're not being dismissed, no question of that but it will take some time to organise your team and install the listening devices. You'll be back one day, just not right now.'

Interpreting C's moderation as a sign of weakness, Fawkes's every instinct was to carry on giving the head of the SIS the benefit of his opinion. He'd never get another chance.

Just in time, Heywood, the man he'd failed to protect, appeared before him, paddling in the water. "*There's a big difference between you in the field, calm, collected and capable and you back in the office putting everyone's backs up.*"

As always, the advice had bounced off him. But the guilt hadn't. Wasn't this setback a just punishment for his failure to protect his old friend?

He stood up abruptly. Caught by surprise, C half expected him to storm out of the room, slamming the door behind him for good measure. When Fawkes held out his hand, saying, 'I understand, sir, I spoke out of turn, I'll do my best in the new posting,' it took C a moment to grasp what he was saying. Once they'd shaken hands, surprised but gratified, he watched Fawkes turn and walk away.

By the time he'd reached the door, Fawkes had used up his meagre supply of diplomacy. Grasping the handle firmly, he tried to slam it shut. But a new C meant a new carpet and the thick pile slowed the door's progress. Hearing the soft thud as it shut, he looked angrily at the door then strode past the secretary in the outer office. Expecting a look of contempt, he was surprised by her sympathetic expression.

Even so, when he left Broadway Buildings, he feared it would be forever.

Chapter 22

High Summer 1940

THE WAAFs STOOD around the large table, each holding a billiard cue with a triangle of wood on the end. The table was a cream coloured map of the Channel coast with a line of little wooden blocks with numbers, waiting to be deployed. Behind and above the WAAFs, the Controller sat in a small room with a window overlooking the table. It had a sliding panel of glass which he could keep closed or open. It was never closed. Biggin Hill was both a fighter station and a Sector Control Room and those WAAFs needed all their powers of concentration to do a job for which they had been specially selected.

One of the WAAFs waiting by the table was Mary Ballantyne. When she'd signed up, she, like everyone else, had known nothing of the advanced system the British had created to defend their island against attacks from the air. The Controller changed all that.

'I see you ride, Ballantyne.'

'Yes sir. I show jump actually.'

'Good reactions then.'

'Oh yes sir.'

'What about maths, any good at that?'

'Pretty good sir.'

'So, quick reactions, good at figures, under twenty-one and female.' He scribbled something on the sheet of paper in front of him. 'We're going to train you as a plotter in our Control Room. Some genius in Fighter Command has worked out that the best people to run our control system are stock exchange traders and bookmakers giving instructions to young women like you. People who can call the odds and make quick decisions. You'll be doing a vital job, Ballantyne.'

The Controller had been a pilot in the Great War, an actor afterwards. Some of the WAAFs called him a fusspot but he'd survived being shot down by von Richtofen and didn't mind what they called him as long as they helped him get the squadrons in the air. Aircraftwoman 2nd Class Mary Ballantyne rather liked the old fellow, with his calm and penetrating voice. He reminded her of her father.

She also liked her job. Single-minded and self-absorbed before joining the WAAFs, she'd had no idea how other people lived. For the first time in her life, she'd had to look up from her own narrow concerns and take a hard look at what was going on around her. Surrounded by women from all walks of life, the naive only child had become a tough, broad-minded woman. Life at Biggin Hill was hard, dangerous and good.

'There's a new lot arriving, Ballantyne, 74 Squadron. Their boss, Malan, has quite a reputation. Make sure you change the Squadron markers in case they have to go up straight away.'

'At once, sir.'

In the Control room, she ran into Winifred, a forty-year-old woman who, being older than most of the other WAAFs, had become something of a mother to them. She was married but childless with a husband who was a professional soldier stationed in Singapore. Finding herself with time on her hands, she'd joined the WAAFs to keep herself busy. A cockney, loud, boisterous and disrespectful of authority, she was quite unlike the genteel, Church-going Mary.

At first, Mary had tried to avoid her but Winifred gave her no choice. She may have been rough round the edges but Winifred was a natural mother who decided Mary needed looking after and took her under her wing, whether she liked it or not. For the first week or two, Mary resented her attention but little by little, she saw beneath Winifred's rough exterior, and started to appreciate her true nature. Within a month, she'd come to love her.

With the marker boards updated, when she stepped outside to watch the new squadron arrive, the Controller called her over.

'Take a good look at this lot, Ballantyne. They're history in the making. Malan's a South African but his squadron contains men from all over the world, not just the Empire, men who've come to fight for what they believe in. There's a couple of pilots from Poland with names so unpronounceable they just call them Sneezy and Breezy. Then there's the bloke who owns that car, some kind of fancy Jaguar.'

He pointed to a green two-seater and carried on talking. But she was gone, striding briskly at first, then breaking into a run. 'I'm sure it's the same one,' she thought. 'Perhaps he sold it before he bunked off to the States. I wonder who owns it now.'

'Her name's Henrietta. You can take her for a spin, if you like.'

When she turned round, it was as if she was looking at a different person. Gone was the slight air of shallowness born of moneyed ease, gone too the beard and every other trace of Ernest Hemingway. She hugged him.

'You're supposed to salute me young lady.'

'Sorry sir.' She stepped back and brought her hand up to her temple.

'That's better. Now you can hug me.'

'I thought you'd gone home.'

'I nearly did. I was on the ship. Then I saw a sight that made me change my mind. I'll tell you about it sometime.'

'That's wonderful. I mean, it's not your fight, yet here you are.'

'It is my fight.'

The firmness of his reply surprised her.

'I've never felt so fulfilled. It's a privilege to be part of it. My fellow Americans a-bed shall think themselves accursed they were not here.'

'I had you down as many things, never a poet.'

'No, that's Shakespeare adapted to the hour but if you want something more modern, the Poles in our squadron call this country "the island of last hope." Pretty much sums it up.'

His face softened. He looked down at the ground then back at her, like a shy teenager.

'Can you come out for a drink tonight? Catch up on things?'

The great American playboy displayed a diffidence that touched her.

'I'd love to.'

The sound of singing could be heard through the doors even before they drew into the car park of the White Hart in Brasted. Brandon gave Mary a rueful look.

'If you need somewhere to take your mind off the fact that you may die tomorrow, there are worse places than a British pub.'

'But?'

'It can get a bit artificial. Everyone's a little too happy, too boisterous. The more determined we are to enjoy ourselves, the more frightened we become.'

'Sounds like it's one of those evenings tonight.'

'Let's see if we can find a quiet corner.'

He bought himself a pint of bitter. She asked for a double scotch.

'It's a warm evening, let's go outside.'

They found a table at the far end of the garden, beside a weeping willow that caressed the ground. She thought of the last dinner in France and found herself shivering at the thought of that lost world.

'Cold?'

'No, just thinking of times past.'

He sat opposite her and shook his head.

'You're the last person I expected to see on a fighter station.

The last time we met, your whole life revolved around show jumping and your dreams of Olympic glory. How do you like being a WAAF?'

'I love it but my parents were very unhappy when I told them. "You should join the Land Army. They need women on the farms and you love the countryside. You'd be in your element," they said. They accepted my decision in the end. They had to, I'd already signed up.'

She grinned, sheepishly.

'I persuaded them that an undemanding job in a quiet airfield in the countryside might not be such a bad idea after all. I don't tell them how bad it really is.'

'How do you get on with the other girls?'

'It's not what I expected. It's silly, I suppose, but I thought everyone would be like me. They're not, of course. There are people from the cream of society who say "dahling" all the time and others from the East End who say "cor blimey." It took some getting used to. And you're right, until I got here, I never realised what a sheltered life I'd led.'

She sat back, surveying him.

'But hark at you talking, you've changed too. What happened to the playboy from last year? You can start with the beard.'

'RAF regulations don't permit one but I wasn't sorry. Shaving it off was a way of telling myself I meant business because, until the very last moment on the ship, I guess I hadn't really been serious about staying and fighting. I learned a lot travelling around Europe. I saw what was going on and thought I couldn't stand by and do nothing. Then Kennedy handed me a ticket to go home and I abandoned those cherished beliefs simply because a young woman had turned me down and left me feeling sorry for myself. It was pathetic.'

'So how come you're here?'

'It's all down to one little girl. She was in a group of Jewish children rescued by the Captain of a liner that delayed sailing from Cherbourg to wait for them. I was already on the boat home when this line of children walked along the quayside. When she looked up at me, I realised this wasn't something you read about in the papers, this was real. She made me see how shallow I was. I only just got off the boat in time.'

'I don't think you're shallow at all.'

She reached for his hand.

'How different things might have been.'

Her words trailed away when the singing started up again. Brandon barely noticed, his expression becoming fixed as he gazed into the middle distance. It was a look she knew all too well, the distracted look of a pilot struggling to control his fear. He could have cleared off back to America but he hadn't, he'd stayed and fought, fought to protect people like her. A feeling came over her like nothing she'd ever experienced, a desire to enfold him, to keep him safe. Every day, he risked his life to protect her, now it was her turn to protect him. She slid round and sat next to him. Gently prising his hand off the beer glass, she held it tightly then pulled him to her. She wasn't sure what this feeling was but it consumed her.

'You're wonderful, you know that?'

'I don't feel wonderful, I feel frightened. If you hadn't come back into my life like this, I don't think I could have gone on.'

'That's why you're wonderful. Real courage isn't being fearless, it's overcoming fear.'

He tried to smile but it was more of a grimace.

'We don't have to stay here,' she said gently. 'We can go back now if you like.'

Taking his hand, she led him in silence to the car and sat him in the passenger seat. When they reached the aerodrome, she drove to the far end of the grass runway and turned the engine off. For several minutes, neither spoke. His heart was thumping but he made no move. Even with his life on the line every day, he remained honourable and that meant more to her than anything else. She kissed his hand then went round to his side and opened the door. Not one word passed between them as she climbed over him.

Afterwards, and for the first time, she kissed him, dressed and drove back. When they reached her barracks, she smiled at him, climbed out of the car and ran inside.

Lying in her hard bed, unable to sleep, she had ample time to reflect on what she'd done and why she'd done it. First, she tried out the idea that she'd acted out of respect for a brave man. Or, giving herself to him had been an extension of her duties, that was all. Both explanations were neat and uncomplicated.

But another one hovered in the back of her head and wouldn't go away.

Chapter 23

'MORNING SIR, LOOKS like a nice one. Shouldn't have any trouble spotting Jerry today.'

It was four o'clock when his batman woke Brandon with a cup of tea.

'Excellent, Rogers. Just what I was hoping for.'

He washed and shaved before shuffling out to the lorry taking him to his dispersal hut on the edge of the airfield. The rest of his flight were already on the lorry as he climbed aboard.

'Good time last night, Doodle?'

'It was OK.'

'The young lady driving your car seemed to get lost on the way back and ended up down the end of the runway.'

Brandon wasn't in the mood.

'Get lost yourself.'

He'd woken up not knowing whether to feel wonderful or terrible. He couldn't ignore what had happened but he didn't want to presume too much. People can act out of character in wartime. She was probably regretting it already. Then again, he might be dead by tonight. That would certainly take care of things.

At eight o'clock, his flight was told they could stand down long enough to have breakfast back at the Mess. As he jumped down from the lorry, he saw her making for the Control room and hurried over.

'I just wanted to say would you mind looking out for my plane? I'd like to think you were watching over me.'

She looked at the shy young man standing in front of her.

How could she ever have seen him as a suave playboy? The dilemma she'd wrestled with in the early hours was resolved.

'It's ZPT just so you know who to look for.'

'Do be careful.'

'Don't worry, when I see the enemy, I'll turn round and head in the opposite direction. It's worked pretty well so far.'

'That's how you got that medal, is it?' She pointed to the ribbon of the Distinguished Flying Cross stitched to his uniform. She was touched to see him flush with embarrassment.

Then a sombre look came over his face.

'If I don't come back.'

She wouldn't let him finish.

'Don't be ridiculous. Firstly, you're coming back and secondly, well there is no secondly. You're to come back and that's an order.'

She touched his sleeve, stood back and saluted. He returned the salute and turned in the direction of the Mess. She hadn't mentioned last night. Was that good or bad?

Deep in thought, Mary was about to enter the Control Room when she was intercepted by Winifred. Her worldly-wise friend could see something was on her mind.

'Penny for 'em, darling.'

'God, you never miss a thing do you. Actually, you're just the person.'

'Oh, "actually" is it? Lah-di-dah. Well, come on Lady Ballantyne. What's on your mind?'

'I think I'm in love.'

'I'm in love too, darling but Clark Gable never replies to my...' She stopped when Mary burst into tears, and took her in her arms.

'Tell me all about it love.'

When Mary had finished, Winifred got straight to the point. 'If you really think you love him, don't waste time. There's a war on and the rules are different. My guess is he'll want to know how you feel so tell him. You'll regret it if you don't.'

It might not have been advice her local vicar would have given her but it was what she wanted to hear. As she touched her friend's arm, an actorly voice boomed out from across the room.

'Ballantyne, where the hell are you. Go to your post. Jerry isn't going to wait for you to finish gossiping.'

The only sound was the dawn chorus of birds for whom this was just another day. The planes had been filled with 85 gallons of high-octane fuel, the battery carts were attached. Everything was ready, everyone was waiting. That was the worst part. The pilots might come from many countries but they all had one thing in common, fear. They dealt with it in different ways but felt it in the same way. Some played football or cards, others pretended to read. A few withdrew to a private corner, away from the others and stared into the middle distance. It didn't matter what they did, they all thought the same thought. Would it be today? Would they crash in flames, leaving only a name tag to identify them or would they float on the sea, the sun burning away their eyes? Either way, they would die alone. And if they didn't? Another night of fun and laughter in the pub before it started all over again tomorrow.

Brandon settled into a deck chair outside the dispersal hut and picked up a tattered copy of Picture Post. After a couple of pages, he threw it down and stared at the blue, cloudless sky. All he could think about was Mary.

Whether the pilots played football, read, or feigned sleep, every one of them stopped when they heard the phone ring inside the dispersal hut. Every one of them heard the loudspeaker click as the microphone was switched on.

'Scramble, scramble.'

When he reached his plane, two cheerful ground crew pulled his waiting parachute off the wing, helped him into it then strapped him into the cockpit. Not too tight, his body would expand at high altitude. He clipped on his oxygen mask, making sure he could turn his head from side to side to see the enemy. When he pressed the starter button, the propellers gave a jerk, a mix of black smoke and flames shot out of the exhaust and the engine roared into life. The needles on the dials in front of him swung to their correct positions. No turning back. But that was alright, he was in control now.

As flight leader, he led the other planes towards the take off point, weaving from side to side to see where he was going. Once they were airborne and had sorted themselves into two sections of four, Control gave him their instructions. The eight of them had to head for two hundred enemy aircraft flying in at twenty thousand feet. Now he could focus on one thing only, doing what he was trained to do. It was always the same. Down on the ground he was terrified, up in the air he was fearless.

In the Control room, Mary heard him calmly issuing instructions. She too was doing what she was trained to do, moving the squadron marker ever nearer the markers for the incoming enemy. Every day, she tried to convince herself that, if she moved the markers correctly, the planes themselves would be safe.

Below him, the patchwork quilt of the Kent fields stretched out before him until it met the grey of the sea. The sky above him was a deep almost violet blue, turning to a pale bluey green on the horizon. Halfway between the two, the vapour trails of the enemy appeared, disfiguring the blue, like knife slashes on a canvas.

'Keep climbing and head for the sun. Red Four, you're dropping back. Keep up.'

A voice suddenly crackled over the airwaves. It was the leader of a squadron from Kenley.

'I say chaps, is that a Yankee voice I hear over the airwaves? Splendid fellow. At least one of you has turned up for the war on time. Good to have you on board.'

'Listen Lord Snooty, you're buying me a drink for that tonight.'

'My pleasure old boy. It's the least you deserve. Good hunting, old chap.'

The girls in the Control room clapped. The controller told them to get on with their work or they'd all be put on a charge. 'They'll be engaging any minute. The least we can do is concentrate.'

As the two sides converged, Brandon gave his instructions to the tiny team he led.

'We'll take the fighters. Leave the bombers for the Kenley Hurricanes. Watch your tails. Here we go.'

He picked a group of German fighters and led his section of four in a dive towards them. The 109s turned to face them. They were doing 300 miles per hour, so were the 109s. At a combined closing speed of 600 miles per hour, there was no time to think. It was all about reaction times. When he selected a target and opened fire, his plane shook from the recoil. Did his burst hit its target? He turned away before he could tell.

The control room filled with the sound of men shouting warnings to each other, cursing the enemy and screaming that they'd been hit. One pilot, too wounded to bail out, called out softly to his mother as his plane went down.

As Brandon climbed to gain the advantage of height, a 109 flashed past his nose, so close the sky darkened. For a fraction of a second, he could see every rivet, every oil smear. He fired. Then it was gone and the sun flooded back into his cockpit. As he stopped firing, his plane stopped shuddering and he put it into a tight turn.

Cannon shells came flying past his cockpit. Someone was on his tail. His plane rocked violently and went into a spin. Instinctively, he pushed the stick forward and applied opposite rudder. Slowly, delicately, he brought it out of the spin and resumed level flight. His engine sounded rough. He'd been hit.

Three more 109s came at him from his left. This was bad. They'd take it in turns to finish him off. The first one opened fire. A loud bang from the engine. Black smoke came through into the cockpit. His plane rolled over and went into another spin. He looked around. He was very low now, too low to bail out. Did he even have enough height to come out of the spin? Magically, the plane seemed to right itself. Who's flying this machine, he thought, Him or me? The smoke stopped. He was over the aerodrome. It must be Him.

In the control room, Mary knew none of this until a voice came over the loudspeaker.

'Anyone seen Red One?'

'I think he was caught by a 109. I'm not sure he made it.'

She froze, the rod she used to move the marker blocks rattling against the table as her hand shook. She wanted to curl up into a ball but she had to stay at her post as, one by one, the planes landed and switched off their engines. All except Red One. When she was given the order to stand down, she walked out slowly, trying not to look concerned. The planes were lined up outside one of the hangars. All the ZPs were there, all except T.

The smoke started again but much thicker this time. Christ, where are the 109s? If they're still there, there's nothing he can do about it. Just get the plane down. He pulled the throttle back but it didn't respond. If he put the wheels down, maybe only one will work and, anyway, he won't be able to stop before he runs out of grass. Keep the wheels up. Tighten the straps or that gun sight will make a mess of your face. Your helmet's connected to the plane by the oxygen tube and radio wires. Take it off. Open the canopy. Christ, it's stiff. The tail is too high. Pull the stick back. Turn off the engine. A thump as the plane hit the ground. He was pushed forward but the straps held. A long metallic slithering noise then a brief silence. Undo the straps. Quickly man. Thank God you opened the hood.

Then a roar as the whole plane went up.

She heard a plane coming in, the engine sounding rough and uneven. The fire engines rushed across the grass. She followed.

A Spitfire was coming in low, its undercarriage still up, the engine misfiring badly, the canopy open. It gradually dropped down, running along just above ground level for what seemed an eternity before the pilot switched off the engine and the plane dropped to earth with a long scraping sound. It came to a halt, so much dust and smoke, she couldn't see the cockpit. A few seconds silence then a whoomph as it burst into flames.

'He doesn't stand a chance,' said one of the ground crew.

Ignoring all orders to stop, Mary ran amongst the fire engines as they sprayed the plane. Her uniform was quickly soaked, her hair clung to her head. Even when the flames had been doused, the mixture of smoke and steam made it impossible to see clearly. All the time, she heard the terrible crackling noise of the fire. When the smoke cleared to reveal the charred remains, she put her hands to her mouth in horror.

A gust of wind blew away the smoke and she looked beyond the wreckage at the figure standing on the other side. She just had time to see him wave before she collapsed onto the sodden, oily ground.

Chapter 24

'WHY DO THEY call you Doodle?'

They were lying in each other's arms in a small bed and breakfast on the edge of the New Forest. 'Forty-eight hours,' Malan had said. 'That's all I can give you, Brandon. Make the most of it.' A year ago, it would have been unthinkable for a respectable landlady like Mrs Presley to allow an unmarried couple to share a room. But things had changed. Besides, they were stationed at Biggin Hill. It was Mrs Presley's way of contributing to the war effort.

'Isn't it obvious? I'm Yankee Doodle. Everybody has to have a nickname in the RAF. I'm stuck with mine.'

She started to smile but it soon faded.

'Why the sombre look?'

She got out of bed and wandered naked to the window. The New Forest ponies were frolicking in the field at the end of the garden. The deer could be seen wandering in and out of the woods, the leaves were already starting to turn. So did she. Framed by the sun shining through the window, her face was solemn. She walked back to the bed, sat on the edge and took his hand in hers.

'Will you marry me?'

He tried to look shocked rather than thrilled but couldn't carry it off.

'Well, I wasn't expecting that.'

'Why not? It's a leap year. A girl's entitled to ask, so I'm asking.'

He took her hands and stroked her cheek.

'I don't want this to be one of those eat drink and be merry for tomorrow we die marriages. I intend to survive this war. If I do, I want to spend the rest of my life with you. I don't want you to marry me because you're assuming I'll be killed and all that matters is loving me while you can.'

She pulled him to her. 'I want us to be together forever but I want us to be married now, whatever the future brings. It's the right thing to do, we both know it.'

'We'll have to get permission from our COs. Supposing Malan says you're not good enough for me.'

She threw a pillow at him.

'My CO's a crusty old bird. She won't want me marrying a colonial rebel.'

He pulled her onto the bed.

'We'll just have to take our chances, I suppose.'

She snuggled up to him. 'In the meantime, Flight Lieutenant Wade.'

'Oh no, you can propose to me but you're not defiling me before my wedding day.'

Chapter 25

'GOD THIS UNIFORM'S hot.'

Harry Ransome stood on top of Norwood Hill, encased in the uniform of an auxiliary fireman. From there, he could see across south London to the City and the docks.

'You'll be glad of that uniform when you get caught in a burning building.'

His new friend Charley was the cheerful cockney from central casting. Harry smiled at him.

'S'pose you're right. God, will you look at that.'

Thirty German bombers were racing along the valley beneath them, just a few feet off the ground, their bomb bays open, their machine guns firing at random.

'I never thought I'd be looking down on Jerry when he attacked.'

'They'll be heading for Croydon aerodrome,' said Charley. 'They'll give it a pasting.'

Harry's role as an auxiliary fireman was a temporary one while he waited for his call-up papers. He could have joined the police but thought the fire service would be nearer the action. It was hard work but only for three nights a week and when he'd come home from work that evening, he'd been looking forward to a quiet night in.

As usual, Lydia was giving little Harry junior his nightly bath. Slipping off his jacket, he rolled up his sleeves, gave his wife a kiss and joined in the fun.

'This is the life. God, I've had a boring day. I can't wait to be called up.'

'Don't say that, the longer it takes, the better. I hate the thought of you going off to war. I want you to stay in your boring job for as long as possible.'

The phone rang.

'I'll get it.'

Lydia watched her husband walk into the hall of their tiny flat. He was only a few feet away. She could hear everything he said.

'Of course I will. Just give me a chance to change and have a bite to eat.'

He replaced the receiver and returned to the bathroom. Little Harry junior splashed the water and laughed. One look at Harry's face told Lydia who the call was from.

'It's not your duty night. Can't someone else go?'

'They're a man short. It's Tomkins, his wife's gone into labour and he's had to take her to hospital. I shan't be long. Stop worrying, we'll be moving to Dorking any day now, it'll be much quieter.'

He and Charley watched the Dorniers whizz by beneath them. It was a clear evening and the crews were plainly visible. 'I wouldn't want to be on the receiving end of that lot,' said Charley.

'We'll probably be sent over there in a minute or two.'

Harry checked his watch.

'Have you got somewhere you need to be?'

'No, I was just thinking I've missed giving my son his bedtime story.'

Harry smiled at the thought of him, curled up in bed. 'I'll look in on him when I get back. Thank God tomorrow's Saturday.'

A boy on a bike came puffing up the hill. He couldn't have been more than fourteen, thought Harry. They shouldn't allow it.

When he arrived, they waited patiently while he regained his breath. 'Give this lad a mug,' yelled Charley. The tea was brought over and the boy took a sip.

'You're to go to Deptford,' the words stumbled out. 'Big warehouse fire.' Another sip of tea. 'It's urgent.'

They hoisted his bike onto the back of the engine and helped him up into the cab. As soon as they were underway, Harry started to question the young lad.

'How long have you been doing this?'

'A month.'

'How old are you?

'Old enough.'

'Oh, come on, you can't be a day over fourteen. You're supposed to be sixteen. Do your parents know?'

'Of course. They think I'll be safer out on the bike than sitting in the Anderson shelter. So do I.'

'I hope you're right,' said Harry. 'I wouldn't like the idea of my son riding around with bombs dropping all around.'

'Look Mister, I've got a bike and they need boys like me to fetch blokes like you. The whole thing's a bloody shambles. We've got a bloody great river running through us but there's never enough water to put out the fires. It's crazy.'

'You're an expert, are you?'

'No, but I've got eyes in me 'ead. If it wasn't for lads like me, there'd never be enough fire engines where they're needed. I'm a bloody 'ero, I am.'

Harry smiled at him.

'You know, I rather think you are. Lead on Sir Galahad.'

When they reached Deptford, it was obvious where they were needed. The warehouse was already ablaze but the fire was not so far gone the building couldn't be saved. They let the boy down and told him to go home.

'Go on, Sir Galahad. You've done a good night's work, now go home and get some sleep. We don't want you late for Saturday morning school so hoppit.'

The boy had no intention of leaving and they had a fire to put out so they set their ladders up against the wall and Harry climbed up with a hose. He struggled to point the hose in the right direction and turned to shout at the crew on the engine.

'Turn it off a minute.'

He looked towards the sky and saw a Dornier flying low along the road, spraying it with bullets. The boy stood in the middle of the road staring at the burning building, unaware of the danger. Harry wanted to shout out his name but he hadn't asked him what it was. He shouted 'get out of the way' but his voice was lost in the roar of the engines. He thought of his own son. No boy was going to die at the hands of the Nazis if he had anything to do with it.

Placing his feet on the outside of the ladder, he slid down, the hose crashing down beside him. Hurling himself at the lad, he turned him round to place his own body in the path of the bullets as they traced an elegant line along the middle of the road. He jumped to one side and collapsed on the pavement, still clutching the boy. As they lay there, they heard a rumbling sound and looked across the road to see the wall of the warehouse collapse, crushing the ladder on which Harry had been standing just moments earlier.

'Blimey, that was a close one, Mister. You saved my life.'

Harry surveyed the pile of bricks that, moments ago, had been the wall against which his ladder had stood.

'Actually, you saved mine. What's your name young fellermelad?'

'Harry, sir. But everyone calls me Harry Junior.'

Harry smiled, not just because he had the same name as his own son. The cheeky little devil had finally called him sir.

Chapter 26

A PHONE RANG, the one linked to Uxbridge Operations Room. The girls exchanged looks as the Controller lifted the receiver from its cradle, listened, put the phone down and gave the order for Dysoe Squadron to scramble. Her stomach tightened. This was the code name for Brandon's squadron. She pushed a yellow flag marked 74 into a marker block.

Malan's voice came over the loudspeaker to say they were airborne and awaiting orders.

'Dysoe leader this is Tophat control. We have some customers for you. Vector zero nine one, angels two zero. Fifty bandits.'

'Better odds than usual, Tophat. You must be getting soft in your old age.'

She put a red 50 and a black 20 into the front of the block and moved it forward. There was complete silence in the Control Room as the blocks moved closer to their target. The loudspeakers on the walls burst into life as first one then another pilot claimed to have seen the enemy. With a calm 'Sailor here,' Malan took over and led his men into the attack. One of those men was her future husband. In a week's time, they were to be married in Bromley Registry Office.

Brandon peered through the haze, still thick at 15,000 feet. No sign of the enemy. One minute they were climbing then Malan led them into a steep dive and there they were, row upon row of bombers, each row above the other, filling the sky. Where were the fighters? No point in worrying about them. He selected a Ju88 and closed in until the bomber's port wing filled his gunsight. A burst of fire from his machine guns produced a puff of smoke then a flash of flame. The pilot banked steeply towards him, turning sharply. Brandon aimed a deflection shot ahead of the plane's nose, firing one short burst, then another and another. No time to see the result as he flashed past the bomber and climbed up, looked around then dived back into the mêlée.

In the control room, the WAAFs heard warnings, curses, shouts of triumph, screams of fear mingled with each other in an indistinguishable melee. When an unmistakable American voice claimed a kill, the other girls smiled at her. She tried to smile back but couldn't.

Black puffs of smoke just above the Spitfire's wing followed by orange balls of fire over the cockpit. Someone was attacking him but Brandon couldn't see who. He went into a climbing turn, the G force pressing him into his seat and pushing him towards a blackout. Just in time, he straightened out and there they were, two 109s heading downwards, tracer curling towards him. A nudge on the Spitfire's controls and one of them crossed his gunsight. He fired but couldn't see if he'd hit him as the 109 passed under his nose.

As so often happened, one minute he was surrounded by planes, both friend and foe, the next he was alone in the sky. As he headed back to Biggin, the empty sky allowed him to look down at the landscape beneath, the sweeping hills, the rooftops, the church spires. His thoughts turned to Mary. Next week, they would become man and wife. He accepted the need to get married quickly in a Registry Office but the sight of the ancient village churches helped him come to a decision. They'd have another ceremony in one of those churches as soon as possible.

His reverie was interrupted by the shaking of his Spitfire as bullets ploughed into the fuselage and wings. The sky hadn't been as empty as he had thought. He'd allowed his concentration to wander. Land and sky changed places as he went into a spin. By the time opposite rudder and stick forward had brought the plane under control, smoke had started to pour from his engine into the cockpit. Nursing his stricken plane into a climbing turn brought a 109 briefly across his path but when he tried to fire a burst, all he heard was the sound of compressed air pumping empty breeches. By weaving and turning, never flying straight, he worked out that there were two 109s who had taken off with three times as much ammunition as his Spifire and had plenty left. As they closed in, he dived and climbed in a desperate attempt to throw them off. They had the ammunition but they must be low on fuel. If he could just keep them at bay. But the 109 pilots knew he'd run out of bullets. They lined up, one behind the other, to take turns at finishing him off.

A mixture of cannon shells and machine gun bullets chased him as he flew over a golf course at zero feet, rounding the dog-leg of the 12th then diving down the steep fairway of the 14th and up towards the immaculately tended green. A group of golfers, thinking he was showing off, shook their clubs at him in anger for interrupting their round then dived for cover as the chasing 109s opened fire, some of their shells ripping up their beloved green. But not every shell. Brandon screamed in pain as a shell smashed into his thigh, sending blood down his leg and into his flying boot. If he didn't get his plane down in the next few minutes, he'd bleed to death. With the 109s still chasing him, there was no chance of that. Determined to take one of them with him, he put the Spitfire into a tight turn and flew straight at his pursuers.

The shock of his action caught the pilots of the 109s by surprise. Realising the mad RAF pilot was intent on colliding with him, the pilot of the lead plane turned across the path of his number two. Reacting too slowly to the RAF man's change of tactics, the number two flew straight into his leader, the explosion sending a shower of wreckage and body parts across the Golf Club car park. When the golfers returned to the club house, they found their cars crushed beyond repair. Commiserating with one another on a rotten end to a rotten round, they agreed the war was a damn nuisance.

He'd escaped death at the hands of the enemy but his engine revs were going up and down, a sign of fuel starvation. He needed to get down fast. Spotting a level piece of ground, he prepared to put the plane down. He'd have to do a wheels-up landing but he'd done that before. Then he saw them. Anti-tank concrete blocks, row upon row. Forced to pull up, he approached the crest of a hill just as the engine cut out for good. At this height, he had no choice but to glide down to earth. Just keep the nose up or that heavy engine will pull the rest of the plane into a vertical dive. Once he'd safely cleared the hill, he found himself approaching a small village. Between him and the village lay a field, perfect for his purpose except for one thing, a line of children walking across the field from the village school on one side to the local church on the other.

Only one child, a small girl at the back of the line, noticed the plane gliding silently down. Saying nothing to her friends, she stared in wonderment as the silent bird swooped down. With blood pouring from his thigh, Brandon grew weaker. Every movement required more effort. Staring at the line of children, his eyesight became blurred, transforming the children before him. Blinking rapidly, he found himself staring at the children walking along the quay at Southampton docks and the little girl with her reproachful look. As his stricken plane closed in on the line, everything became clear. Once again, he knew what he had to do. This was how it started, he thought, this is how it ends. Clicking the switch on his r/t, he cried out 'Mary,' and pushed his control stick full forward.

With no fuel left, there was no explosion as he hit the ground. He'd given the plane full left rudder to turn it sideways on, making the impact short and sharp. As the disintegrating plane slithered sideways through the earth, the engine broke away and the fuselage bounced across the field, coming to a halt just yards in front of the children.

Before the teacher could stop her, the little girl ran over to the plane and stared anxiously at the pilot, crumpled up in what remained of the cockpit. Silently, she took his hand. The stranger smiled weakly as he uttered two words.

'Worth it.'

The girl looked around anxiously as the teacher approached.

'I don't think he's very well.'

The teacher looked at the pilot's vacant eyes and gently closed them.

'He's tired. I think we'd better let him sleep.'

Clutching the little girl's hand, she led her back to the other children and gathered them in a circle.

'The pilot of that plane fought up in the sky to protect us and died on the ground to save us. We must never forget him.'

Chapter 27

THE BATMAN HANDED the cardboard box to Mary with a sigh.

'I'm really sorry to lose this one Miss. He was one of the best.'

He didn't know whether to stay and continue the conversation or leave her to grieve alone. She touched his arm and nodded her head. Gratefully, he took it as a sign to leave. When he reached the door, he turned and added, 'The boss would like to see you. When you're ready, of course.'

She found Malan seated at his desk, signing a letter. She knew at once what it was, stood to attention and saluted. He stood up, came round the desk and took both her hands.

'What can I say, Mary? Brandon was one of the best.' He picked up the letter and handed it to her. 'I want you to have this.'

'But I'm not his next of kin.'

'He listed you as his next of kin when he joined up so you're entitled to it. I didn't realise he already knew you.'

If he'd named her when he doubted he'd ever see her again, he must have known he was going to die. She started breathing faster.

'I'm sorry sir.'

Malan led her to a chair. 'Don't worry. Sit down and get your breath back.'

He went over to his desk and picked up an envelope and a set of car keys.

'This is his Will. He also left instructions that you were to have his car.'

'I'll have to sell it. I can't even afford the petrol.'

'I'd read the will first. Besides, with a car like that, every officer on the station will want to use you as his driver. That'll keep you in free petrol for the rest of the war.'

Keys in one hand, envelope in the other, she walked outside, unable to think. The car stood forlornly outside the Mess window. Malan was right, she couldn't possibly sell it. She climbed in and looked blankly at the controls. The corner of an envelope peeked out from the pocket in the door. As she pulled it out, she saw the single word 'Mary' on the front. She opened it and unfolded the page.

Darling Mary

So I didn't make it then and I'll never know how things turned out but I've an idea my sacrifice will have been worth it. I don't regret a thing.

Look after my lovely Henrietta and give her the love you so briefly gave me. What a wonderful woman you are. I was coming to the end of my tether before I came to Biggin and we met again. You will never know what a difference you made.

I have something important to say. One day, you'll meet someone. When you do, I want you to be happy with him. Don't lose hope and don't do anything dangerous in the meantime.

Think of me now and again, but not too often. You've got a life to lead. Go out and live it.

Vitae Summa Brevis Spem Nos Vetat Incohare Longam

Brandon

A single tear fell onto the page. The ink of his name started to run. She dabbed it with the cuff of her uniform but this only made it worse. One day, she would ask someone to translate the Latin message but not yet. The letter was too private to show anyone. She folded it carefully and placed it inside her uniform, vowing to keep it by her always.

She pressed the starter button and let the engine run for a while before summoning up the nerve to engage first gear and creep nervously onto the grass of the aerodrome. Then she accelerated, faster and faster. As the green monster tore across the grass, she felt him beside her. Slowing down, she crawled over to the far side of the runway, turned the engine off and sat there thinking, the silence broken only by the sound of the engine ticking as the metal cooled. It was all her fault. He'd survived until she'd come back into his life and distracted him when he'd needed to concentrate on staying alive.

She thought about his final words to her. She had a choice, avoid all danger, survive the war, meet someone else. Or take what risks came her way and play her part in fighting for what he'd believed in.

Do as he said or do as he did?

She already knew which one it was going to be.

Chapter 28

SHE WAS OFFERED leave but it would have taken her away from the world she'd shared with Brandon and the battle in which they'd both fought. Day after day, the bombers pasted the aerodrome, trying to put it out of action but, like the Windmill theatre in London, the station could boast "we never closed." When the Luftwaffe unexpectedly switched to attacking London, the breathing space was welcome to everyone else. It only gave her more time to grieve.

When all available aircraft were scrambled to meet a formation heading for London, Winifred, who had re-doubled her efforts as a surrogate mother, led Mary to the canteen where she tried to persuade her ward to eat.

'I feel sorry for the civilians on the receiving end of that lot but I'm glad they're leaving us alone now. A bit of peace and quiet is the least you deserve, dear.'

With all planes over London to protect the capital, a staffel of Heinkels peeled off unexpectedly and headed for the aerodrome. The first the two women knew of the attack was when the windows of the canteen were blown out. Expecting more, they dived under the tables but it was over as quickly as it started. When they walked outside, they found the runway littered with craters.

'There's a job for the men,' said Winifred. 'Just as well there's enough grass left for the fighters to land.'

'Never mind the craters, look at all those unexploded bombs. Some of them may be duds but a lot of them are on delayed action fuses.'

Mary clenched her hands, horrified by the danger awaiting the pilots, her pilots. A few weeks earlier, she might have said 'Somebody must do something' but Brandon had bequeathed more than a car to her, he'd imbued her with his philosophy. Now, it wasn't 'somebody' who should do something but Mary herself. She ran to the shed where the red flags were kept.

'I've got to show the boys where those bombs are,' she said to Winifred. 'You go back to the NAAFI. I won't be long.'

'Don't be so bloody silly, dear, you can't possibly do that on your own. Here, give me some.' Winifred grabbed some of the flags and the two of them set out across the runway.

The Controller was surveying the damage when he saw two women running across the grass. His actor's voice penetrated every corner of the room.

'What the hell are those women doing? Have they no idea how dangerous that is? They must be mad. Christ, they're wonderful.'

They started out walking side by side, sticking a flag by each bomb, working further and further apart. Mary carried out her task with a zeal born of obsession. No one else was going to die, not if she could help it. Her logic was simple, the more flags she could put in the ground, the more lives she could save. The further across the field she worked, the more frantic she became. She was taking the risks he had taken. She felt alive and needed.

Winifred called to her. 'I think that's about it, love. Let's go in.'

Mary pointed to one final bomb behind her friend. 'I'll do it,' she said. Winifred held up her hand. 'No darling. You've run out of flags, leave it to me.' She walked over to the bomb and planted the flag. Mary watched as the mother hen gave her a cheery wave, then turned to head back.

She felt the blast before she heard it. Then the full force of the explosion hit her and she felt and saw nothing more.

When she regained consciousness, she found herself in a hospital bed. Seeing her eyes open, the nurse called the surgeon over.

'You're back with us at last.'

'Where's Winifred?'

The expression on their faces answered her question. Then the surgeon's face brightened.

'There is one piece of good news though, you'll be able to go to full term.'

'What do you mean?'

He patted her hand.

'The baby.' He paused and gave her a big smile. 'It's fine.'

Chapter 29

ALTHOUGH OF SOUND military stock, the late, lamented head of the SIS had never been a great landowner. His successor, by contrast, owned estates producing an income so large he neither needed nor drew a salary for doing a job he considered to be his duty. It was, however, an acknowledged truth of the society in which he lived that however high a man might be, there were always others still higher. He knew this and it irked him.

On his first day in the job, he was handed the file given to all new Cs when they take up the post. As he turned the pages, he came to a loose sheet with the hand-written message "*You will be contacted by the Fishing Club*" and nothing else. Assuming it referred to one of his predecessor's clubs, he turned the page over and gave it no further thought until, at the end of May1940, he received his first summons, framed as an invitation to a day's fishing followed by dinner in a nearby pub. He'd been working non-stop while France collapsed and, as the river was one of the finest chalk streams in the country, he decided to reward himself with a day out. The new C may have been a snob but he wasn't a fool. He doubted the day's activities would be confined to fishing.

When his driver dropped him off, his first surprise came as he entered the pub to be greeted by Sir Baldwyn Lestocq, father of the man he himself had recruited. Sir Baldwyn introduced him to the members, all fifteen of whom had turned up. The setting was a simple Hampshire pub but the gathering was the grandest he had ever attended. While an opening snifter was served, they all expressed their pleasure at his elevation to the top job. Now we were at war, he was the right man at the right time, they assured him. Then it was down to the river for a day's pleasure, giving C an opportunity to return the compliment.

'The water's looking particularly clear today, Sir Baldwyn.'

His host, tall, thin, stooped and balding stared mournfully at the water and sighed.

'But for how long? Word is there'll be soldiers billeted up river. God knows what they'll dump on us. The chalk acts as a filter, you know. They say the rainwater takes sixty years to work its way through the chalk and find its way to the river. That's why it's so clear.'

'Can't you put a stop to it?'

'The rainwater? Of course not.'

Sir Baldwyn was the head of one of those families who, by avoiding a title too grand, had survived the twists and turns of history for nine hundred years without losing their heads or their lands. They'd been Catholic when it was appropriate,

Protestant when it was not. Tory then Whig, then Tory again. In any given age, the family knew where their best interests lay and pursued them discreetly but vigorously. It had come as a surprise when his son, Roland, had expressed a wish to join the SIS but events in Europe had quickly shown the advantages of this move.

'I mean the troop billeting. Can't you put a stop to it.'

'The club would never interfere with something like that. We know where our duty lies. As, no doubt, do you.'

An excellent day's fishing was followed by dinner in an upstairs room. Not a mention of his job or the war, until the port was circulating. Then one of the members, a character straight out of P.G. Wodehouse, told him how glad he was to see the SIS in the right hands after the unfortunate death of his predecessor.

'Of course, we kept in close touch with him.' A slight pause. 'We hope you'll permit us to do the same with you. We have excellent contacts with our European counterparts. You never know when these may come in useful. You now have Baldwyn's son Roland working for you. I must say, that came as much of a surprise to him as it did to us. I don't want you to get the impression he's been foisted on you.'

C made no reply. It had never occurred to him that young Lestocq had been foisted on him, until now. Finally, the old man came to the point, not just of this conversation but of the whole day.

'It's such a shame we got ourselves into this war. So unnecessary. Obviously, it's not our place to interfere but I hope something can be done about it before things go too far. There are people on the other side thinking the same thing, I'm sure.'

The old fellow sat back and, as if they were working as a relay team, which they were, Sir Baldwyn took over.

'No false casting. We liked that.'

C accepted the compliment and responded with one of his own.

'Splendid stretch of river, Sir Baldwyn.'

'We like to think so. Of course, we're only looking after it for future generations. Like everything else we do.'

Though he was the equal of these men in terms of land and wealth, C's family was nouveau by comparison with men whose estates had been in their hands for nearly a thousand years. They were where he wanted to belong but not quite where he did belong, their ranks as closed to him as the upper ranks of the SIS were to underlings like Fawkes. That was his weak spot and both he and they knew it. Dinner in a room above a pub. So understated but so intoxicating. The purpose of today's outing had been to dangle the bait in front of him. The war must be stopped and social advancement awaited the man who stopped it.

'You're just the sort of chap Six needs for this war. Your predecessor's death was most regrettable but your appointment has come just in time. You're a man with a large estate, made larger by the addition of your wife's estate, of course. That gives you a real stake in the country and gives us confidence in you. Frankly, I'm surprised you don't have a title to go with it. When the time comes, we must do something about that.'

Sir Baldwyn raised his eyebrows to query whether C had understood. He gave no sign of having done so but understood perfectly. It was an offer to become 'one of us,' on conditions that Sir Baldwyn was about to reveal.

'Things can't go on like this. We went to war assuming the French would hold the line on land while we controlled the sea. The French soldier is as brave as they come but half his Generals were in favour of capitulation and cosying up to the Nazis. Did you know there were more fascists in France before the war than there were in Germany? I'm told they kept seventeen hundred planes in the south which they never committed to the battle.'

'We're the secret service, Sir Baldwyn, it's our job to know these things. It's because we knew about the strength of fascism in France that we were in favour of encouraging a coup against Hitler. Unfortunately, no one else was.'

Sir Baldwyn ignored the remark and resumed his lecture.

'We assumed Hitler could be appeased, he couldn't. We assumed he'd expand in the east, he's expanded in the west. We've got everything wrong and we're now fighting a war that will bankrupt us.'

He paused to give C an opportunity to agree. He obliged.

'That is all too evident.'

'Of course, Winston's right to show defiance and a determination to fight on.'

He fixed C with a stern gaze.

'But we have to consider an alternative.'

Now, C felt real alarm. "Consider an alternative" could only mean doing something without the government's knowledge. In other words, commit treason. He spoke calmly, as if discussing the filtering capabilities of chalk.

'What do you have in mind?'

'How's my son coming along? Not making a fool of himself, I trust.'

If someone like Fawkes had been on the receiving end of this blatant non sequitur, his displeasure would have registered on his face. C, cut from different cloth, found nothing surprising or irritating in the question. Apart from anything else, it gave him time to think. It also gave his host time to assess C's reaction to his opening gambit.

'Splendidly, he has an appetite for information that is second to none. I'm grooming him for the top, of course. I have high hopes for him.'

Sir Baldwyn returned to the subject at hand.

'There's a clear division between the SS and the Wehrmacht. The latter believe in the old way of doing things, the SS are no better than Al Capone. We've got to open a line of communication with the Wehrmacht. Any ideas?'

C disguised his relief. Making contact was both easy and carried no treasonous connotations. Even if it got nowhere, he'd have shown the club he was willing to do their bidding.

'Szymańska.'

'What?'

'Polish woman. Works for us out of Switzerland. She's in contact with Admiral Canaris and his people. The Gestapo call them the Schwarze Kapelle.'

'I thought that was their name for the communists. We want to keep well away from them.'

'No, that's the Rote Kapelle. It's quite simple, black orchestra for the good guys, red orchestra for the baddies.'

'Whichever bloody orchestra it is, we want you to make personal contact, face to face as it were. Meet him somewhere neutral, d'you see? No point in beating about the bush, make it clear we want to work with them.'

'It won't be easy. They lost a lot of confidence in us when we rejected them in '38.'

'We lost a lot of confidence in them when they kidnapped your top men at Venlo in '39. How could you have been so stupid as to let two of your top men be lured into a trap thinking they were dealing with people conspiring to overthrow Hitler only to be captured and reveal your entire agent list in Europe.'

'They were doing exactly what you want me to do now. The Swedes, the Dutch, they were all trying to negotiate with German industrialists and others to get the war called off. In that atmosphere, there was always a risk of that happening. Besides, that was the SD, the security arm of the SS. Canaris is Abwehr, the security arm of the Wehrmacht. As you say, quite different. They'd rather fight each other than the enemy. Doesn't alter the fact that I'd be taking the same risk that they took at Venlo.'

Sir Baldwyn displayed the merest trace of irritation. C knew this meant he was decidedly irritated.

'Just go and meet him, sound him out. If he offers to cooperate, tell him Churchill can be persuaded. The matter is urgent.'

'I didn't realise Churchill was involved. That should make it more convincing.'

Sir Baldwyn gave Control what passed as a reassuring smile, a slight widening of his thin lips, but the absence of any verbal confirmation of the PM's involvement was noted.

He had to admit that Sir Baldwyn's proposal had merit. The SIS had been short of success after the Venlo debacle – how did the cunning old devil know about that? Surely young Lestocq hadn't told his father. Or was this another of the father's little ways of showing how powerful his group was? Either way, a bit of decisive action, spiced with danger, might start the process of restoring the department's reputation.

When, armed with the Club's very best wishes, he climbed into his car at the end of the evening, C assumed two things. His induction was over and he was now on the team.

Only one of these assumptions was correct.

Chapter 30

THE UNIMPOSING BUILDING bore the faded legend "Funicular de Monte Igueldo" over its green doors. Ticket in hand, C climbed the steps to the front carriage and sat facing backwards to keep an eye on any other passengers. Being in San Sebastian in the north of neutral Spain did not guarantee his safety. It was his job to send people on dangerous missions, his job to do bad things for a good cause, but this was a mission only he could undertake. More than that, it was a way of putting something on the other side of the scales, a way of showing that he didn't ask others to do something he wasn't prepared to do himself. He patted his jacket pocket to feel the cyanide capsule and remind himself where this might end. The funicular started off with a jerk. It was too late to turn back.

The wooden slatted bench was hard but the journey would be short. As the little train emerged from the station, he had a brief view of the bay before it climbed into the trees that lined the track to form a tunnel of greenery. He turned round to look up the steep slope, noticing it was single track except for a loop where the down train and the up train crossed each other. This was where he would be most at risk. He watched carefully as the down train approached. The doors of the carriages were open, allowing a breeze to waft through but giving an intruder easy access. As the train creaked by, he could see just one passenger, a well-dressed, middle aged man. With his nose buried in a newspaper, he gave C not so much as a glance as they passed by. Realising he'd been holding his breath for several seconds, he sat back, exhaling sharply.

At the top, the train gave one final jerk before halting. Once the other passengers had disembarked, he stepped out and started to climb the steep steps that would take him into the open air and a measure of safety. Halfway up, he realised he was being followed. He sensed it at first then heard the sound of soft footsteps. He could feel the hairs on his forearms standing up. Whoever it was, it was too late to do anything about it. He'd chosen to take this risk.

They wouldn't kill him. They would take him prisoner. And what a prisoner he would make. He slipped a hand into his jacket pocket and fingered the cyanide capsule. He'd only have a few seconds to swallow it so he pulled it out. At the top of the steps, he paused. So did the footsteps. He didn't turn round, that would show weakness. If he showed weakness, the mission would fail. Silence for a few seconds then a voice, soft and cultured.

'You won't be needing that, Colonel. Nor, I hope, shall I.'

C turned to see a man in his fifties, short, with thick grey hair and a solemn face. He nodded his head.

'Good morning, Herr Admiral.'

No smiles were exchanged. He half expected his adversary to click his heels but they were in Spain. No point in drawing attention to themselves.

'Shall we?' Admiral Canaris gestured towards the café across from the station.

'My turn to follow you, I think.' C spoke with the merest hint of a smile.

'Quite so,' said Canaris as he walked solemnly ahead.

The jousting continued as they sat down. Canaris sat facing the square. With a brief 'if you will permit,' C sat next to, rather than opposite him, giving himself the widest field of view. After admiring the view across the bay, Canaris spoke softly.

'Our mutual friend said you wanted to see me.'

C wasted no time.

'The war is a disaster. Our masters have no idea what they're doing. Somebody has to sort this mess out.'

Canaris let C's remark hang in the air, then gave out a sigh.

'It's the little things that upset me most, the inconveniences and small irritations. You can't buy the clothes you want, the food you like, new cello strings for my wife. Don't you find?'

Neither man looked at the other, both staring out across the square as if something fascinating was taking place on the other side. Eventually, C took up the theme.

'And the deaths of people you know. It's all so random, friends, children of friends, people you like, people you dislike. One man takes enormous risks and emerges unscathed, another sits in an office preparing statistics and is killed by a bomb.'

He banged a fist on the table. People at the other tables turned to look. He held up his hands, palms facing outwards, to placate them. Then he whispered to his companion.

'And all this is happening in a war against a country who should be our ally in the fight against Communism.'

Silence, a long silence, a silence that didn't bother C. He was a fisherman, patient, used to waiting. He felt a tug on his line.

'But what can we do about it?' Canaris turned to face his adversary, giving C the opening he needed.

'Someone has to take decisive action. We can't move in the right direction till he's out of the way.'

There was no need for a name.

'I have to convince the doubters that such a step will be for the benefit of Germany.'

'I have to convince my doubters too. Venlo seriously damaged their willingness to trust so-called conspirators. Then there's the politicians. I serve my country. They serve their careers.'

Though he looked straight ahead, C could feel the other man's eyes upon him, the eyes of a man used to conspiratorial conversations. The Admiral's reply was soft and low.

'If we don't do something, we face a long war with both our countries losing and the yanks and commies coming out on top.'

'Indeed, but it's no good daydreaming. We won't get anywhere without the cooperation of my master and the destruction of yours. We can make our plans together but, eventually, I have to convince Churchill you will not only work with us but will succeed in overthrowing Hitler.'

Canaris held his hand up.

'And I have to convince the doubters that Churchill will support such a coup. Back in '38, the people running your country were much less warlike but even they refused to support us. It's hard to believe a man like him will be more amenable.'

'Be fair, Admiral, Churchill was never in favour of war. He warned us that we would end up with one if we failed to stand up to Hitler. And he was right.'

As if to end the meeting, Canaris rose from his chair. Before he was even halfway up, C caught hold of his forearm. The tone of his voice altered.

'Sit down, Admiral. I admire you and your circle, we share the same beliefs. Germany must be strong to save Europe from Communism. It is your duty to the fatherland.'

Canaris continued to look across the square. After a long pause, he said, 'let's go for a walk.'

He's testing me, thought C. How serious am I, enough to be prepared to walk into danger?

'By all means.'

They walked across the square, down the sloping path towards the gardens below. Once the lush foliage had absorbed them, Canaris led the way to a stone seat and sat down. Without looking at his adversary, he said, 'why now?'

Game on. C sat down, his stomach fluttering in anticipation.

'Churchill is working tirelessly to bring the Americans into the war. If he succeeds, the game is up for both Britain and Germany. As you said, the Yanks and Soviets will end up in control of everything. We need to do this now.'

Canaris looked around, as if he'd come here to admire the plants. At length, he turned and looked C in the face.

'I need a letter.'

'Certainly, I'll guarantee our support for a coup and promise an immediate ceasefire. You can show it to your allies.'

Canaris laughed.

'Not from you, from Churchill. Nothing less will do, not after the rejection in '38. Without a guarantee from the one man who won't compromise, no one will take your approach seriously.'

C had considered many demands that Canaris might make but not that one. He couldn't turn him down on the spot so he sat in silence, as if considering the German's request.

'I'll do my best. I can't promise more than that. There are limits to what the two of us can achieve but we have to try, don't we? We're not so far apart, you and I.'

Canaris ignored the invitation to join in the expressions of good faith. C continued.

'Where shall we meet?'

'Back here. It's quiet and I like getting out of Germany.'

C didn't need to ask why. Canaris had more important things to worry about than cello strings for his wife. The SD and their masters in the SS hated the Wehrmacht in general and the Abwehr in particular. Canaris was a thorn in their side, a thorn they'd seize any opportunity to remove.

'Back here it is, then.'

Canaris stood up, gave a quick bow of his head and turned to climb back up to the funicular. Once he was out of sight, C returned to the café to consider his next move. He had to obtain a letter that Churchill would never agree to and return here to deliver it himself. For C this was an excellent result. Not only had the meeting passed off without incident, even Sir Baldwyn would have to abandon his crazy project once he realised how impossible those demands were.

He was relaxing with these thoughts when a man emerged from the gardens, looked around and headed straight for the café. Of medium height and thickset, he didn't look Spanish and his suit had a north European cut to it. C watched him scan the tables. Had the whole thing been a trap after all? He was surprised Canaris had done this but, if this was the end, so be it, the risk had been worth taking.

When the guard's whistle announced the departure of the train, two things happened: the man turned towards the funicular and started running and C realised he wasn't one of Canaris's men. Which meant he could only be SD. When he reported back to Heydrich, the operation would be blown, Canaris would be hanged, Hitler would be secure. Furious with himself for being so stupid, C sent his table flying as he rushed towards the station. The train was already moving as he ran down the steep steps and jumped into the last carriage.

C had fought in the Great War, been wounded and decorated. But he'd never worked as an agent in the field. Death held no fears for him but if this man exposed Canaris, the consequences were unthinkable. He had no choice. The man would have to die.

Sitting on the slats of the wooden bench, already writing busily on a notepad, the man looked up sharply as C scrambled into the carriage. The recognition was mutual, one with a look of horror, the other with a steely determination. As the man reached inside his jacket for his pistol, C remembered Fawkes's exploits in France. The dark red paint of the wooden walls was faded and peeling. It was a far cry from the Blue Train but the outcome would have to be the same.

His first task was to neutralise the pistol and prevent the man from firing it and alerting the other passengers. The best way to do that was to force his hand to remain in the jacket pocket without leaving the man's other hand free to do him damage. Having the advantage of surprise helped and he was able to jam both arms against the man's chest as both men tumbled onto the wooden floor. But the other man, younger and stronger than C, started to roll over, forcing C to stand up. Thinking he had the better of C, the German was taken by surprise when C sank back down onto the man's chest, trapping the man's arms with his knees. Knowing he had only a second or two before the man three him off, C used both hands to twist the man's head till his neck snapped and all resistance ceased.

Though the struggle had been brief, it had exhausted him but he still had work to do. Seeing the writing pad lying on the floor, C picked it up and scanned the page, dreading the possibility that it was nothing to do with the meeting and he'd killed an innocent man. The notes were in German, a near verbatim report of C's conversation with Canaris. He sat back on the seat shaking, not from the shock of killing the man but from the realisation of how close he'd come to disaster.

He looked at the body. There were three compartments on the train and just two other passengers, both, including Canaris, in the front compartment. He could sit him up on the bench seat and simply walk off the train as if nothing had happened but the presence of a dead body might be discovered even before he'd left the station. He needed to get it out of the train before they arrived but this was a slow-moving train with no long dark tunnels in which to operate.

A clanking and groaning sound told him the up train was approaching. In a few seconds, the trains would be side by side. The doors of his own compartment were open because of the hot weather but were the doors of the up train? He manoeuvred the dead man into position, waiting for the train to draw alongside. The driver in the front was the only crew and there were just two passengers talking to each other in the front compartment. As the trains started to pass, they looked across, puzzled by the sight of one man with his arm around another but C's train jerked from the uneven pull of the cable giving the impression they were drunk. The passengers shrugged and resumed their conversation.

The second compartment had open doors but was too close to the people in the front. Then the third compartment rattled alongside with open doors and no passengers. C was not a young man but his adrenalin was in full flow and he all but threw the man into the open compartment of the up train. The thud of the body hitting the floor caused the passengers to look around but they saw nothing. Sweating profusely, he sat down heavily and turned once more to the report. He was in for one more shock.

He'd got it all wrong. Yes, the man was German but he wasn't SD, he was a communist. The report wasn't for Heydrich, it was for Moscow Central. Its message was simple, Canaris was doing a deal with the British and must be eliminated. The shock hit him like a blow to the solar plexus.

Chapter 31

'IF YOU IGNORE the need to kill a Soviet spy and throw him out of one moving train and into another, it all went pretty smoothly.'

C was looking forward to delivering the line he'd been preparing on his walk from Broadway Buildings to Suffolk Street. San Sebastian had boosted his already abundant self-esteem and Canaris's demand for a letter which he couldn't possibly provide meant the matter would go no further. He'd succeeded in ingratiating himself with a powerful group without compromising his position. A satisfactory result all round.

No chalk river and country pub. This time, a London Club but not Boodles or Whites. Instead, the understated charm of a small back room in the United University Club in Suffolk Street.

Sir Baldwyn was sitting in one of three red leather armchairs. Next to him sat another man. Immaculately tailored, with an abundant head of beautifully cut silver hair, he stood up as C entered, offered his hand and addressed him in an American accent.

'It's an honour to meet you sir. My name is McKittrick.'

Robbed of delivering his opening line, a lesser man would have responded frostily. C hid his irritation behind what passed for him as a smile.

'Mr McKittrick, I've heard a lot about you and the Bank of International Settlements. What is it you call yourselves, "the bank to the central bankers"?'

McKittrick smiled warmly and changed the subject.

'Sir Baldwyn was telling me how impressed he was with

your fishing skills. I'd consider it an honour to be able to join you next time.'

'McKittrick is a keen anglophile,' Sir Baldwyn chimed in. 'Has a butler and reads an ironed copy of The Times every morning.'

Sir Baldwyn gave C a look that said, 'American y'see.'

C played along, using the time to consider why this man was here. One thing was certain, the mad plan C had come here to close down had further to run and the people behind it were more powerful than he'd realised.

'You're wondering why I'm here.'

'To talk about fishing?'

'I'd like nothing more.'

McKittrick paused.

'But there's another reason. Admiral Canaris has asked me to pass on his sincere thanks for saving his life in San Sebastian. You went above and beyond the call of duty. He won't forget that.'

As a way of demonstrating his influence, it was a line that took some beating. It also served to increase C's sense of alarm. As if reading his mind, McKittrick moved swiftly on.

'I'm here to explain the value of the BIS as an intermediary trusted by both sides.'

'From what I hear, you're trusted by the Nazis much more than by us. I'm told the Vice President of the Reichsbank calls you their only overseas branch.'

McKittrick smiled, the discreet glow from a table lamp highlighting some expensive dental work.

'It's because we're trusted by the Nazis that we're valuable to you. I'm a banker dealing only with other bankers. Even in war, international banking must go on. I'm learning a lot about Nazi strengths and weaknesses and passing this on.'

'To whom?'

'Right now, mainly to the US Government via the Dulles brothers. I tell them what the Nazis are thinking, they tell me what the US government is thinking.'

Another, and starting to irritate, smile.

'Which brings me to the main reason I'm here.'

McKittrick looked across at Sir Baldwyn, seeking approval to continue. He received a nod.

'The United States has significant economic interests in Germany and a powerful strategic interest in the existence of a strong Germany as a bulwark against communism. Americans don't want wars and, if there are any, they certainly don't want to be involved in them. They want strong economies with which they can trade and in which they can invest. If the Poles hadn't defeated the Soviets in 1920, the whole of Europe might have become communist by now. That was too close a call. When they look across the Atlantic, what they want is a German run Europe to keep the Soviets at bay.'

'What you've got right now is a German run Europe.'

'The problem is it's being run in the wrong way, by the wrong man.'

No smile, this time.

'Which is where you come in. Churchill's policy of continuing the fight assumes that, sooner or later, the US will join the war. Believe me, unless the US is attacked, that's not going to happen. The American government will happily take your money and supply you with weapons but that's all. Germany is funding the war by appropriating the assets of the occupied countries. Your country will bleed to death unless a peace deal is arranged and quickly. You and I have an important role to play in arranging that peace deal. It's in everyone's interest.'

C had come to Suffolk Street to close things down and with good reason. The first meeting with Canaris could be justified as being within his remit. Without approval from Churchill, a second would be regarded as treason. He was considering how to make his position clear when McKittrick resumed.

'The President of the Reichsbank has produced a blueprint for Europe. I've obtained an English translation which Sir Baldwyn will let you have. They're looking to create a federation like the US and we intend to assist this. Everyone will benefit. You will still have your empire and navy. Europe will be a powerful defence against the Soviets as well as a reliable place in which to invest. Removing Hitler is the key. You are the man who can insert that key into the lock.'

'You want me to return to San Sebastian?'

'Ideally, yes but the furore created by a dead body in the funicular has persuaded Canaris to switch to France. You'll be quite safe. It's Abwehr only in France, no SD allowed.'

'I'm aware of that. Whereabouts in France?'

'When the Abwehr was given responsibility for security in France, Canaris insisted the SD hand over details of all places where intelligence activities were logged.

C raised an eyebrow.

'How did he manage that? They hate each other.'

'He appealed directly to the Führer. Even then, the SD held the files back. He had to send an Abwehr section into the SD headquarters armed with an order from the Führer and instructions not to leave without the files. Hitler likes playing people off against each other.'

McKittrick clearly enjoyed revealing how much he knew about the internal politics of the Nazi Party.

'He's suggested a place one of your men went to last year, La Dame Brave. You'll be quite safe.'

Enough was enough. It was time to bring this insane conversation to an end.

'I can't possibly do that. Canaris may be a man of honour but it only takes one person in his circle to reveal the meeting, whether deliberately or otherwise, and I'll be captured. I'm sorry, it's too great a risk.'

Sir Baldwyn intervened.

'I agree. It's out of the question. You're far too valuable.'

Surprised by this unexpected show of support, C assumed Sir Baldwyn had finally seen sense. Appearing to read the room, McKittrick backtracked.

'You're quite right, Sir Baldwyn. It wasn't Canaris's idea C should go in person, it was mine and it was a foolish one.'

'So what do you want me to do?'

The question was addressed to McKittrick but the reply came from Sir Baldwyn.

'You'll have to send somebody else. Supply Canaris with what he asked for in San Sebastian, a letter from Churchill promising support for a coup against Hitler followed by an immediate cessation of hostilities.'

'I can't persuade Churchill to sign such a letter.'

The American brushed an imaginary piece of fluff from his Savile Row suit.

'Of course you can't and nobody expects you to. I'm sure you can come up with a convincing forgery. That's all that's needed. Canaris will never know.'

Seeing the shocked look on C's face, McKittrick continued.

'If you will permit me, I'd like to give you some advice. We're at one of those turning points in history that occur very rarely. In this situation, you need to decide if you want to be an insider or an outsider. As an outsider, you're free to speak your mind and do what you think is right but you won't be one of the people shaping the future of the world. As an insider, you won't be able to speak so freely and you must never betray your fellow insiders but you will have a chance to influence the course of events while enjoying the protection of your fellow insiders. I'm sure you will agree there's never been a time when the right people were more needed to step forward and do just that. But be clear on one thing, if you decide to become an insider, your support must be complete and unconditional.'

He stood up and held out his hand.

'I've said my piece. It's up to you to decide your future.'

He turned to Sir Baldwyn.

'I'll leave you gentlemen to sort out the details.'

The assumption that, one way or another, he would do as he was told wasn't lost on C.

Once McKittrick had taken his leave, a club servant appeared, seemingly without being summoned, bearing a tray with a decanter of port and two glasses. Placing the tray on the table, he went over to the curtains and pulled them back, allowing the sunlight to flood in. Moving swiftly to switch off all the lamps, he made to pick up the decanter. Waving the man away, Sir Baldwyn filled the glasses. With the American out of the way, both men felt less constrained.

'Is he a friend of yours?'

'Never met him before. He called me yesterday. Told me he'd been put on to me by friends of Canaris and was anxious to meet you. I'm sorry I foisted him on you without warning but what he told me last night convinced me you needed to meet him.'

Sir Baldwyn took a sip of port to allow C to respond. He ignored the opportunity.

'As he explained, there are powerful forces at work wanting peace. Granted their motives are material rather than altruistic. Just as we want to keep our lands, the Americans want to make money out of a stable Europe. But if those motives bring peace, does it matter? If we fail to remove Hitler, a war could lead to communist revolutions all over Europe. You've seen how angry the people in the East End are at being bombed while the toffs in the West End are untouched. That could easily spread to the whole country. We're sitting on a tinder box.'

He paused to refill C's glass.

'But he made one big point and that was the reason I agreed to bring him here today. Churchill's strategy is to stay in the war at any cost because the Americans will join in eventually. You heard what he had to say about that. It'll never happen.'

He allowed C a moment to reflect then got down to business.

'No time to waste then. Who will you use to produce the letter? One of your best people, I trust.'

C couldn't fail to notice the change in Sir Baldwyn. Not just his words but the manner in which he was saying them. No more non sequiturs, no more beating about the bush to avoid coming to the point. The change in his demeanour and the self-confidence that went with it alarmed C at least as much as anything the American had said. He needed to get out of this and quickly.

'What about your own contacts? The British aristocracy has links with its German counterparts; the Royals are related to half of them. Prince George's activities have been watched by both Five and Six for years.'

'That's why we can't go down that route. The German aristocracy pretends to hate Hitler but, like the ordinary citizens and soldiers, they'll support him as long as he's successful. Besides, they're the ones with their eyes on our estates. No, it's got to be the Wehrmacht.'

'When they examine the letter, they'll see it's forged.'

'Come now, Canaris is hardly likely to pass it over to his experts. He'll show it to a couple of his closest allies. After that, I'd be surprised if it ever sees the light of day again.'

Aware of the need to push C further, Sir Baldwyn stood up and walked over to a bookcase. After a leisurely examination of its contents, he turned round and set about telling him how many beans made three.

'No British government has ever taken the SIS seriously. For years, your entire annual expenditure has been roughly the equivalent of keeping one Royal Navy destroyer in commission for one year. Your so-called Passport Control Officers devoted more time to stealing visa fees than in maintaining spy networks. Focusing entirely on the threat from the Soviet Union, you ignored the threat from the Nazis. When your predecessor woke up to this and formed Z section, you established a network of worthwhile agents only to lose them all at Venlo.'

With McKittrick out of the way, C had assumed he would have no trouble in closing things down. Instead, he found himself facing Sir Baldwyn's icy self-assurance and it puzzled him. It couldn't simply be explained by the confidence that comes from a thousand years at the top of the tree nor from the possession of far more information than he had realised. There was something else powering the man's assumption that he would do as he was told. Sensing his alarm, Sir Baldwyn sweetened the mixture.

'I know I sound critical but you've proved yourself with that trip to Spain. What you did there was heroic but you've done your bit and you're one of us now. For the next stage, you should send someone disposable and deniable, with a forged letter that's equally deniable.'

For all Sir Baldwyn's mixture of bullying and flattery, C had been resolved to call the whole thing off. As intended, the words "you're one of us now," weakened that resolve. Sir Baldwyn pressed home his advantage.

'It's for the good of the country. We can't afford the luxury of petty scruples. If we lose this war, it will be like the Norman Conquest. People like us will face not only death but the seizure of our estates. We know, because that's how our ancestors obtained the estates in the first place. We just want to protect British interests and maintain the status quo. We need someone who can see the big picture here. We think you're that man.'

He reached into his jacket pocket and produced a sheet of paper.

'This is the wording for the letter.'

He watched C's face darken as he read it. Anticipating his alarm, Sir Baldwyn had an explanation ready.

'Churchill's got it all wrong and he's ruining us in the process.'

He could see C was wavering.

'You may be surprised to know we helped your predecessor finance the purchase of Bletchley Park.'

'I thought he paid for it out of his own money.'

'And in a sense, he did, using money we gave him. The point I'm making is that everything we do is for the good of the country. We gain nothing personally. No political gains, no financial reward. That's rather rare these days, don't you think? Politicians are here today, gone tomorrow. Families like us, people who think in terms of generations, are the ones who really matter. This war threatens our position and we have to do something about it. In helping us, you're joining us, becoming one of us. A title will be the least you deserve.'

Unsure whether the man opposite was very clever or very mad, C steered the conversation back to the matter in hand.

'If we're talking about petty scruples, what happens if there's a successful coup in Germany but Churchill refuses to work with the new men in charge?'

Sir Baldwyn took a sip of the port and grimaced.

'This port's bloody awful. The first thing everyone does in wartime is drink all the best vintages, leaving us with this muck. Human nature, I suppose.'

He smiled benevolently.

'What did you think of our stretch of the river? You must come down again soon.'

This time, C wasn't prepared to play Sir Baldwyn's game.

'No doubt but that doesn't answer my question.'

'If the mission is a success, Churchill won't be able to object but if he does, well, those planes he's always flying around in,' he looked C straight in the eye, 'they're awfully prone to engine failure, don't you know.'

Giving him no time to protest, Sir Baldwyn stood up.

'Look, I must dash. Promised my gamekeeper I'd look in on him. One of his assistants has had his call-up papers. Damn nuisance. While you're thinking things over, you might like to have a look at the contents of this.'

He pulled a battered briefcase off the floor and withdrew two manila envelopes, one thicker than the other. Selecting the thicker one, he handed it to C.

'This is the Reichsbank's blueprint for Europe that McKittrick mentioned. I've added something myself, nothing to do with McKittrick.'

When he reached the door, he turned, as if a thought had just occurred to him.

'We wouldn't pressure you like this if it wasn't important. Nine hundred years of our history, everything this country stands for is at risk. Someone has to deal with this before it's too late. Sort the letter out, sort a courier out and agree a date with Canaris via the Polish woman. And remember what I said about SOE. Pull this off and you won't have to worry about them.'

'I'm not sure I can do this.'

'Oh, I'm sure you can.'

C watched the door close. Thanks to McKittrick's unexpected intervention, he now knew the attempt to manipulate him went far beyond a domestic group of ancient families. It was international and powerful and their objectives of peace, prosperity and a bulwark against communism were sensible. Did that entitle him to act without the government's knowledge and against the government's policy?

The decanter of what, to him, was a perfectly satisfactory port lay on the table in front of him. He re-filled his glass and sank into the Chesterfield to weigh his options. It didn't take long. There was only one. He'd have to tell Churchill, make a clean breast of it. These people were too dangerous to play with. Sir Baldwyn would deny the whole thing and probably question his mental stability. Better to lose his job than lose his head.

He stood up and pulled the envelope towards him, intending to read it in his office. The flap was open, revealing a set of photos. Assuming they were of Canaris or some other German conspirators, he was stunned to see himself and his secretary. Six photos, each one more compromising than the previous one. So that was why they were so sure of his cooperation. As Sir Baldwyn had intended, fear easily outweighed anger. And with good reason. Attractive as the promise of social advancement might be, he'd never really believed it but the threat contained in the photos was all too real. Half his lands had come to him by his marriage and had remained in his wife's name. If she divorced him, he'd lose the lands and the social standing that went with them.

He had to admire Sir Baldwyn's skill, the same skill that had enabled the family to survive and prosper for nearly a thousand years. While seeming to offer him social advancement, he was really threatening him with social and financial ruin. But the man had made two mistakes. The first was to assume the letter would be forged inside MI6. That was out of the question. No one in Six could know about it.

His second mistake was the wording of the letter. Instead of a vague promise of support, the letter offered Canaris a golden opportunity to rise in the ranks of the Nazi Party, leaving Hitler in place. It was all too obvious that it wasn't Hitler Sir Baldwyn and McKittrick wanted to overthrow, it was Churchill. They were counting on Canaris publishing the letter and destroying Churchill, leaving his successor to negotiate a peace treaty. Hitler would be left to invade the Soviet Union. Sir Baldwyn and his chums would keep their lands.

But if Sir Baldwyn thought he could tempt a wily spymaster like Canaris, he was wrong. Canaris knew Hitler's appetite could never be sated. For Germany's sake not his own, he wanted him gone. When he read the letter, Canaris would do two things, destroy it and end all communication with the British. That would be a shame but not much more.

And C wasn't the only one with a weak spot. Sir Baldwyn had one too, one that could be used to deter Sir Baldwyn from trying to bring him down if things went wrong.

He started to see a way through this but it depended on his judgement of Canaris being correct. Feeling a little better about the outcome, he turned his mind to the one missing piece.

He needed someone "disposable and deniable" to take the letter.

Chapter 32

From a distance, Trent Park looked like any other classic British country house, set in its own ample grounds. Only when you approached it did you notice the coils of barbed wire and the metal perimeter fence. If you ignored them and went inside, the rooms were magnificent. The staff were deferential to the guests, leaving them to themselves until required. It was as if the Edwardian era had never ended. Apart from one oddity: every guest wore the uniform of an officer in the German armed forces.

If you ventured round the back, you might notice a small door. If you were one of the few who knew how to open that door and walked down the steep wooden steps that lay behind it, you would find yourself in a large cellar that ran the full length of the house and had been partitioned into small offices. The ceiling was festooned with pipes for water, heating and sewage. Hidden amongst these pipes were wires that led down to the recording machines that had been installed on the desks in the small rooms. At each desk sat a man, dressed this time in the uniform of the British army. It was all a far cry from the luxury enjoyed by the men above, a luxury that encouraged them to relax and speak freely to one another. While the men in the basement listened to every word.

Freddie Fawkes would much rather be upstairs, engaging the captured airmen in conversation and using his skills to draw them out but that would have given the game away. So here he was, below stairs, in a small office of his own, searching reams of verbatim conversations for the occasional nugget. It occurred to him that C might as well have sent him to prison until he realised that that was pretty much what he had done.

When he'd walked out of Broadway Buildings, Fawkes had tried to disguise his dismay by setting off with a spring in his step, telling himself he was a free man. But the Department had been his whole life and by the time he'd reached the end of the street, he was feeling a lot less jaunty. In the months that followed, he'd missed not only his old job but the very people he'd loved to hate. What was it that silly girl at the hotel had said about everyone doing what they were best at? The SIS wasn't just what he was best at, it was the only job he was fit for. By the late summer, he'd lost all hope. Until one morning, a batman approached, waving a letter. It contained an invitation.

The drab, lower middle-class respectability of Kennington made a welcome change from the lavish surroundings of Trent Park. Though he'd written to her from time to time since his exile, he hadn't visited Maud Heywood since the funeral. Feeling guilty, he'd been surprised but delighted by her invitation to lunch.

Maud opened the door and led him into the hall. Nothing had changed. Everything brown and cream, the photo of Heywood and Fawkes still taking pride of place on the hall table. She led him over to it.

'He would have been so proud of you, Freddie. I mean, he always was proud of you, but especially now we're fighting this terrible war. I know you can't tell me anything but I'm sure you'd do anything for the security of this little island of ours.'

She heard the sharp intake of breath, saw the look of pain in his eyes, pretended she'd seen and heard neither.

'Anyway, you go on into the parlour and help yourself to a drink while I finish the meal. The cupboard's a little bare I'm afraid but I've managed to rustle up something.'

When he opened the sitting room door, it was as if he'd never been away. He could feel Heywood's presence in the armchair he'd always occupied after Sunday lunch. In the weeks following his death, Fawkes had been riven with guilt. Now, he almost envied his old friend for having had the opportunity to die on active service.

Over lunch, Maud steered the conversation round to his future, asking him if he would ever go back to his old job.

'If only I could. I can't get over how I let George down. All I want is a chance to avenge his death but they won't have me back.'

'Don't be so sure. They need people like you and they'll realise it sooner or later. When that day comes, you need to be ready for it.'

'No, I should have listened to George. He told me to play along with the office politics. I didn't and it cost me my career.'

Her reply surprised him.

'Well I think you should carry on doing what you think is right. That's all you can do, dear. You're not cut out to be like the others so don't even try. Carry on the way you are. Things'll turn out right in the end, you'll see.'

He tried to resist her optimism but, by the time he left, his spirits had brightened. Maud had told him what he wanted to hear. As he walked down the street, a little of the old spring returned to his step.

Once he was safely out of the way, Maud phoned the number she'd been given.

'I gave him a pep talk, just like you said. He sounded desperate to get back to his old job, if only to avenge poor George. I'm sure he'll be glad to hear from you, even if he doesn't show it.'

She put the phone down and turned to the photo of her beloved husband. Helping his old employers had kept his name alive, if only for a day. She picked the photo up and kissed it.

'Have I done the right thing, George? It's what you'd have done isn't it?'

She was right about Fawkes on both counts. He was glad to be summoned and he didn't show it. When he knocked on the outer door to C's office, the secretary directed him along the corridor to a narrow door that opened to reveal a flight of stairs.

'He's waiting for you up there.'

The stairs opened onto the roof. Stepping into the sunlight, his eyes squinting in the glare, he could see the head of the secret service at the far end. He seemed to be talking to himself. As he drew near, he realised C was standing in front of a coop full of pigeons, whispering sweet nothings in their ears. Continuing to stroke one of the pigeons, C started the conversation.

'Wonderful creatures don't you think?'

He turned to Fawkes with an enquiring look.

'Absolutely sir.'

'Oh ye of little faith. Do you know the difference between a pigeon and a wireless message?'

'You can't decode a pigeon?'

It was all he could think of.

'True.'

C turned back to the pigeon.

'But the wrong answer. The correct answer is a wireless message can be intercepted, a pigeon can't. In an age of electronic wizardry, I find that rather reassuring. Don't you?'

'And they live on rooftops, sir, where conversations can't be overheard.'

C gave the pigeons some seed.

'Quite so, Fawkes, quite so.'

Turning back to Fawkes, he gave him his best attempt at a sympathetic look.

'You're feeling neglected. I want to bring you back into the fold but not like before. They speak well of you at Trent Park but we need your German skills here in the office. Your absence has made that all too obvious.'

'You mean as a desk man?' Fawkes made a half-hearted attempt to conceal his anger.

'The war won't last for ever. You must be patient.'

C had chosen the setting deliberately. The rooftop, the pigeons, had raised his underling's expectations, as they had been intended to. The offer of a desk job had sent them plummeting, as also intended. He watched Fawkes's anger bubble up.

'If it's all the same to you, Sir, I'd rather be a desk man in the comfort of Trent House. I've grown quite fond of the place. They appreciate me there.'

He turned round and strode at a firm but not too fast pace towards the door. With the pigeon clucking in sympathy, C waited till Fawkes was halfway across the roof then moved on to the next stage.

'Now just hang on a second.'

The tingle in the base of Fawkes's spine felt like the return of a long-lost friend. He knew what this was about. They needed him but they didn't want him. He turned to face his master. C beckoned him back then got down to business.

'You should be thanking me, you know.'

Fawkes tried to give him his most insolent stare but it didn't work. This was the kind of conversation he used to have with his contacts in the field.

'How so?'

'By sending you to Trent Park, I saved your life. If I hadn't, you would have been in the field when the Venlo incident occurred and the SD rolled up our entire network. Instead, here you are, still alive, still an aggressive little sod.'

Fawkes didn't take up the challenge.

'And, as it happens, I have a job for you, a real job.'

He watched Fawkes's shoulders relax. The man would do anything to be recalled to the colours. C laid it on thick.

'Things are desperate. The RAF are doing a grand job but we need to consider alternatives. Six needs to take direct action.'

'In what sense?'

'Outside normal channels, no one must know. And I mean no one. Do you want to be part of this? It means taking a considerable risk.'

'Of course, sir. It's what I'm trained for.'

C could hardly stroke Fawkes's stomach so he stroked the pigeon's instead. It had the same effect, heightening Fawkes's anticipation.

'I'm supposed to go to France to meet Canaris and deliver a letter from the PM but we've decided it's too risky. Are you willing to take my place? It would mean a lot to me if you agreed but you'd be going into the lion's den, as it were. I can't guarantee you'd come out again.'

The sight of Fawkes's smiling face told C he was home and dry but his own expression gave no sign of this. Time to add a little more sugar.

'By the way, I've seen for myself that the Germans have been penetrated by communists at the highest level. Apart from one man weeded out by Lestocq, we don't have that problem, but it makes secrecy even more important.'

Fawkes wanted to laugh. With only the pigeons as witnesses, the wily old bird was playing on his own obsession to bind him more closely into a mission so secret, no one must know. And it was working. His desire to get back in the game overrode his caution, as C knew it would. Whatever was going on must be better than listening in on German POWs.

'Your job is to be a carrier pigeon with a very important message, one that mustn't be intercepted.'

He fixed his underling with a steely gaze.

'Do you think you can be a carrier pigeon?'

Fawkes looked at the pigeons cooing contentedly in the coop.

'As long as I can find my way home, sir.'

Pleased with the way things were going, C turned towards the door. But Fawkes hadn't finished.

'What's in the letter?'

'You don't need to know that.'

C saw the doubtful look on his face. Time to give his carrier pigeon some seed.

'Carry out this mission and you can come back here permanently.'

'Under Lestocq?'

'No, we'll make other arrangements.'

Things were going so well, Fawkes was tempted to raise the

question of the rotors. Being lied to about the success of that mission still infuriated him. Heywood's advice to be diplomatic held him back. He'd save that discussion for his return from this mission.

Just as well. When it came to using Fawkes, C had had to wrestle with his conscience. Not about lying to Fawkes about the rotors but about ignoring the Commander's advice not to send him back into the field. His need to use Fawkes for this mission had led him to convince himself that, as long as Fawkes believed the rotors had been of no value, the risk to the Enigma decrypts was minimal. Minimal, but not non-existent. He petted one of the pigeons.

'A small point, but important. This mission is so sensitive that, if you are captured, you'll have to use your suicide pill right away. If you don't, I don't need to tell you what sort of a death you'll face. Is it true what they say about you, that you're semi-suicidal anyway?'

'That's a lot of nonsense. I only take risks when they're necessary. But I agree, whether I commit suicide or not is a small matter to the Department.'

C let out a sigh of relief.

'That's more like it. You've been so diplomatic, I was beginning to wonder what had happened to the insolent little sod of old. Glad to see you haven't lost your touch.'

Even Fawkes had to smile at that one.

'One more thing. I know you feel responsible for Heywood's death. Don't even think of using this mission as a revenge trip.'

So Maud Heywood had been recruited to reel him in. Was there nothing C wouldn't stoop to?

'Of course not, sir. I'm a professional.'

'Good. Let's go down to my office and plan things with Lestocq. He's the only other man in on this.'

Bend the knee to Lestocq and be prepared to kill himself if he was captured. A year ago, he would have stormed off the roof. Not anymore. It was a price worth paying.

He was back.

Chapter 33

ROLAND LESTOCQ WAS everything Freddie Fawkes was not, well dressed, well mannered, diplomatic and charming. The archetypal "one of us". As C entered the outer office, Lestocq stood up, giving C the opportunity to put an arm round him and shepherd him into his office. Fawkes assumed Lestocq had been brought in to put him in his place but he was wrong. He was C's insurance policy. If things went wrong and the Fishing Club abandoned him, C would make sure he took Sir Baldwyn's son and heir down with him.

But he correctly interpreted the absence of C's secretary. This one really was off the books.

C beamed at Lestocq.

'How's your aunt these days?'

'Bearing up under the strains, sir but she's pretty put out at not being able to go to the villa in Sainte-Maxime this year. She misses it badly.'

'Still, she's got the horses to occupy her.'

'Yes, but for how long? Her local Council are threatening to plough the polo field for vegetables. She's really suffering.'

'I've brought Fawkes into the picture and explained a little of what he has to do but we must be careful. If there's one thing I learned from my recent trip, it's that the Germans have been penetrated by commies at the highest level.'

Fawkes wondered what trip C was referring to but knew better than to ask. Once they were seated, C got down to business.

'Anyway, the upshot is that Fawkes has agreed to take my

place and will return to La Dame Brave carrying a letter from the PM promising to support any coup against Hitler.'

After a brief silence, Lestocq spoke in his most obsequious manner, as if pointing out a tiny detail that had been overlooked.

'I thought the PM was to be kept out of this.'

'Correct.'

'Then how?' Lestocq's voice trailed away as he realised the implication of what his boss was saying. Which pleased his boss. His father really had kept him in the dark.

'A forgery. It's what we do, after all.'

So it wasn't a genuine letter from Churchill. Fawkes made his first contribution to the meeting.

'Don't you think it likely the recipients of the letter will check it thoroughly?'

C shook his head.

'How can they? They're conspirators and can hardly call upon their experts without betraying themselves.'

'Conspirators? Are we trying to remove Hitler? If the letter falls into the hands of the SD, it would be highly embarrassing to Churchill. He'd be the one forced out of office, not Hitler.'

'France is Abwehr territory. The SD won't be allowed near it.'

Fawkes noticed Lestocq listening intently. C, as he liked to do when creating an impression of shared intimacy, leaned forward.

'The Prime Minister has his hands full and this sort of thing falls naturally to us. We'd be failing in our duty if we didn't do it. Once Hitler is overthrown, we have two nations under arms, and ready to fight. Instead of fighting each other, we can join forces against the real enemy, the Soviets.'

'It's a good idea, sir,' said Lestocq. 'Fawkes knows La Dame Brave well and his languages will come in handy.'

Fawkes listened to his superior both praising him and putting the boot in about his obviously untrustworthy ancestry.

'But, does Canaris know it's Fawkes who'll be bringing the letter and not you?'

'He does.'

'Supposing Canaris's motives aren't as pure as we would wish. If he was trying to lure you into a trap, he'll feel thwarted. At the very least, he'll arrest Fawkes. May even shoot him on the spot.'

'He won't feel thwarted. There are powerful people behind this.'

'But, if things do go wrong, it's alright for Fawkes to defend himself?'

'If absolutely necessary but it won't come to that.'

'I'm just trying to protect Fawkes's interests here. As his superior, I feel responsible for him.'

'Quite right. I'm sure he'll be glad to have that reassurance.'

Fawkes was astonished by this sudden concern for his welfare by a man who he knew loathed him. But Lestocq hadn't finished.

'So, to be clear, we can't rule out the possibility that Canaris may end up dead.'

'In a hypothetical situation that will definitely not arise, that is correct.'

Knowing how surprised Fawkes must be by his change of attitude, Lestocq turned to him.

'Time to draw a line under the past. Mistakes were made, I'd be the first to admit that. But this is a vital mission. Time for a fresh start.'

He held out his hand. Seeing it as a further sign of his return to favour, Fawkes shook it, eagerly. Then Lestocq got back to business.

'What if I go too, but separately? I could keep an eye on things from a distance. Intervene if necessary.'

'You're too valuable here, dear boy and the fewer of us there are, the better. Canaris suggested a meeting in the Pole's house and I've agreed to this.'

By now, even the desperate-to-be-back Fawkes could hear alarm bells ringing in his head. The first principle of agent briefing was that the agent was only ever told as much as he needed to know to carry out his part of the mission. The meeting on the roof had obeyed that rule. The second principle was that as few people as possible were told of the existence of the mission. In C's office, both rules had been broken. He'd been told far more than he needed to know. He'd assumed Lestocq had been part of the planning but he clearly knew nothing about it. Why was he being told so much and why was Lestocq being told anything at all?

But right now, he had a more immediate worry to deal with.

'Anywhere in the village will do, won't it?'

'No, it has to be the house where you went last year. He's gone to a lot of trouble to extract the address from the SD. Had to get Hitler's support. If we change the meeting place, he'll smell a rat. What's the problem?'

'The thing is, I never went to the house. Heywood was given a detailed map but it was a complicated route.'

That was the bad news. He paused before delivering the really bad news.

'And he left the map showing how to get there in the house.'

The change in C's demeanour caught both men by surprise. He stood up, knocking his chair over, and marched round the room, coming to a halt behind Fawkes's chair.

'Why the hell didn't you tell me this before? I've just sent him a message saying we'll meet in the house. We must keep to that and I'll tell you why. Do you trust Canaris? No, nor do I. Does Canaris trust us? Of course not. He's taking a hell of a risk meeting us at all and he's jumpy. If we change the venue, he'll call the whole thing off. I'd do the same and so would you. We have to meet in the house. Why don't you know the address?'

'We were going to meet in the house then Koslowski changed the plan. Heywood went to the house and I met the Pole in the factory. With respect, sir, I explained all this to the Commander in your office. I never even saw the house. Had no reason too.'

C righted the chair and sat down again.

'You can't just wander round a small village guessing which house it is.'

Believing his knowledge of the house was the sole reason

he'd been recalled, Fawkes could feel his return to favour turning to ashes in his mouth. Without that knowledge, he had nothing to offer. Unless, unless…

Like a gambler down to his last chip, he placed one last, desperate bet.

'There's one person who would know.'

Chapter 34

For Jean-Paul Durand, the sight of Mary's name on the decoded message summoned up that last summer with Juliette. He wasn't told why her surname and address were needed but it seemed a simple enough request. Allowing himself a brief sigh, he picked up the hotel register and flicked the pages back. When he came to Juliette's name and address, he gently ran his finger over her writing. But there was no separate entry for Mary. She was listed under the Poitrenaud's address in Paris. His report back to London received an immediate response. 'Do whatever is needed to obtain the woman's address.'

There was only one way to do this.

He disliked dealing with the Resistance, too many leaks, too many traitors. MI6 had told him to stay away from them and he was only too happy to obey. Now, however, he faced a dilemma. To make a legal passage from the unoccupied zone to the occupied, he needed an Ausweis, a pass issued only by the Germans and all but impossible to obtain. If he was going to cross the demarcation line, he would have to do it illegally. To do that, he would need the services of the very people he wanted to avoid.

There was one man, just one, he trusted - the restaurateur Yann. Telling his receptionist he was going to arrange a food delivery, he went round to see the big man. Using the alleyway behind the restaurant, he approached the back door to the sound of Yann and his wife arguing. They stopped as soon as he walked in. Yann smiled warmly, his wife retained her scowl.

Not the start he was hoping for.

'Good morning, Jean-Paul. What can I do for you?'

'It's a delicate matter, Yann.' He paused and looked across at Yann's wife. 'In connection with your other activities.'

His wife piped up.

'You see? Everyone knows. It'll be the death of you one day and me too.'

She'd been preparing a monk fish while they were arguing. Chopping its ugly head away from the body, she tossed it into a soup pot and stormed out.

Yann gave his visitor a shamefaced look and invited him to sit down.

'She doesn't like me getting involved but I can't stand by and do nothing. What's this about?'

'I have to go to Paris. Immediately. Can you help?'

Yann sat back in his chair, staring intently at his guest. He'd always had an indefinable air of mystery about him so the approach wasn't a complete surprise but could he be trusted? Durand knew what he was thinking; he'd have asked himself the same question.

'I'm not trying to trap you, Yann. We're on the same side, just working in different areas. I'd tell you more but it's better you don't know.'

'You'll need someone to take you to Loches. You can cross the zone line at the river there but only if you use the right people. More than a few have paid good money to be taken across only to be handed over to the Boches for a reward. Betrayal is a lucrative business up there.'

'Who do I use?'

'There's only one person you can use, me. You can't trust anyone else and they won't trust you. When do you want to go?'

'Right away.'

Yann decided the less his wife knew about it the better. There'd be the mother and father of a row when he returned. He'd face that when the time came.

'We're just going out for a while,' he said, ushering Durand through the door before she could reply.

Starting out in daylight suited both of them. A drive at night, without lights up the winding roads into the hills and down the other side, was unthinkable.

'So we're on the same side,' Yann said, as they started their climb into the hills.

'Yes, but I don't work with the Resistance.'

'Lucky you.'

'Not much fun?'

'It was when we started, we were all patriots pure and simple. The communists won't touch us with a barge pole because of the pact between Hitler and Stalin. Then a guy from Germany, a communist who fled before the war, took over in the Marseilles region and suddenly he wants to work with us, says he doesn't agree with what Moscow are doing. I think I can trust him but I'm not sure. That's what my wife and I were arguing about.'

They carried on, past La Dame Brave, higher and higher. The rocks turned from brown to grey, the vegetation ceased. Once they'd reached the highest point and were starting their descent, Yann returned to his subject.

'If you don't work for us, you must be an SIS man.'

He waited for a reply. None came.

'I understand. The less I know, the better.'

'Look, I'm just a conduit, a money man, if you like, that's all.'

'Is that why we're going to Paris?'

'Something like that.' A pause. 'Hang on, what do you mean "we"?'

'You've got to get into the Occupied Zone and out again. You can only do that if I'm with you. 'I'll have to come with you all the way. Besides, we'll be less conspicuous if there are two of us.'

Durand was a natural loner and had assumed he would be leaving him at the crossing. But Yann was right about looking less conspicuous, it might make all the difference.

'OK but this is going to be dangerous. When we get to Paris, you must do as I say.'

'You're the boss.'

Durand might be the boss if and when they reached Paris. When it came to making the dangerous crossing into the occupied zone, it was Yann who gave the orders. By the time darkness fell, they'd reached the flat farmland to the south of Loches. As they approached the river, he took charge.

'Wait here.'

The farmhouse Yann was looking for lay at the end of a narrow, winding lane. It would have been hard to find in daylight. That Yann could find it in the dark meant he must have done this before. Durand tried to find that reassuring as he watched Yann tap quietly on the farmhouse door.

After a long wait, during which Durand could hear shouting, Yann emerged with an unshaven old man and a younger man in his forties. They looked Durand up and down.

'Stop worrying, he's a good man.'

He turned to Durand.

'These gentlemen are the only ones we can trust. They'll take us across and bring us back but they don't like the fact that we turned up without notice. They're worried you work for the Germans.'

Durand said the only thing he could think of.

'People of my race don't work for the Germans.'

He turned towards Yann. 'You really want to come? You're taking a big risk.'

'We've already discussed this, it's my duty.'

'Pity there aren't more like you.'

The boat crossing was the easiest part of the journey. The oars, wrapped in cloth, made little noise, the water, glistening in the moonlight, was smooth.

The younger man whispered as he rowed. 'There aren't many guards round here. As long as you know when to go, it's quite safe. It'll be a different matter when you get near Paris. You'll have to be more careful then and you'll need plenty of luck.'

'Yann told you we need a car?' Durand whispered as they climbed out on the other side. The younger man smiled.

'Wait here. I may be some time.'

The oarsman clambered up the riverbank and disappeared. They sat in silence for a while then, as much for his own benefit as Durand's, Yann whispered, 'he knows what he's doing.'

"Some time" turned out to be an understatement. Durand remembered what Yann had said about ferrymen who betrayed their clients for cash.

'Are you sure we can trust him?'

Even Yann had started to wonder by the time the man finally appeared at the top of the riverbank and beckoned to them.

'We're about to find out.'

Yann helped Durand up the slippery bank, his expensive shoes far from ideal for the task.

'Here you are gentlemen.'

They looked in astonishment.

'What the hell's that?'

Durand pointed to the shiny black Mercedes, gleaming in the moonlight, engine purring softly. A small swastika flag was mounted on one wing.

'Are you mad?'

'If you want to get to Paris without papers then drive round a city swarming with soldiers without being stopped, you can't do better than this. You,' he pointed to Yann, 'will do the driving and you,' he pointed to Durand, 'will sit in the back like a Gestapo officer. No one will touch you. Don't forget to put your watches forward an hour. In the occupied zone, they're on Berlin time, not GMT.'

Durand turned to Yann.

'What are we going to do? He's either mad or a genius.'

'We're here now, I think we should give it a go. How much petrol is there?'

The oarsman beamed with pride.

'That's why it took so long. I filled her up with two cans of petrol and put two more in the boot. He's away for the weekend. You'll be gone long before he returns. He'll never know.'

'Who won't know?'

'The local area commander.'

'Oh shit,' said Yann. 'You don't do things by halves, do you.'

A brief handshake with the oarsman and they set off into the night. Yann saw Durand's worried face in the rear-view mirror.

'Relax and enjoy the ride, mein Kommandant. They're good, these cars, aren't they?'

Once they'd settled in for the long drive ahead, Durand started to relax and, without intending to, drifted off into a dreamless sleep. When he awoke, it was daylight. Hearing him stir, Yann said, 'not long to go, we're almost there.'

To enter Paris, they had to pass through one of the city gates which were sited at intervals around the city. Since the removal of the defensive Thiers wall, after the end of the Great War, the gates themselves had always been kept open. They chose the Porte d'Orléans but, as they approached, they could see the gates were both firmly shut and manned by guards. If they had to show papers, they had none. The mission would come to an end there and then.

Durand spoke first.

'What are we going to do? Should we turn round?'

'We can't do that,' said Yann, 'they're bound to notice such a suspicious move. We'll have to take our chance. Look as if you're asleep. If they ask for papers I'll say you've got them and you'll be furious with me and them if I wake you. This is a senior officer's car. It might work.'

Durand was far from convinced but it was their only option. He slumped down in his seat and closed his eyes.

The car continued at a steady pace towards the gates. Yann noticed they were manned by French gendarmes, less inclined, he hoped to disturb a senior German officer, especially one in civilian clothes who had obviously come to Paris for pleasure.

To encourage the gendarmes to let them through, he maintained his speed, not accelerating but certainly not slowing down.

It worked. Seeing the swastika bedecked Mercedes speeding towards them, the gendarmes opened the gates to make way for the important passenger, whoever he might be.

The oarsman had been right when he'd said they wouldn't be stopped and it soon became clear he'd been right again when he'd said the city would be swarming with soldiers. They were everywhere. But these men weren't armed and marching around, they were strolling along the streets like tourists. It was all very relaxed with the shops doing good business. On the other hand, almost all the cars driving around were German, rendering their own swastika bedecked Mercedes inconspicuous.

Durand was planning how to handle Juliette when his thoughts were interrupted by Yann.

'Vincennes, you said?'

The car rolled to a halt.

'We're here. You know where to go?'

'Down there on the left. I looked it up on a map.'

'Well, don't take it with you. You'll draw attention to yourself.'

Driving along the avenue where Juliette lived, Durand experienced a tension far greater than anything he'd felt when they'd driven through the city gates. He was used to people passing through his life but Juliette was different. He'd never felt such an affinity with another human being, always known he shouldn't have accepted her departure from his life so passively. Was fate giving him a second chance?

'Stop here, I'll walk the rest. Keep the engine running, we may need to get out fast.'

It was a pleasant area of solid, bourgeois apartment blocks. As he walked the last steps towards her building, he wondered what would he find. Her husband had a reasonable job in a bank so there was a good chance she'd still be there but she might have fled Paris for the country.

Their name was still on the board against the bell push for

flat seventeen, fourth floor. In days gone by, there would have been a concierge but he was long gone. Ignoring the lift, he took the stairs. At the door of flat seventeen, he paused, took a deep breath, rang the bell and waited. No one came. He inserted his skeleton key into the lock. If it turned twice, there was no one there, if it turned once, there was. It turned twice. Saddened, he pushed on the door and entered.

The flat was clearly lived in but there was no one around. Feeling deflated, he set about searching drawers, cupboards, anywhere that might contain an address book. His search became increasingly frantic as it became increasingly fruitless and repetitive. Moving from a small desk back to a cupboard he'd already searched, his arm swept carelessly past a photograph on the desk, knocking it over. He managed to catch it before it hit the floor and started to replace it. As he did so, he realised it was a photograph of a family and that one member of the family was the British girl. In a moment of inspiration, he opened the back of the frame. The photograph fell out together with a single sheet of paper, a letter from the girl's mother with their address and phone number.

He slipped it into his jacket and put the photograph back in the frame. He wanted to stay but ought to get back to Yann. Feeling both cheated and relieved that he'd got what he came for, he buttoned his jacket and made for the door. As he reached for the door handle, he heard a key slip into the lock. He longed to see Juliette's rich brown curls but the woman who walked through the door had a brassy blonde mane. He moved to grab her. As he did so, the woman called his name.

'Jean-Paul?'

Chapter 35

THEY DRANK COFFEE, real coffee, of good quality. Durand wondered how she'd come by it. He watched as she poured, feeling embarrassed and angry at what he saw. Her lovely auburn hair had been dyed in the cheapest possible way and allowed to grow far too long. Her eye makeup was overdone, her lipstick too garish. She was unrecognisable as the woman he'd known. She knew what he was thinking and looked away hoping the less he saw, the less he would be offended by the change in her. He gently turned her towards him.

'My love, what has happened to you? Are things really that bad up here? They seem surprisingly normal.'

'They're anything but. My life has changed beyond recognition.'

She paused then poured forth her troubles.

'When Gamelin set up his headquarters here in Vincennes, so far from the front line, my husband lost all faith in the General's determination to fight to the finish and when Sedan fell, he decided we had to get out of Paris fast. While Audrey and I packed up as many of our belongings as we could, he went out to bring our car round.'

She shook her head.

'But he never returned. To this day, I don't know what happened to him. Perhaps someone murdered him to steal the car. I sent Audrey to relatives in Bordeaux and stayed on here hoping my husband would return. I tried to draw money from our bank account but it's in his name. I was penniless and alone.'

He saw the shame on her face. There was no point in asking the question that was on his mind. She'd been dishonoured enough without him adding to it.

'Pack your bags. You're coming with me.'

The look of gratitude mixed with relief should have made him feel good. Instead, he felt ashamed that he'd neglected her for so long. That would change, starting now.

'Is this why you came here?'

'No, but if I'd known all this I would have come sooner.'

He held her hands and stroked her face as he explained who he really was and why he'd come.

'So those chance events last summer have brought you here to rescue me. I was due a little luck.'

'We can't hang around. I'm here illegally. If we're stopped I don't have the correct documents. They'll shoot me and probably you too. Pack a small bag. Yann is waiting outside in a car.'

'Yann? The restaurateur? Does he work for the British too?'

'No, he's in the Resistance. If it wasn't for him, I'd never have made it here.'

She went to her wardrobe and pulled the back out to reveal a hidden section where she'd kept her best clothes. Their secret existence had been something to cling to in her wretched state. Now it had all been worthwhile and she lovingly packed each item, ready to start a new life. With barely a backward glance, she picked up her bag and headed for the door. He followed her onto the landing.

As she turned to double lock the door, they heard the sound of the lift ascending. Her hands fumbled the key, the lift drew closer. Taking the key from her hand, he pushed it into the lock, turning it twice. As they turned to head for the stairs, the lift stopped. They were on the top step when the doors slid back to reveal a German officer. He had a bag of coffee in his hands.

'Madame, I've just caught you,' he said cheerily. 'That was lucky.'

It was obvious why he he'd come. Durand guessed it was a regular visit. Ignoring him, the officer continued.

'It seems I've come at a bad time but perhaps you could spare me a few moments.' It was charmingly spoken but obviously not a request.

'I'm sorry, Herr Hauptmann but I can't see you at the moment. Why don't you come back after lunch?'

'I prefer now.' Still smiling, not quite so affable.

'Forgive me intruding Herr Hauptmann, but the lady really does need to be somewhere urgently.'

He should have stayed out of it but he didn't like having the reality of Juliette's situation so clearly spelt out to him. The German looked him up and down.

'Show me your papers.'

Juliette intervened.

'Herr Hauptmann, I don't think we need this, do you. If you come back later, I promise I'll make it worth your while.'

Durand should have allowed the German time to consider Juliette's offer. Once again anger at what was taking place in front of him overruled his judgement as he thrust his papers in front of the Herr Hauptmann, trying to take control in a situation where he was a mere onlooker. He knew they were all in order but he also knew one vital piece of paper was missing. Yann was down below, waiting. If they could just get past this man, they'd be alright. The German studied the papers minutely. Then looked him up and down, slowly.

'You live in the south?'

'I used to but I've been in Paris since before the war. I never got around to updating my papers, I'm sorry, I'll attend to it tomorrow.'

The officer looked at him then back at his papers, shrugged and held them out for Durand to take.

'You should keep your papers up-to-date.'

Durand reached forward, exposing his wristwatch from under his shirt cuff. The German looked hard at the watch, the one his uncle had given him. Was he going to steal his most precious possession? Too late, he realised why the German was staring at it.

'If you live in Paris, how come your watch is on GMT?'

Without waiting for an answer, the officer drew his pistol from its holster. Durand had a choice, accept arrest with both he and Juliette being marched off to be questioned - he was only too aware of where that would lead - or try and neutralise the German's weapon.

Death now or death later.

Juliette had other ideas. In the few seconds it took the Hauptmann to draw his pistol, everything seemed to slow down. She was looking forward to her new life in the south and nothing was going to stop her. She saw herself on the roof of the hotel that first night with Jean-Paul. She could smell the mimosa, hear the cicadas. Her hatred of all the men who had reduced her to her current state was focused on the one man who stood in her way. Shouting to Durand, 'go on, run,' she emitted a piercing scream and leapt at the startled officer.

Yann was waiting outside, his motor running. If Durand obeyed Juliette's instruction, he'd be out in the road in no time and on his way. He had the information he'd been sent to acquire. All he had to do was leave Juliette to her fate.

The Hauptmann, still clutching his bag of coffee and reluctant to shoot Juliette, decided the best way to get rid of her would be to hoist her onto the ledge of the bannisters, confident she would see the danger and let go of him to save herself. Durand, knowing he had to neutralize the gun, ran at him. Going in low, he placed his arms round the man's hips and stood up, hoisting him onto the balcony ledge with such force that the man started to topple over the edge.

Juliette, focusing solely on the need to distract the German while Durand escaped, ignored the danger and wouldn't let go of the Hauptmann. He, thinking she was helping to throw him over, fired his pistol at her in a futile attempt to save himself. Durand heard the sickening sound of the pistol being fired at point blank range and watched helplessly as the two of them tumbled down four floors to the hall below.

Horrified, not just by what had happened but by the speed of it all, Durand stared into the stairwell. The German's head was at an impossible angle to his body. The bag of coffee had burst, the beans spread across the floor. Juliette lay next to the German, whimpering. Jumping whole flights of stairs at a time, he ran down to her in desperation. With tears in her eyes, she reached out, her arms covered in bruises, blood trickling from her mouth.

She murmured weakly.

'I'm sorry. I couldn't let him kill you. Now I've spoilt everything. Please hold me, I'm so frightened.'

Durand held her gently in his arms and stroked her hair.

'You're going to be alright. I'll call an ambulance.'

'We both know you can't do that. You have to go. Promise you'll find my daughter after the war and look after her. Promise me.'

With the little strength she had remaining, she clutched his arm.

'I promise, my darling.'

'Smell the mimosa for me.'

She gave him the faintest of smiles as, clutching her to him, he felt her fade away.

Yann was gazing at a sign in a restaurant window, *Essen Mit Wein Komplett 30F.* He was wondering how long it would be before he had to put a similar sign in his window when he heard a shot. If he'd heard it, so, probably, had half the neighbourhood. He waited, his hand on the gear lever, his feet poised over the pedals. No one came out. He eased the car forward. He could see a police car coming down the road but it was held up by a pedal taxi, laboriously making its way across the road junction.

He swung the car across the traffic, narrowly missing a cyclist, and drove down the side of the building. If Durand had any sense, he'd come out the back way. If he didn't, the bullet must have been for him. He moved slowly up the road while he decided how long to give him. As he drew abreast of the back of the building, Durand emerged and leapt in. As Yann moved off, smoothly but not too fast, he looked sideways at Durand. He was as white as a sheet and his hands were shaking.

'I take it that didn't go too well.'

'I got what I came for,' he sighed.

'But I lost the only thing I really wanted.'

Chapter 36

C HAD NEVER been to the East End, never had any reason to. If he'd been a middle ranking trader in the city, he might have gone there to have a suit made. Brick Lane was teeming with Jewish tailors offering high quality suits, as good as anything in Savile Row and at a fraction of the price. The head of MI6, however, had no need to make such economies or go anywhere near this hotchpotch of humanity. Then war broke out and the SIS found itself in need of the services of one particular tailor. Naturally, he delegated the task of creating the relationship to a minion. Now, he needed to give the tailor a commission so secret, he had no alternative but to visit the man himself.

It was to this particular establishment that he now headed as he made his way past the delicatessens, past the Jolly Butchers pub, all the time weaving between the mass of people wandering, some with purpose, some without, down not just the pavements but the road as well. It was ten o'clock in the morning and the crowd in Brick Lane was so great, he had no choice but to accept defeat, abandon his manly pace and allow himself to be hustled along the street like everyone else. As a result, he walked past the number he was looking for and only noticed when he reached a pawn shop with its number clearly shown. Once he'd managed to switch from the tide of humanity flowing north to the one flowing south, he worked his way back until he arrived at his destination.

He expected to be greeted by a shop with the name "Isaac Gold Tailor" above a window with examples of his wares on display. What he found was a narrow door with brown peeling paint and nothing but the number to identify it. Unsure if he'd come to the right place, he knocked and waited. Nothing happened. He tried the handle and it opened with a scraping sound as the wood dragged itself across the uneven tiles of a narrow alley. At the far end, past the body of a dead rat, another door awaited him. This time, his knock was answered by a woman's voice.

'Who's there?'

'Mr Gold?'

'Do I sound like Mr Gold?'

'I'm looking for Mr Gold.'

'Is he expecting you?'

'Tell him Mr C sent me.'

The sound of slippered footsteps padding across the room grew louder until they stopped and were replaced by the sound of bolts being slid back. When the door opened, he was confronted by a woman dressed entirely in black, black dress, black shawl and black slippers. In her hands, a pair of half-finished trousers. After looking him up and down, she turned round and walked back to her sewing bench. Taking this as an invitation to enter, he followed her into a room that stank of cigar smoke. The paint on the walls was peeling, the floor covered in bits of material and discarded newspapers. Against one wall, a row of half-finished suits hung on a rack, the tacking thread visible on each. He was wondering if the thread was an essential part of the suit-making process or really just for show when a door opened on the far side of the room. An elderly man, also wearing carpet slippers, shuffled in. A pair of shiny trousers hung below an ash covered cardigan through which the flesh of his belly protruded. C tried not to look but his eyes kept returning to the unsavoury sight. The cigar responsible for the ash hung from the man's lips, even as he spoke.

'I don't know any Mr C. Who the hell are you?'

Having adjusted to his surroundings, C now had to adjust to

the fact that the man he was speaking to was not quite what he'd expected. When the SIS had asked a contact in Special Branch if they had their eye on any currency forgers, they'd been told there were plenty of them around, none of them any good. 'Except old man Gold. He's really good but we can never pin anything on him.' The man from the SIS had asked where Mr Gold could be reached and mutually beneficial business had followed. Now the head of the SIS found himself standing in this stinking room looking at the least likely forger he'd ever imagined. But needs must and the devil, in the form of Sir Baldwyn, was certainly driving. To prove who he was, he reached into his wallet and produced a bank note for fifty Reichsmarks.

'One of yours, I believe. Excellent work, if I may say so.'

Mr Gold relaxed.

'I take it you're the boss.'

'I am indeed. I've come in person this time because the job I have for you is rather different from our usual requirements.'

He glanced at the woman, sewing busily and seeming not to be listening as she took in every word.

'Can we go somewhere private?'

Having considered how to put his proposal to Mr Gold, C had decided to use a story that no one would believe if Gold should ever be foolish enough to relate it. Once inside the tailor's inner sanctum, he launched into his spiel. When he'd finished, there was a long silence while Gold considered the preposterous tale.

'You need to contact a group of Germans who want to overthrow Hitler and need me to forge a letter from Churchill pledging his support?'

'Exactly. I don't need to tell you how important this is both to the British people and to the future of your fellow Jews in occupied Europe.'

'This isn't part of our deal.'

'It is now. I think you will agree that our deal is very favourable to you. In return for forging various currencies for us, we allow you to continue forging British pounds. This little letter is hardly a problem for a man of your skills but, if you don't want to do it, we can always tell Special Branch that we have no further use for you. I think you know what that means. As I say, it's up to you.'

'In other words, or I help you, or you hang me. That's the real message here.'

For the first time, C felt sorry for the man he was dealing with. The continental use of or instead of either spoke of Gold's origins, of his family's flight from persecution.

'I am loath to put it so directly.'

'How much?'

'One thousand pounds. After this, we return to business as usual. Provided you don't do anything silly.'

'How do I know the pounds aren't forged?'

'If they're some of your own work, you won't.'

Both men smiled.

'When do you need it?'

'The day after tomorrow.'

Gold nodded his agreement, C gave him the wording and a copy of Churchill's signature. He was thinking of shaking his hand, had second thoughts, turned and left. Outside, the hubbub of Brick Lane came as a relief. He sniffed at his jacket. It reeked of cigar smoke. Realising the odour was clear evidence of his visit, he thought of having the suit cleaned, then decided to throw it away.

Chapter 37

HEAD BOWED, SHOULDERS slumped, Mary nearly stumbled into the stocks in the centre of Woodstock, as her mind played her last day in uniform over and over again. The brusque way her CO handed out her discharge papers and told her to get her uniform off still burned in her memory. She hadn't even bothered to look up as Mary left the office. Miserable old spinster. Oh God, is that what I'm going to be? When she met the Controller on the way to her hut, she'd expected more of the same. How wrong she'd been. As he nudged her to one side, the penetrating voice he'd used in the operations room was replaced by a gentle, fatherly tone.

'I'm sorry to see you go. You were an excellent plotter and God knows we need people like you. When you first turned up I thought you were just another spoilt little madam, like some of the actresses I encountered in rep, the ones who didn't stay the course. But you proved to be so much more than that, particularly when that wise old bird Winifred took you under her wing.'

Her CO had been so unpleasant, she'd nearly convinced herself she was glad to be leaving. Hearing the Controller's gentle words made her realise how much she was going to miss. He saw the tears well up in her eyes and took a chance.

'Look, it's not my place to say this but, if you need someone to get you out of your situation, I can put you in touch with an excellent surgeon who did that sort of thing as a sideline for the many actresses I came across who found themselves in the same position. It really is quite safe, not some nasty back street affair. No one will ever know.'

He saw the shocked look on her face.

'I'm sorry, I shouldn't have spoken.'

She touched his arm.

'No, not at all. I appreciate your concern.' She paused. He saw the anguished look on her face. Was she trying to come to a decision?

'I'm well aware my situation isn't going to be easy. Not now, not for the rest of my life and nor is that of my unborn child. But our situation is infinitely preferable to that of the father of my child. He died fighting for freedom in a fight that wasn't even his to fight. However much dishonour I suffer, I cannot dishonour his memory and will not do so.'

She caught his shamefaced look and pecked him on the cheek.

'But thanks all the same. It's good to know there's someone here who wants to help.'

He smiled.

'I'm so glad you said that.'

He paused.

'May I make another suggestion?'

'Of course.'

'You should be an actress, you know.'

'Thanks, but that's not for me.'

'I'm not being flippant. They need actresses for propaganda films. You'd be making a real contribution to the war effort.'

She wrinkled her nose.

'Well, if you change your mind, let me know and, if there's ever anything you need, anything I can do, you only have to ask.'

Remembering the soft centred old fellow's kindness helped make up her mind. By the time she turned into her parents' road, she'd reached a decision. It was time to face the music. She'd tell Mummy first. Heaven knows what Daddy would say. Brandon, why did you leave me in this mess?

She knew why and knew it was her fault. He'd survived until she'd come back into his life, until he'd been distracted by thoughts of her and their forthcoming wedding. That was why he'd been shot down. She'd as good as killed him herself. More than anything, she needed to atone by carrying on the fight for which he had died. Now, she'd never get the chance.

Her daily walk always took the same route, down Market Street, along Park Street and round the corner as far as Blenheim Town Gate where she stood for several minutes looking up the drive that led to the Palace. Anyone standing next to her would have seen an empty drive stretching before them. Mary saw a green Jaguar SS roaring up the drive with a lone driver. Moments later the same car would drive back down again, this time with someone in the passenger seat. The driver was a young man in the uniform of an RAF pilot, the young woman in the uniform of the Women's Auxiliary Air Force. They were happy and laughing as the road stretched out before them. But, as they grew nearer the gates, a change occurred. One minute, there were two of them then, only one. One minute, the pilot was driving then, the woman was at the wheel and on her own.

Every day, Mary repeated this ritual, hoping, every day, the outcome would be different. Afterwards, she would retrace her steps until she reached her parents' home, her home. Today, as usual, she walked up the gravel path that led round the side of the house to the gabled back door. As usual, her mother was in the kitchen and smiled at her.

'Nice walk? You look tired.'

'Not tired, just a little tearful.'

She saw the anxious look on her mother's face.

'Don't worry, I'll be fine. I'm tougher than you think. I'll get by.'

'Will you? You've changed. I know you see yourself as a battle-hardened service woman, a better person than when you left home. I see a woman damaged by her experiences. The small kindnesses, the consideration for others that used to be such a feature of the old you, they've all but gone. Oh, I don't doubt you're more mature and more business-like but you're suppressing too much of your natural self. You complain that the people you meet in the street don't like to talk about Brandon but you've hardly mentioned him all the time you've been here.'

'I'm just keeping things under control, that's all. Someone has to, there's a war on. Thousands of women have suffered the loss I've suffered. We just have to carry on.'

When she turned away, her mother feared she'd lost her forever. Then Mary fell into her arms, sobbing helplessly. Holding her silently, she eased her onto a chair and knelt beside her, resting Mary's head on her shoulder.

'I can't seem to speak about it. I meet people in the village and they say nothing about him and I'm angry with them. But I don't say anything either. And, when I get back here, I still can't say anything. What's the matter with me?'

'You mustn't think like that. You've had a terrible experience and you've been waiting for the right time. Now it's here.'

'It was all so quick. Does that mean it was pointless or wrong? Am I being punished for loving him? I feel I should have died instead of Winifred. I keep wondering if I was trying to get myself killed when I planted those flags. I shouldn't have let Winifred help me. I'm a bad person.'

'You're nothing of the kind.' Her mother hugged her even closer. When she judged the moment to be right, she whispered, 'I have a little confession to make.' Mary looked at her wondering what she could mean.

'When I was nursing in France, a young man came in, badly wounded but terribly brave about it. I shouldn't have done it but I made a special fuss of him. I wasn't in love with him or anything like that, but I suppose I had a bit of a crush.'

She stood up, walked over to the sink and busied herself with washing the vegetables.

'Anyway, he died one night when I was off duty. I felt terrible, guilty because I hadn't been there. But what made it so much worse, I felt responsible for his death because I'd had a crush on him. I thought that, if I'd gone about my duties in a more professional, detached way, he would have lived. I felt so bad, I couldn't work properly and they sent me home.'

She pulled a chair up and sat beside her daughter.

'I think you feel the same way. That Brandon died because you weren't doing your job properly.'

She took her hands and held them to her cheeks.

'It's not true for you, just as it wasn't true for me.'

Mary wiped away her tears and looked tenderly at her mother.

'What happened?'

'When I'd recovered, I returned to my duties. I'd got it out of my system and I needed to go back.'

'But that's it, don't you see? I need to avenge his death. I want to kill Germans, but I can't, not now.'

When she'd returned home, it hadn't taken her mother long to realise the truth about her condition. It was time to say something. She opened her mouth to speak but was interrupted by a sharp rap on the door knocker.

'Who on earth can that be?'

Her mother went to the front window and saw a car, a black official looking Humber. Cautiously, she opened the door.

'Good morning. Does Miss Mary Ballantyne live here?'

The question came from the older of two men. Dressed in a city suit, he had the look of a provincial bank manager. The other man looked a good twenty years younger than his colleague and tough with it. Mary appeared from behind her mother.

'And you are?'

'We're from London. Would you mind coming with us please? We're instructed to take you to meet someone who thinks you can help the war effort.'

To emphasise that it was a rhetorical question, he started to usher her down the path.

'We'll have you back here by evening, I assure you.'

When she said, 'there must be some mistake,' he said, 'please, not in front of the neighbours. We're on official business and request and require your complete discretion.'

As they led her out to the car, she heard her mother saying, 'we'll continue this conversation this evening.'

Glad of the short stay of execution, she climbed into the back of the Humber.

After a drive, in complete silence, she was deposited outside a building by St James's Park tube station. The well-dressed man wound down his window and smiled for the first time.

'If you'd be so kind as to go in there, they'll see to you.'

Before she could reply, the Humber drove off leaving her to read the only nameplate on the front door, 'Minimax Fire Extinguishers.'

The dingy hall offered no clues as to how or why the government should think she had vital information on the use of fire extinguishers. When she gave her name to a woman sitting at a desk in the far corner, she was directed to a room on the ground floor with bare, cream walls, and a Venetian blind, half closed. In the middle, a cheap wooden desk with a hard, wooden chair on one side and another upholstered but badly worn chair at the desk itself. Demand for fire extinguishers must have soared during wartime, couldn't they afford better furniture?She'd barely had time to sit down when the door opened and a man came in, clutching a thin file.

She recognised him at once and in the time it took for him to walk from the door to the desk, she worked out what this was all about. Those two men at the hotel really had been in films and the dear old Controller hadn't taken no for an answer. They wanted her to appear in a government propaganda film. She touched her hair quickly then smiled warmly.

Fawkes had been looking forward to the interview. It was an opportunity to show the childish girl that he was a master spy, not the film company buffoon she'd met a year earlier. He was also aware of the irony in the situation. A year earlier, he'd been irritated when she'd gone to the house with Heywood's briefcase, now her knowledge might save his career. Trying to ignore the powerful effect her looks were having on him, he got down to business.

'Thank you for coming in, Miss Ballantyne. You'll be wondering what this is all about.'

'I think I can guess.' Another warm smile.

Ignoring both the remark and the smile, Fawkes opened the slim file as if it contained useful information rather than the single sheet of paper staring up at him. It gave him time to digest the change in her.

The looks were still there but the hair wasn't so glossy and were those lines he detected around her eyes? Was it possible she was no longer the laughing child of last year? Then she smiled foolishly and patted her hair, removing his doubts. He looked at her in silence.

She looked at him in eager anticipation.

'You're not doing anything at the moment, not in employment, I mean.'

Was there a hint of recrimination in his voice? If she told him the truth, she'd have to admit she was pregnant and that would be that.

'I'm thinking of joining the Land Army but I can delay that if necessary. I don't have any acting experience but I'm sure I could improvise and I have a good memory so I'll be able to remember my lines. I'll do anything to help the war effort.'

A puzzled Fawkes stuck to the script and pressed on. It shouldn't take long. All he needed was an address and she'd be in a car on her way back to Woodstock.

'The thing is, we think you have some information that could be of use to us. First, though, I need you to sign this.'

He extracted the solitary sheet of paper from the file. Thinking it was a strange way to conduct an audition, she nevertheless took the sheet and the proffered pen and dashed off her signature.

'Don't you want to know what it is you've just signed?'

'Is it important? I assume it's something to do with the film.'

'It's the Official Secrets Act. It requires you not to reveal anything you hear or see today.' He paused. 'On pain of imprisonment or possibly death.'

His voice trailed off and neither of them spoke as he realised she had misunderstood the nature of the interview and she realised that, whatever this meeting was about, it wasn't an audition. There was no film and he wasn't in the film industry. Juliette had been right all along. Was the Controller in on it too? How else could they have found her? Was there *anyone* she could trust? She put the pen down and stood up.

'I'd like to go now please.'

He held up his hands with his palms towards her.

'Miss Ballantyne, this is entirely my fault. I should have explained at the beginning what I really do and why you are here.'

'Yes, you should.'

She remained standing.

'The film making was a deception, a very necessary one, to disguise the work my late colleague and I were doing last year.'

'So who are you?'

He gestured with his hand for her to sit down. She didn't.

'I work for a very secret part of the government. What I need from you is your memory of the trip you made last year to La Dame Brave. Do you remember it?'

Remember it? How could she forget? Her mind was transported from this dingy office back to that unforgettable day, the drive in Brandon's car, the walk along the narrow winding lanes. Without thinking, she stroked her stomach and nodded.

'You remember my colleague who went off for a meeting?'

'Of course I do. He seemed rather sweet but we were told he was some sort of gangster. He killed three men, didn't he? Perhaps because I was rather immature at the time, he and the other man were a huge embarrassment to me. There's nothing worse than staying in a foreign hotel with a couple like that. Even the people I was on holiday with were laughing at them.'

She knew perfectly well the man sitting opposite was the "other man" and he'd already told her he was a secret agent. But she needed to express her anger, anger that he hadn't come clean from the start, anger with herself for jumping to the wrong conclusion. Delivering the insult made her feel better.

She sat down.

Fawkes didn't mind the insult directed at him but bristled at the slur on his old friend. He said softly, 'I can assure you he was a brave man who died in the service of his country. The men he killed and who killed him, were German agents.'

'I'm sorry, I had no idea.'

Fawkes softened his tone.

'Of course not, the whole idea was to create the impression we were rather stupid Englishmen from a film company. Clearly we succeeded.'

'I remembered you immediately because everyone laughed at you the most. Remind me, which one were you, Heywood or Fawkes?'

'I'm Fawkes, the one who survived, I'm ashamed to say.'

Anxious to make amends, Mary softened her tone.

'Well I'm glad one of you did. And I'm impressed to hear it was all a cover for your work. You were very convincing.'

'Convincingly stupid, you mean.'

She laughed nervously. 'Well, yes, I suppose I do. But that's obviously your job.'

Fawkes tried to make his next question sound casual but his career was on the line. He spoke slowly, to delay the moment of truth.

'You took a briefcase to my colleague. Do you think you'd remember which house you went to?'

She relaxed. They just wanted information, an address, that was all. Now she knew what it was all about, she looked at him more closely. Undeniably good looking but with a look of permanent sadness on his face. He'd hidden that well in France but she wondered if there was a story behind that face.

'It was one of a group of houses inside a sort of courtyard.'

'We need a bit more than that, I'm afraid.'

'The houses were obviously for living in but they looked as if people also did some sort of work in them. There was a symbol over the door. I can't quite remember what it was.'

She paused.

'But I'd recognise it if I saw it again. It was rather unusual.'

She smiled, then realising what she'd just said, her mouth dropped open and her breathing turned shallower. She could feel the fear as it spread like liquid through her veins. He sensed it too. She obviously thought he was trying to recruit her. Nothing was further from his mind. An immature girl was the last person he wanted around him on a mission on which his future depended.

When C had offered him the opportunity to get back into the game, he'd been furious with himself for blurting out that he didn't know the address. He should have kept his mouth shut and used his initiative once he was in the village. If he sent her on her way and pretended she'd given him the address, he could still do that. But he'd have to be quick about it.

'Please don't worry, we just wanted your help with the address, that's all. I'll tell them upstairs you don't remember enough about it. Thank you for your time, I'm sure we can make use of the information you've given us. I'll arrange a car to take you back.'

She couldn't decide if she was relieved or irritated. The idea of being sent into danger with her unborn child terrified her. But she'd thought she'd never get a chance to avenge Brandon, now the opportunity to do so was being stolen from her.

Fawkes was wondering why she wouldn't move when the door opened and C walked in, smiling broadly, his hand outstretched.

'Good morning Miss Ballantyne, I'm a colleague of Freddie's. I hope he's been looking after you. Has he explained our little dilemma?'

Chapter 38

THE THREE OF them sat down. One out of her depth, perplexed by this sudden turn of events; one furious that his boss had been listening in to the conversation; one exuding urbane charm as he opened a file with several pages in it, pages which Fawkes had never seen.

'It says here you were blown up by a bomb on the RAF station where you were serving. Have you fully recovered?'

'Yes, completely, thank you. Unfortunately, my companion was killed but I escaped rather lightly.'

'I'm sorry to hear about your companion but delighted you survived. You were planting flags to show the pilots the unexploded bombs. Surely that wasn't your job, was it?'

'Somebody had to do it, the fighters were due back any minute. They risk their lives in the air and shouldn't have to risk them coming in to land. I just feel guilty it was I who survived and my friend who was killed.'

'Your friend got a posthumous medal but you got nothing. Does that upset you?'

'It was the least she deserved, I was happy to survive. I was only doing my duty.'

C stood up and walked round the room to give the impression he was trying to make his mind up, even though that moment had long passed. His prey sat motionless in her chair while Fawkes struggled to conceal his surprise at what he was hearing and his anger that C had deliberately concealed this information from him. Clearly, the questions had been asked to brief him about the true nature of the woman he had tried to hustle out of the building.

C turned and smiled at Mary.

'I'll get straight to the point. You've already done your fair share for the war effort, would you be willing to do more than your fair share? You see, we have a job for you, in fact, we need your help rather badly.'

C's performance had given Mary time to sort out a list of her priorities. In the comfort and security of Woodstock, it had been easy to believe that top of that list was the need to seize any opportunity to avenge the father of her unborn child. Faced with a real opportunity to do just that, the words "unborn child" pushed themselves forward. How could she possibly put her child at risk? She needed to know more.

'I'll do anything to help the war effort but could I possibly know what this is about?'

'Last year, Fawkes's late colleague collected some valuable documents from the house but we believe his contact didn't give him everything. We think he was planning to ask for more money and that those documents are still there.'

He gave her a searching look.

'We need those documents.'

Mary saw a brief flicker of alarm, or was it disgust, on Fawkes' face. Then it was gone. Not used to the world she was being drawn into, she paid no attention to it as C continued.

'I'm sure Freddie here has explained the situation but, knowing him for the gentleman he is, I suspect he hasn't told you the full story so you can leave without feeling guilty about letting your country down.'

C paused, leaving her to fill the silence that followed "letting your country down." Fawkes also said nothing but for a quite different reason. This mission wasn't just his route back into favour, it was his last chance. She might be a lot more courageous than he'd imagined but she was still an amateur. Was C seriously thinking he should take her with him? And lying to her to persuade her?

Mary knew she should come clean and tell them of her condition but, she was torn between fear and exhilaration. But if they knew about her WAAF service, they must know she'd been discharged because of her 'condition.' She faced the problem head on.

'How did you know I was in the WAAFs?'

'I know a young lady, an actress.'

I bet you do, thought Fawkes.

'She knows a fighter pilot at Biggin Hill and he spoke highly of you. We've asked for your service record, of course, but, knowing the RAF and the strain they are under at the moment, it'll be quite a while before it reaches us. Obviously, if there's anything you want to tell us.'

She knew what she had to do. End this now. Tell them you're pregnant. Get out of here. If they won't drive you back to Woodstock, catch a train to Oxford. Whatever it takes. Just go home. Your baby is your priority, nothing else is half as important. It was now or never. Get out while you can.

Then her mind wandered to those last days with Brandon when she realised how frightened he really was and how bravely he'd overcome that fear. She thought of smiling, motherly Winifred. Above all, she thought of the young life she was nurturing inside her and felt a burning hatred for the men who had robbed that life of a father. She'd been longing for some way to take her own personal revenge for the deaths of her husband and a sweet little woman who should never have worn a uniform in the first place.

But she'd never dreamt of this.

Hardly realising what she was doing, she blurted out the words.

'No, nothing,'

C went over to the window again, this time to conceal his pleasure. Everything had depended on her being able to identify the house. If she'd said no, he faced possible ruin. He'd given her the chance to take the obvious way out and she'd rejected it. He was home and dry and his conscience, such as it was, was clear. He turned and gave her an encouraging smile, she smiled back.

'I'd like to help but I'm worried that you're placing too much reliance on my memory and I'll let you all down.'

Her eyes followed C as he wandered across to the window. After peering briefly through the blind, he nodded to Fawkes as if to say, 'over to you.' Reluctantly but skilfully, he obeyed.

'The thing is, Miss Ballantyne, we need to get back into that house and you're the only one who can identify it.'

She looked from one man to the other. One last chance to climb into the car waiting outside to take her home. Just three words, 'I am pregnant' and she and her unborn child could be safe inside it. Then she thought of the note Brandon had left her. *Don't lose hope and don't do anything dangerous in the meantime.*

Do as he said or do as he did? Her fear didn't lessen but it was accompanied by a surge of adrenalin.

'I want to help, it's my duty. Everyone understands that nowadays.'

C smiled broadly.

'You have no idea how important you are to this mission or how much I admire your courage and dedication. Now, if you don't mind, I'll leave you in Freddie's capable hands. I'll see you when you return from France.'

When he was gone, Fawkes asked her gently.

'May I ask why?'

'I lost someone in the Battle of Britain, someone who understood what we were fighting for better than I did. I'll be doing this for him.' Once more, she stroked her tummy. 'But I think we should get on with it before I change my mind. What happens next?'

'You'll be prepared for the mission, given clothes, identity papers, everything necessary to pass you off as a native. All being well, we'll leave immediately. I'm afraid you won't be able to tell anyone you're going, in fact, you won't be let out of our sight until this is over.'

'My parents will want to know where I am.'

'We'll come up with a suitable story. They won't be worried.'

'I should have realised you were involved in something like this when we were in the village.'

'How come?'

'I overheard you talking to your colleague in the back of the café. You were a different person, almost normal.'

'You flatter me.'

They both laughed, easing the tension, for a brief moment.

'You don't have to do this, you know.'

'No, I want to. I have a score to settle and I intend to settle it.'

So do I, thought Fawkes but he kept the thought to himself.

He escorted her to a fitting room for her French clothes, then returned to the interview room. He'd hardly had time to gather his papers when C stormed in. The charm he'd displayed to Mary was no longer in evidence.

'Just what the hell did you think you were doing?'

'I'm not sure I understand, sir.'

'Stop pissing me about Fawkes, you know perfectly well what I mean. You were about to let that woman go until I stepped in. What's your problem?'

'I've met this girl under more normal circumstances, you haven't.'

'Oh come on, her behaviour at Biggin Hill shows she's good under pressure, both in her job as a plotter and in the incident with the unexploded bombs. Admit it, if we were recruiting someone you'd never met who had had her experiences, you'd have been all for her.'

'Yes, but I have met her. I know what she's really like. She's a silly little thing, head in the clouds. And she's been blown up by a bomb. Thanks for not telling me about that, by the way. I take it the bit about not having her service file was a lie.'

C ignored Fawkes's allegation.

'You can see the bomb hasn't affected her. Not a scratch on her.'

'On the outside, but what about in her head? Being blown up is no small matter. How do we know she won't fall apart if there's any trouble? Three things worry me.'

'And they are?'

'As I said, I saw a lot of her at the hotel. She's a flibbertigibbet, not right for this sort of thing at all. Secondly, she sabotaged last year's mission by leading the Germans to the house simply to be alone with some American playboy she fancied. That's why she won't necessarily be able to identify the house. She was too busy making eyes at him.'

'And the third thing?'

'She wants revenge. What happens when she realises she's not going to get it, that this mission isn't about attacking the enemy, it's about cooperating with them? By blackmailing her into going with all this talk of not letting people down, you've put us all at risk.'

'We've all been at risk, ever since this war started. What you'll be doing down there is intended to decrease that risk for millions of people. The risk to you, Durand and her is minimal, Canaris will see to that. But only if you go to the right house. It'll all come back to her when she's there.'

He stood up to make his final threat.

'Look, if you think you're not up to this mission, you can always go back to the RAF. In fact, I'm not sure I need you now. She and Durand can deliver the letter.'

'Is Durand reliable? If our entire network was rolled up after Venlo, how come he's still there?

'He's a money man.'

'Meaning?'

'He was never on our list of agents. No doubt a fair bit of what we send him for onward transfer is siphoned off into his own account but that helps to keep him on side.'

'You mean it's not in his financial interest to betray us. But he could carry out his work for us and be getting orders from the Abwehr at the same time.'

'He could be, but since it's the head of the Abwehr you're

going to see, it would almost assist matters if he was working for both sides.'

'That's hardly reassuring.'

'Do you want the job or don't you? The young lady can go on her own if necessary.'

The alarm on his underling's face told C the threat had worked. He sat down and softened his tone.

'I wasn't expecting Canaris to demand a letter from the PM but he has and we have to go along with him. He may not deliver on his promises but we have to try, for everyone's sake. You do see that, don't you?'

What Fawkes saw was that his return to the fold depended on him going along with C's plan. His resistance evaporated.

'I'm happy to play my part, sir but, if my experience at Trent Park is anything to go by, we're wasting our time. The officers I listened to were divided by their attitude to Hitler. Some were fanatical Nazis, some thought he was a disaster but none of them, not a single one, talked of taking any action. An oath is sacred to them and they'd all sworn an oath to Hitler. Canaris can plot all he likes and I'm not saying we shouldn't encourage him but I doubt he'll get anywhere unless someone kills Hitler.'

C stood up.

'You may be right, but we've got to try. I've arranged for a submarine from the Canadian Navy to take the pair of you. The Captain has experience of this sort of drop. God knows where we'd be without the Canadians.'

Fawkes recognised his cue and stood up to leave.

'She was telling me what a buffoon she thought I was last year. I was thinking what a shallow thing she was for not doing anything for the war effort.'

'She's proved you wrong. Now's your chance to prove her wrong. I must say, she's a good-looking girl.'

He could have added, 'And she doesn't work for us so she's completely deniable. In fact, she's the icing on the cake.'

Wisely, he refrained.

Chapter 39

MARY WAS DRIVEN down to Portsmouth in a car C had made a great show of ordering while telling Fawkes to make his own way there. It served a dual purpose, keeping them apart until it was too late for Fawkes to persuade Mary to change her mind and giving him another little hint that he wasn't so necessary now.

C needn't have worried. Fawkes had come to a decision. It was time to break the habit of a lifetime and become a team player. Not because he was a team player but because, on the journey down to Portsmouth, he'd realised that she could be useful to him. She would be required to make a report when they returned and what she said about him could make or break him. He'd use the outward journey not only to be friendly and charming, two words not normally in his vocabulary, but also to draw her out, discover her strengths and weaknesses. He prided himself on his ability to draw information out of other people without giving anything away about himself. Friendly and charming. He had it all worked out.

As she stepped onto the quay, Mary's nostrils were assailed by the smell of fuel oil vying with the salty tang of the sea. The atmosphere in the naval base was in sharp contrast to her RAF station. Everything was just that bit tighter here, that bit more formal. She made her way up the gangplank and was taken down below where the Captain greeted her with a salute and a handshake.

'We'll be leaving within the hour. The bosun will show you to your quarters. They're a little cramped, I'm afraid.'

He wasn't exaggerating. Large on the outside, the sub was tiny inside. She stumbled along the gangway, past narrow bunks separated by thin curtains on either side, pipes and valves everywhere. At the far end, the Officers' wardroom was just big enough to hold a dining table and chairs, with barely enough room to stand up. Slumping into a chair, she surveyed the sight with dismay before rushing to the Heads, a term she had made sure to learn, to throw up. When she returned, a familiar voice greeted her.

'It's not the Ritz but we won't be here long.'

Fawkes stood there, smiling and holding, of all things, a violin case. She gave him an enquiring look. He didn't enlighten her. Placing it on the table he sat down opposite her and prepared to do a bit of team building.

Things didn't start well. In London, he'd made it clear he didn't want her. She wasted no time in tackling the problem head on.

'Look, I know you don't want me here. If it's any consolation, I don't want me here either but I am, so we may as well try to get along.'

He held up his hands to placate her.

'Forget everything I said in London. A decision has been taken and it's my job to implement it. You're part of the team now.'

If he thought that would satisfy her, he was wrong.

'That's hardly reassuring. All you're saying is you'll go along with your boss's decision even though you think I'm a liability.'

'You think I'm not being fair to you but you're hardly being fair to me either. I knew nothing of your WAAF service and your bravery. All I had to go on was the impulsive young girl I'd met at the hotel. Normally I'm briefed about these things in advance.'

'But not this time?'

'It was a rush job.' He paused. 'But that's no excuse and I'm sorry.'

He gave her a rueful smile.

She'd steeled herself for a confrontation and he'd disarmed

her. It was her turn to give him a smile. He could almost hear the ice cracking as she continued.

'I'm sorry if I've misjudged you. I'd assumed you'd carry out this whole mission while making it clear I wasn't wanted.'

'Entirely my fault. I should have treated you with more respect.'

'Don't worry, I'm battle hardened.'

'Rather more than me, it seems. I was against taking you because I saw you as an amateur. I took an amateur to the hotel last year and he ended up dead.'

'I thought Heywood worked with you.'

'Yes, but only as a desk man. He shouldn't have been there.'

She gave him the softest of smiles.

'Well, we'll just have to do better this time.'

Just as his plan was getting underway, the Captain summoned Fawkes to his cabin to discuss the journey, leaving Mary alone as they cast off. No turning back now. The noise from the engines was deafening, the heat and the smell of diesel overwhelming. She'd been rushed off her feet and had joined the mission in an adrenalin fuelled desire to avenge Brandon but as the sub sank below the waves, Mary's spirits sank with it. All she could think about was the child inside her. What on earth had she been thinking? With Fawkes out of sight, her face crumpled and she sobbed.

When he returned, there was no sign of her, just the sound of someone throwing up. When Mary emerging once more from the Heads, he asked the obvious question.

'Sea sick?'

'I'll get used to it, don't worry.'

'You've changed.'

She laughed.

'So much has happened. I've had to grow up whether I wanted to or not.'

She gave him a long, inquisitive look.

'Seems to me I'm not the only one. You're different now

you're on the sub. And I don't mean different from the buffoon you played last year. You seem more relaxed now you're out of the office. Is it because you're away from that awful man?'

His thoughts drifted back to the beach in Fort Sarrasin and Heywood telling him the same thing. He realised Mary was waiting for a reply.

'Sorry, I was thinking of Heywood. What you said reminded me of a conversation with him when he said much the same thing.'

He shifted in his chair. He'd been sitting with his arms crossed, now he unfolded them.

'I've been kept off operations since La Dame Brave, cast aside as it were. I thought my career was over and I was desperate to get back. Six is a rather snobbish organisation but though I've never been "one of us," I've always loved the work. Being here, right now, means everything to me.'

He paused.

'In spite of my reservations.'

'Reservations?'

'That awful man, as you put it, has made it clear this operation is off the books, so secret, no one knows anything about it. If it goes well, my future should be assured. If not, I'm eminently deniable. I don't like it but it's my only way back in.'

'Sounds to me you're so desperate to re-join the fold, you'll do anything they ask. What have you lured me into?'

Seeing her words strike home, she pressed home her advantage.

'When your boss was briefing me, I saw a look of disgust on your face. He was lying, wasn't he. What's this mission really about?'

Her perceptiveness caught him off guard. She could almost see his brain ticking over as he considered how much to tell her. He decided to stick to the golden rule that C had broken when briefing him.

'I have to meet someone and give him something. The

meeting has to take place in the house.'

'Well, that clears that up. Now I'm fully informed, I won't need to worry.'

Seeing the look of disappointment on her face and knowing he had to keep her onside, he reached for her hand.

'I'm trying to protect you, the less you know, the better.'

It didn't take a mind-reader to see she wasn't convinced.

'I had the same problem last year with Durand. Like you, he resented my reluctance to tell him anything but it was for his own good. One of the basic rules of my kind of work is never tell anyone anything they don't need to know.'

'Durand?'

'He's our man down there.'

'How many more people in that hotel weren't what they appeared to be?'

'That's the lot. Don't worry, you'll be perfectly safe.'

'That's all very well but, the last time we were here, your colleague was killed and we weren't even at war.'

'That was the SD, the intelligence section of the SS, real bastards. They aren't allowed into France now. German military intelligence is in control.'

'And they're perfect gentlemen, I suppose.'

Giving him a sympathetic smile, she stood up and tried to walk around in the confined space. Realising the effort was futile, she sat down again.

'How can you risk your life like this when you have such a low opinion of your bosses?'

'A question I keep asking myself and always get the same answer.'

She gave him a questioning look as she waited for him to continue.

'It's my job, it's all I know. They're not completely useless, you know. They're good at clever projects, not so good at the spade work. Fortunately, the Germans aren't either. The people who are really good are the Soviets but my people are blind to the threat and so, I think, are the Germans.'

'Sounds to me you're someone who takes pride in being a bit awkward.'

The conversation wasn't going the way he'd intended. Seeing his crestfallen look, she sought to make amends.

'I'm sorry, that was unkind. It's just that you do seem to be at odds with your bosses rather a lot. Would you like to tell me about it?'

He sighed.

'Where to begin?'

'Try the beginning.'

'My mother was German.'

Expecting her to focus on the German bit, he was surprised to hear her say, 'Was?'

'Everything was fine till the war broke out in '14. Until then, no one thought twice about me having a foreign mother and neither did I. If anything, I felt a little superior to my friends. My mother,' he stopped as her face appeared before his eyes, 'my mother was lovely, I adored her but, when war broke out everything changed. Overnight, I became the boy with the kraut mother and went from loving her to resenting her for putting me in such a embarrassing position. Then my father, an officer in the Navy, was killed at Jutland. I'm sure the Navy meant well but they deemed it inappropriate to leave me in the care of a kraut so they sent me to Naval College. She was devastated. I'd deserted her in her hour of need, left on her own in a foreign country. I failed completely to appreciate what she was going through.'

He paused and held her gaze.

'I can't forgive myself for that.'

Mary watched his face come alive with the pain of his memories. It was the first time she'd seen real emotion on his face and it took her by surprise. But he still hadn't come to 'was.'

'So, your poor mother lost her husband and son, one after the other. I remember now, you told Juliette she died of cancer. How sad.'

For several moments, he stared down at the table and said nothing. He'd planned to do some team building, not soul-baring. He should stop but he couldn't. He needed this conversation. When he lifted his head, he held her gaze.

'I lied. She didn't die of cancer. She hanged herself. She'd lost everything, including me and had nothing left to live for.'

'And you had no idea, no warning signs?'

'If there were, I was too self-absorbed to notice them. Her letters were always full of good cheer and were only concerned with my well-being, not hers. The Navy took complete control of me. When they told me what had happened, I was consumed with guilt.'

Mary gasped and reached for his hand.

'That's awful. You'd lost your father and your mother, one after the other. How did you survive?'

'The usual way, work. I left Naval College with top honours and, by the age of thirty, I was a First Lieutenant but, all the time, I knew I had failed the only woman who meant anything to me. Then it all went wrong. I was put on an obviously trumped up charge and was dismissed from the service. Immediately afterwards, I was approached by the SIS. Back then, my being half German was seen as an asset, the opposite of the Navy's attitude, and I felt immense gratitude to them for rescuing me.'

'Do you ever kill people?'

'Only in self-defence. I never set out to kill. It draws attention to me which is the opposite of what I want.'

'Does it worry you? That you might have to do that?'

'No, simply because the other person is trying to kill me.'

'You say "person," does that mean women as well as men?'

'If necessary, I would kill a woman but I never have. When I came back from France last year, I thought I'd have to but it wasn't necessary in the end.'

'But if need be, you would.'

'Yes.'

'Is any part of killing people a form of revenge for what

happened to your mother?'

'Of course not.'

'You look unsure.'

'Well, I've never thought about it before.'

'I'd understand. I want revenge for what happened to someone I loved.'

Her expression hardened briefly then softened again.

'Anyway, you were telling me your bosses used to like the fact that you're half German. Then what happened?'

'What happened was a man called Lestocq. When he joined, things changed. He had C's ear and started questioning my loyalties. The worst part is, he pretends it's my German blood that's the problem but I'm sure it's my constant reference to communist infiltration.'

'Why?'

'He's from the top drawer and I mean the very top. People like him don't owe their position in the world to anyone. It's theirs by right. He says I'm undermining morale, simply because he resents the suggestion that people like him could ever be attracted to communism. Not having to deal with him on this mission came as a great relief to me.'

'Might he have come?'

'He wanted to. Thankfully, C said no. I really couldn't have faced that.'

'Sounds to me like you've got a good old-fashioned inferiority complex. You need to stop feeling sorry for yourself and start looking out for number one. You are what you are. Don't change.'

'You're the second woman to tell me that in the last few days.'

She was surprised to feel a tinge of jealousy.

'Well, go on, who is this other woman?'

He experienced a little thrill at her need to know. Unskilled in the art of wooing, he was, nevertheless, wise enough not to play on it.

'Dear old Heywood's widow. The other day, she gave me a gentle talking to. I'm not sure she wasn't put up to it by C.'

Worried she was betraying Brandon, she changed the subject.

'What was your mother's name?'

'Ilse.'

'That's a lovely name. Perhaps one day, you'll have a daughter and you can call her Ilse.'

For a moment, she saw a look on his face, the look of a little boy lost. Then he recovered and tried to laugh it off.

'I doubt that. How can I court someone who doesn't know what I do for a living? I can't lie to her for a couple of years then tell her I'm not who I appear to be. Besides, I've been in this game so long, I've lost the art of wooing women. Or perhaps I never really possessed it. Either way, women can tell and they stay clear of me.'

'Are you sure you're not using your job as an excuse not to have emotions? Perhaps your dreadful experience with your mother has made you frightened to have feelings for someone because they only lead to loss.'

Knowing Fawkes would speak when he was ready, Mary didn't interrupt the long silence that followed.

'I worry I wasn't sufficiently loveable to….'

His voice trailed away. Now, she spoke.

'To make her want to go on living? And if your own mother couldn't love you enough, how could any other woman?'

She gave him a reassuring smile.

'You've got it all wrong. I think it was precisely because she loved you so much and was so sure she would never see you again. That's what made her life not worth living.'

Sensing she had given him enough to think about, she stood up.

'Well, let's hope this mission is a success and that awful man C appreciates what you've done for him. In the meantime, I need some sleep.'

Things had not gone to plan. She'd been the one doing the team building, the one drawing him out while telling him next to nothing about herself. On top of that, he knew he should have regretted being so indiscreet, but he didn't.

Her departure forced him to turn his mind back to the mission and the next thing to worry about. Durand would be waiting for them at the hotel. C was confident he hadn't been turned but was that confidence justified?

Apart from one trip to the conning tower when the vessel surfaced to re-charge its batteries, the two of them stayed below until they were woken at one o'clock one morning and told to prepare to disembark. When Mary reached the conning tower, she found Fawkes, violin case in hand.

After the stale air and relentless heat of the sub, the light breeze acted like a drug to Mary's system, sharpening her mind for what lay ahead. For several minutes, nothing happened then a dinghy slid silently out of the darkness. Nerves tightened her stomach so much, she feared she was damaging her child. She'd hated being in the sub but hated leaving it more. Now, they really were on a mission and the danger was all around. Struggling down the rope ladder, she flopped into the dinghy and drew her knees to her chest. The full moon allowed her to catch a glimpse of the familiar sight of the French coast and the island. Feeling the bile rising in her gullet, she swallowed constantly to keep it down.

The sailor in the dinghy let go of the rope ladder and they moved away, to a whispered 'good luck' from the Captain and an 'I'll look after you' from Fawkes. The sailor, huge and dressed from head to foot in black, put a finger to lips obscured by a balaclava. He doesn't want to reveal his face so I can't identify him under interrogation, she thought. I'd do the same. She noticed him studying her intently. Then he did something quite unexpected. He pulled the balaclava off to reveal his face.

'Well, well, well. If it isn't young Mary. I should have brought some scotch with me.'

For a brief moment, she was back on the terrace drinking whisky with a man who'd said he was going to join the RAF and a man who'd sworn to do anything to fight the boches.

'If I'd known it would be you, Yann, I'd have brought you a bottle.'

'I wonder what happened to that young American.'

'He died in his Spitfire, doing what he always said he would do.'

Fawkes saw the anguish on her face. So this was the man she'd been talking about, the American with the fancy car. He felt more than a tug of jealousy as the two of them shared their private memories.

'I'm sorry to hear that,' said Yann. 'He was a good man. We must avenge him.' He paused. 'One way or another.'

As they drew near the shore, Mary could see nothing but coils of barbed wire preventing a landing. Then Yann turned the small craft towards a narrow gap free of wire, the sewage outlet on the edge of the town. After lowering the sails, he handed a cloth covered oar to Fawkes and the two men paddled gently up the inlet until they could scramble onto dry land. Even in the dead of night, the cicadas maintained their relentless chorus as they were led along an alleyway behind the beachfront shops then up a path and into the gardens at the back of the hotel. Yann ushered them into the covered area at the back of the hotel and with a silent wave, disappeared into the night.

As part of his role in transmitting money for MI6, Durand was required to send and receive messages on a wireless set which he kept on the roof. He'd assumed that once he'd found Mary's address and made the dangerous journey back from Paris, no more would be required of him. When he received a message giving him further instructions, he felt these went far beyond his duties and seriously considered resigning.

Unfortunately, C knew him too well. In addition to his long-term dalliance with one particular female guest, he had one further vulnerability. His role as the conduit for money in exchange for information between MI6 and Szymańska was highly lucrative and the longer the war continued, the more he stood to make. C, aware that he was skimming from each transfer, was confident that, however much Durand disliked this instruction, he would obey it.

The possession of a wireless set, however, put him constantly at risk and, once he knew two SIS agents were arriving, he decided to ignore his instruction to tune in every night at midnight and not to use it until the mission was over. It was a sensible decision. An unexpected detector van mooching around the hotel at the wrong time would be a disaster for both him and his visitors.

Told to expect two visitors, he'd assumed they'd both be men, like last time. The first thing he noticed as the two figures crept across the grass was that one of them was a woman. Since his return from Paris, he'd developed a strong feeling of resentment towards Mary, holding her responsible for Juliette's death. If she hadn't flirted endlessly with that American playboy, she wouldn't have gone to the house, finding her wouldn't have been necessary and Juliette would still be alive. Having assumed her sole contribution would be to give the SIS the information they needed, as the shadowy pair move closer to the back of the hotel, he was shocked to see the woman was Mary herself. And worse was to come. The man was none other than the fellow who'd made such a mess of things a year ago. He sighed, crept down the stairs and entered the covered area.

His attitude changed as soon as he saw Mary, forlorn, vulnerable and just as much a victim of this bloody war as he was. He walked over and clutched her in a warm embrace.

'Welcome back', he whispered. 'You must be tired.'

His attitude to Fawkes, however, did not change.

'After all the trouble you caused last time, I assumed they'd send someone else.'

Fawkes knew nothing of Juliette's fate and thought his words were harsh and unjustified particularly as Heywood had given his life in the line of duty. There was, of course, another explanation but if Durand really had been turned, he would surely have gone out of his way to seem friendly. He decided to reserve judgement.

In the safety of his office, Durand continued to ignore him, addressing his words to Mary.

'Why are you of all people here?'

'I have to identify a house,' said Mary. 'That's all I know.'

'Join the club. I've worked for the British for years but they never tell me a damn thing either. All I know is we're going back to La Dame Brave. Quite why we're doing so is something no one has seen fit to tell me.'

Mary touched his arm and took a leaf out of Fawkes's book.

'It's probably better that way. When do we leave and how will we avoid being discovered? Aren't there roadside checks of cars?'

My goodness, she's a fast learner, thought Fawkes.

'We'll drive up there tomorrow. There aren't too many roadside checks. If we meet one, let me deal with it, they all know me.'

As he led them out to the unlit foyer, Mary asked Durand if he had any guests at all and was surprised to be told the hotel was full.

'So it's business as usual. It's quite different from the world I've just left.'

She tried not to sound too accusing.

'Nothing could be further from the truth. Most of the people staying here are Jewish. They're not on holiday, they're here because it's safe. Some French gentiles are helping us so we've got a well organised network of boarding houses, even private homes that are housing Jews who've fled from other parts of France.' His face came alive with pride as he spoke. 'And not just Jews. We've even got a few Italians.'

'Italians? What are they doing here?'

'They're anti-fascists. The Resistance has many foreigners in it, anti-fascists from Spain and Italy, even Vietnamese who were working in France and faced deportation to German labour camps. I expect you've been given a simple view of what's going on here. Good guys equals the French Resistance, bad guys equals the Germans. It's more complicated than that. This war has divided people as much on ideological lines as national ones. In the Marseilles region, the leader of the Resistance is a German and the leader of German Intelligence is a Frenchman.'

'So this place is a Mecca for all these different people,' said Mary. 'Perhaps Mecca isn't the right word.'

'Mecca will do fine. We Jews can't be fussy in these times. I'm lucky I live in the south. Further north, people are looking forward to deporting Jews to Germany.'

He gestured to the cheap prints that festooned the walls.

'You see these paintings?'

'I noticed there are a lot more than last time I was in here', said Fawkes. 'They look so much cheaper than that chrome framed one you used to have? Did you have to sell it?'

After a brief silence, Durand finally acknowledged Fawkes's presence.

'No, it's still here, but not obviously so. Behind each of these cheap paintings, lies a real work of art. The best place to hide them was behind other paintings, typical of the sort of rubbish you'd find in a hotel. Most of them are from German Jews but some are from Polish gentiles driven out of Poland. The paintings are probably worth more than the hotel itself.'

Mary stroked his arm.

'So you're not just lounging around in the sun waiting for the war to end.'

Durand smiled.

'I wish I could do more.'

He paused.

'I'll show you to your rooms. Get some sleep. Big day tomorrow.'

Chapter 40

UNDETERRED BY THE London rain, the motorcyclist overtook the car in front, swung across the car coming in the opposite direction and pulled up outside Broadway Buildings. The drivers of the two cars didn't hoot or even wave a fist. The motorbike was painted in khaki green no. 3 and the driver wore a leather jerkin over his uniform, leaving his sergeant's stripes plainly visible. Best not to hoot a man on official business. But they suspected he'd rather enjoyed cutting them up.

They were right. The despatch rider rode a special Triumph Tiger 100 which he'd collected himself from the Triumph factory in Coventry. It was fast because it needed to be. Every day, he made this trip, from Bletchley Park to Broadway Buildings with none of the usual canvas document bags hanging either side of the rear wheel. The documents he carried were always strapped inside his leather jerkin. Cutting up cars was a privilege that went with the job.

Pulling off his gauntlets, he strode inside to deliver the document bag, sealed and unopened. But not to the man at the desk in the entrance hall. Giving him a brief nod, he took the lift to the top floor and handed the bag to the secretary who sat in the outer office of her boss, the man known as C. Job done, the despatch rider returned to his beloved bike.

As she did every day, the secretary carried the sealed bag into C's office and placed it on his desk

'It's a thin one today. Less to worry about, I hope.'

She gazed softly at his strained face, watching it darken as he read the single sheet of paper that he'd withdrawn from the bag, his eyes working from top to bottom, three times.

'You need a rest. The PM asks too much of you.'

'Is the outer door shut?'

She nodded.

'Lock it.'

When she returned, she could contain herself no longer.

'What's happened? Is an invasion on the way?'

'If only it were that simple.'

He gestured to the chair opposite his desk. Before she'd even sat down, he started to tell her about the Fishing Club, Sir Baldwyn's approach and McKittrick. But not the blackmail. Conflicting thoughts ran through her head as she listened.

'You've kept this very quiet. Didn't you trust me?'

'It wasn't about trust, I wanted to protect you. If this goes wrong, they'll come for me and they'll have a go at you too. It was important that you knew nothing about it.'

'Peace would be a wonderful thing. It's a shame you can't do as he suggests.'

'But I have.'

Time to come clean about the blackmail. Then he told her where Fawkes was, who he'd gone with and why. Trying not to think of the benefit to her of his wife divorcing him, she concentrated on his well-being.

'So that's why you've looked so strained lately. Have you discussed this with anyone?'

'How could I? I was protecting you by not telling you and there wasn't anyone else I could tell.'

He handed her the newly delivered document.

'And now this.'

Once she'd got beyond 'MOST SECRET FOR YOUR EYES ONLY,' she learned that a radio intercept of a message sent from SS headquarters in Berlin revealed that no fewer than two teams had left for the south of France to track down a British agent, believed to be heading for La Dame Brave. Watching her puzzled look as she tried to make sense of it all, he gave her a rueful smile.

'This little French village seems to be rather popular at the moment.'

'How could they have known about this mission when no one here knew?'

'A good question but looking into that will be for another day. There's a Soviet mole somewhere but is it here on in Berlin?'

She looked thoughtful.

'Do they know our team is there to talk to Canaris?'

'Possibly. Often, it's not what's in the message that really matters but what's left out. It would be a real coup for the Soviets if the SS were to capture our team and Canaris conspiring to remove Hitler. Stalin thinks Hitler will honour his promise not to invade Russia so he wants him kept in power.'

'I'm afraid I'm not being much help.'

'On the contrary, your mere presence is helping me think straight.'

Emboldened by the compliment, she continued.

'It seems to me there are two issues here, your interests and the country's.'

'Correct. And if Fawkes had been able to carry out the mission without interference, those interests would have coincided. We can't afford this war. It's already bleeding us dry and it's hardly begun.'

'Is there nothing you can do?'

He turned to looked out of the window and across St James's Park. She could see he was trying to come to a decision. When he turned back, he shook his head.

'I can't put my career before the needs of the country.'

'When the PM learns of your involvement, what will happen to you?'

'Depends. I've made sure young Lestocq's as deep in this as I am. His father won't let him go to the gallows. That might save me too.'

'If he's so important, why did you send him on a mission?'

'What are you talking about? I haven't sent Lestocq on a mission.'

'The armourer mentioned it to me in the canteen. He was hoping I'd tell him where Lestocq was going.'

'The armourer?'

'He's taken a pistol. I assumed you knew.'

'That bastard.'

'Lestocq?'

'No, his father. He doesn't trust me so he's sent him down there to make sure Fawkes turns up. Probably been told to kill the team when they've done their job.'

He stood up and went over to the window. Sir Baldwyn's deceit energised him, even bringing a smile to his face.

'The team lands at 2am. Durand tunes in every night at midnight. We've plenty of time.'

'To do what?'

'To hell with Sir Baldwyn, I'm calling it off.'

Now the decision had been taken, C had no difficulty in convincing himself that he'd never really believed the promises of social promotion or been influenced by the crude blackmail threat. All along, his real motive had been to do the right thing for the country. Self-interest had never entered into it. That night, for the first time in months, he slept soundly.

When he arrived at the office the next morning, he greeted the doorman with a cheery wave and headed straight to the radio room. Two minutes later, the doorman watched as, ashen-faced, he emerged and rushed to the lift. Expecting confirmation that his message, *await further instructions before proceeding,* had been acknowledged, he'd watched the radio operator shake his head.

'What's happened?'

'The message to Durand never got through. He didn't log on as usual. Was it important?'

Chapter 41

SHE'D FORGOTTEN HOW hot the nights were. Exhausted, she flopped onto her bed, pulling off her clothes at intervals until she was naked. Bathed in sweat, she lay there, waiting for sleep to come, wondering what the day would bring.

The next thing she knew, a blinding light filled the room making her sit up with a start. She'd forgotten to draw the curtains and the sun was streaming in. Her sleep had been dreamless but the moment she awoke, the knot in her stomach returned, one thought filling her head. Would she still be alive this time tomorrow? She dressed carefully, as if for her execution.

Outside her bedroom door, she found a tray of croissants and coffee together with a little note, *Have your laundry ready by 9.30.*

At nine-thirty precisely, she walked through the door into the laundry area to find Durand and Fawkes standing by Durand's car. To her relief, they were talking amicably. Unknown to her, that was entirely due to her presence. Durand had planned to protest to the SIS team about being dragged into this type of operation, hoping they'd see him as a liability and leave him behind. Mary's presence changed all that. He felt he owed it to Juliette to protect her. It was what she would have wanted. To honour her name, he would drop the hostility and cooperate with the bloody Englishman.

But he told the Englishman none of this and Fawkes was all smiles as Mary climbed into the back of the sensible saloon. A week ago, he'd been in Trent House, bored to death. Now he was about to meet the head of the Abwehr. He had every reason to beam at Mary as she settled herself into the back. It looked like Durand was still on their side so the mission should be completed without difficulty. As long as everyone played their allotted role. As long as he called the shots. Seeing the happy couple, Mary smiled at Durand.

'What happened to your little two-seater?'

'Long gone, I'm afraid. After the war, perhaps the British will buy me one as a reward for services rendered. Mr Fawkes, you could mention it in your report.'

'If this mission succeeds, we'll show our gratitude in the usual way, old boy. You may be sure of that.'

'That's what I was afraid of.'

Mary laughed, trying to sound relaxed.

'What's the plan?'

Wanting to get the show on the road as quickly as possible, Fawkes tried to make it sound like a repeat of last year's outing.

'We're going to the house to meet a man called Canaris and give him a letter assuring him of our support. Then it's back here and onto the sub tonight.'

'What letter? Who is this Canaris?'

Surprised by the sharp tone of Mary's questions, Fawkes turned round and saw the determined look on her face, a quite different expression from the one she'd displayed on the sub. But he wasn't alarmed. She just needed reassuring. Time for some teamwork. He'd break the golden rule and give her a little background information.

'Admiral Canaris is the head of the Abwehr. That's the military intelligence I was telling you about. He's in control of the whole territory, so we'll be perfectly safe.'

Feeling pleased with his explanation, he gave her a reassuring smile.

'And the letter?'

'Don't worry about that. It's to assure him of our support, something to show his fellow conspirators.'

He turned to Durand.

'Let's get this car started.'

'No, hold on a moment.'

Mary leaned forward, her head between the two men.

'Who's the letter from?'

'Churchill, that's why this meeting is so important.'

He pulled the letter out of his inside pocket and, thinking it would satisfy her doubts, showed her the Downing Street crest. She reached forward and snatched it from his grasp.

'You mean he's been lying to us? All this talk about never surrendering and here he is selling out to a bunch of German Generals?'

Clearly, more reassurance was needed.

'Relax, it's a forgery, Churchill knows nothing about it.'

Having established a rapport on the sub he was confident Mary would accept what he'd said. No need to trouble her with the details. Feeling just a little less sympathetic towards her, he held his hand out for the letter's return.

She held on to it.

A very faint warning bell sounded in the back of his head. So faint, he paid no attention to it. Until she spoke again.

'You live in a world of your own, constantly play acting. Film executive one minute, master spy the next. You've forgotten what reality is. Well, I haven't. After all we've been through, the idea of making some sort of deal with these people will never be accepted by the British people. The Germans have lied to us at every turn. "Give us this and there'll be peace, give us that and there'll be peace. Oh no, hang on a second, we need this too." Can't you see that this letter is just an invitation to Hitler to eat us last? Right now, things are on a knife edge. If this letter is made public, morale will collapse and we'll lose the war. For God's sake use a bit of common sense.'

She was in full flow now.

'The man I knew could have gone home, avoided this war altogether, but he stayed, fought and died to stand up against fascism. And for what? To let your bastard of a boss do a deal with them?'

'Oh, come on, he's not such a bad chap.'

'For God's sake, he was ghastly. So manipulative.'

'Manipulative?'

'Well, he certainly had you wrapped around his little finger. One minute, you were trying to get rid of me, then he snaps his fingers and you're recruiting me. You'll do anything to get back into his good books.'

Thinking about that report Mary would have to make when they got back, Fawkes remained affable.

'He's not trying to change British policy, just add another arrow to our bow, an escape clause if you like. You were keen on this mission when we interviewed you, when you thought you were coming here to kill Germans. All those questions on the sub about me killing people, you just wanted to make sure I was the right man for the job. Now you know this isn't the sort of mission you were hoping for, surely you don't want to sabotage it?'

He smiled and reached for her hand. She pulled it away.

'You really don't get it because all you're interested in is your precious career. The East End is being bombed to blazes while the West End is untouched. Now, to add insult to injury, the people who live comfortably in the West End are proposing to sell the country out. If you want a revolution on your hands, you're going the right way about it. In fact, the revolution starts here. I don't mind you pledging our support for a coup but you're not giving him a forged letter from the one man the British people believe in. It'll be made public immediately. Surely you can see that.'

Fawkes still thought he could talk her round. Her outburst was understandable, she'd been through a lot. She just needed to calm down.

'I really think we should leave this sort of stuff to the experts and just do our job. The sooner we get this over with, the better.'

She couldn't read his mind but she could see the anger and

the pain written on his face. He'd been lovely on the sub and she knew how important the mission was to him. She felt awful for being so awkward and a large part of her wanted to back down but she couldn't betray Brandon and the other pilots. She turned to Durand.

'You've been very quiet M. Durand.'

'Given what we're about to do, I think you might start calling me Jean-Paul.'

He gave her a gentle smile.

'I can see both sides of the argument but the fact is, this is what we do, Mary. We're given a task and we carry it out. If every agent sat down and considered the merits of his instructions, we'd never get anything done.'

Durand had intervened at just the right moment. Fawkes nodded to him to show his pleasure. Durand looked away. Why does this bloody Englishman cause trouble everywhere he goes?

Mary sat back and, for a brief moment, Fawkes naively thought her silence indicated acquiescence. When she resumed, her words were addressed to Durand.

'Do you remember our dinner in that magical garden?'

He nodded.

'Do you remember what Brandon said about it being hard to get a man to understand something when his salary depends on his not understanding it?'

When Durand nodded again, she turned to Fawkes.

'Don't you think that's the situation we have here? This is wrong and you know it but you can't admit it because the price you think you'll have to pay is too high.'

The heat of the car was stultifying but they couldn't open the windows in case they were overheard. Beads of sweat formed on Fawkes's forehead, long beads ran down his back. Knowing he should have stuck with the information-free version of the mission he'd given her on the sub, he went on the attack.

'It's alright for you, you're only here to identify the house. When you return home, you'll go back to your normal life. This is my job. If we do what you want, when I return, I'll be fired. But it's not just about my job. We're already at war. Taking this letter to Canaris won't change that. But supposing it brings peace. What right have you to allow your anger at being deceived to overrule your duty to save lives by bringing this war to an early end?'

He had a point. Mary looked out of the window.

'Have you read the letter?'

'No.'

'Don't you think you should?'

'It's more than my job's worth. I have to deliver it unopened.'

'It's not your job we're talking about, it's the future of the country. You keep saying how much you despise your bosses but you leap at the chance to do their bidding. For God's sake think for yourself for a change. There's something not right about this and you know it.'

'No, I don't,' he lied.

'I'll make it easy for you. Either we read it or I won't identify the house.'

Without waiting for an answer, she slid her nail under the flap and along the top edge. The two men could only watch in silence as she extracted the letter and read it. Fawkes watched her eyes move along the lines and his career go up in smoke. When she'd finished, she looked at him.

'They must be mad.'

She held the letter out for him, then watched his face go white as he read it. In that moment, everything changed. He stopped fooling himself that Mary was the problem, stopped fooling himself that C had been offering him a way back.

The contents were nothing more than a surrender note, offering Germany some of Britain's colonies in Africa, the restoration of Edward VIII in return for peace, a guarantee that the City of London would remain the centre of world finance and an undertaking to give Germany a free hand in any war against the Soviets. It made no mention of Hitler's overthrow.

He turned round to face Mary. As he did so, she opened the

car door, ran over to a corner of the laundry area and threw up.

'That's a bit extreme,' said Fawkes.

'How could you bring someone in her condition on a mission like this?'

Fawkes stared at Durand.

'What do you mean?'

'She's pregnant for God's sake. Don't you know anything?'

'I was an only child,' was all Fawkes could come up with as he struggled to come to terms with the letter and now this. He'd had it all worked out, how the day would go, the return to London and a grateful C. He'd even pictured himself driving Mary back to her parents and arranging to stay in touch, quite with what end in mind, he hadn't yet thought out. Now this. Desperately wanting to stick to the plan, he watched her walk slowly back to the car while he struggled to follow the moral course, even though he now knew what it was.

'Why didn't you tell C you were pregnant? Even he couldn't have used you then.'

As he spoke, he remembered the thick file in C's possession, compared to the non-existent one in his. C had known all along.

'Would it have made any difference? Your boss was going to use me, come what may.'

'Over my dead body.'

'Almost certainly,' said Mary. 'It rather proves my point.'

'The father, where is he?'

'He died in his Spitfire. You both met him here last year, Brandon, the American who said he was going to fight but none of us believed him.'

Fawkes sat completely still, saying nothing, just staring through the windscreen. When he opened the car door and stepped out, his sudden move caught the other two by surprise. Mary whispered to Durand.

'What's he doing?'

'Hard to tell. What you said about Brandon seemed to have triggered something, as if he was jealous, but it can't be that trivial.'

'He's deciding whether to throw me out and continue the mission without me.'

After pacing around, with occasional glances at the car, Fawkes climbed back in. Mary watched anxiously as he settled into his seat then turned to address her.

'You're right.'

His voice trailed off.

'Go on.' Mary stroked his shoulder.

'I've let my ambition cloud my judgement. We can't betray people who have fought and died for us.'

She stared back, wide-eyed.

'So we're not going up to the village?'

'You're not but I'll have to go. Canaris knows we're here. If I don't turn up, he'll think I've used the pretence of seeing him to carry out a real spying mission. I'll have to think of something to say to him to explain why there's no letter. Best if you wait in the hotel. If I don't return, you must go back to the sub tonight.'

'What about me?'

Durand's question forced Fawkes to confront the other doubt in his mind.

'You can come too, as long as I know whose side you're on.'

Durand laughed.

'I'll say one thing for you, you're consistent. You haven't trusted me since the day we met and you still don't trust me now.'

He stared through the windscreen, his hands gripping the steering wheel.

'Weren't you told how I obtained Mary's address?'

'I assumed it was from the hotel register.'

Durand gave a hollow laugh.

'If only.'

He turned to look at Mary.

'You remember Juliette?'

'Of course. I hope she's alright in Paris. I often think of her.'

She saw the look on Durand's face, a look of utter devastation.

'What's happened?'

'I went to Paris to ask her for your address.'

His voice tailed off.

'And?'

'She gave it to me then died saving me from a German officer.'

Mary sobbed as she saw a tear rolling down Durand's cheek. Still staring forward, he spoke calmly to Fawkes.

'Does that answer your question?'

'It does and I apologise for doubting you. Would you rather I went on my own while you stay here with Mary? You'd be safer.'

'No, I was furious when I was told what was expected of me. Mary has changed that. I need to do this, for Juliette.'

He looked at Mary.

'But you should stay here.'

She was still thinking about Juliette.

'Why did you have to ask Jean-Paul? Wasn't the information available in London?'

'Probably but that would have left a trail. Not a risk C could take for an off-piste mission.'

'Christ, what people you are. Well, that settles it, neither of you is going anywhere without me, not now I know how Juliette died. We're in this together. Besides, you need me to identify the house. You'll look suspicious wandering around the village not having a clue where to go.'

'Mary, this isn't your fight. C bullied you into coming here.'

'I'm not doing this for that bloody man. I'm doing it for Juliette and my pilots. We had Poles at Biggin Hill. They call us the "island of last hope." They didn't escape to Britain to live, they came to die so that Poland would one day live again. I can't let them down.'

'Alright but once you've identified it, I want you to go back to the car. There's no telling how Canaris will react when he learns there's no letter. If he turns nasty, I want you to have a chance to escape.'

Durand turned the ignition key.

'If we don't leave now, there won't be any meeting, with or without a letter.'

As Durand slipped the car into gear and drove out into the morning sunshine, Fawkes turned his thoughts back to his meetings with C, the man's anger when he needed the address of the house and the way he'd swiftly intervened to stop Mary going home. Why was he so desperate to ensure the letter was delivered and if Churchill wasn't behind it, who was? As the car moved on towards the distant hills, he re-assessed his priorities. The Department's reputation was at stake, so was the survival of his team. He'd do his best to protect both but if it came to the crunch, the team came first. He'd worry about the consequences if and when he returned to Broadway. At least his doubts about Durand had been disproved. That had worried him more than he'd cared to admit.

His thoughts were interrupted by Mary, riven with guilt that Juliette had died because of her.

'If we're meeting the head of German intelligence but not giving him what he wants, the mission will be a waste of time.'

She paused.

'Unless we change its purpose.'

'What do you mean?'

Durand asked the question but Fawkes already had a good idea of the answer.

'We could kill him. That's got to help the war effort. I mean, if they killed C that would help them.'

Fawkes turned round to look at her.

'You really want to kill Germans, don't you?'

'More than anything.'

'Three points. Firstly, it wouldn't help as they'd simply replace him with someone else. Canaris isn't that good at his job so his successor might be more effective. Secondly, if we kill him, none of the plotters against Hitler will have anything more to do with us.'

'What's the third?'

The tone in her voice suggested she was unconvinced.

'You liked that village last year?'

'Of course.'

'Well, they'd massacre the entire village as a reprisal.'

Realising what had prompted this thirst for blood, Durand spoke gently.

'It wasn't your fault. She didn't die because we needed your address, she died because she was determined to save me from a German soldier. The truth is, if I'd come for her sooner, none of this would have happened. If anyone is to blame, it's me.'

Mary stroked the back of his shoulders to comfort him then sat back in her seat. But she hadn't finished.

'At least we've messed up the plans of the people behind this letter. I've been blown up by a bomb, watched my friend being blown to pieces and listened to pilots dying in the air, knowing all the time it was these people who got us into this war. God I'll be glad to mess up their little scheme.'

'You're right,' said Durand. 'France collapsed because everyone knew the elite wanted to make a deal with Hitler so what was the point in continuing to fight? The same will happen to you British if this ever gets out. Whoever is behind this letter doesn't care about the ordinary man.'

'Or woman,' added Mary. 'Ironic, isn't it? Though we're in enemy territory, visiting the head of their secret service, there's little risk in that. Do you think we'll be as safe when we return to Britain?'

Shocked that she'd already worked that out, Fawkes resisted the urge to tell a comforting lie.

'I'm sorry, I should never have brought you here. But I'll do my damnedest to protect you.'

'We've already been through this. I'm here because I want to be, so stop apologising. We've got a job to do.'

'Do you keep any weapons in this car?'

Fawkes looked out of the window to make the question sound as casual as possible.

'Of course not. If the shooting starts, perhaps you could accompany us on your violin. Is it a Stradivarius by any chance?'

'Not quite, it's made by a man called Thompson.'

Fawkes opened the violin case with a flourish to display a Thompson sub machine gun and four box magazines. He tapped the case.

'Useful disguise for occasions like these.'

It was only ten o'clock but Mary felt as if she'd been up for hours. As she looked out of the window, the movement of the car and the rapidly rising heat combined to make her drift off. She was back with Juliette and Audrey, listening as Juliette scolded her for being too forward with the young American. It was a different age. A man clutching a bunch of grapes drifted before her. She reached out to him but he faded away.

Feeling the car slow to a halt, she opened her eyes to find a barrier blocking their path and a policeman walking towards them. She'd barely looked at the false papers they'd given her in London. What if they didn't pass muster? Oh God, what was her cover name? Supposing they dragged her off on her own leaving the others to continue their journey? Instinctively, she placed a hand on her stomach.

'Stay calm and say nothing. I'll do the talking.'

Durand's instruction didn't reassure her, nor did Fawkes when he unclipped the catches on his violin case. The policeman leaned through the window. After a cursory glance at the passengers, he spoke to Durand.

'Security check. Show me the papers for everyone in the car please.'

'Look, we're in a terrible hurry. We're late for a funeral and my companion here has promised to play the violin over the grave. Can't we show them when we return?'

A Citroën was parked on the other side of the road. When the door opened, Durand was pleased to see his old friend Charles, the policeman who'd investigated the deaths of Heywood and the three Germans. Charles strolled over smiling broadly.

'And what brings you out here J-P? I never had you down as a country boy.'

'I'm taking my friends to a funeral. It's up in the hills and we're running late so we really need to get a move on.'

'Well, I should ask for all your identity papers and study them carefully but, seeing as it's you, be on your way. You know J-P, I sometimes think you'd be late for your own funeral.'

He waited for Durand to finish his artificial laugh then reached through the window to shake the hand of his old friend. His solemn expression took Durand by surprise.

'*Tire pas trop sur la corde*,' he said as Durand slid the car into gear and moved slowly off.

Fawkes had also noticed the sudden change in the detective's manner.

'You know him, do you?'

'Yes, I've known him for years.'

'Were you expecting him to say "don't push your luck"?'

'He probably meant that I shouldn't always expect not to show our papers. We were lucky it was him or we might have been in trouble.'

Charles had set up the road block next to a café and while the policeman dismantled it, he sought a coffee. At the zinc counter, he gestured to the owner to pass him a token then went over to the phone on the wall and gave the operator a number. When he got through, the café owner heard him speaking in German.

'They're on their way. They should reach the village in under an hour.'

'Did they suspect anything?'

'They thought they were in trouble until Durand saw me, then he knew he could talk his way out of it. He's probably congratulating himself right now.'

'Good,' said the German. 'Now I have something else for you to do.'

As Charles listened to his new instructions, his anger welled up.

'You said just a roadblock on the way up. You have no jurisdiction over me.'

'You've done well so far. Don't be a silly boy now.'

When Charles said nothing, the German tried to soothe him.

Don't worry, they won't escape from the village. You won't be involved. Then we'll go back to Berlin and leave you alone.'

The German put the phone down and turned to his colleague.

'He'll do as he's told. Meantime, let's pay a visit to that perfume factory.'

'What do we do if we find something?'

'Whatever needs to be done. We've got silencers and can always blame it on Mirbeth. It'll be one more nail in her coffin. Schellenberg will like that.'

Back in the café, Charles took his anger out on the poor policeman by leaving him in the baking sun while he sat down to a coffee. This was his first encounter with the SD and he'd hoped it would be his last. He'd been a fool to believe them.

Fawkes shut the clips on the violin case and sat back in his seat. As he did so, his eyes came to rest on the car's wing mirror. The roadblock was already being dismantled. It had been set up just for them. The doubts about Durand, doubts he'd told himself could be dismissed, now returned. The story he'd told about Juliette's death had sounded convincing but wasn't it a little strange that the authorities had let him fill the hotel with Jews? The Vichy government was making life increasingly difficult for Jews elsewhere, why not here? Was Charles's strange warning some sort of code?

If Durand had been turned, it was a problem to be dealt with later. He stopped looking in the wing mirror and slid down in his seat to consider a much bigger problem.

How would Canaris react when he found out there was no letter?

Chapter 42

MARY WAS SURPRISED how much of the route she'd forgotten. The view she remembered was the sight of Brandon at the wheel of his car. Now she was on the same road, with his child inside her. The vineyards, the dense woodland, so much had slipped from her mind. Only when they drove up into the hill did she start to remember. The road twisted and turned until Durand drove round one final bend and the scene changed. Fields of lavender and jasmine spread out before them. Suddenly, she was back. Only a year had passed but it seemed like a lifetime. The sun blazed down but she felt a shiver run down her spine. The sight before her was enchanting but she could think of only one thing. What on earth had she let her unborn child in for?

Up ahead, a car was parked in one of the fields. The driver, leaning against the bonnet, stood up as they approached.

'Who's that?' Mary asked, clutching Durand's shoulders.

'I didn't tell you before because I didn't want to alarm you,' said Durand. 'This is the man they call "the German." Yann introduced me to him. He's a communist who fled Germany before the war and now leads the Resistance round here. Don't show your distrust, we'll need him if things turn nasty.'

This was the kind of unexpected development Fawkes had worried about. Had he been too anxious to believe Durand? He felt for his Webley in the inside pocket of his jacket.

'What have you told him?'

'That we're recruiting a Wehrmacht officer to spy for us.'

Durand stepped out of the car and walked over. A brief

handshake, then they spoke for a couple of minutes. Fawkes's suspicions increased. When Durand led the German back to the car, he pulled the Webley out and cocked it. The German poked his head through the window, started to speak, saw the Webley and stopped. Durand said, 'go on, tell them.'

'I know you don't trust me but listen to what I have to say before you use that revolver. I'm a communist but I'm not happy with the pact Stalin has made with Hitler. An alliance with fascists can never be justified.'

He paused, waiting for a reaction. Fawkes un-cocked the Webley and smiled.

'It can't be easy for you. Though I don't agree with your beliefs, I realise they're sincerely held.'

His turn to pause.

'Does this have something to do with today?'

'I've been told a Soviet agent is here, someone from London.'

'Do you know why he's here?'

There could only be one reason but he wanted to hear it from the German.

'That's the strange thing, normally I'd be kept informed. This time, my orders are to keep away and offer him no assistance. I wouldn't be told that unless it was something big.'

Then, as an afterthought, 'all I know is he's staying in Sainte-Maxime.'

'Perhaps he's not coming here, then.'

'Oh, he is. Just because they don't tell me something doesn't mean I can't find it out.'

'Well, thanks for telling us. We'll keep a lookout for him.'

'Good luck,' said the German. 'We'll be around if you need us.'

While Durand engaged first gear, Mary wanted to know more about the mysterious communist from London.

'What can we do about this man?'

'Nothing,' said Fawkes. 'He's probably here to observe, nothing more. We'll keep an eye out for him but we must focus on the job in hand.'

As they entered the village, Mary felt the tension grip her. The tall buildings shaded them from the heat and glare but reminded them that they were near their destination.

She wasn't the only one feeling the tension. When they entered the square, her tap on Durand's shoulder made him jump.

'Stop.'

He braked sharply.

'The house was down that lane, remember? We parked over there. It all comes back to me, I can just picture poor old Heywood disappearing round the corner.'

Durand pulled over, applied the handbrake and turned the engine off. Unlike a year ago, the square was deserted. Some shops were open but the ones aimed at tourists were firmly shuttered. Fawkes climbed out and looked around.

'Place seems deserted. Don't know if that's a good thing or a bad thing.'

He opened the door for Mary.

'Either way, we'd better get a move on. We're running late.'

He turned to Durand.

'Best if you stay here while Mary and I find the house. Then she'll come back to the car while I go in. If anything goes wrong, the two of you should get out as fast as possible.'

Durand stepped out into the blazing sun.

'I don't agree.'

Fawkes shook his head.

'I'm trying to protect you. If Canaris sees you, he won't do anything about it now but he'll come after you later.'

'He knows who I am and what I do. I'm the money conduit to Szymańska. She's the conduit between Canaris and the British and a lot of other people too. He needs her and that means he needs me. He'll leave me alone.'

He placed a hand on Fawkes's shoulder.

'Now you're not giving him the letter, you'll carry more weight if I'm there.'

'You're starting to sound like Lestocq.'

'Who?'

'Never mind, he's my problem not yours.'

No more than six feet wide, the lane wound its dark way past the windows of the medieval houses. Two small children, sitting at a table, looked up at the sight of strangers. Across the way, a wife was shouting at her husband but stopped to watch suspiciously as they passed by. In this village of narrow streets, everyone knew what everyone else was doing. Feeling watched every step of the way, he understood why C had insisted he take Mary with him. They would attract just a little less attention if she could quickly identify the house. As they strolled along, he took the opportunity to get things straight with her.

'You're living with your parents. Do they know about your, er?'

He looked down at her tummy. She shook her head.

'I was about to tell Mummy when your men arrived and whisked me away. The funny thing is, I'd been thinking my condition prevented me from doing anything to avenge the death of the father when you solved that little problem for me.'

'I'm sorry Brandon's dead.'

'Perhaps you shouldn't be. If he was still alive, I wouldn't have come on this mission.'

'I was furious with you for following Heywood, that day.'

'That was you're fault.'

'How come?'

'I was furious with you when you turned up at the hotel acting like a pair of Englishmen Abroad, embarrassing me in front of everyone. When you turned out to be in the film business, I was so grateful, I leapt at the chance to help you. With Juliette, of course, it was the other way around. She loved mocking the original you and was not at all happy when you turned out to be people everyone wanted to know.'

She shook her head.

'I can't believe what happened to her. First Brandon, now Juliette.'

Without meaning to, she let out a sob.

'Sorry, I promised myself I wouldn't do that.'

'No, a little of that sort of thing can be a great help at a time like this.'

'It's just that I know Brandon died because of me. He was safe until we met and I distracted him. Juliette's death is my fault too.'

'It's the war that caused their deaths, not you and you mustn't allow your desire for vengeance to distract you. It's important we all focus on the job in hand.'

'Don't worry, I just want an opportunity to do my bit.'

To avoid being probed any further, she changed the subject.

'I'm sorry if I was abrupt back at the hotel. I can see it's come as a terrible shock to you.'

'It was a shock I needed. I didn't want you on this mission because I thought you'd be a liability. I couldn't have been more wrong and I apologise.'

'Apology accepted.'

She smiled at him.

'But I keep the letter.'

It was his turn to smile at her.

'You should do this job full time, you know.'

'While you go into films.'

The narrow lane led them to a crossroads. Fawkes looked anxiously at Mary. Would she fail at the first test?

'I remember this. A man pushed past us just here. A nasty piece of work but it has served to fixed the route in my mind. Follow me.'

'I believe I made the gentleman's acquaintance later that day. He'd be furious if he knew of his vital contribution to this mission.'

Mary strode with increasing confidence down the winding lanes, the twists and turns showing Fawkes that he could never have found the house on his own. When they arrived at the courtyard, it was just as she remembered it. Even the blazing sun reprised its role. She remembered being aware of Brandon's eyes on her as they stood in the baking heat. Glowing with pride, she turned to Fawkes.

'These are the houses. We need to find the one with the symbol.'

'Take your time.'

She climbed the steps of each house in turn, checking the door frames of each. Nothing. She was about to give up when she took a closer look at one of the frames. The oak had a diagonal split that ran through the symbol, dividing it in two.

'This one.'

'Sure?'

'Positive.'

'Well done.'

He smiled at her.

'Now go back to the car and wait for us. It shouldn't take long. If we don't come out after an hour, drive back to the hotel.'

Durand handed her the keys. Assuming, wrongly, she was being sent back to the car to stop her shooting Canaris, she said 'I couldn't do it, you know. I haven't got a gun.'

She turned to walk away.

'Hold on.'

He produced his Webley British Bulldog from the capacious inside pocket in his suit.

'You'd better have this.'

She was mortified.

'I'm sorry, I shouldn't have said that. I'll behave, don't worry.'

'Cock it first, then squeeze the trigger. At the first sign of trouble, don't wait for either of us. Just drive to the coast and go to Yann's restaurant, not the hotel.'

He handed the revolver to her and watched her set off down the narrow lane, relieved to have her out of harm's way. Noticing there weren't any locals around, let alone a communist agent, he nodded to Durand, took a deep breath and grasped the door handle. It was unlocked. Opening the door, he led the way inside. Had Canaris turned up? Had the communist beaten them to it? He felt no fear, only excitement. This was what he did and he was good at it.

The room where Heywood had met Koslowski was shuttered and dark. At the far end, a wingback armchair faced the unlit fire. By its side, a leather briefcase, obviously new. As they walked across the uneven floor, a head popped around the side of the chair and the man who would decide his fate stood up. Short with thick grey hair, he was wearing a well-travelled beige linen suit and a weary look. He pulled a pistol from his jacket and held it up.

'Weapons on the table, shall we gentlemen?'

Durand held his hands open to show he had no weapon. Fawkes placed his violin case on the table. Straightening up, he bowed his head and spoke in German.

'Good morning, Herr Admiral. I trust you've not been waiting long. We were held up by a roadblock.'

He'd expected a tough, militaristic Prussian type but the overwhelming impression was of a man tired of what he was doing. He'd heard Canaris travelled nonstop and had assumed it was because he loved his job. Perhaps it was really because he liked to be out of the office for the same reasons he did? Fawkes had to make a rapid re-appraisal of how to handle him. Canaris bowed his head slightly then spoke abruptly and in English.

'I did not order that. I'm disappointed you should think I would.'

If he's like this now, how will he react when I tell him there's no letter? Take it slowly and don't give the impression they were anxious to get away.

But it was Canaris who wanted to hurry.

'You'll be wanting to get out of here as quickly as possible, as do I, so there's no need to prolong this meeting. I believe you have a letter for me.'

If Fawkes could reach into his pocket and produce the letter, he'd earn the undying gratitude of his boss. He kept his hands by his side and proceeded with the words he'd chosen on the journey.

'Herr Admiral, I'm embarrassed to say this but I'm afraid my master overreached himself. He cannot produce the letter you require, not at this time. I am, however, authorised to say that your efforts will have his full support when the time comes.'

For what seemed like an age, Canaris stared at him. Saying nothing, he went over to the window and peered through the shutters. Was he signalling to his men to come up? When he turned back, his look was sombre, distrustful.

'First no C, now no letter. Why then are you here? An offer to rescue me if I get into trouble, perhaps?'

Not a good start. The fate of the mission would be decided in the next few minutes; the kind of situation Fawkes was made for.

'No, sir, you are a patriotic German just as C is a patriotic Briton. You would never accept such an offer, nor would he in a similar situation.'

The expression on the German's face gave no clue as to what he was thinking.

'Do you know why I asked for this letter?'

During the car journey, Fawkes had thought of little else. He'd decided he had no choice but to bet the farm on his answer.

'As a test. You knew Churchill would never put his signature to the sort of letter you were seeking so any letter C produced would be a forgery. C is an honourable man and has sent us here without the letter to prove his reliability. You need have no doubts about him.'

When Canaris smiled, it was like the sun emerging from a dark cloud. But the sun quickly went in again, to be replaced by a searching look. This was the decisive moment. Without saying anything, Canaris walked over to the armchair. Fawkes looked across at Durand as the German bent down to pick up the leather briefcase. A moment's hesitation, then he lifted the flap to produce a pile of letters tied up with a red ribbon.

'I can't tell you where these letters come from but I can assure you they are genuine.'

As if to prove the point, he pulled one out of the bundle and opened it up.

'They were written by the Duke of Windsor and reveal his

attitude towards the Nazi leadership. They also complain about the anti-Nazi views of your Queen. Your Royal family will be relieved to get their hands on them.'

Fawkes took the letters with a nod.

'May I ask why you are giving them to us?'

'There is a powerful faction in your country that would happily put the Duke back on the throne as part of a deal with Hitler. I wish to rid my own country of Nazis. The last thing I want is a Nazi sympathiser on the British throne. These letters will keep them quiet, I think.'

'You don't mind our failure to produce a letter of support from Churchill?'

'I am surrounded by people who would happily use such a letter to betray me in order to curry favour with Hitler. If you had handed me such a letter, I would have burnt it in that grate in front of you.'

He pointed to the fireplace to emphasise his point.

'As you say, Churchill would never sign such a document. Only someone who was out of touch with the British people would have done so. I only decided to ask for such a letter when I saw how wound up C was during our meeting in Spain. I knew something wasn't right.'

He walked over to the window.

'This changes nothing, you understand. We shall still have to wait for the right moment. Just as Churchill understands the British people, so Hitler understands his. The common soldier is right behind him and will remain so, even when things turn nasty. That is our biggest problem.'

Fawkes nodded.

'C understands that. The important thing is that you know where we stand. In '38, you didn't. We realise that now.'

'You must also understand that I am doing this, not for myself but for the Fatherland.'

The words took Fawkes back to his meeting with Koslowski. The Pole had felt the same need to justify himself. He'd let him say his piece then. He let the German do so now.

'Our two countries should not be at war. My country has fallen into the hands of a madman and it is my duty to remove him so we can join together in the fight against communism. It is important that you realise this. I don't want my motives misunderstood.'

'There is no danger of that, Herr Admiral. Even if your countrymen don't understand that now, one day they will.'

Canaris picked his hat off the table.

'Well, I think that concludes our business.'

Fawkes was trying to digest the extraordinary turn of events. Mary hadn't destroyed his career, she'd saved it. He was starting to picture a triumphant return to C's office, bearing the incriminating letters, when the front door opened and he heard the sound of footsteps crossing the hall.

Chapter 43

HE SHOULD HAVE taken the warning about a communist agent more seriously but things had gone so smoothly, he'd allowed his guard to drop. The violin case was out of reach, Canaris had placed his revolver on the table, Mary had the Webley.

The door opened to reveal the newcomer. In any other situation, Fawkes would have watched in fury as Roland Lestocq slithered across the uneven floor. He'd just pulled off the greatest coup of his career and saved C's bacon only for the archetypal "one of us" man, the embodiment of everything that was wrong with the SIS, to turn up and steal the glory. Instead, a wave of relief swept over him.

Needing to maintain appearances in front of Canaris, Fawkes gave Lestocq a warm smile.

'I thought you were too valuable to be sent down here.'

'Me? No, not at all, old chap.'

Lestocq favoured the room with the self-deprecating smile of a man who knew exactly how valuable he really was. Then he got down to business.

'After you left we learnt there was a communist agent in the area, planning to kill you all. We tried to warn you but couldn't get through, so C sent me down here to tell you.'

Like hell, thought Fawkes, the wave of relief starting to subside. C sent him down to make sure I carried out his instructions. Any moment now, Lestocq will check that the letter had been delivered and the mission will fall apart. Just keep him talking while Canaris puts his hat on and walks out. Say anything.

Just keep Lestocq off the subject of the letter.

Lestocq had entered the house with a gun in his hand, a reasonable precaution in the circumstances but no longer necessary. Fawkes pointed to the pistol.

'I don't think there's any need for that, old man.'

'Yes, clumsy of me, old boy but I wasn't sure what I would find.'

Lestocq made a show of trying to fit the pistol into one of his pockets but none was large enough. Giving Fawkes a contrite look, he dropped his arm so the weapon hung by his side.

'Sorry, old boy, the whole thing was arranged in a hurry and they didn't give me one of those suits with a large inside pocket.'

Thinking only of getting Canaris out of there, Fawkes ignored the explanation. For God's sake, put your bloody hat on and go. But Canaris made no sign of leaving and Fawkes knew why. The opportunity to study one of the top men in the British Secret Service was an unexpected bonus. In desperation, he came up with the only topic he could think of.

'Where are you staying?'

'Sainte-Maxime. My aunt has a villa down there. Lovely to see the place again.'

Fawkes remembered the conversation with C and the resentment he felt when they spoke in front of him about the villa and his poor aunt's travails with her polo field. This time, it didn't bother him. He had a success under his belt, a success that no one could deny.

As long as Lestocq didn't mention the letter.

He was trying to think of a third delaying tactic when something clicked at the back of his mind and replayed the words of the man they call "the German" warning about a communist agent in the area.

'He's staying in Sainte-Maxime.'

Fawkes had told Mary he was sending her back to the car for her own safety but she knew it was because Fawkes didn't trust her messing up his delicate discussion with the head of the Abwehr. And she didn't blame him. She felt so much anger and bitterness towards the people who had ruined her life, even she didn't trust herself. Fawkes had told her to drive to the coast if things went wrong but the only way of knowing what was going on in the house was by keeping it in sight. She couldn't do that from the car and, if she waited in the street she'd stick out like a sore thumb in a village where everyone knew everyone else.

A little way down the lane, a small café offered a clear view of the courtyard. Taking a seat in the window, she ordered a coffee. Aware she might have to make a hasty exit, she paid for it immediately.

She'd barely taken her first sip when a man walked past and came to a halt in the courtyard in front of the house. He struck her as too well-dressed for a communist but who else could it be? The man looked around then crept up the steps and disappeared inside. Her orders were perfectly clear: return to the car and head for the coast. Wrapping her hand round the revolver in her pocket, she made for the house.

The front door was ajar. She couldn't risk opening it further, in case it creaked so she slipped in between the narrow gap and crept across the hall towards the sound of voices. Fawkes was speaking.

'Funny you should mention that, a mutual acquaintance told me you were staying there. Jolly tiresome for her not being able to come down this year.'

'A mutual acquaintance? I didn't think we moved in the same circles.'

Canaris interrupted.

'Could someone tell me what is going on?'

The intervention forced Fawkes's hand. He was used to taking risks with his life. What he was about to say risked something far more valuable to him, his reputation with both the SIS and the Abwehr. The next few seconds would decide if his career was over, this time for good.

'Admiral, I apologise for my bad manners. This is Roland Lestocq, seemingly a senior man in the SIS.'

He paused for what was only second or two but seemed like an eternity. Taking a deep breath, he continued.

'But actually, a communist agent. I'm afraid he's here to kill you.'

Lestocq tried to hide his dismay but he lacked Fawkes's experience. The plan, such as it was, had been to walk in and shoot the two of them before Fawkes worked out his real purpose. Pretty straightforward.

But there were three men, not two, all presumably armed and, thanks to that upstart little bastard, they now knew why he was there. Even if he succeeded in shooting Canaris, one of the others would kill him. He'd come here to further his career, not end it. Fawkes, the professional, had reached the same conclusion and knew what he had to do. Keep him talking, make him feel good. Thank God Mary wasn't here.

From her position in the hall, Mary saw the beads of sweat form on Fawkes's forehead and tried to make sense of the conversation she'd just heard. Lestocq was the hated boss. Why was Fawkes calling him a communist?

'It was clever of you to find the house. How did you do it?'

'We have people at the heart of the Reich. They found the address for me.'

'Where are you going afterwards? You can't return to London.'

'I'm going back all right. The Party has big plans for me in Six.'

'But your family's one of the oldest in the land. Why are you doing this?'

Though Lestocq could see what Fawkes was doing, the delay was just as welcome to him, still trying to work out how to carry out his orders and survive. But there was more to it than that. He'd operated in complete secrecy ever since he'd been recruited at Cambridge. This was the first time he'd had an opportunity to talk to anyone other than his handler about why he had joined The Party. The situation was far from ideal but it gave him a much-needed opportunity to justify his actions.

'It's precisely because I come from such a family that I have embraced communism. I spent my early years being relentlessly indoctrinated by my father about the importance of maintaining the status quo with us on top. And it worked, I completely accepted his version of how things should be.'

'So what made you change your mind?'

'Going to Cambridge. It opened my eyes. People think universities like Oxford and Cambridge are entirely populated by people from my world. I found that all the most intelligent, the most interesting people came from a section of society I knew nothing about. They helped me see the world as it really is.'

'It never occurred to you that they were simply making use of you.'

'That's exactly why I joined them, to be made use of by someone other than my father for the first time in my life. They knew my social position would get me into the SIS with ease. You thought C and others were blind to the threat of communist penetration. In fact, they were obsessed by it and assumed that the best way to prevent it was to recruit splendid chaps like me. Little did they realise that people like me have all the fervour of converts. For us, communism isn't a passing fad of youth, we really believe in it.'

'We? There are more of you?'

Lestocq smiled.

'I've spoken too freely. I'll say no more.'

Lestocq's self-confidence worried Fawkes. It was time to puncture it.

'If you manage to kill all three of us and survive, you'll have carried out your mission and we won't be around to tell C what you've just told us. But how do you think you'll get back?'

'Moscow Central will organise something for me. The local Resistance leader is a German communist, you know.'

Lestocq smirked at Canaris while delivering this piece of information. Fawkes saw a glimmer of hope.

'Sorry to disappoint you but I met him on the way here. It was he who warned me there was a communist from London who was staying in Sainte Maxime. He doesn't approve of what you're doing. You'll get no help there.'

Lestocq's attempt at a contemptuous laugh sounded like a hollow gargle.

'You're lying.'

Fawkes's hopes rose, but only a little. He pressed his attack home.

'Why do you think he's never made contact? He was ordered not to help you. You're not as important to Moscow as you think. They just want to use you to kill the Admiral and blame it on MI6. They know you can't take on three armed men and expect to come out alive.'

The grin remained but Fawkes could see the doubt in his eyes.

'For God's sake wise up, Lestocq. Moscow Central have got trained assassins living full time in Berlin. They can kill the Admiral whenever they want. They chose you because they wanted to pin his death on the British. You've been taken for a ride.'

He pressed on.

'You joined shortly after the Admiral tried to do a deal with us in '38.'

Lestocq nodded, the grin starting to disappear.

'They've been planning this ever since, it's all they ever wanted you for. They've made you feel important when all along you've just been a pawn in their game. Letting you think you weren't being manipulated was their way of manipulating you.'

As Lestocq's doubt turned to anger, Fawkes saw the change in his expression. Had he gone too far? Time for a little flattery.

'I'll give you one thing, you had me completely fooled. If I hadn't spoken to that German and he hadn't mentioned Sainte-Maxime, I'd never have guessed. Seems to me, Moscow Central are wasting your talents on a pointless assassination. Forget the whole thing and come back with us. C will never believe me over you so there's no point in me trying. You can carry on where you left off as if nothing had happened.'

For a moment, it seemed to work, then Lestocq's gun start to wave about once more. Fawkes knew he was losing control as Lestocq shouted defiantly.

'Nice try but I'm more important to them than some little man down here. Central will get me out, don't you worry about that. Silly of me, I was forgetting, you won't have to worry about that because you'll be dead.'

Having worked out what was going on, Mary knew that once he'd disposed of the others, Lestocq would kill her too. She had to do something and do it quickly. She had the revolver but the sound of cocking it would alert him. She looked around for another weapon.

The house had been built by Protestants to withstand attack from Catholics. Metal slots had been screwed into either side of the front door to hold a solid oak beam that would prevent the door from being broken open. She looked around and saw the beam, propped up against the wall to her right. While Fawkes kept Lestocq talking, she picked it up with both hands and crept through the open door.

'I'm trying to help you here, Lestocq. You've got to kill a lot of people in this room, escape arrest and rely on a man who has already betrayed you to get you back to London. That's not a plan I would rely on and I've been in this game a lot longer than you. Abandon it and come home with us. We'll say you were here to help us and, as you say, no one will hear a word against you.'

A look of absolute calm spread over Lestocq's face, a look that worried Fawkes more than the gun-waving. He'd lost and he knew it. Then he saw Mary crouching in the doorway, clutching the beam. As soon as she made the slightest sound, Lestocq would turn and shoot. His only option was to charge at Lestocq and take the bullet himself.

Durand beat him to it. He'd also seen Mary and reached the same conclusion. Shouting, he moved towards Lestocq. As

Lestocq turned towards him and fired, Mary slammed the beam into his back. The bullet that would have hit Durand between the eyes lodged harmlessly in the ceiling as Lestocq slumped to the floor. Even the experienced Fawkes was stunned by the speed with which the situation had changed. Pocketing Lestocq's gun, he turned to Canaris and spoke like a butler apologising for a tray being dropped.

'My apologies for the inconvenience, Admiral.'

Canaris acted as if he'd merely watched an embarrassing dispute between two old friends.

'I'm glad that's resolved. Now, if you'll forgive me, it's time I was on my way. Shall I leave you to deal with this gentleman or do you want me to take him into custody?'

'With your permission, he's coming back with me. I apologise again Admiral, this was not what C had in mind.'

On his way to the door, Canaris passed Mary. He smiled at her then turned to Fawkes.

'I don't know who this young lady is but she saved my life. I won't forget that.'

'And mine,' added Durand, smoothing down his hair.

Fawkes took a different line.

'You disobeyed orders.'

His words thrilled her. No amount of team building on the sub, or agreeing with her in the car, meant as much to her as those three blunt words. Now, she really was on the team.

'That shot will have been heard,' warned Canaris. 'You'd better be on your way too.'

Fawkes hauled Lestocq up and ushered the other two towards the front door. He'd squared things with the Admiral without handing over the letter, had a live communist to take back to London and letters that would save the Royal Family's reputation. On top of that, Durand had been prepared to take a bullet for the team. Things had gone better than he could possibly have hoped.

He opened the door with a flourish, to be greeted by the sight of the woman who had tried to kill him on the Blue Train.

Chapter 44

Mirbeth was halfway across the rutted cobblestones when she found herself looking at the man who had ruined her career. While they stared at each other, Grüber, the man in charge of the SD squad she'd brought with her, raised his pistol. Seeing the pistol in her peripheral vision, Mirbeth pushed his arm up sending the bullet harmlessly into the door frame. As Fawkes slammed the door shut, Grüber turned on Mirbeth.

'Why did you do that?'

'I want him alive. He's got the answers to all my questions. He's not getting away this time.'

The truth dawned on Grüber.

'He's your English gentleman. They told me about him and you. Well, well, well.'

'Shut up and surround the house.'

Fawkes was planning to tell the others he'd recognised the woman outside. Fortunately, his first task was to take the beam that had already saved their lives and press it into service a second time. While slotting it into place, he realised telling Canaris would reveal that he'd been on last year's mission and might tempt him to interrogate him about Enigma. Damn Lestocq. If he hadn't turned up they'd have been gone by now.

Or had Lestocq saved them from walking straight into the arms of Mirbeth?

'If it's the police,' said Canaris, 'I can deal with them.'

'I doubt it. They're in plain clothes and armed with machine pistols.'

Canaris frowned.

'They must be SD. In that case I can definitely deal with them.'

The situation was spinning out of control. As soon as Canaris confronted Mirbeth, he'd learn of Fawkes's role in the Enigma mission. How could he keep the two of them apart?

It was Durand who saved the day.

'Forgive me Admiral but I don't think that would be wise.'

Canaris and Fawkes both turned towards the hotelier. Durand started with Fawkes.

'Is one of them a woman?'

Fawkes responded solemnly.

'I believe so.'

'Admiral, I think this is nothing to do with our meeting and everything to do with a failed British mission last year. If it's the same woman who led that, I suspects she thinks we're here, not to meet you but to follow up on that mission. In that case, it would be unwise to reveal yourself, don't you think?'

Fawkes struggled to conceal his delight at Durand's intervention.

'He's right, we can't be found together Admiral. I suggest you go out of the back door while we hold them off.'

Canaris shook his head.

'No, I invited you here, you are my guests. Either we leave together or we fall together. Let's see what it looks like at the back.'

Their entry into the kitchen was greeted by a bullet that flew through the window and embedded itself in the dresser. Canaris pointed to a table in the centre of the room.

'We should put that across the window for protection, propped up on the chairs.'

As they pulled the table across, the rug underneath caught on the legs, revealing two small rings attached to the floorboards. When Mary pulled on them, two sides of a trapdoor opened up, releasing a smell of damp, musty air. She peered into the darkness then turned to Durand.

'When we visited the perfume factory, you said there was a network of escape tunnels. Do you remember?'

'Yes, but I never knew if it was true.'

Durand peered down.

'It's got to be worth a try.'

Mary asked the obvious question, 'What about Lestocq?'

Fawkes pushed him forward.

'I'm not leaving him to the SD, he knows too much. We'll have to take him with us but only as long as he cooperates.'

Lestocq was still in shock at being foiled by a slip of a girl but that didn't stop him calculating the odds. Being left here meant certain death but if he could get back to London, he was confident he could bluff it out. He adopted a beaten look.

'I'll cooperate. I have no choice.'

Fawkes handed the briefcase with its letters to Mary.

'You'd better look after that. What you did back there was wonderful. You saved all our lives but you did it by disobeying orders.'

'I learnt that from you.'

'Yes, but you've now got all the important documents. That makes you the key member of the team. Whatever happens, you have get back to London so you must obey orders from now on.'

While Mary nodded her agreement, Fawkes handed Lestocq's gun to Durand and Canaris led the way down into the airless pitch black. As his eyes accustomed to the gloom, he noticed a small gap partially hidden by a dust covered altar.

'You're right, this is the start of the tunnel.'

He crawled through and the others followed. Fawkes went in last and pulled the altar back into place. Once inside, the tunnel enlarged and they were able to stand up and feel their way along its narrow and winding course. Progress was slow but Fawkes recognised that the twists and turns made it a hard place in which to mount an attack but a good place to defend. When they reached a fork in the path, Durand stopped and pointed to the left-hand tunnel.

'That way must lead somewhere near where we left the car, the other must lead to the perfume factory. Which way do we go?'

Lestocq intervened.

'If we stay in the centre of the village, we'll be caught. Isn't this factory on the edge of the village?'

Fawkes signalled his agreement by pushing him towards the right-hand fork. As he did so, they heard a noise behind them. He put a finger to his lips and held his other hand up. There it was again, a soft scraping sound and the occasional clang of metal on rock. Mirbeth's men had found the tunnel. Silently, he signalled to the others to continue then turned to face the other way. Only when Durand shook his hand did a shocked Mary realise what he was doing. Unable to cry out, she pulled Fawkes towards her like an actress in a silent film. When, with a sorrowful smile, he pushed her gently away, something snapped inside her.

'Why are you doing this? Why can't we all escape together? You're just making a futile gesture.'

His first instinct was to ignore her questions and carry on back down the tunnel but his need to tell was as great as her need to know.

'The tunnel is the one place I can hope to hold them off. If it works, you have a real chance of escaping back to the coast, if we carry on, they're bound to catch up with us. This has to be done and I'm the only person who can do it.'

Before she could answer, he turned and went back the way they'd come. Tugged along by Durand, she looked back until they rounded the next bend and Fawkes disappeared from sight.

Choosing a position where the already narrow tunnel curved in a tight bend, he crouched down to wait. It was a sound tactical move but there was more to it than that. Seeing Mirbeth had awakened an old emotion. Just as Mary wanted vengeance for Brandon, he needed to avenge Heywood.

The tap, tap grew louder. Without a lamp, his pursuers had been reduced to feeling their way along like blind men going down an unfamiliar path. Now they were nearly on top of him.

He didn't want to die but with the men closing in, death had become a certainty and with that certainty came the end of fear. Life went from being complicated to being very simple. He had to hold off Mirbeth's men long enough to give the others time to escape; it was all he could hope for. He crouched down to offer the smallest target and waited.

They were starting to wonder if the tunnel would ever end when it opened out into a storage area full of boxes. Pushing them aside revealed a flight of steps and a trap door similar to the one in the house. Keeping Lestocq in front of him, Durand pushed it open and found himself confronted by a familiar scene, the despatch bay of the factory. As they finished climbing the steps, they heard the sound of gunfire echoing down the tunnel, two short burst of rapid fire, a long silence then a single shot. Mary let out a piercing cry and felt a terrible wrenching in her stomach, a sensation she hadn't felt since Brandon's death.

'There wasn't much shooting. They must have got him.'

Durand shook his head sorrowfully.

'That last shot sounded like an execution.'

Lestocq chimed in.

'Listen. There's someone in the tunnel.'

They took up positions round the trap door, Durand and Mary pointing their weapons at the dark space. Mary, now bent on revenging the deaths of two men, cocked the Webley and held her breath. When Fawkes emerged, she expressed her relief by hugging him. As he was holding a tommy gun with the safety catch off, instead of hugging her back, he let his arms hang by his side. Misinterpreting his response, she hurriedly withdrew.

Canaris placed a hand on his arm and drew him to one side.

'I'll leave you now.'

'Which way will you go?'

Canaris walked over to a door at the side of the storage area, and peered out. It opened onto the loading area. There was no one around.

'Out this way and on foot.'

'Is it safe?'

Mary's concern was greeted with a warm smile from Canaris.

'They'd have been happy to shoot me while in pursuit of British spies but not on my own. This is my territory and, unlike the woman from the SD, I'm entitled to be here. I'll be alright but you need to find a vehicle and get down to the coast immediately. It's strange that there doesn't seem to be anybody around. Perhaps they're closed today. That should make it easier to borrow a vehicle.'

He raised his hat in farewell and walked confidently through the front door. As she watched him go, Mary said, 'shouldn't we just hide here till the Germans have gone?'

Durand looked at the others. 'I don't see what else we can do. If there's nobody here, how can we get the keys to a vehicle?'

Lestocq had more advice to offer.

'That's no good. We'll be swapping one trap for another. We've got to keep moving. Even if they're shut, there'll be a delivery van somewhere and the keys are bound to be in an office. Let's look around.'

As they started their search, Fawkes took Durand to one side.

'You did well back there. I didn't know how I was going to keep Canaris in the dark about my attendance last year. You're full of surprises.'

'It's called teamwork, old man. You should try it.'

Their search was soon rewarded. In the yard on the other side of the storage room, they found a Peugeot 201 painted in lavender and white. When Mary walked round to the other side of the van and let out a scream, they discovered why there was nobody around.

Hanging out of the driver's door was the body of a man.

Chapter 45

A TRAIL OF blood led into the main room of the factory. Against the far wall were seven more bodies, the expression on their faces telling the story of their last moments. On some, a look of defiance, on others of fear, on others of resignation. Mary looked up at the raised floor where the old man had sat at his desk with the wonderful view of the lavender fields. Now, he lay slumped over his ledger, clutching a sprig of lavender, his pince-nez still in place. Sobbing, Mary ran to Durand who held her in his arms. To suppress the jealous pain that shot through his body, Fawkes concentrated on the need to answer the question posed by this horrific scene. Who had done this and why?

'No wonder Canaris left in such a hurry.'

Lestocq did his best to hide the smirk on his face as he shook his head in mock sorrow. Fawkes wasted no time in disabusing him.

'He had nothing to do with this. Drawing attention to his visit is the last thing he needed.'

Durand had been calm and efficient until now but he'd known these people. Over the years and the many factory visits, they had become his friends. Grabbing Lestocq by his lapels, he dragged him up the stairs and held him over the lavender still. The fire in the boiler had gone out but the water was still hot. He pushed him hard against the ancient wood, forcing him to gaze into the water below.

'This is your doing. The people chasing us were tipped off by your lot. They came here first and when they couldn't find us, killed these people, purely for the sake of it.'

Fawkes restrained Durand to stop him pushing Lestocq over the edge.

'Mirbeth isn't supposed to be in Abwehr territory and this would only have drawn attention to her.'

Reluctantly releasing Lestocq and shoving him aside, Durand vented his anger by pummelling the still, his head bowed. After a moment or two, he stopped and bent down. When he stood up, he was clutching a magazine from a sten gun.

'It was lying beside the still.'

He looked more closely.

'This thing has a compartment.'

He tugged a panel loose to reveal two sten guns and four grenades.

'This is why they were shot. My dear friends were in the Resistance.'

Fawkes picked up the grenades, leaving the sten guns to Durand. When he'd picked them up, he pointed to Lestocq.

'Why are you so determined to bring him with us? It's obvious we've been set up by the commies. We've been betrayed and he's behind it.'

'He may swagger about but he's just a pawn and by the look on his face, he knows it. He told his handler about our mission, the handler passed it on to Moscow Central and they fed it to the SD who sent Mirbeth down here to capture me, knowing she'd find Canaris with me.'

'Spying used to be so simple,' said Durand.

'There's more to it than that,' Fawkes grimaced.

'What are you saying?'

'First the roadblock, now this. Someone else is operating down here.'

He looked at Durand.

'And with a different agenda.'

Grüber wasted no time telling Mirbeth the bad news.

'They've killed two of my men and escaped.'

'Can't you send more men down?'

'The tunnel is narrow and twisting. They'd be picked off one at a time and I don't have enough men to risk that.'

Can't we go to the other end of the tunnel?'

'We don't know where it comes out.'

Mirbeth paced up and down.

'So what do we do now?'

'If they came by submarine, they'll make for the coast. We'll search the village to make sure they've left then follow them down. In our fast Mercedes, we'll soon catch them.'

Mirbeth continued her pacing, now adding a continuous clenching and unclenching of her fists. Grüber watched her anxiously.

'Why don't you wait here and we'll bring them to you. That way, if things get messy, you won't be involved. The two men your boss sent ahead of us are probably down at the coast. If they get past us, they'll catch them.'

'What two men?'

'From Special Operations.'

'You mean killers?'

'Correct.'

'I wasn't told about them.'

'Well, I was.'

'The bastards still don't trust me.'

'All the more reason for you to stay here. If it all goes wrong, you won't get the blame this time, they will.'

'I'll need one of the Mercedes.'

'Of course.'

Durand urged the little van on, expecting trouble round each bend but finding none. Then the road straightened out. At the far end, a flimsy barrier, like the one on the outward journey, stretched across the road. This time, a car was parked sideways behind it. Without waiting for instructions, Durand turned into a field and brought the van to a halt.

'They're bound to have seen us,' said Mary.

Durand tried to sound reassuring.

'They won't be interested in a perfume van pulling into a lavender field.'

Fawkes picked up one of the grenades from the factory and pulled his tommy gun out of its violin case.

'Wait here while I deal with them.'

With the tommy gun on his back and the grenade in one hand, he crawled silently between the rows of lavender. As he drew near, he heard a voice he recognised.

'I don't like it any more than you do but if we catch this lot, the Boche have promised to leave us alone.'

He'd never thrown a grenade before but the little he knew told him not to throw it immediately after he'd pulled the pin as the delay before it exploded would give them time to throw it back. But how long should he wait? He decided four seconds, pulled the pin and counted the longest four seconds of his life.

Mary was surprised to find Lestocq watching as anxiously as she was. He'd dismissed as a bluff Fawkes's claim that Moscow had abandoned him but it was obviously true. They hadn't expected him to survive and he was on his own. Aware of her gaze, he lowered his head.

'I was a fool to put my faith in Moscow.'

'Don't try that one on me. Faith never came into it. If you want to confess your sins, I'm no priest. You'll have to find absolution another way.'

Lestocq looked at the beautiful young woman who, like him, would shortly be dead. Then he looked across at Fawkes, crawling through the lavender fields.

'How much do you know about him?'

'Virtually nothing. Why do you ask?'

'The SIS had their eye on him from the day he was born. Naval officer father, German mother. They knew he'd make the perfect agent so, when his father was killed, they got the Navy to take him away from his mother, in case she took him back to Germany and he grew up to spy for them against us.'

He scrutinised her face to see if she knew any of this. It was a blank canvas.

'Then, when he was well-established in the Navy, the SIS arranged for him to be thrown out on a trumped-up charge, offered him a sympathetic ear and recruited him. Clever really. He fell for it completely.'

He thought for a bit.

'Just like I fell for Moscow's line, I suppose.'

Fawkes watched the grenade arc silently through the air, exploding on impact. As the dust and debris settled, a man in civilian clothes, the only one to survive the blast, crawled towards the car, even though it was obviously wrecked. Emerging from the lavender, Fawkes watched Charles tug at the twisted door. As Fawkes approached, Charles looked at him, saying nothing but pleading for his life with his eyes. The car was a wreck so the only reason Charles was opening the door must be to find a weapon. Fawkes couldn't take the risk. The tommy gun burst into life.

Stepping over his body, Fawkes inspected the inside of the car. No sign of a weapon. Durand was already angry at him for bringing Lestocq with them. As the gaudy perfume van drew near, he looked around, saw a rifle belonging to a dead policeman and quickly placed it beside Charles. When the others arrived, they found him pulling the bodies of the policemen into the ditch at the side of the road. He left the other body to Durand. Turning the body over, Durand gazed at the lifeless face of Charles staring up at him.

'Poor bastard, that's why he shook my hand. He knew one of us wouldn't survive the day.'

Fawkes placed a hand on his shoulder.

'I'm sorry. It was him or me.'

Durand turned away. Juliette was dead, now Charles. His

world would never be the same. While he closed Charles's eyes, Fawkes issued fresh orders.

'Help me push this car out of the way. We can still reach the hotel in good time. We'll look like just another delivery van driving in through the back entrance without attracting any attention.'

Mary tried to imagine that moment but didn't want to tempt fate. Lestocq imagined himself back in Broadway Buildings, talking his way out of trouble.

Fawkes wondered how long it would be before Mirbeth's men caught up with them.

Chapter 46

THEY WERE STILL surrounded by lavender fields when Durand checked his wing mirror.

'Two Mercedes coming up fast.'

Fawkes looked at the van's flimsy rear doors and told Lestocq to help him pile the perfume cases against them. When the front passenger of the leading Mercedes leaned out of his window and opened fire, the glass bottles inside the perfume cartons were shattered, soaking the two men but absorbing the bullets.

Noticing a panel above him, Fawkes clambered on to the cartons and slid it open. Resting his tommy gun on the roof, he fired at the front car. When his first burst landed short, he yelled to Durand.

'Slow down.'

Thinking they'd damaged the slowing van, the first car closed in for the kill. Fawkes's second burst hit the radiator. His third moved up to the windscreen, killing the front seat passenger. As the first car came to a halt, the second car pulled alongside to pick up its crew. Knowing the Mercedes would soon overhaul the cute but underpowered van, Fawkes looked around. They needed a side road but the rows of lavender seemed endless on either side. Then he saw a stone shed in one of the fields, set well back from the road. He pointed to it.

'Make for that. If we can hide the van behind it, they may drive on by. You'll have to go over the fields.'

It was a bad decision. The lavender presented no obstacle but the ground was flinty. One by one, the tyres were torn to shreds until they could feel the metal rims spinning against the hard ground, the flints hammering against the floor beneath them. All Durand could do was keep the accelerator pressed to the floor and hope. When he'd worked the vehicle over the last few yards and turned the engine off, he collapsed over the wheel, sweat pouring from his face.

Their relief was short-lived. As they clambered out, Fawkes surveyed the carnage wrought by the van on its journey across the lavender.

'Christ! We might as well have put up a neon sign pointing them in the right direction.'

He shook his head.

'I'm sorry.'

Hearing the distant sound of the second Mercedes, he pointed to Mary and Durand.

'There must be a road on the other side of the field. You two must go on ahead. Lestocq and I will stay here.'

Mary suddenly dropped to the ground and started shaking. Lestocq looked at Fawkes in alarm.

'What's happened to her?'

'Shock, she's been pushed too far.'

Fawkes knelt beside her.

'I thought you were going to make me an actress,' she sobbed.

For a man so used to deceit and lies, Fawkes was cut to the quick by her words but their pursuers weren't far behind. Kneeling beside her, he held her shoulders firmly.

'Look at me. We agreed you'd be a team player from now on and get those letters back to London. That means leaving right now. They don't know how many of us there are so chances are, they won't come looking for you. There must be a road at the back of this field, when you reach it, head south.'

He reached into her jacket pocket and pulled out the Webley.

'Remember to cock it before you pull the trigger.'

He demonstrated the motion then put the revolver back into her left-hand jacket pocket.

'I'm not leaving you.'

'Mary, if you want to stop the plotters back home, you've got to survive this and get those letters back.'

'Stop doing this!'

'Doing what?'

'Always trying to atone for your mother's death by sacrificing yourself. One minute your Mr Ambition, the next you're doing your best to get killed. No wonder they think you're odd.'

His instinctive reaction was to bring her to her senses with a slap.

Instead, he kissed her.

'What you have to do is get these letters back to London. What I have to do is hold these people off. We can't both escape and we can't both stay and fight. That's just the way it is. Please, please go. You'll get your revenge in carrying out your task.'

'And you'll get yours in dying here.'

'Like I said, that's just the way it is.'

She stood up.

'Alright, have it your own way, I can't stop you.'

The briefcase was lying on the ground, beside her. He picked it up and handed it to Durand.

'Look after her and make sure she takes this to the sub.'

Hearing the plaintive tone in which the request was delivered, the Frenchman placed a hand on Fawkes's shoulders.

'You have my word as a Jew. That word is sacred to me.'

Durand turned to Mary.

'Come on, let's get out of here.'

'Hold on.' Fawkes reached into his jacket. 'Take this.'

She looked at the pill in his hand.

'What's that for.'

'If all else fails.'

'If that's what I think it is, I don't want it.'

'It's up to you whether you take it. I just want you to have the option.'

She pocketed the pill with a sigh. As they moved off, she

called out.

'I meant what I said and you know I'm right.'

After a few paces, she stopped, turned round, ran back and kissed him.

When they were out of earshot, Durand asked, 'what was all that about?'

'I was just kissing him goodbye. Nothing more.'

'No, all that about him having a death wish.'

She told him about Fawkes's mother.

'Well, he never told me that.'

'Perhaps I'm better at drawing information out of people.'

'You like him, don't you?'

'Don't be bloody ridiculous.'

Durand made no comment as they continued up the hill. When a road appeared in front of them, she said, 'he's not as bad as I thought he was last year.'

He smiled.

'He's a brave man.'

He paused.

'Honourable too. We learned that when he sacrificed his career to agree with you about the letter.'

He gave her a sly grin.

'I hope it's not catching.'

'Oh, you'll be honourable when the time comes. I don't doubt that.'

Relieved she was on her way, Fawkes pushed Lestocq into the hut. Telling him to stay at the back and lie low, he placed his tommy gun and the grenades on the windowsill. While he did so, he watched Grüber's men arrive and spread out across the lavender. It wouldn't take long but with any luck, Mirbeth would assume that, like last year, the two of them composed the entire team. Once they'd been dealt with, they'd consider their job done. Losing his life didn't bother him, he didn't have much of a life to lose. But he was surprised to realise how much he regretted that he'd seen Mary for the last time.

Lestocq's plaintiff voice interrupted his thoughts. Of all the people to die with.

'What about me?'

'You've lived as an aristocrat. Now's your chance to die like one. Stay at the back. When I'm down, you can do as you like.'

'You've got to give me a weapon. We're not going to get out of here and these people are my enemies just as much as yours. Even if I'm lying, the worst thing that can happen is that I'll kill you shortly before they do. Give me a chance to do something worthwhile, the chance to go down fighting.'

Fawkes looked at the man who would have happily killed him an hour ago. He'd be mad to give him a weapon but if he did join in the fight, it would give Mary more time to escape. He passed him a sten gun.

They held fire till Grüber's men were within range but as they were spread out, the grenades had a limited effect. When the first grenade took out just one man, the advance was halted and both sides exchanged fire, Lestocq using short bursts of the sten gun to good effect. Though he and Fawkes had the advantage of stone walls to protect them, Grüber's men had the advantage of numbers. Fawkes knew how this would end. His sole aim was to give the other two time to reach a road.

As Canaris drove away from La Dame Brave, the relaxed image he'd projected to the British fell away. If Mirbeth captured them, she'd torture the truth out of them. When that happened, he'd be hanged. There was only one way to protect them but it meant recruiting an unlikely ally. He turned his car round and headed back to the village.

In the main square, only one café was opened. Sitting in the blazing sun, he'd not long finished his first cup when that sun was blotted out. Finding the café owner looming over him, he pushed his cup towards him for a refill. Instead of coffee, the old man produced a Great War revolver from under a napkin.

With a trembling hand, he pointed it at Canaris.

'I spotted you right away for what you are.'

'And what's that?'

'Gestapo. I'm handing you over to the Resistance for them to do to you what you did to those poor people in the perfume factory.'

The former U boat captain remained calm while he considered his options. They were alone. In a fight, he'd probably win but that wasn't why he was here. First, though, there was the little matter of the gun. He pushed the table hard against the old man and watched his knees buckle and the gun clatter across the ground. Ignoring it, he lifted the man up and sat him on a chair.

'By all means hand me over. The gun's over there, all you've got to do is pick it up but you'll have to accept the consequences for your fellow villagers. I don't know what happened in the perfume factory but I can assure you the SS will do much worse to all of you if you kill me.'

The man rubbed his bruised stomach.

'Now listen carefully, I'm Abwehr, not SS, and I need your help. I want you to contact the leader of the Resistance and tell him to come here. Tell him that when he and I have spoken, he can either kill me or work with me. In the meantime, you have my word that I won't try to escape. Now pick up your gun.'

The old man stared at Canaris, nonplussed by this unexpected turn of events but aware of the consequences for the rest of the village if he shot him. After a brief pause, he went inside to the phone, spoke at some length then returned to Canaris.

'He says he'll come.'

He walked back to his counter, leaving the gun lying on the ground.

An hour and two cups of coffee later, the man they called "the German" arrived. Expecting him to walk over to his table, Canaris sat still with his hands visible. Without acknowledging him, the man went inside to a table by the far wall. Canaris followed him, sat down and started talking softly but rapidly in German.

Chapter 47

THEIR RELIEF AT reaching a road was interrupted by the sound of gunfire. For the second time that day, Durand saw an anguished look on Mary's face.

'He's doing his duty. It's what he wants. We should respect that. Your duty is to get these letters back to London and make his sacrifice worthwhile.'

Mary's shoulders slumped in acquiescence.

'I know. I just wish things were different.'

Using the sun to work out their position, they headed south. They'd barely started when they heard the sound of a lorry behind them. Mary grabbed Durand's arm.

'Supposing it's soldiers. What are we going to do?'

'Supposing it's not. If we hide, we may miss an opportunity to hitch a lift. If they are soldiers, they're bound to stop when they hear the shooting and they'll find us anyway. Shall we take a chance?'

Fingering the pill she'd been so reluctant to accept, she nodded reluctantly.

The lorry seemed to be full of agricultural workers but what from a distance looked like agricultural implements turned out to be a motley assortment of weapons. When it drew up beside them, the man they called "the German" jumped down. Grabbing his arm, Mary pointed towards the lavender field.

'Our colleague is in that stone shed down there, holding off a squad of soldiers so we can escape.'

'That's why we're here. Leave it to us.'

With a cheery wave, the motley band headed off in the direction of the gunfire.

Out of ammunition, Lestocq laid down his gun. Resigned to his fate, he stared out of the window just as one of Grüber's men stood up and pulled the pin from a grenade. Fawkes responded to Lestocq's warning shout by pulling the trigger of his tommy gun, firing off three bullets followed by a dull metallic clack as the magazine ran out. The bullets hit their target but not before he'd released the grenade. They watched helplessly as it arced through the air, crashed through the window, spun across the floor and came to rest in the middle of the room. For no more than a second, the two men looked at each other, then Lestocq remembered Mary's words, *"you'll have to find absolution another way."* With the briefest of smiles, he leapt across the floor and smothered the grenade with his body. As it detonated, his body lifted slightly then subsided. Shocked by the sight of blood spreading slowly across the floor, Fawkes was slow to realise Lestocq was trying to tell him something.

'The Fishing Club.' Lestocq spoke in a whisper.

'What?'

'Tell C you know all about the Fishing Club.'

The words made no sense to him. Hoping to hear more, he placed an ear close to Lestocq's mouth.

Lestocq's vacant eyes stared back at him.

Certain no one could survive the grenade, Grüber's men stopped firing. In the silence, Fawkes looked enviously at Lestocq. His orders were clear. He couldn't be taken alive but he'd given Mary his cyanide pill. Left with no choice, he'd have to charge the enemy with his empty tommy gun to make sure they killed him. As he reached the door, a volley of shooting and shouting erupted then just as quickly stopped. Amid the silence, the sound of the cicadas accompanied a familiar voice.

'You can come out now, it's quite safe.'

Through a narrow opening in the door, he saw "the German",

standing over the body of a soldier. By the time he'd accustomed his eyes to the bright sun, Durand and Mary had arrived. The Frenchman walked over and put his arms around him. Not sure what to do and anxious not to betray Brandon further, Mary hung back. Fawkes pointed to the shed.

'He smothered a grenade. Saved my life. Damn the bastard, now I don't know what to think.'

His unexpected display of emotion touched Mary deeply. Overcoming her doubts, she stepped forward and hugged him.

'You're safe, that's all that matters.'

She turned to "the German".

'How did you know where to find us?'

'Canaris contacted me and told me to go after you. He's the one you really ought to thank. Look, my men and I need to disappear fast. How will you manage from here?'

Durand asked one last favour.

'Can you take us to the village just down the road? I think I can get hold of another vehicle there.'

Before they left, after carefully surveying the dead, Fawkes went over to the body of one of the dead men and removed the identity tag from his neck. When they reached the lorry, they looked back at the lavender, trampled by feet, blown up by grenades and littered with bodies. He tried to lighten the atmosphere.

'We've ruined this year's crop, I'm afraid. I doubt they'll be inviting any more hotel guests to visit.' Then he remembered the fate of the people who'd welcomed them just a year earlier.

'I'm sorry, that was callous.'

He glanced guiltily at Durand.

'Over the centuries, that village has seen many tough times. The factory will re-open one day. When it does, I hope I'll have the honour of showing some guests around.'

On the outskirts of the village, they thanked their saviours and climbed down from the lorry. As she watched the lorry drive away, Mary's shoulders slumped.

'I don't think I can take any more of this. We were lucky back there but they'll get us in the end, I know.'

Durand saw the beaten look on her face and leaned forward.

'No, they won't. The man who drives the hotel laundry van lives here. We'll use that. Yann will hide us till dark then take you out to the sub. We've done the hard part, we just need you to stay strong a bit longer.'

He led them through the maze of narrow lanes till they reached a single storey yellow stone building with a narrow front door, fringed with wisteria.

'This is the one.'

While Fawkes kept out of sight, he gave the knocker three sharp raps. An unshaven man in trousers and a vest opened the door, a cigarette in one hand, a beer bottle in the other. His sullen expression changed to one of surprised embarrassment when he saw who the caller was.

'Aristide, I'm sorry to trouble you but we need your help.'

'What on earth are you doing here Monsieur?'

'I was taking this young lady out for a drive.'

Aware of Durand's interest in women, Aristide showed no surprise but the strong smell of lavender made him step back.

'Some bastard Boches stopped us and commandeered my car. Apparently, theirs had broken down so they took mine. Heaven help us if this is what it's going to be like from now on.'

'What are the Germans doing round here?'

'Looking for someone, probably a spy. It could have been worse, at least they didn't suspect us.'

'You want me to drive you back into town?'

'Or you can give me the keys and I'll drive myself. Someone can come up here tomorrow and collect you.'

Durand tried to sound as if either course of action was fine by him but he didn't want Aristide to see Fawkes. He needn't have worried. Aristide had already decided the woman must be married and knew an opportunity when he saw one.

'I suppose I could go to the bar in the village. But drinks are so expensive there. It's those bloody artists. All they do is paint and drink.'

Durand reached for his wallet and handed over a couple of notes.

'There you are, enjoy yourself. Someone will pick you up tomorrow. Thank you, Aristide, you've saved my life.'

Once they were back on the road, a new plan started to form in Durand's mind. He turned to give Mary an encouraging smile.

She was fast asleep.

Chapter 48

SHE WOKE UP to find the road down to the harbour stretching out invitingly before her. Durand had stopped the van outside a row of shops. Apart from two women leaning out of the windows of their flats to discuss their useless husbands, the place seemed deserted. Fawkes and Durand were deciding what to do next.

'We could drive into the back of the hotel as planned,' Fawkes was saying, 'but we've drawn a lot of attention to ourselves today. They may be waiting for us.'

Mary had been hoping for a bath before being consigned to the claustrophobia of the submarine but said nothing.

'The two of you could go to Yann's restaurant,' said Durand, 'while I see if the hotel looks safe.'

Their conversation was interrupted by a tap on Durand's window. Reaching for the door handle, he found himself looking into the face of a policeman. Fawkes stayed out of sight in the back.

'Where have you been, Monsieur?'

Another policeman emerged from an empty shop, stubbed out his cigarette and wandered round the vehicle.

'Out in the country with this young lady.'

Noting their dirty clothes, the policeman whispered to his colleague. Mary ostentatiously brushed the dirt from her skirt.

'Next time, take me somewhere decent,' she snapped at him.

'Go on, arrest him, the dirty old man,' shouted one woman from her window.

'And you can arrest my husband while you're at it,' added

the other.

The policeman laughed and was about to wave them on their way when his colleague pointed to the side of the van. In his door mirror, Durand could see he was pointing to the writing on the side.

'Are you Durand?'

Durand shrugged. The policeman un-holstered his gun.

'Step out of the van please, Monsieur.'

He weighed their chances. If he drove off, the policemen would shoot but they only had pistols. They'd been through much worse and got away with it. As his hand moved towards the gear lever, a Citroën saloon pulled up alongside. The driver was in civilian clothes, thick grey hair and solemn eyes, a familiar face. Manoeuvring slowly as if making a bad attempt at parallel parking, he peered up at Durand. One of the policemen went up to him.

'Move your vehicle, please sir, you're hindering an arrest.'

The car door opened and Canaris stepped out, holding his identification aloft. The policeman read it, saluted and stepped back. Canaris turned to the occupants of the van and spoke in a loud voice.

'Come with me, please.'

Then, softly and in English, 'Get in the car. Look frightened. Say nothing.'

Canaris held up his hand to emphasise the need for complete obedience. When all the doors were shut, he spoke again.

'You can't go back to your hotel so I'm taking you to the old fort. You'll have to stay there until it's time to leave.'

They sat in silence until they passed the village graveyard with the inscription *Hodie Nobis Cras Vobis*. In an effort to control her nerves, Mary turned to Durand.

'What does that mean?'

He shrugged his shoulders. 'I don't know much about Christian graveyards.'

Seeing her discomfort, Canaris laughed.

'It means "today this place is for us, tomorrow it will be for you." Simple but effective.'

Mary shuddered.

'I don't think I'd like to live in a village where I had to walk past that every day knowing it was getting nearer and nearer to coming true.'

'It doesn't matter if you walk past the sign or not,' said Canaris, 'it's still true. And, for a lot of us, tomorrow *is* coming a lot sooner than we expected.'

He parked the car at the foot of the steps and led them into the tower where Heywood had fought and died. Mary shivered from the cold of the bare room. Fawkes shivered too but for a different reason. Canaris clicked his heels.

'I must leave you now. I've done all I can and it's important I disappear.'

He turned and walked towards the door. As he neared it, Mary called softly to him.

'May I ask one last favour?'

He turned and nodded.

You read Latin. Can you tell me what this says?'

She pulled a folded piece of paper out of a pocket in her jacket and handed it to Canaris. He studied the Latin sentence "*Vitae Summa Brevis Spem Nos Vetat Incohare Longam*" and smiled.

'I recognise this, it's the title of a poem by Ernest Dowson, the one with that famous line, "they are not long, the days of wine and roses." For the title, he used a line from the poet Horace. I would translate it as "the short span of life does not permit us to have long hopes." Whoever wrote this down is well read.'

'Was well read. He was killed in action.'

'Then he was both brave and well read. I see there is a tear stain on the page. I'm sorry for your loss.'

'I thought he was just a playboy.'

'A playboy can be well read. May I read the rest of the letter?'

She nodded. Fawkes had sworn not to let Mary get under his skin but he felt the by now familiar pang of jealousy as Canaris read the lines of a dead man, a man with whom he could never compete. When he'd finished, Canaris looked up. 'And what you're doing now, is this your idea of *Don't lose hope and don't do anything dangerous in the meantime?'*

The head of the Abwehr, one of Hitler's most trusted men, took Mary's hand.

'You are a fine young woman. I wish you a long life and happiness but when you get home, promise me you'll start following his advice. I think he deserves it, don't you? And, if you will permit, I should like to copy this Latin phrase. I find it strangely comforting.

When he'd finished writing, he clicked his heels once more. This time, Mary let him go. He walked down the steps with a military bearing but when he reached his car, the mask fell away. The trip to San Sebastian and this mission in the south of France had been welcome distractions from all the plotting and counter plotting. Now, he must return to Berlin and its nest of vipers. His shoulders slumped and he sighed.

When they heard his car drive off, Durand broke the silence.

'I must get back to the hotel. I have some matters to attend to.'

Without waiting for a reply, he slipped out of the door. Fawkes soon followed.

'I need to check with Yann that he can take us out tonight. I won't be long. Don't open the door to anyone while I'm gone.'

As he stepped onto the pavement, apart from the overpowering smell of lavender, Fawkes looked outwardly like any other citizen of Fort Sarrasin out for a stroll. Inwardly, his mind was focused on two points. He and Mary were supposed to go home together in the sub. That was one issue. There was another. He'd examined the dead bodies. Not one of them had been a woman. Mirbeth was still out there.

But where?

Chapter 49

HER INSTRUCTIONS COULD not have been clearer: stay in the tower, out of sight and safe. While they'd been on the move, she'd longed for a break from the action and the danger but her mind had gone into overdrive and wouldn't slow down. The silence gave her time to think a thought she'd pushed to the back of her mind. In trying to avenge Brandon, had she damaged his child? In the cold room, with nothing to stare at except bare, stone walls, the thought overwhelmed her. She desperately needed something to take her mind off that terrible thought, something that reminded her of the life she'd once led. They'd kicked her off the RAF station she'd shared with him. Now this place, the haunts they'd shared, were all she had left of their time together. Leaving the briefcase on the stone floor, she opened the door of the tower and peered out. There was no one to be seen. Just a quick walk around. It wouldn't take long.

The cobbled street brought her down to the side of the hotel. She longed to step out onto the terrace just once more but it would be too risky. Giving it a fond look, she turned left towards the town. In the days following Brandon's death, she'd often pictured herself wandering among the shops again, such daydreams sustaining her while the world she knew fell apart. As she passed those same shops, she tried to summon up her memories but it wasn't the same. It had been the people, not the place that had made last year so memorable.

Feeling guilty for disobeying Fawkes, she turned round and started back up the hill to the tower. Near the top, she found the little wooden door that led into the green oasis where they'd had that last dinner. Imagining the scene she would find, she tried the handle. It was unlocked. The door scraped on the flagstones as she pushed it open, allowing her to gaze forlornly at the scene that greeted her.

The once immaculate lawn was now a wild meadow, the table at which they'd sat now covered in lichen. Only the beautiful cypress trees still bore testament to the elegance they had once enjoyed. She closed her eyes and was back at the cloth-covered table, laughing her way through a dinner she would remember for the rest of her life.

In La Dame Brave, Mirbeth paced around her car. She'd recovered from the shock of seeing the Englishman from the Blue Train, the man who called himself Freddie. Now, all her thoughts were focused on taking him back to Berlin, dead or alive. But there was no sign of Grüber or his men. If Freddie had escaped their clutches, there was a real risk those two SD killers would catch him and take him back, making her a laughing stock again. That would be too much. She started her car and set out for Fort Sarrasin.

At the top of the hill, she parked behind a van from the hotel with the funny name to consider her options. She'd start with the hotel. She'd only gone a short way down the hill when she saw a figure walking towards her, a figure she recognised as the young woman she'd encountered in the hotel entrance a year ago. At the time, she'd dismissed her as just a young girl on holiday. Clearly, she'd been wrong. Slipping the safety catch on her pistol, she waited for the woman to draw level only to see her stop at an oak door, look around furtively and stepped inside. Mirbeth let her car roll down silently to the door and climbed out.

Durand slipped into the rear of the hotel and headed for his office to put his new plan into action. Though he hated the idea of abandoning his lucrative role as an SIS go-between, the day's events had convinced him that his time in France was up. He needed to be on that sub tonight. Allowing himself a brief moment to look round the room, he placed Lestocq's pistol on his desk, walked over to the now disguised Tamara de Lempicka and lifted it off the wall to expose his safe. He'd barely turned the dial two clicks when the door burst open and two men barged past his embarrassed receptionist.

'I'm sorry, M. Durand. They ignored me completely.'

Saying, 'I'll deal with this,' he waved Agnes away. She knew who they were and so did he. Glad to be out of it, she withdrew. Expecting them to question him about the events in the village, he was surprised when they started to talk about something quite different.

'M. Durand, your hotel seems remarkably full considering there's a war on.'

'I don't think we've been introduced. You can't be too careful you know, there's a lot of spies around in the south of France.'

One of the men came right up to him and flourished his Gestapo card, repeatedly poking Durand in the chest.

'That's why we want to know where these people have come from.'

He was the hard man. Durand ignored him and turned to his companion.

'Look, I run a hotel. If guests want to stay here, I'm only too glad to have them.'

The other man adopted a gentler tone.

'You realise almost all your guests are Jews.'

'Of course. Without them, the hotel would have had to close. If they ever leave, it probably will.'

The soft man smiled, a smile more chilling than the hard man's chest pokes.

'M. Durand, we're not here to give you a hard time. Just tell us who runs the Jewish network round here and we'll leave you alone. We can be reasonable you know. We might even overlook what you've just been up to with your British friends.'

'I have no idea. I didn't even know there was a "Jewish network", as you put it. Word got around and people came here because they felt safe. Once they no longer feel safe, they'll leave. It's as simple as that.'

The hard man took over.

'Yesterday, my colleague and I executed your Resistance friends. If you want to avoid the same fate, I suggest you stop being a smartarse and tell us what we want to know.'

Had they killed Yann, the only man who could get them out to the sub? He fought to control his breathing.

'You've been killing people down here in this peaceful little town?'

'No, your friends in the hills, eight of them,' boasted the hard man.

'You forgot the old man at the desk,' added the soft man.

'My mistake. I was never very good at maths. Nine of your friends, then.'

The hard man leered at Durand.

Ashamed of the relief he felt, Durand looked away. He might yet talk his way out of this and onto the sub.

'Look, I'm not a member of the Resistance. They're the last people I'd have any dealings with.'

As soon as the words left his mouth, he knew he'd made a fatal mistake. The men exchanged looks. The soft man spoke.

'So you're SIS, an even bigger fish. My, it's been a useful couple of days.'

Durand edged towards the door. Without waiting for the soft man to finish, he rushed out and made for the lift. Slamming the lift cage shut and holding it with both hands, he used his elbow to press the button for the roof terrace. As the lift rose, he sank to the floor, preparing himself for what he had to do.

By the time the lift reached the roof, he'd composed himself. Straightening his tie, he pulled the cuffs of his shirt down and stepped out into the hot sun, smiling at the handful of guests as if it was an ordinary day and he'd come to check on their wellbeing. Exchanging the usual pleasantries, he moved over to the front wall and glanced into the bar. What a success that had been. As he looked around, he remembered coming up here after his interview for the job of manager and the life he'd led since that day. He'd been a playboy with women, played at being a spy and been rather pleased with his performance in both roles. But they were just roles and it all seemed rather empty now. Though he was proud of what he'd done to help his fellow Jews, he knew that one day, the authorities would come for them and when they did, he'd be powerless to prevent it.

There was one thing, one big thing he could do, one thing he wanted to be remembered by. He thought about the brave young girl he'd left in the tower, his promise to Fawkes to protect her and her own words to him. *You'll be honourable when the time comes,* she'd said. The game was up for him but she could still get out on the submarine that night. Provided he kept his mouth shut. There was only one way to guarantee that.

He heard the sound of footsteps and men panting. Taking one last look, far across the sea, towards the land of his birth, he turned to face his pursuers. The smiles of the guests turned to alarm as the men from the Gestapo approached him.

'Alright, gentlemen, I'll tell you what you want to know but you must arrest me and handcuff me in front of the hotel guests. I don't want anyone thinking I gave you this information willingly.'

He held out his hand. The hard man stepped forward and attached one end of the cuffs to Durand's wrist and the other to his own. As the handcuffs snapped shut, Durand asked if he might take one last look at the rooftop view.

'I know I'm not coming back.'

'Sensible fellow,' the hard man said as they turned him round to face the sea.

'You're very kind.'

He felt them relax slightly. Seizing the soft man under the armpits he dragged him up and over the wall. The hard man screamed, desperately trying to cling to brickwork but the weight of Durand and the soft man was too much. The three of them tumbled downwards.

The roof terrace was on the seventh floor. On the ground floor, directly beneath them was a small restaurant open to the street. In the last summer of peace, Durand had installed a canvas awning so people could sit outside and had been gratified by the amount of passing trade it had attracted. Now the full value of his investment was realised when he landed, not on the pavement but on the awning. It took most of the force of his landing before catapulting him onto the pavement. He landed on one German, breaking his own fall but killing the man. The other man landed on his head, narrowly missing Durand. Durand's back was broken in three places. His legs were shattered. But he was alive. The men who had murdered his friends in the perfume factory were dead.

A passing Catholic priest, seeing the three men, came over to attend to their souls. Two of the men were obviously dead but one was still breathing. He started to administer the last rites.

'Do you believe in God the Father, God the Son and God the Holy Ghost?'

'This is no time for riddles, Father, just unlock me from these men and get me into the hotel.'

Showing a worldly appreciation of the situation, the priest searched in the pockets of the dead men, found the keys and un-cuffed him. A group of hotel guests repaid their debt to their protector by carrying him into the hotel on a makeshift stretcher. The priest stood up to leave then had a further thought. Bending down, he cuffed the two dead men together, making it look as if one had arrested the other. Crossing himself, he departed the scene.

Fawkes had debated whether to enter Yann's restaurant by the front or the back. If Yann was already known for his Resistance work, the police would be watching both entrances and trying to slip in by the back door would attract more attention. Knowing they served meals all day, he arrived at the main entrance at the same time as an elderly couple. Assuring them he was delighted to see them looking so well, he linked arms with them and marched inside. They were relieved when this strange man, reeking of lavender, left them and walked through to the kitchen.

Yann was surprised to see him.

'I'd heard there was a big gunfight and assumed your little team wouldn't survive. Are you all here?'

'Durand has gone back to the hotel, Mary's waiting in the tower.'

He helped himself to a bread roll but declined a glass of wine. Then he got down to business.

'I need some notepaper, an envelope and a pen.'

Yann's wife fetched them and he started writing. When he'd finished, he addressed the envelope to the captain of the submarine and sealed it.

'I want you to give this to Mary when you take her out to the sub.'

'Aren't you coming too?'

Fawkes shook his head.

'If she and I go back together, she's a dead woman. Tell her there are too many patrols for you to use the big dinghy we came in and that she's to hand this letter to the Captain as soon as she boards the sub. When you hand her over, tell her you're going back for me.'

'It's dangerous for me to make two journeys.'

'You'll only make one. All you have to do is get Mary and the letter out to the sub.'

'As long as you know what you're doing.'

'That'll be the day.'

Giving a cheery wave to the couple with whom he'd come in, he left by the front entrance.

Just one more task. He couldn't be sure Mirbeth would come down to Fort Sarrasin but she knew what had happened in the tower last year and he knew she was a woman who would never give up. If he was in her place, that's where he would go.

He set off up the hill and was rewarded immediately by the sight of a Mercedes heading towards him. From the seclusion of a shop doorway, he saw the car glide silently to a halt by a door in the wall running underneath the tower. Expecting her to walk up the hill to the tower, he was surprised to see Mirbeth walk through the door.

That was good. But she'd be armed and, though Mary was safely tucked up in the tower, so was his Webley, in Mary's pocket. Everything depended on catching Mirbeth unawares.

He quickened his pace.

Chapter 50

MARY'S REVERIE WAS interrupted by the sound of the door creaking open. Watching anxiously to see if the police had come for her, she was relieved when a smiling blonde woman stepped through.

'Sorry to disturb you but I'm lost. I'm from Sweden and I'm looking for a hotel, the one with the funny name.'

Mary had the strangest feeling she'd met her somewhere before but the woman's friendly manner disarmed her and she decided she must be mistaken. As L'Hirondelle des Isles was the only large hotel for miles around, Mary was surprised the woman hadn't found it but was happy to help her, if only to get rid of her.

'Let me show you.'

Mirbeth looked around, her eyes resting on the table and chairs.

'Actually, do you mind if I have a little sit down? I've been wandering around looking for the hotel and I'm a bit pooped.'

Anxious to return to the safety of the tower, Mary would have preferred the woman to be on her way.

'Of course.'

As if reading her mind, Mirbeth whispered, 'it's that time of the month, I'm afraid.'

'Oh please, take as long as you need, then I'll show you.'

'Please, sit down too,' beckoned Mirbeth. 'You make me feel guilty, standing there.'

Again, Mary felt compelled to comply but couldn't help stealing a glance at her watch.

'I'm sorry, do you have to be somewhere?'

'No, I'd just lost track of time, that's all.'

'You speak French very well but you don't sound French.'

'I'm American.'

Given that she couldn't say she was British, it was the only answer she could think of.

'We can speak in English if you prefer.'

She knew she'd never manage a convincing American accent. For the first time, the thought briefly crossed her mind that she'd walked into a trap but she quickly dismissed it. The woman was just being friendly.

'Thank you but no, I need to keep my French up to scratch. I'm the only woman on my team and have to do twice as well as the men just to stand still.'

If the woman asked her why, she was in trouble but she needn't have worried. Mirbeth felt she'd softened her up sufficiently.

'Not another one! It's exactly the same for me. If I don't come up with the right result on this trip, I'll be for it. It's so unfair.'

Mary took another look at her watch, this time not so surreptitiously. It seemed to work. Taking the hint, Mirbeth stood up.

'I'm sorry, I've taken enough of your time.'

A relieved Mary went to the open door and gestured to the woman to go through.

'Please, I prefer that you should go first.'

Mary started to move then froze. The words conjured up a clear image of the hotel entrance last year, the woman coming in just as she was going out. When she turned round, the woman was no longer smiling. Pointing a gun at her, she pulled Mary back into the garden and kicked the door shut.

'Sit down young lady. You and I are going to have a little chat. I think you'll agree, we've a lot to talk about.'

Mary tried to sound defiant but it wasn't the talking that worried her. The briefcase with the letters from Canaris was safely in the tower but the forged Churchill letter was still in her jacket. When that was found, the mission, everything they had gone through that day, would come to nothing.

And there was no way out.

'I won't tell you anything, no matter what you do to me.'

Mirbeth tutted.

'Why do you people always assume you're going to be tortured? I'm sure there'll be no need for that.'

Pushing Mary into a chair, she forced her hands onto the rough lichen of the table.

'I'll let you into a little secret, we constantly arrest British agents, question them and let them go. When they go home they're not going to tell their superiors are they? Why be any different? It's quite simple really, you're going to tell me everything then I'm going to let you catch the sub that's waiting for you. You're hours away from safety. What do you say? That's fair, isn't it?'

Mary spat in Mirbeth's face.

As he drew near, Fawkes was surprised to hear two voices, stunned when he realised one of them was Mary's.

'You can go to hell.'

Mirbeth wiped the spittle from her face and shook her head.

'Now that's a pity. It means I have to move to plan B. You're a spy and you're of limited use once I take you into custody. You'll be tried and shot. We do things correctly, you know. Right now, I'm offering you a deal. Why not be reasonable?'

Fawkes had a decision to make. Mary was where she was because she'd disobeyed orders but he had to assume she still had the forged letter on her. And the Webley. He could leave her to her fate, telling C he'd given the letter to Canaris but the SS must have got their hands on it. When he presented C with the Royal letters given to him by Canaris, his own future would be secure.

Or he could, unarmed, step through the door and by distracting Mirbeth, almost certainly dying in the process, give Mary a chance to use the Webley.

Mr Ambition or Mr Doing Your Best to Get Killed?

He stepped through the door.

'Ingrid, how are things in Norrköping?'

Mirbeth looked at him as if she'd seen a ghost but, ever the professional, she recovered quickly. Pulling Mary out of the chair and holding a gun to her head, she used her as a shield. When Fawkes spoke, the charm he'd displayed on the Blue Train was absent.

'I don't think you realise your position. The Resistance have killed your entire team. You're on your own but if you leave now, we'll let you escape. I'd get on with it if I was you, you're not in a strong position here.'

'Come now, Freddie, it's your position that's weak. If you had a weapon, you'd have used it by now.'

Mirbeth smiled broadly, as if addressing an old friend.

'I have a better idea.'

The pistol remained firmly pressed against Mary's head, the smile firmly in place.

'She's a pretty little thing, I'll give you that.'

The smile evaporated. Her eyes hardened.

'Tell me why you're here or I'll kill her.'

Fawkes adopted a defiant look.

'You know perfectly well why we're here. Last year, the Pole promised to give us some top-secret material but when he realised you were following him, he panicked and fled back to Poland. We went back to the village to see if he'd left anything behind but there wasn't. I failed last year and I've failed again this year so you win. Are you satisfied?'

Mirbeth scoffed.

'You're a good actor but when I get you back to Berlin, I rather think you'll tell me the truth. I gave you a chance to save the girl. Say goodbye to her, Freddie.'

'Oh what the hell, Ingrid, go ahead and kill her. I never wanted her on the mission in the first place. But before you do, you might want to take a look at this.'

Fawkes produced the identity tag he'd pocketed in the

lavender field and tossed it at her feet, ready to lunge at her as she looked down. As Mirbeth saw Grüber's name on the metal disc, Mary felt the pistol ease away from her head. Seizing his opportunity, Fawkes launched himself at Mirbeth. From the moment he'd walked through the door, Mary had known what he had in mind - summon up his mother's memory one last time and make the ultimate sacrifice. She wasn't having that. Allowing herself to be tricked by Mirbeth had made her angry. Drawing Fawkes into the same trap made her furious. If this was where it had to end, so be it. Brandon had gone down fighting, so would she. While Mirbeth focused, first on the identity disc then Fawkes, Mary slipped her left hand into the pocket containing the Webley. Leaving it in the pocket, she cocked it, turned and fired two shots. Fawkes saw a brief look of surprise on Mirbeth's face before she dropped to the ground, twitched then lay motionless.

Mary gazed down at her for a second or two then collapsed to the ground herself. In shooting Mirbeth, she'd finally avenged Brandon but she had nothing more to give. Seeing only one wound on Mirbeth's chest, Fawkes feared one of the shots had been fired by her and had hit Mary. Pulling Mary to him, he held her tightly. To his relief, she started sobbing.

'It's alright, you'll be fine. You had to do it. But we've got to get out of here. Those gunshots could be heard all over town.'

He'd barely finished speaking when the sky darkened as a giant figure filled the doorway and Yann stepped through. Looking down at Mirbeth, he turned to Mary and spoke quickly and with authority.

'The police will be here any minute. That must be her car. Get the keys off her.'

His firmness of purpose was what Mary needed. Leaning over Mirbeth, she searched her pockets till she found them. Snatching them for her, Yann headed for the door.

'I'll go outside and wait for them. Shut the door and push the table across it. With luck, they'll assume it's too rotten to open and give up.'

From behind the door, they heard him open the bonnet of Mirbeth's car just as a police car pulled up.

'I heard a shot. Did it come from here?'

'A shot? I never heard a shot.'

An appropriate pause, not too long.

'Oh, you mean the backfire from my car. It's this bloody cheap petrol. It's not good enough for a car of this quality.'

'What's behind that door.'

'Search me. As far as I know, it's been shut for a long time.'

Fawkes and Mary heard the inevitable sound of footsteps approaching. They leaned hard on the table as the door handle rattled and the door was pushed from the other side.

'I told you, it's a long time since anyone went in there.'

'Your car definitely backfired?'

'I told you. Bloody loud it was.'

As he prepared to leave, the policeman had a parting word for Yann.

'I'd keep that car out of sight, if I was you. If the Mayor sees it, he'll want it for himself and confiscate it. That's the way things are nowadays in this country.'

'Thanks, officer. That sounds good advice.'

With the policeman safely out of the way, Yann tapped on the door.

'He's gone.'

As the door scraped open, he continued to take charge of the situation but this time, with a script written by Fawkes.

'You'll have to hide in my restaurant until it's time to go out to the submarine. They'll be scanning the sea with searchlights and using patrol boats so it's too dangerous to go out in the large dinghy, I'll have to use my racing craft. It's small and fast but I can only take one person at a time.'

Yann spoke his lines with conviction but Mary wasn't taken in.

'I'm not having that. Either we both go together or we both stay.'

Yann pulled Mary close and spoke softly.

'There's something you don't know. The Gestapo came to the hotel looking for you. Rather than betray you, Durand jumped off the roof. It's your duty to get away now to justify his sacrifice.'

Mary gasped in anguish.

'Is he dead? Oh God, that's awful.'

'No, he's not dead but he may never walk again. Now come with me.'

Fawkes led her gently towards the door.

'This is important. When you get back, go to your father's family in Scotland and stay there. Don't talk to anyone. C won't like it but he can't risk sending people out to find you. Is that clear?'

She looked at him in a way she'd never done before. As his heart soared, his resolve not to join her weakened.

'You're talking as if I'll never see you again. How can you saying that after what happened back there? I thought we meant something to each other.'

He wanted to tell her that, after "what had happened back there," she meant everything, not something, to him but her survival depended on going back without him and placing herself beyond C's reach. He used the only words he thought would work.

'I got carried away back there. Take my advice, forget me and everything that happened here. Go home and bring your child up.'

If he wasn't coming with her, she wanted to give him something to make him angry, something that would make him determined to get home safely so he could confront the organisation that had used him so cruelly.

'Lestocq told me something while you were crawling through the lavender.'

'I know, he mentioned the Fishing Club.'

'He wasn't talking about fishing. This was much more serious. He told me the SIS had had their eye on you since you were born and arranged for the Navy to take you away from your mother. Then they got you thrown out of the Navy so they could recruit you.'

'I wouldn't pay any attention to the lies of a communist agent. God knows what he would have said if we'd got him back to London. But thanks anyway.'

He did his best to sound nonchalant but her words hit home, as she had intended. She had supplied the missing piece in the jigsaw, the piece that explained everything. He needed to bring this conversation to a close before he surrendered to the emotions swirling about in his head.

He turned his back on her and walked through the door.

Chapter 51

YANN HAD A decision to make. The Captain of the submarine had agreed with Fawkes that he'd surface at 10pm and 2am each night for two nights. If no one turned up by then, he was to abandon the team and head for home. Should he go for the earlier time or wait till dead of night when things should be quieter?

He decided to go for the earlier time and for one simple reason. Mary worried him. On the surface, she'd recovered well since her collapse after shooting Mirbeth but the signs were there. She smiled a lot and nodded vigorously at everything he said but she hardly uttered a word. He respected Fawkes for sending her home the easy way while he drew away any remaining pursuers by taking the long route. He also hoped Mary would keep things together better in front of a relative stranger like himself.

But would she? The Vichy police were bound to conduct searches both on land and sea. She'd been chased all day long. How much more could she take? All he could do was not show Mary how worried he was. And do his duty. He was determined to get her safely on board that submarine as quickly as possible and at whatever cost to himself.

He wasn't the only one with feelings to hide. She'd returned to France fuelled by a desire for revenge and the chance to kill Germans. Until she'd killed one. Now, instead of elation, she felt soiled by what she'd done. The sight of Mirbeth twitching on the ground played over and over again in her mind until all she could think of was getting out of this place and never coming back.

'Going for a 2am rendezvous is the obvious thing to do but,

because it's so obvious, I think we should go for the earlier time,' he told Mary. 'You've created a hell of a stir today. The police will be under instructions to search the town but they'll probably wait till dead of night as they'll assume that's when we'll leave. The one thing we've got in our favour is that the exit via the sewage outlet is always left unguarded.'

'Why is that?'

'It's the start of the route for smuggling to and from French North Africa. The Mayor is one of the leading smugglers so they leave it unguarded.'

When darkness came, they crept along the alley at the back of the restaurant. The tiny sailing dinghy was painted black with black oars and a black sail. Even the lifejacket Yann handed her was black. Once she was on board, he lifted a panel in the stern and pointed to a sten gun. Before leaving the restaurant, he'd given her clear instructions.

'Complete silence at all times. Lie flat on your back and don't lean to one side or the other. If we're caught by a searchlight, it must look as if I'm alone. That way, they'll assume I'm a smuggler and ignore me. This little beauty is fast. It won't take long.'

Yann used his cloth-covered oars to paddle through the sewage until they were far enough from the shore to raise the mast and unfurled the sail. Immediately, the little dinghy leapt into life. Lying in the bottom of the boat, Mary felt the water thumping the sides, just inches away.

With her life in Yann's hands, all she could do was gaze up at the stars and the light of the full moon. It was hard to believe so much evil could exist alongside such beauty.

'We're passing the island,' whispered Yann. 'Not long now.'

Yann's search of the horizon was rewarded when the submarine's conning tower emerged from the water, silhouetted against the moon and less than half a mile away. Three swift flashes from a lamp followed. He beckoned Mary to sit up but as she did so, the sub disappeared below the waves.

'What is it?'

'It was the sub but it's submerged again. Something has disturbed it. Stay down.

Don't worry.'

They needed to be less visible in the moonlight. As he pushed her back down, she felt the abrupt turn of the little craft as Yann steered it close in to the shoreline.

The tactic worked too well. As they rounded a promontory, a Vichy patrol boat swept out of the darkness, the roar of its engine replacing the gentle lap of the waves. The stars and moon disappeared, the sky went black as it clipped Yann's invisible craft on the stern. Mary let out a cry as she clung to the sides to stop herself falling out. The patrol boat continued on its way while the dinghy spun round, taking on water rapidly. Only Yann's skill and the fact that they were so close in enabled them to make it to a shoreline ringed by a shelf of rocks, interspersed with channels of water.

He steered the shattered dinghy into one of the channels then pulled Mary out with one hand, grabbing the sten gun with the other.

'Help me raise her up onto this shelf before she sinks.'

They stepped knee deep into the water and hoisted the dinghy up, turning it over to drain. One corner of the stern was smashed in.

'I'll see if there's anything I can do to patch it up.'

He pulled out a knife and started stripping any spare pieces of wood whose removal wouldn't let in water.

'You can't possibly, can you? The stern's been smashed open.'

'If I can make it seaworthy enough and you can bail out the water fast enough, we can make it to the sub before we sink. It's close by but you may have to swim the last few yards.'

'What about you?'

'Don't worry about me, I can swim back to the island.'

'You're taking a terrible risk.'

'I said I would and I will. I won't let you down, not while there's breath in my body.'

He started working the strips of wood into the shattered corner, while talking to take Mary's mind off their predicament.

'Do you remember the first time we met, that evening on the hotel terrace?'

'I remember every detail. You were very angry about the boches and what you'd do to them.'

'That was just talk. This is me, putting those words into action, this and taking Durand to Paris to find Juliette.'

'I didn't realise you'd gone too. That was very brave of you.'

Yann completed his handiwork.

'At least the patrol boat has gone away. I don't think they even knew they'd hit us.'

He sat back to survey the repair.

'This might work.'

The smile on his lips froze at the sound of an engine growing louder. A searchlight clicked on and swept across the shoreline.

'They're coming back.'

They lay flat on the rock shelf but there was no time to hide the dinghy and the searchlight soon picked it up. A machine gun opened up but its first burst fell well short of them. Yann stood up.

'We'll have to run for it. Pick up your weapon.'

As he dragged her towards the trees, they heard men climbing down the side of the patrol boat.

'Our only chance is the monastery.' He gestured towards the rising ground in front of them. 'They'll give us sanctuary.'

'And if they won't?'

'We'll have to make a stand or swim for it. Which do you want to do?'

'Let's head for the monastery. I'd rather die on dry land, wouldn't you?'

He looked at the young woman he'd sworn to protect.

'We're not dead yet.' He pulled her into the trees. 'I know this island and they don't.'

They ran and kept running, through the pines, into a field

which sloped up towards the comforting sight of the monastery silhouetted against the moonlight. Long lines of bushes pointed the way to the top of the field. She remembered the vineyard and Brandon's stolen grapes.

Yann told her to get down and crawl.

'If we stand up, they'll see us against the moonlight.'

Bullets started to thud into the soft earth. Seeing smears of red on her clothes, she thought she'd been hit until she remembered the clumsy kiss with Brandon and the red grape stains. As they neared the top, Yann whispered encouragement.

'Keep going, they can't see us. They're just firing wildly.'

At the top end of the vineyard, the first thing they came to was the well, halfway between them and the monastery. Covered in dirt and grape stains, they scrambled past it to the monastery door. Yann tried to open it but it wouldn't budge. Mary hammered on it with her sten gun. No one answered. Behind them, their pursuers trampled through the vineyard. Every second brought them nearer. For the first time, she saw a look of defeat on Yann's face.

'We'll have to go back to that well and make a stand there.'

Mary looked at her sten gun. If it was over, she'd go down fighting.

'No, I'll hold them off while you keep knocking.'

She stumbled back to the well. When the soldiers burst through the vineyard, she fired a fearful, tentative burst to distract them from Yann. When they fired back, bullets slammed into the well sending up shards of stone and brick, one shard slicing her cheek. With anger replacing fear, she fired back and kept firing until her magazine was empty. Throwing the gun down, she ran towards Yann in despair. As she reached him, the door of the monastery creaked open, revealing a hooded figure in the doorway.

'Sanctuary, brother, we seek sanctuary.'

The monk looked at the extraordinary sight of a man and a woman, a sten gun lying on the ground and, behind them, the sound of his beloved grapes being crushed. He pulled them through and slammed the door shut.

Gesturing with his arms, he showed them the monastery.

'I think he's saying we're safe here but he's taken a vow of silence. It's hard to tell. The monk nodded warmly but his unspoken words were contradicted as machine gun fire rattled across the wall of the monastery and through the windows, taking chunks out of a fresco of Jesus delivering the Sermon on the Mount.

'Jesus,' said Yann.

Delighted that his visitor had recognised Our Saviour, the monk beckoned them to follow him across the courtyard.

'I need to get this young lady out to a submarine. How can she get down to the sea from here?'

With the sound of splintering wood adding urgency to his request, the monk led them through the refectory towards a room containing latrines. Shutting the door, he waved Mary over to look at the wooden planks with their round holes.

'I can't climb down there. It's a sheer drop to the rocks below.'

The monk shook his head as he tried to think how to explain matters. Exasperated, he turned his back on her and walked over to the far side of the room.

Mary clutched Yann's sleeve.

'Is he abandoning us?'

Seeing the pitiful look on her face, the monk crossed himself before breaking his vow.

'The sea is right below us, that's what I was showing you. If you go through this door you'll see a long, low wall. At the end of the wall, you'll find the top of a path that leads down the cliff. It's steep, narrow and dangerous but it's your only chance. They'll be here any moment and they clearly have no regard for the sanctity of this place.'

As he finished speaking, they heard the sound of raised voices coming from the other side of the door. The monk raised a finger to his lips and whispered, 'you'll have to hide and wait till they're gone.'

While he looked around for a way to hide them, they heard another monk break his vow and speak.

'There's no one here who isn't supposed to be. Apart from you.'

Another voice said, 'Where does this lead?'

'To the latrines, you're welcome to look but please act with courtesy.'

As the monk spoke, the door opened and three monks emerged from the latrines. Avoiding eye contact, they joined the others at the dining table. Having searched the latrines, the officer returned to the refectory and paced around the length of the table. When he came to a halt behind one of them, the monk saw that her women's shoes were protruding from under her habit. Feeling his eyes on the back of her head, she drew her feet back, her fingers clasping Fawkes's revolver, all the time trying desperately to prevent her legs from shaking. Just when she thought he would never move, he walked over to the monk sitting at the head of the table.

'Gentlemen, this is a house of God. I mean no disrespect to you or your traditions but you are harbouring spies. If you don't tell us where they are, it will be necessary to shoot this venerable old man. I will shoot him with regret, I assure you, but I will shoot him.'

The monks looked at each other but no one spoke. The officer cocked his pistol. Finally, the monk who'd hidden them stood up.

'Put your gun away, officer. I know where they are. I have taken a vow of silence but I'm willing to speak because I don't approve of traitors.'

Mary wasn't particularly religious, but she'd been a regular churchgoer at home and had instinctively placed her faith in this man of the cloth. It seemed that faith had been betrayed.

'They went out of the door on the far side of the hall. It leads to the cellars where we store our wine. I think they're hiding there but you'd better be quick. Follow me.'

As the police left the room, Yann beckoned to a contrite Mary to follow him back through the latrines and out into the night air. They halted by the long, low wall.

'The sub is out there. It's not that far and you've got a lifejacket. It's not what we planned but you'll see it in the moonlight. It's your only chance.'

'What if they capture you?'

'They won't, not alive anyway. Go on, they'll soon realise they've been tricked.'

When she didn't move, he sighed.

'Alright, I'll show you the way.'

'No, you've done enough. Go while you can.'

She pushed him away and, with a last look back, he disappeared into the night.

Slipping off the habit, Mary crept along the wall. When she reached the end, the path turned out to be a steep and rocky slope half hidden by bushes. It would have been difficult to negotiate in daylight. In darkness, it was madness. She stared at the steep drop, looked back at the monastery and froze to the spot. There was only one way out, a route she had been convinced she'd never take. When she pulled out the pill Fawkes had given her, it gleamed invitingly in the moonlight. She couldn't put her unborn child through the ordeal they would both suffer when they captured her. Another look at the pill. Was it like this for Brandon in those last few seconds when he knew he was about to die?

As she brushed the pill against her bottom lip, a metallic scraping sound interrupted her. She turned to see a grappling hook embedding itself on the wall. The sailors from the patrol boat must be cutting off her last hope of escape.

'Oh, Brandon, teach me how to do this.'

As her lips parted, an arm reached out to whisk her over the wall. The pill slipped from her fingers and tumbled into the darkness. She saw the insignia of the Royal Canadian Navy on the man's shoulder as a gentle Canadian voice spoke in a whisper.

'Hold on tight Ma'am, we're taking you home'.

Chapter 52

'WHERE THE HELL have you been?'

That was what C wanted to say when the door to the roof opened to reveal his prodigal agent walking unhurriedly towards him, carrying a smart leather briefcase. He restrained himself. Something about that unhurried walk told him the Fawkes walking towards him was not the man he'd recruited on this same roof.

C concealed his anxiety and he had a lot of anxiety to conceal. The submarine had docked on the west coast of Scotland instead of Portsmouth. The Ballantyne woman had promptly disappeared. There was no news of Durand or Fawkes and, to cap it all, Lestocq had disappeared. The Fishing Club wanted answers and he had none. He was a frightened man, a man under pressure from equally worried men fearing for the loss of their estates.

The slow journey back had given Fawkes time to think. Aware that C visited his pigeons every morning at 11 o'clock, he'd taken the lift to the top floor and headed up the narrow staircase. When he emerged into the daylight, a new, diplomatic Fawkes prepared to deliver a few surprises to the man standing there, framed by the autumn sun and caressing the creatures he loved more than any human.

'Fawkes old man, good to see you. I was worried.'

'Sorry I'm late sir. There wasn't room for me on the dinghy out to the sub so I had to come home the slow way but I expect the young lady has already told you that.'

'The young lady has told me nothing. She walked off the sub and disappeared into thin air.'

Fawkes made no reply, hoping the relief he felt wasn't reflected in his expression as he watched C turn away from his birds long enough to give him an accusatory look.

'Who put that idea into her head?'

'Not me sir. I made it quite clear she needed to be debriefed. Of course, women in her condition can be, you know, unpredictable. But now I'm back, I can fill you in. I don't think we need trouble her anymore.'

'Her condition?'

'Pregnant, sir. The father was an American, serving in the RAF. He was killed in his Spitfire before he could do the right thing by her.'

C stopped stroking the pigeon to give the impression all this was news to him.

'That explains it. Women in that situation usually prefer to disappear from the public gaze.' He resumed his stroking. 'Fact is, Lestocq's disappeared and I wanted to find out if she knew anything about it. He was disappointed not to be going on the mission and I was wondering if he was down there with you.'

This was one of the three matters Fawkes had given most thought to on the long journey home. Though he suspected C's ignorance was feigned, his reply was fluent and convincing.

'He was there, sir and I'm afraid he didn't make it back.'

He looked his boss firmly in the eye.

'But you can tell his father he died for his country. I was there when it happened. We owe our lives to him.'

'What on earth was he doing there?'

'He said you'd heard a communist, an SIS man, was in the area bent on assassinating Canaris. As there was no way to warn me, he came down to deliver the message personally and make sure the handover of the letter went smoothly. He was a dedicated servant of the department, his death will be a great loss.'

Encouraged by the look of relief that swept over C's face,

he pressed on.

'It all went wrong when the meeting with Canaris ended and a bunch of plain clothes thugs appeared, obviously SD and led by Mirbeth, the woman I encountered last year. I remember you saying the SD had been penetrated by commies. As usual, you were right.'

After a brief look around the roof, he summoned up a solemn face.

'When we came under attack, Lestocq was the bravest of us all. While we were trying to escape, he fought off Mirbeth's men before throwing himself on a grenade to save the rest of us. It is impossible to exaggerate his courage.'

Keeping a pigeon balanced on the index finger of his left hand, C stepped back from the coop to put an arm round his underling.

'Thank you for telling me that, Freddie, it makes my task much easier.'

Slowly, he eased the pigeon back into the coop and shut the door, giving Fawkes time to absorb his promotion to "Freddie."

'The King announced a new award while you were away, the George Cross. It's to be the highest civilian award for bravery and it seems to me young Lestocq should be its first recipient. Don't you think?'

My God, the man's got a bloody nerve, thought "Freddie."

'Absolutely sir. I can't think of anyone more deserving. If you like, I'd be happy to visit his father and tell him of his son's courage and devotion to duty.'

'That won't be necessary.'

C changed the subject.

'What happened to Durand?'

'He jumped off a hotel roof.'

'Good God, I'm sorry to hear that. But the handover went smoothly?'

'Yes and no.'

'Meaning?'

'There was a slight change of plan.'

He prepared to bid farewell to his fleeting "Freddie" status.

'I thought about this a lot on the way out. Instinct told me this wasn't right so I decided to take a risk. I told Canaris that Churchill had refused to sign a letter.'

C's expression was inscrutable but Fawkes thought he saw the merest trace of relief on his face.

'How did he react to that?'

'He said the demand for a letter was a test of your sincerity. If you produced it, he'd know you weren't sincere since anyone showing it around would instantly be betrayed. He said it would be used by Hitler to inflict a humiliating peace on our country. I wasn't sure if I was doing the right thing but it worked because he did something quite unexpected.'

Expressionless, C waited for the next surprise.

'You wanted me to be a carrier pigeon, sir.'

He scrutinised C's face. A blank canvas.

'I went beyond that and used my judgement. I felt it was my duty to do so.'

This time, he avoided eye contact, gazing instead at the barrage balloons floating in the London sky.

'It not only saved the mission, it gave us a bonus.'

He opened the briefcase, produced the bundle of letters that Canaris had given him and handed them over. C perused them carefully, his expression growing more and more amazed as he proceeded. Fawkes pushed home his advantage.

'My report will say that the mission was to collect these letters. No one need know about the letter I was carrying. You're in the clear. These letters guarantee your safety.'

He paused.

'Just as your letter guarantees mine.'

'So you've still got the letter?'

Fawkes nodded.

'Did you read it?'

This was the second thing he'd thought through on the journey home. "Freddie" knew too much, so did Mary and Durand. Accidents could easily be arranged. He needed something that would protect all three of them. He nodded again.

'Did the other two read it?'

'Of course not, sir. They never knew there was a letter.'

'Why did you read it?'

'Instinct again. An essential ingredient in an agent's makeup, wouldn't you say sir? That and knowing what to do with a document that's too hot to handle.'

'You destroyed it?'

He couldn't fail to catch C's hopeful look.

'I've lodged it somewhere for safe keeping. It's important to keep your name out of it so I won't embarrass you by telling you where. I've also included a full and accurate report of Lestcoq's actions. I thought it important to make a record of everything he'd said and done. For example, he was anxious I should know about the Fishing Club.'

'I know nothing about a fishing club. What on earth was he talking about?'

The new Fawkes knew when to pursue a matter and when to let it go.

'They were his dying words, sir. I may have misheard.'

For several seconds, C scrutinised Fawkes's face, admiring the highly misleading picture of calm and repose. Then he walked over to the edge of the roof. Fawkes decided it would be safer to remain with the pigeons. After a long silence, during which Fawkes guessed he was coming to an important decision, C turned and addressed his underling.

'You've come back a very different man from the one who left.'

'Well, I'm sorry about that but the mission changed me.'

'No, I'm impressed. You were right about the letter. While you've been away, the Duke of Windsor has been spotted in Lisbon canoodling with known Nazi sympathisers and we've learnt that Hitler has called off the invasion to prepare an attack on Russia. There's more in that head of yours than I gave you credit for. Well done.'

C paused to select a pigeon from the coop then granted Fawkes the highest accolade of all, placing the pigeon on the young man's finger. "Freddie" felt as if he'd been anointed.

'You've come on a lot as a result of this mission. I see a brighter future for you from now on. Your handling of the Lestocq business makes you one of us now.'

The Lestocq business. So, C knew the truth after all. Fawkes's opinion of the man went up.

'You were right all along about communist penetration, Freddie.'

'Yes, but I never, for one minute, saw Lestocq as one.'

'That's the dilemma.'

'How do you mean, sir?'

'The Soviets win either way. If we don't unmask them they do untold damage. If we do, it damages morale and introduces a permanent climate of suspicion throughout the service.'

'Yes, sir but that's the nature of the business we're in. We need a permanent climate of suspicion. It was the lack of it that enabled men like Lestocq to succeed.'

'Talking of trust, there's one more matter to be dealt with.'

Fawkes gazed steadfastly at the pigeon. He didn't need the pause nor did he need to feel C's arm around him to see where the conversation was leading.

'With Lestocq and Durand out of the way, I can inform the PM that one of my top men went to France to obtain some compromising letters from Canaris. He can use them as he sees fit but I believe he will want to make sure they never see the light of day.'

He looked benignly at his underling.

'Of course, he'll want an assurance that we've tidied up any loose ends. Pregnant or not, Freddie, the young woman is one such loose end. We can't leave her out there. I don't care how you do it but that must be tidied up.'

The offer to become "one of us" had strings attached. If he

really wanted to belong, he had to pass one more test. That was the third matter he'd been thinking about on the journey home. He replied promptly and with assurance.

'I understand sir. Leave it with me.'

If Lestocq had told Fawkes about the Fishing Club, what else had he revealed? To buy his silence, C had even more to offer.

'We must get you into a decent club. It'll do you a world of good. Oh, and we'll clean up your service record. Wipe all that nonsense about a court martial and restore your rank. We owe it to your father.'

'And to my mother.'

'Indeed. Her death is a permanent stain on the Department's record. All I can say is we meant well.'

C looked genuinely contrite, probably a first, thought Fawkes.

'You know, Freddie, if she was alive today. I'm quite sure she would be very proud of you, and justifiably so.'

Fawkes nodded then turned to cross the roof. He was halfway to the door when he heard C speak again, in a voice barely above a whisper.

'I let my ambition overrule my judgement but I only wanted what was best for my country. The situation really is desperate. The invasion may have been called off but we're bleeding to death.'

The pain on C's face was all too evident. Fawkes gave his devious spymaster a sympathetic look.

'But I don't think it was the right thing to do. I can see that now, Freddie.'

'I know sir. It's a pity the whole of Europe collapsed without much resistance, leaving it to us to carry on the fight but we have to take a stand against this terrible tyranny, no matter what the cost to us. It's our national destiny, whether we like it or not. As someone said to me, if we make a dishonourable peace now, all we will be doing is making sure Hitler eats us last.'

He'd come a long way. If he handled the Ballantyne matter in the right way, he'd go a lot further. As he turned the handle of the door, he heard the sound of the pigeon coop being firmly shut.

Chapter 53

THE LUSH LANDSCAPE of the Scottish borders made a sharp contrast to the rocky soil around La Dame Brave but the principle was the same, a village set in the middle of the land on which it relied. Only this time, smaller, much smaller. As he turned off the main road and headed up a gentle slope, he passed a group of houses on each side. At the top, he came to a stone built two storey house with a single storey on one side, also built of stone. Two chimneys rose from its roof giving a clue as to its use. Beyond that, nothing but grassland and sheep grazing. He parked the car and walked towards the front door, feeling more nervous than when he'd approached the head of the Abwehr.

The woman who answered might once have borne a close resemblance to Mary but life as the wife of a blacksmith had taken its toll. Dressed in a simple frock, covered by an apron, she was stooped and wrinkled. Her hair, long since turned to silver, was tied in a bun on her head. When she saw the smart gentleman on her doorstep, she instinctively straightened up to reveal eyes that still sparkled like her granddaughter's. Fawkes bowed his head.

'Mrs Ballantyne? My name is Fawkes, I know your granddaughter, Mary. Is she, by any chance, staying with you?'

Mary's grandmother, also called Mary, had been warned to be careful if anyone called and not to take what she was told at face value. She'd also been given a question to ask. The problem was, she'd forgotten it.

Flustered, she said, 'I'm sorry, I have to ask you a question but it's been so long since she told me, I can't quite, er, hold on, I wrote it down. Wait there.'

She went into the kitchen. Fawkes heard the rustle of papers before she emerged, clutching the vital question.

'Who made the violin in your case?'

Fawkes smiled broadly.

'An excellent question. A gentleman by the name of Thompson, Mrs Ballantyne.'

'She's out in the fields at the back, tending to the sheep. I hope you're not going to upset her.'

'Mrs Ballantyne, I'd do anything not to upset Mary.'

Fawkes followed her through the kitchen and out of the back door.

'Don't keep her standing around too long.'

With a quick, 'I quite understand,' Fawkes stepped out into the green field to be confronted by a flock of sheep but no Mary. Had she seen him and felt it prudent to hide? He turned round to seek guidance from her grandmother but the other Mary Ballantyne had stepped back inside. He turned back and there she was, standing in the middle of the flock. He waved and walked towards her.

She didn't wave back.

He'd be the first to admit he'd stayed away longer than necessary because he wanted to delay the inevitable moment when he experienced the rejection he knew was coming. Knowing this, he'd come up with an alternative and very reasonable offer he was sure she'd accept. To start things off on the right foot, he held his hands, palms outwards, to show he had no weapon, a gesture that came naturally to someone in his line of work.

But she wasn't in that line of work. The gesture was not well received.

'How did you find me?'

'I went to see your parents. There was something I needed to ask your father. Once they accepted that I posed no threat, they told me where you were. I think they were relieved. How was your journey home?'

'The sub was more bearable this time. I suppose I must have got used to it. And you?'

'Slow but sure, which was what I wanted. It gave me time to prepare a suitable story for C.'

And pluck up the courage to face her.

'So where do we stand now? Are our lives in danger?'

'You'll be thrilled to know that C, knowing I possess a letter that can ruin him, has started calling me Freddie. I even found myself standing there with a bloody pigeon on my finger. Apparently, I'm now one of us.'

'Except you don't possess the letter, I do.'

Her condition was more noticeable and the country air had brought a bloom to her cheeks. But there was something else. She seemed calmer, more self-contained. Aware, perhaps of the power the letter gave to its possessor.

'As always, you go straight to the heart of the matter. To be truly one of us, I have to do one more thing, carry out one more task. Then I'm well and truly on the inside track.'

'Sort out the Ballantyne woman.'

'Can you see through me that easily?'

'It's obvious. This whole operation was off the books. Whether it succeeded or failed, we were to be eliminated. I suspected that from the beginning.'

She turned her attention to the sheep munching contentedly on the lush grass. Working from animal to animal, she stroked each one in turn. When she'd finished, she gave him a quizzical look.

'You said there was something you needed to ask my father.'

He turned round and looked back at the house as if hoping for support from Mary's grandmother. When he turned back to face her, anguish was written all over his face.

'This is all I know.'

'Sorry?'

'This job, it's all I know, I can't do anything else, I don't want to do anything else. It matters to me. I believe in it.'

A shiver of fear ran through her. Was he trying to explain why he had to kill her?

'Were you looking round to make sure there were no witnesses?'

'Witnesses? What are you talking about?'

'You don't want anyone to see what you're about to do.'

'Well of course I don't want anyone watching me make a complete fool of myself.'

Best to get it over with. Trying to remember the script he'd prepared, he resumed.

'I'll never marry in the usual way. No woman would put up with me. I explained that to your father. I think he understood.'

'You've completely lost me. Why were you having this conversation?'

She knew perfectly well what the answer was but she was as frightened of where this was going as he was.

'Look, the war won't last forever. When it's over, your position will be difficult. I'd like to help. God, I'm not doing this very well, am I?'

'I rather think you're not.'

'I won't trouble you in any way. You don't need to see me or have anything to do with me but your situation will be much better this way. More to the point, you'll be safe and so will your child.'

'So you're doing me a favour, is that how you see it?'

Knowing he was making a mess of it, Fawkes took refuge in anger.

'Oh for God's sake. I thought we were having a conversation between two adults but if this is what you want.'

He knelt down on the lush grass and took her hand.

'Mary Ballantyne, will you bloody well marry me or won't you?'

From her kitchen window, Mary's grandmother caught her breath as she watched the scene unfold. She loved having her granddaughter living with her but it was a small village and Mary's all too obvious condition was the subject of comment. She watched expectantly for a sign that Mary had accepted what was obviously a marriage proposal. She couldn't hear her reply but the words Mary spoke, delivered in a cutting tone, were heard loud and clear by the man on bended knee.

'No I bloody well will not. Christ you've got a nerve. It's all been a big act, hasn't it, right from the first time we met in the hotel. You'll play any role, say anything to get the job done. And that's all you're doing here, isn't it, just getting the job done.'

She looked down at the lush grass beneath her feet.

'When we kissed in France, I thought you cared for me. Well that was pretty stupid of me.'

A pause.

'But I'm not completely stupid, you know. There's only one reason you're proposing marriage and it's not to "rescue" me or save me from social disgrace. You've been told that if you want to keep your job, you must get hold of the letter. You could just ask for it, you know, I'd give it to you. You don't have to marry me. You saved my life three times, after all and don't think I'm not grateful. But, as you said at the time, you were simply doing your job. Come inside and I'll give it to you. That'll really put you on the inside track, Mr Ambition.'

He stood up and surveyed the grass stain on his knee. She'd expressed her anger, now it was his turn.

'You only liked me when you thought I was about to die. Now I've survived, you've gone off me.'

Since he'd taken the gloves off, she did the same.

'My God, you've got a bloody nerve. Everything you did, everything you said to me was designed to get me through the day. Once I'd killed Mirbeth, you'd completed the mission and had no further use for me. Rather than come home on the sub with me, you handed me over to Yann and cleared off on your own to plan how to save your career. Do you think I didn't realise what was going on? You couldn't get rid of me fast enough.'

Stunned by the bitterness in her voice, he turned away and started pacing around the field, just as he had paced around the car before coming to that momentous decision about the letter. Convinced he had no chance with her, he was about to admit defeat when Heywood's words on the beach came back to him.

'The right woman will only come your way once. When she does, if you don't tell her how you really feel, you'll lose her.'

He approached her slowly, and tentatively took her hand. Knowing how important the next few moments were, she didn't resist.

'I enjoyed talking to you on the journey out in the sub but it wasn't till you fought me tooth and nail over the letter that I realised I'd fallen for you in a big way. When I did, it frightened me. We were on the biggest mission of my career and the last thing I needed was a distraction like that.'

He gazed into her eyes. She didn't look away.

'Every time we faced a life and death moment, you thought I was needlessly sacrificing myself to atone for deserting my mother. It wasn't that at all. All I could think about was protecting you, whatever the cost to me.'

He shook his head in despair.

'But all the time, I knew we had no future together because your heart belonged to a dead man. You proved that when we argued about the letter. As for sending you home like that to get rid of you, nothing could have been further from my mind. It was because I wasn't sure how C would react when I told him the letter hadn't been delivered and what he would do if he had both of us together. I wanted you safely out of the way while I found out.'

She smiled briefly but he gained no encouragement from it.

'I couldn't believe you really cared for me. On the journey home, I'd convinced myself the signs you gave of doing so were simply the product of the life and death situation we were in. Once you returned to safety, you'd return to the opinion you had of me before. I offered you a marriage of convenience because I knew your heart would always belong to Brandon and all I could hope for was to help you out of your situation. You confirmed this with your angry rejection of my proposal.'

He released her hand and turned to leave. He'd taken a few steps when he heard her speak, her voice barely above a whisper.

'Don't go.'

Fawkes had faced death time and again. Each time, his heart had pounded as the adrenalin poured through his bloodstream but that was nothing compared to the thumping in his chest as he rushed to her side.

'When Durand said I'd fallen for you, I told him he was talking nonsense. When Granny said the same thing I was angry with her. They were both right but out of duty to Brandon, I couldn't admit it not just to them but to myself.'

In the silence that followed, Fawkes sensed that the rest of his life was about to be decided. After what seemed an eternity, she pulled him towards her and wrapped her arms round his neck.

'Not anymore.'

Then she whispered in his ear.

'Frederick Fawkes, will you bloody well marry me or won't you?'

South of France August 1964

THREE MINUTES TO eight.

The sun had slipped behind the hills; the champagne had been flowing for nearly an hour. A minuscule breeze wafted the scent of jasmine across the terrace, to the accompaniment of the seamless chirrup of the cicadas.

Was it really so long ago? The jasmine had ignored the passing years, its flowers still covering every inch of the railings that bordered the terrace. The bougainvillea still glowed like a flame in the evening light. Immaculate waiters glided, like the best waiters always do, imperceptibly among the guests. How could this one place change so little when everything else had changed so much?

From her bedroom window, she could see the island, peaceful and inviting, the yachts anchored for the night, their cabin lights glowing in the fading light. The beaches had emptied of tourists. It was a view to delight any hotel guest. She shuddered and turned away.

Returning reluctantly to the dressing table, she sighed at the sight that confronted her, the southern light, though fading fast, illuminating every line in her face. Even with her elbows firmly planted, her hand shook as she applied her lipstick. The last time she'd sat in this room, there'd been every reason for her hand to shake but not today. Then, her very life had been at stake, today of all days, she had nothing to fear. This is silly, she thought, it was all a long time ago and tonight she was among friends. But she'd been among friends then. A few more moments wouldn't do any harm.

There must have been thirty of them on the terrace. Every Tuesday, the manager held a cocktail party, a last link with the pre-war era. But this wasn't a Tuesday and these weren't ordinary guests. They'd come here for a reason, to celebrate the twentieth anniversary of the Allied landings in the south. There were Frenchmen, Italians and Spaniards, one was German, the rest, British and American. But they all spoke to each other in just one language, French.

A last look in the mirror, a quick check that she had her key. It was time to join the others. As the lift rushed down, she wished she'd taken the stairs to delay the moment a little longer. She crossed the hall and stood at the open French doors, pausing before taking a few tentative steps onto the terrace just as she'd done all those years ago. Enveloped by the soft, jasmine-laced air, she looked across at the guests, most of them with their backs to her. A waiter offered her a drink, an old friend turned and waved. She relaxed a little as a welcome voice intervened.

'Come along Mother, everyone's been waiting for you. This is your night. We're so proud of you.'

She gave her son a warm smile as he took one arm and her daughter took the other, leading her over to Durand, still handsome, still immaculately groomed, now trapped in his wheelchair. From the other side of the terrace, a man watched the daughter walking by her mother's side, the image of the girl he'd first seen on this very terrace, all those years ago.

Durand held his arms open. As they embraced, he whispered in Mary's ear.

'I always hoped you'd come back.'

There was no reproach in his voice. He knew why she'd stayed away.

'I should have come back sooner but I couldn't face it. I could barely leave my room to come down here.'

'You're here now, that's all that matters.'

As he spoke, she became aware that someone had stepped

out of the crowd to stand next to the old hotelier. She looked up to see a woman of her own age, smiling nervously. Mary stared at her until recognition dawned.

'Is it really you?'

The woman held her arms open.

'Yes, it's me. Hold me tight.'

'Oh, Audrey, I thought you were dead. This is too much. I wish I'd known Jean-Paul had invited you.'

'He didn't invite me, I live here. After the war, he found me and became a father to me. I've lived here ever since.'

'I feel so ashamed. I should have kept in touch. I've let you down.'

'Don't be so silly. Jean-Paul told me it was your courage that inspired him and made him determined to find me.'

Someone came up behind her, grabbed her and swung her round. Even before they came face to face, she knew who it was. There was only one man with that sort of strength.

'You will dine with me tonight, no arguments. The table is already laid in your honour.'

The hair had gone, the waistline had thickened, otherwise, Yann hadn't changed. But his wardrobe had. Gone were the colourful shirts and sailor's trousers. An expensive suit fitted his huge figure like a glove. She beamed up at him.

'I'm so glad you survived, I hated leaving you like that. Tell me what happened.'

'I hid down the well for three days, that's how long they searched the place. They couldn't believe you'd escaped.'

'Didn't they think to look down the well?'

'Of course, it was the first place they checked but I was still in the monastery then. Once they'd searched it – they even sent a man down on the end of the rope – I climbed in, was lowered down onto a ledge and tied to the rope in case I fell asleep and fell off. Those lovely monks lowered food down every day in the bucket.'

'It must have been awful.'

'Well, it was a lot better than being shot, which I would have been if they'd caught me.'

'Did you continue working for the Resistance?'

'No, I didn't. My wife was right about them, too many traitors, too many people pretending to join just to avoid doing forced labour. No, the events of those days changed my life.'

'In what way?'

'Once Jean-Paul had recovered enough, he was taken to La Dame Brave and hidden there for the rest of the war. But the British needed someone to continue as their banker down here so I handled all the work, under his direction. I also took over the running of the hotel when the owners were rounded up and sent off to the camps. After the war, J-P and I bought it.'

'Where did you get the money? Or shouldn't I ask?'

'You shouldn't ask. But, believe me, we earned every penny of it.'

She laughed.

'You're a very bad man.'

She gave him a reproachful look.

'But you're right, you earned it.'

He hugged her again.

'And you have earned the right to be guest of honour at this celebration.'

'I will be your guest of honour,' said Mary, 'on condition that you are mine. You saved my life.'

While Yann's face beamed with pride, a distinguished gentleman walked over. No bear hug for him. Yann bowed his head respectfully.

'Hello Freddie, long time no see. Still up to your old tricks? Congratulations on the knighthood, by the way, richly deserved.'

'Much appreciated, Yann my good friend. May I borrow your companion for a moment?'

He escorted Mary over to the corner where they nearly disappeared in the bougainvillea.

'Are you alright? You were a long time coming down.'

'I'm fine, don't worry about me. I'm glad I came now.'

'I'm proud of many things I've done for my country but I've never forgiven myself for exposing you to the unnecessary risk of that mission.'

Mary laughed.

'Well, I survived to tell the tale, or rather not to tell the tale.'

She paused.

'Now we're back, I can't help thinking about the enigmatic Admiral Canaris. We haven't talked about him for years, you and I. Do you think he was a good guy? Should we have done more to encourage him?'

'I wouldn't go that far. He was one of several people who opposed Hitler but were reluctant to do anything about it and you can see why. Even today, twenty years later, most Germans regard the July plotters as traitors. We, on the other hand, owe him our lives.'

'Yes, I remember the day you told me he'd been hanged.'

Fawkes looked away.

'What is it? Something you haven't told me?'

'Yes, and I'm not sure I should tell you now.'

She gave him a searching look.

'Go on.'

'The Nazis hanged him with piano wire. It took thirty minutes for him to die. The war was already lost but they did that. They say he went to the gallows clutching a sheet of paper with a single Latin phrase which he read out as they placed the wire round his neck. So in a way, you were there with him, right at the end.'

The breeze fluttered briefly. Just as briefly, Canaris seemed to be standing before her, his stiff manner softening to give her a last piece of advice before he turned and left her life forever. She shuddered.

'Is it turning chilly or are there a lot of ghosts around tonight?'

'I shouldn't have made you come.'

She gave him the softest of looks.

'I'm fine now. This is Durand's party, let's go and talk to him.'

Durand was shifting in his chair. It was never much fun being confined to the wretched thing and today had been particularly tiring what with first arranging, then attending this party. But he had something to get off his chest. With one hand, he pulled Audrey close. Using the other to hold Fawkes in a firm grip, he turned to Audrey.

'You remember that old fellow, Heywood?'

Audrey nodded.

'The old guy who had a gunfight in the tower?'

'That's right but what you don't know is that when Freddie here was offered the customary title awarded to men who reach the pinnacle of his profession, he replied that he would be delighted to accept but with one condition. "And what, pray, is that?" said the toffee-nosed gentlemen who run the Honours list. "That a certain George Heywood be awarded the George Cross," said plain Mr. Fawkes.'

The no longer plain Mr. Fawkes shuffled awkwardly.

'Come on Jean-Paul, you're embarrassing this delightful lady.'

'The only person I 'm embarrassing is you and you'll just have to put up with it.'

He turned back to Audrey.

'As I was saying, the Honours people didn't know what to make of it. They'd never heard of Heywood and thought he was joking. When he made it clear he was deadly serious and told them about the mission, they said this Heywood chappie couldn't have a medal because there was no record of him ever going on a mission. "We've checked and he was strictly a desk man. Sorry and all that but it just can't be done. We're sure you'll understand," they said.'

Durand's strangled attempt at an upper-class British accent served its purpose admirably. He was warming to his subject and, for him at least, the discomfort had all but gone. Fawkes's discomfort increased with every word but the old Egyptian Jew maintained a firm grip on his arm.

'Well, like the rest of us, they underestimated our mutual

friend. You know how blunt Freddie can be, no respect for authority, even when he is the authority. "I've got a letter from Churchill that will be very embarrassing if it ever sees the light of day. If you don't make the award immediately, I'll decline the knighthood and tell the world why." Needless to say, he got his way and Heywood has received the medal he deserved. Sir Frederick here must have a hold over some powerful people.'

Durand released Fawkes from his iron grip, allowing his embarrassed victim to make a great show of rubbing his arm. As he did so, a man and woman stepped out onto the terrace and looked round at the assembled guests. Behind them, Agnes, once Durand's receptionist, now his wife, shrugged her shoulders to signal her failure to prevent them gate-crashing the party. The woman pointed to the far corner of the terrace.

'Oh, look darling, the bougainvillea is still there.'

Beaming from ear to ear, the husband led her over to the group gathered around Durand.

'I say, you still do these cocktail parties, how splendid. We haven't been here since '39. It's amazing how little has changed.'

Noticing Fawkes, a glimmer of recognition crossed his face.

'Forgive the impertinence but weren't you here then? Aren't you one of the chaps from the film company? We gave you a lift to that village, I'm sure it was you. What do you say, Lydia?'

'Now don't bother Mr Hawkes. I'm sure he won't remember us.'

Fawkes burst out laughing.

'Of course I remember you, Lydia and Harry Ransome isn't it? How could I ever forget the stylish lady who deliberately got my name wrong then and remembered to do the same again a quarter of a century later? I'm delighted to see you looking so well. Are you still in the insurance game?'

'Not any more,' said Harry.

'Good for you. As I recall, you hated it.'

'Ah well, when I said not any more, I meant as of last week. When I was called up, I ended up in a tank regiment. While we were working our way across Normandy, one of my colleagues and I took our mind off things by planning to go into business together as brokers after the war. I must say, we never looked back and finally sold the business for a tidy sum. Lydia and I have left the children at home and thought we'd re-visit the scene of a holiday that had such an effect on our lives.'

He paused to let his satisfaction sink in.

'And you, are you still in the film business?'

'Sadly, no, I've been doing government work for some time, I'm afraid. But I'm delighted to hear of your success.'

Lydia cut in before Harry displayed too much satisfaction at this reversal of fortune.

'And how is your colleague? The last we saw of him was when he jumped out of our car and ran off rather suddenly. He seemed desperate for a drink.'

Fawkes had long wondered how Heywood had come to be in the tower. Quite unexpectedly, the Ransomes had turned up and filled the gap in his knowledge. George had led his pursuers away from both the box of rotors and the Ransomes, sacrificing his own life to do so. His determination to get him a medal had been more justified than he'd realised. He exchanged looks with Durand who nodded in appreciation.

'I'm afraid he died not long after.'

'Oh dear,' said Lydia. 'And he was such a nice man.'

'Yes, he was. It was an honour to have known him.'

Noticing a tear in Mr Hawkes's eye, Lydia took her husband's hand.

'Come along, Harry, I want to take a closer look at that lovely old bougainvillea.'

Once they were out of earshot, Mary whispered to Fawkes, 'you never mentioned having a run-in with the Honours people.'

'That's because I didn't. It was a rumour I allowed to circulate to draw attention away from what really happened. When I was offered the knighthood, I had a quiet word with the Fishing Club, reminding them that I'd saved the Lestocq family honour and got Roland a wholly undeserved George Cross. I told them the same medal for Heywood would wipe the slate clean. They didn't argue.'

'I'm glad you did that. It mattered to you.'

'I wouldn't be where I am today but for George Heywood.'

He kissed her.

'And you of course, Lady Fawkes, you above all.'

'The stupid Englishman Abroad who turned out not to be so stupid after all. Did he ever make a reappearance?'

'Just once more, when I proposed to you in that foolish way.'

'And I rejected you in that foolish way.'

He pulled her close and kissed her.

'Well, so long as we may be fools together, I think we'll be alright.

Mary surveyed the guests just as she had done all those years ago. Instead of separate groups of people all ignoring each other, everyone was moving around from group to group. Durand had finally been given the party he'd always wanted. Then she thought of someone else and the words he'd written. *Think of me now and again, but not too often. You've got a life to lead so go out and live it.* She looked across the silver sea towards the island then turned back to look up at the hills that contained so many memories and hid so many secrets. As if reading her mind, Fawkes said, 'do you think we can leave the children here while we take a short drive up into the hills?'

She called to her son.

'Brandon, we're going for a short drive. Can you look after Ilse?'

'Of course, Mother. We're not children anymore.'

Mary kissed Durand on the cheek.

'We're going for a drive, we won't be long.'

'There won't be a porter to help you into your car, I'm so sorry. They're all here on the terrace tonight.'

'Don't be silly, we can manage. I'm perfectly capable of shutting my own door.'

Durand was right, the front of the hotel was deserted apart from a single pre-war car, in racing green. Mary opened the door and took the wheel while Fawkes eased himself into the passenger seat. As she reached to close the door, she became aware of a figure standing over her. There had been a doorman after all. She looked at his polished black shoes then at the RAF blue uniform. As her eyes moved up, she took in the jacket with the top button undone and the ribbon of the Distinguished Flying Cross. Her skin tingled as she moved up and gazed straight into the eyes of her beloved Brandon. She felt no shock, only pleasure, a feeling of being cocooned in warmth. When she smiled at him, he stood to attention and saluted, a tear running down his cheek. As she drove away, she looked in the mirror and watched him standing in the middle of the drive, watched him wave then watched him fade away into nothingness.

The eternal sound of the cicadas filled the soft evening air.

Printed in Great Britain
by Amazon

29392963R00218